New York Times and *US*~~A~~
Caridad Piñeiro is a Jerse~~y~~
and is the author of nearly
loves romance novels, superheroes, ᴉ ᵥ
For more information on Caridad and her dark, seᴧy
romantic suspense and paranormal romances, please
visit caridad.com

Cindi Myers is the author of more than seventy-five novels.
When she's not plotting new romance storylines, she enjoys
skiing, gardening, cooking, crafting and daydreaming. A
lover of small-town life, she lives with her husband and two
spoiled dogs in the Colorado mountains.

Also by Caridad Piñeiro

Crooked Pass Security
Cliffside Kidnapping
Defended by the Bodyguard

South Beach Security: K-9 Division
Sabotage Operation
Escape the Everglades
Killer in the Kennel
Danger in Dade

South Beach Security
Biscayne Bay Breach

Also by Cindi Myers

Eagle Mountain: Unsolved Mysteries
Wilderness Search
Peak Suspicion

Eagle Mountain: Criminal History
Colorado Kidnapping
Twin Jeopardy
Mountain Captive

Eagle Mountain: Critical Response
Killer on Kestrel Trail
Secrets of Silverpeak Mine

Discover more at millsandboon.co.uk

COLD CASE K-9

CARIDAD PIÑEIRO

HIGH COUNTRY ESCAPE

CINDI MYERS

MILLS & BOON

First Published in Great Britain 2025
by Mills & Boon, an imprint of HarperCollins*Publishers* Ltd
1 London Bridge Street, London, SE1 9GF

www.harpercollins.co.uk

HarperCollins*Publishers*
Macken House, 39/40 Mayor Street Upper,
Dublin 1, D01 C9W8, Ireland

This book contains references to emotional, psychological and sexual trauma as a result of being kidnapped and held captive as a child.

ISBN: 978-0-263-39739-0

1225

MIX
Paper | Supporting
responsible forestry
FSC™ C007454

This book contains FSC™ certified paper and other controlled sources to ensure responsible forest management.

For more information visit: www.harpercollins.co.uk/green

Printed and Bound in the UK using 100% Renewable Electricity at CPI Group (UK) Ltd, Croydon, CR0 4YY

COLD CASE K-9

CARIDAD PIÑEIRO

Prologue

The early spring sun bathed her face as she stood on the mountain trail. She walked to the lip and peered down a nearby ravine to the creek at its base. Along the edges of the crystal-clear water, spring was coming alive with the first hints of green and purple. Before long, those little slips of color would unfurl into mountain bluebells and the tall, hairy leaves of cow parsnip.

In the trees nearby, bright green buds were bursting open as life returned to the Colorado mountains.

She loved this time of year that held so much promise.

Shielding her eyes against the sun, she glanced up the trail, reviewing how much farther she had to go before reaching the summit.

Not far, she thought, but the day was still early, and she didn't want to rush her hike. She wanted to savor the day. Tomorrow she'd be trapped behind walls of glass and cement while at work.

Walking to the other side of the trail, a challenging one for more experienced hikers, she sat on a boulder warmed by the sun and laid her knapsack at her feet. Rummaging through it, she hauled out a baggie with trail mix to satisfy the hunger in her belly.

The snap of a branch behind her snared her attention.

Something dark and menacing charged at her before she could react.

Peanuts, chocolate and raisins went flying as she was slammed onto the ground.

The force of the impact drove her breath from her. Before she could take another breath, a gloved hand covered her mouth.

She fought for breath and freedom, but he was just too heavy. Too big. Too strong.

Circles of black whirled before her eyes. In her mind, a silent scream rang out.

I don't want to die.

As the blackness thickened, taking her away, that small desperate voice pleaded.

Please, I don't want to die.

Chapter One

"I'm really sorry we have to do this, Diego. My hands are tied on account of what happened with the senator," said Police Chief Jackson Whitaker.

"I understand, Jax," Diego Rodriguez replied. Ever since the senator had been arrested for crimes including alleged rape, money laundering and kidnapping, any project in which the senator had been involved was being reviewed and reassessed.

"I feel bad. You just relocated for this gig," Jackson said. "If you're not sure about making that rental permanent, you're welcome to stay with Rhea and me until this is all cleared up."

Diego appreciated the offer, but since his friend had a new baby, he didn't want to intrude. Waving off the invitation, he said, "I appreciate it, but I'm sure I can get a job as a security guard or something until everything is straightened out."

"Actually, I thought this might interest you," Jackson said, and passed a business card to Diego.

Crooked Pass Security. The company had a Denver address and indicated that it was a branch of South Beach Security. He'd worked with SBS before when Jackson had been investigating the disappearance of his wife's twin sister and more recently, during the kidnapping case involving State Senator Oliver.

Diego held the card up. "I don't get it. What's SBS doing here?"

"SBS tech geniuses Sophie and Robbie Whitaker helped us with the Oliver case, and they've decided to put down roots in Colorado," Jackson explained.

Not strange considering Sophie and Robbie were Jackson's cousins and visited regularly. Plus, he'd heard that the two had found love with the people who'd helped them during the investigations. Robbie was involved with Jax's sister-in-law Selene while his sister Sophie had fallen for CBI Agent Ryder Hunt.

"What does this have to do with me?" Diego asked, and tried to return the business card to Jackson, but his friend urged him to keep it.

"They need good investigators and are also hoping to build a K-9 division here. I think you'd be a perfect fit."

Diego examined the card again. From what he knew of the SBS agency and the brother-and-sister tech experts who had been such a help during recent investigations, they were bright, hardworking, successful and friendly. He did not doubt they'd treat anyone who worked for them well.

As he met Jackson's gaze across the width of the heavy old oak desk in his office, he finally realized that it might be some time before Jackson would be able to allow him and his K-9, Poppy, onto the police force again.

Slipping the card into the pocket of his shirt uniform, he said, "Thanks for this. I'll check it out."

GABRIELLA RUIZ LAID the reports and photos with details of a missing hiker on her desk. The young woman had disappeared the day before, and the local police department had reached out to the Colorado Bureau of Investigation for help.

She diligently reviewed the information, flagging details that might be helpful. It was impossible not to notice the similarities to two other cases that she could not forget. Women who had also gone out for just a day of fresh air and sunshine only to disappear.

Just like her sister had disappeared, she thought.

Standing, she grabbed a photo of the missing woman, Jeannie Roberts, and walked over to the murder board she had on one wall of her office. She tacked Jeannie's photo beside those of the two missing women. All twentysomething brunettes. All beautiful. All avid hikers and athletes much like Gabriella herself.

And much like her sister Isabella, except she'd only been twelve when she'd gone missing.

A few taps on the frame of her door drew her attention.

"Heard you caught the Roberts case," said her colleague Ryder Hunt as he sauntered into her office.

"I did. I need a partner on this one. You interested?" she said, and gestured for him to take a seat.

His gaze drifted from her to the board and then back to her. "Depends," he almost drawled.

She arched a dark brow. "On what?"

He gestured to the board. "You still trying to connect those two cold cases? And now this one?"

Gabriella did a slow turn and scrutinized the board, wanting to be certain of the answer she gave her friend and colleague. With a decisive nod, she faced Ryder and said, "I am."

His eyes opened slightly wider. "Because of Isabella?"

She couldn't deny that every case like this brought reminders of her sister. It was the reason she'd decided to go into law enforcement. Isabella had never received justice, and her family had never gotten closure. She wanted to keep other families from a similar fate.

Unfazed by her colleague's obvious worry, she said, "Yes. For Isabella and these women. Someone has to figure out what happened to them."

Ryder did that slow perusal again. Her. The board. Her, before he finally said, "These disappearances happened over six months apart and it's been what, two years since they took place?"

"Numerous serial killers—"

"Whoa, that's a big leap. Plus, those are only two," Ryder shot out.

Gabriella pointed at the board. "In 2008, the FBI defined serial murder to be the unlawful killing of *two* or more victims."

The flush of angry color swept across Ryder's cheeks as with a slow dip of his head, he said, "I know, Gabby. You don't have to quote scripture to me."

Gabriella muttered a curse beneath her breath and shook her head in apology. "I'm sorry, Ryder. I'm just so..." She hesitated, searching for the right word, and finally gave up and said, "Determined. I'm determined to find out where they are. What happened."

"That kind of determination can lead you to lose focus," Ryder reminded.

Ryder wasn't wrong. "Which is why it's even more important to have a good partner to keep me in line."

Ryder hesitated but then dipped his head in agreement. "If the chief agrees, you've got your partner."

Chapter Two

I love watching them wake up.

I love that look that joyfully says, I'm alive.

I love seeing that joy fade as reality registers and fear sets in.

He wished he could experience those looks again and again as the days passed. But he couldn't hold on to her for too long even with all the precautions he'd taken.

The root cellar in the cabin was soundproof, protection against any screams alerting distant neighbors or hikers to what was happening.

He'd learned that the hard way many years earlier when he'd had a screamer. Even though he was a good distance away from any real civilization, he'd worried someone might have heard and come to spoil his pleasure.

That night's fear of discovery had morphed into disappointment at having to get rid of his toy earlier than planned.

But not this time, he thought as he eased on the black hood, grabbed his camera and slipped down the stairs. At the base of the steps, he flipped a switch and bright stage lights snapped to life.

She shot awake, eyes opened as wide as a deer in the headlights. Pulling up her knees, she wrapped her arms around them to hide her naked body from his gaze. In a tiny voice, she said, "Please. Please don't hurt me again."

Pleasure filled him at her fear. "You know what to do," he said. At her hesitation, he reached for the large bowie knife at his side and held it up so that the light from the powerful spotlights made the sharp edge glint with menace.

Her breathing raced and her body trembled, but she slowly opened her arms and legs wide. The metal shackles on her wrists and ankles rasped against the cement floor of the cellar with her movement.

He sheathed the knife and took the photo. The click of the shutter was loud in the otherwise silent room.

At the second click of the shutter, she turned her face, averting her gaze.

"Look at me," he said, and was about to reach for the knife again, but she instantly complied.

It disappointed him that she had been complacent so far. He liked his women with a little more fight, and she'd been like a cold, dead fish as he'd satisfied himself with her the day before.

"You're weak. Stupid," he challenged, hoping for some spirit, and it finally blossomed.

Her back straightened slightly, and her eyes narrowed, fear fleeing as strength flooded into her. "I'm going to get out of this and when I do…" Her voice trailed off as he snapped another photo, wanting to capture that spirit forever.

"What are you going to do?" he goaded, wanting the dangerous animal everyone had inside them to emerge.

"I'm going to kill you," she said, her voice deadly cold. Fire blazing in her eyes.

He laughed, snapped another photo and then laid the camera on the nearby table. Easing the knife from the sheath on his belt, he held it up again.

"Not if I kill you first."

DIEGO SAT ACROSS the conference room table from Sophie and Robbie Whitaker, the South Beach Security tech geniuses who had decided to stay with the Colorado branch of the family and form Crooked Pass Security.

"We're just getting started so it's a little slow, but we're optimistic things will pick up soon," Sophie said, twined her fingers together and laid them on the leather portfolio before her.

"Where do I fit in?" Diego asked, wondering how a company that had just opened and had little or no work could afford to take on more personnel.

"We sometimes need K-9 handlers in addition to smart investigators. You fill both those slots," Robbie said, and shot a glance at Sophie before he passed a set of papers across the table.

An employment contract, Diego realized as he picked up the papers. His eyes almost bugged out at the salary they were offering. Nearly twice what he'd been getting paid at the Regina Police Department.

"You know the old saying, if it's too good to be true," he said as he skimmed a finger down the terms in the contract. But the terms all seemed reasonable.

"We have the backing of the Miami cousins and luckily, both Robbie and I are financially secure, if that's what you're worried about," Sophie explained.

That was part of it, Diego thought. The other part was that he didn't want to leave Jackson in a lurch if his town council found that there hadn't been any wrongdoing thanks to the senator's involvement with the new police hires. But the salary they were proposing would let him be financially secure and maybe even have enough left over to help other veterans rebuild their lives.

Peering across the table at the siblings, he said, "When do I start?"

Ryder and Gabriella had reviewed all the reports on the hiker's disappearance. But as far as she was concerned, nothing was better than a real-life visit to the scene. Plus, there was the added benefit that it was a glorious spring day.

She sucked in a deep breath and imagined how the hiker must have felt the day she disappeared. The weather had been much like it was today, Gabriella thought as she and Ryder trudged up the trail they had identified as the one where Jeannie Roberts had disappeared. Her car had been found at the trailhead after she'd been reported missing by her partner.

A partner who was still a person of interest until they could eliminate him as a suspect.

But first Gabriella wanted to get a sense of the crime scene and the other information they'd gleaned from the police reports.

They were halfway up the trail, one usually only traveled by more experienced hikers, when they reached the spot where Roberts had allegedly been taken. Police tape marked off an area and as Gabriella examined it, she concurred that this had likely been the spot.

The ground showed signs of a disturbance. There were some nuts and raisins on the ground that local animals and birds hadn't yet scavenged. A nearby boulder provided a perfect place to sit and view the beauty of the landscape.

"She stopped to enjoy the day and get some fuel before she continued to the summit," Gabriella said, and pointed up the trail with the tip of her hiking pole.

Ryder shielded his eyes against the sun, examined the trail and nodded. "Sure looks that way."

Gabriella did a slow pivot and perused the area around them. On the far side of the trail was a drop-off to the ravine below where a mountain creek flowed at its center. A forest of pines and aspens lined the other side of the trail.

With a shake of her head, she said, "How did he get her down the trail without being noticed?"

Ryder mimicked her action, scrutinizing the scene before he pursed his lips and blew out an exasperated sigh. "Slow day on the trail maybe, but he'd have to be strong to carry her out," he said, and gestured with his pole to the difficult path they had taken.

"Maybe he didn't carry her. If he subdued her and had a weapon—"

"She hiked back down with him. Even if they'd met someone on the trek back, they might not have noticed anything was out of the ordinary," Gabriella finished for him and then pushed on. "Roberts has been gone nearly thirty-six hours now. Every hour that goes by is an hour closer to her death."

Ryder met her gaze. "We've got every possible person working this case, but I know some people who might see something new and also help us with those cold cases you want to reopen."

"The chief nixed spending any time or funds on those older cases," Gabriella reminded.

Ryder grinned and used air quotes as he replied, "He said we couldn't spend any time 'on the clock' and don't worry about the cost. My friends love a challenge."

"Really? Who would they be?" Gabriella asked as she started back down to the trailhead. She was eager to return to the office and run through all the information they had so far to see if anything could help them save the missing hiker.

"Crooked Pass Security. They've got connections and capabilities that you wouldn't believe. Are you game?"

Was she game to locate Jeannie Roberts and find out who had killed the other two women? Maybe even finally know what had happened to her sister Isabella?

"I'm game."

HER PHOTO WAS plastered across every local newspaper, television station and social media.

It didn't worry him. No one had seen them hike down that day. He'd done well by choosing that trail since it was a harder hike that few people would do, especially that early in the season when there might still be traces of ice and snow at the higher elevations of the summit because of last week's unseasonable snow.

He'd done well this time, unlike some of his experiences with earlier women. He'd started by taking them in their homes, but he hadn't liked it as much. The fast kills hadn't given him time to enjoy their fear and their bodies.

That's when he'd decided to use the trails to take his victims.

At first, he'd worried that people had seen him hiking with his victims and that someone might connect the two incidents and identify him, but it hadn't happened.

And much like he'd learned about the screams, he'd learned to be more careful and to hide his face beneath a baseball cap, mask or neck gaiter.

Finally, thanks to various television shows and news articles, he'd known what to do to not leave any DNA behind after the first one.

Well, not really the first one. The first one had happened nearly five years earlier.

He'd been a teen then. Young and inexperienced. He hadn't even meant to kill her. He'd just wanted to have some fun. Explore some of what he'd seen online and in the magazines his father kept hidden in his office desk.

I didn't mean to kill her, he thought again, but admitted to himself that once it had happened, he'd liked it. A lot.

So much so that he'd kept her around for nearly a week before panic and the smell had begun to set in and he knew he had to get rid of the young girl's body.

He still visited her every now and again. Firsts were always special, and it thrilled him that they'd yet to find her. He didn't think they ever would. Or the others either. They were buried close by so that he wouldn't have far to go when he visited.

He'd hidden them well, he thought as need rose in him, so strongly that he couldn't just sit at his desk anymore, looking at sheets with numbers that meant little.

Jumping to his feet, he slipped on his jacket, straightened his tie and hurried out of his office.

The receptionist at the front desk smiled as he pushed through the doors. "Have a nice night," she called out.

He smiled and did a friendly wave. "I plan to do just that."

Chapter Three

Diego prowled the conference room restlessly, his German shepherd K-9, Poppy, at his side. He'd spent his first two days at Crooked Pass Security in meetings with the family members who ran South Beach Security, the main branch of the company.

He had been impressed by the Miami cousins, whose grandfather and father had built the agency and turned it over to the next generation to run. He'd also been surprised with what they could bring to investigations, from a brand-new K-9 training facility to incredible technology thanks to the marriage of one of the cousins to John Wilson, a well-known tech billionaire with an innovative program and seemingly endless capabilities.

But Diego wasn't used to sitting in meetings, which was why he was now pacing back and forth in the conference room, waiting for yet another meeting. But at least this one was about an investigation, and he looked forward to helping in any way he could.

As the door to the conference room opened, Diego whirled to face it.

Sophie and Robbie Whitaker entered, followed by a handsome dark-haired man he recognized from the case he'd worked on a few weeks earlier involving the kidnapping of Sophie and Robbie's parents.

A second later, a woman entered. But she wasn't just any woman.

Dark, nearly black hair drifted down against the bright white of her shirt and the lapels of her serious navy-blue pantsuit. Her eyes were just as dark, bottomless almost, as her gaze locked with his.

Something passed between them, and it tugged at his heart more than his gut.

She'd known loss.

He didn't know how he knew it, but he did, and it awoke a similar emotion in him.

But as quickly as that connection came, it evaporated as her shields went up.

Sophie, ever-observant Sophie, must have caught the moment, since she held her hand out in the direction of the woman and man who had entered and said, "Diego. I believe you know CBI Agent Ryder Hunt already. This is his partner, CBI Agent Gabriella Ruiz."

Gabriella. A beautiful name for a beautiful woman, he thought, and as he shook her hand, that feeling of connection swept through him again.

"Nice to meet you, Agent Ruiz," Diego said, and reluctantly released her hand.

"Likewise, Agent Rodriguez," Gabriella said, and was instantly all business as she faced Sophie and Robbie. "I know Ryder has already sent over the information."

Sophie nodded and gestured for them to sit. Once they were all settled, him with Poppy at his feet, he sat back as Gabriella reviewed the materials.

Gabriella displayed information from her laptop on a large television on the far wall of the conference room.

"I came across these cold cases about a year ago during a regular review, and I couldn't forget them," she said, and brought up photos of two women along with pertinent info.

"Missy Cornerstone and Alyssa Nations were twenty-two and twenty-four, respectively, when they were taken. Both Caucasian. Both attended the University of Denver, likely at the same time."

"Lots of similarities. Do you think whoever took them might have been there also?" Robbie jumped in to ask.

"Possibly. Files show that local police and CBI spoke to their boyfriends as well as several persons of interest. But they did not find any overlap between the two cases," Ryder advised.

Lots of similarities but also differences, Diego thought as he skimmed through the copies of the files Gabriella and Ryder had provided. "The women were taken from hiking trails but at different times of the year," he said, and gestured to the television where the photos of the two women almost screamed at them.

Look for me! Look for me!

"They have very similar features," he added as he perused the photos and then slipped a snapshot of the missing hiker from the papers. He held it up and said, "Just like Jeannie Roberts."

"Just like her, which is why I think all three of these cases are connected," Gabriella said with a nod and tight smile.

Diego couldn't argue, but he also couldn't wholeheartedly agree. "It's been two years since these other women disappeared. Plus, there's what…a gap of six months in between these two older abductions."

"BTK had cooling-off periods of as much as ten years between killings. The Grim Sleeper had one gap of almost fourteen years between murders," Gabriella advised.

"Are you saying you suspect a serial killer took Jeannie Roberts?" Sophie asked as she, too, flipped through her copy of the files.

GABRIELLA SHARED A long look with Ryder, aware that he wasn't necessarily on board with her designation of the cases.

"I believe so, but Ryder isn't as sure as I am," she admitted, wanting full disclosure with the team that might help them.

"I'm no expert on serial killers, but aren't they rare?" Diego asked, his gaze fixed on her intently.

His eyes were a deep brown, open and welcoming. When their gazes had locked earlier, she'd felt that welcome and something more. Something she couldn't define, which bothered her, so she dragged her gaze away, nodded and explained. "Less than 1 percent of all murders in the US are connected to serial killers, but the FBI estimates that there are between twenty-five and fifty serial killers at work each year—"

"Twenty-five to fifty! Without being caught?" Diego said, those expressive eyes wide in disbelief.

"It was higher in the 1970s and '80s, when almost three hundred were active at one time. Many are eventually caught, like the alleged Long Island Serial Killer, who was recently arrested. But there are still open cases. The West Mesa Bone Collector investigation comes to mind," Gabriella said, and flipped the images on the screen to show maps marked to reflect the trails where the three women had been hiking.

Using a laser pointer, she circled it around the areas. "These locations are all less than ten miles apart. They're trails that would have been used by more experienced hikers."

"I don't want to be a wet blanket, but Selene Reilly disappeared not far from there. Not on a trail but still, it didn't turn out to be a serial killer," Robbie said, and closed the file that had been sitting in front of him.

Gabriella was familiar with the Reilly case. The local police and CBI had closed it as a suicide. If it hadn't been for
her very determined twin sister and these SBS tech geniuses,
Reilly might not have ever been freed from the mountain men
who had abducted her. Still…

"Selene Reilly's case is an aberration. Sadly, in most disappearances, the victim is likely dead after forty-eight hours,
but something inside me says Jeannie Roberts is still alive,"
she said, and skipped her gaze across all seated at the table,
almost daring them to refuse the case.

The four gathered around the table all looked at one another, and then Sophie slowly came to her feet. "If you don't
mind, Robbie and I would like a private word with Ryder."

"Of course. Shall Agent Rodriguez and I step outside?"
she said, curbing her anger and worry.

Robbie popped to his feet and waved for them to stay.
"We'll just go to my office," he said, and in a flurry of activity, the trio hurried out, leaving her staring at Diego.

"I get the feeling you're not on board with these all being
related," she said, needing to know where he stood.

She didn't know why it mattered so much to her, but it did.

He shrugged impossibly broad shoulders and met her gaze.
"Serial killers are above my pay grade, but I can tell you've
done your research."

With a dip of her head to confirm it, she said, "I have. It's
important to me that we not only solve these cases but find
this missing hiker."

Diego narrowed his gaze and inspected her features,
clearly assessing her. "I can tell it's important to you, but
not just because of this missing hiker. Do you mind sharing why?"

The why of it wasn't something she normally shared with
others, because it still hurt too much.

Luckily, she was spared from answering as the door

opened and Robbie, Sophie and Ryder returned and sat at the table.

Sophie spoke up first. "We may not all agree with your serial killer theory, but we're all determined to find this missing hiker. If you're okay with that, Crooked Pass is eager to help."

It was less than she had hoped for, but she would take it. "I'm okay with that. Where do you want to start?"

JEANNIE HUGGED THE blanket tight, trying to stay warm against the cold from the stone walls and floor. The fact that he'd given her a blanket gave her hope that he intended to keep her alive for just a little longer.

She knew he didn't plan for her to leave this room alive. A large black bag sat in a far corner of the room. Large enough for a body.

Peering around in the dim light cast by the small overhead bulb, she searched for any way to escape besides the stairs off to one side of the room, but there were no windows or other openings.

Probably an old root cellar, she thought. That would explain the slight mustiness, dampness and constant chill.

Chill kept things from decaying.

Like a body, she thought, and fought back a sob.

She had to stay strong. She had to fight to survive. Whether it was for only another minute or another hour, the longer she stayed alive, the greater the likelihood the police would find her.

The creak of a door and slip of light from the top of the stairs warned he'd be joining her soon.

She sucked in a breath and prepared herself, bracing for his abuse. Praying that she had a clue on what pleased him so that he might keep her alive a little longer.

The bright lights, almost like stage lights, snapped on, jolting her into fearfulness.

The freak liked seeing her fear. But he also liked her fight as well.

As he came into view, face hidden beneath the black hood once again, she steadied herself and prayed.

Just let me live for one more minute, she thought. The minutes would become hours, and the hours might become another day of life.

It had to be enough for now, because help had to be on the way.

It just had to be.

Chapter Four

Since Crooked Pass Security had decided to help, Gabriella shared detailed information on all the individuals who had been interviewed in the prior cases. She placed their photos and basic data on the murder board at the front of the large conference room they were using as their war room.

As they reviewed the individuals and the bios of the missing women, they found connections between all three men and women to the local university.

"We'll reach out to the university's human resources department to see if they're willing to provide info on anyone employed during the time frames the women were there," Gabriella said, hoping that they would release the information without a warrant.

"What about getting info on any students in the classes that the women took?" Diego asked as he perused the photos on the board.

"Student privacy is regulated by FERPA," Ryder advised, and then tacked on, "The Family Educational Rights and Privacy Act."

"Which means we'll need a warrant," Diego said, and everyone around the table nodded.

"Right now, we don't have enough info to get a warrant," Gabriella said with a heavy sigh.

"But we have John Wilson's program, which is like a gigantic internet vacuum. He might be able to suck up enough info from publicly posted info to give us some leads," Sophie advised, and jotted down some notes on a pad.

"Do you think he could search their places of employment as well?" Gabriella asked.

Robbie nodded eagerly. "If it's out there, the program can bring it in."

"What about the hiking club that Roberts joined last year?" Diego asked as he flipped through the papers in the file the CBI agents had provided.

"Like I said, if the info is out there—" Robbie began, but Diego finished for him.

"The program can bring it in," he said, and waved his hand in apology. "Sorry, but I'm an old-school investigator."

Sophie smiled and said, "There's nothing wrong with boots on the ground. I think it's important to do that as well as using whatever technology is available."

"I agree," Gabriella said, and gazed in Diego's direction. "I'd like to revisit some of the earlier witness statements together and after, talk to these possible witnesses in person as well as the main persons of interest at the time."

"I'm game. If it's okay with you, I'd like to check out photos and maps of the trails at some point also," Diego said.

"It's okay with me," she said, and glanced around the table. "I understand that Wilson's program can also do a predictive analysis of possible suspects. Would it take long to run it against the current persons of interest and see what the program says?"

"We'll reach out to him and see if he can't prioritize that given the circumstances," Sophie said with a quick look at Robbie, who nodded to confirm that action.

"Great," Ryder said, stood and walked up to the murder board. Tapping the photos of the possible suspects and witnesses in the earlier cases, he said, "Let's split up these interviews."

Gabriella glanced at the board and considered the various individuals until one caught her eye. She walked up and pointed to his photo. "This was Cornerstone's boyfriend at the time of her disappearance. He would also have been at the university at the same time as all the missing women."

"The university has how many students at one time?" Diego tossed out for consideration.

"About five thousand. If there is a connection, it's likely because they had the same major or some other common interest like hiking," Gabriella responded, aware that the university connection might not amount to a pivotal clue.

Diego nodded. "Hiking for sure. I guess that's why I'd like to review those trails. See if they're dogworthy."

"Dogworthy?" Gabriella replied, a dark brow arched in question.

"Sorry for the lingo. It means checking out a crime scene to determine whether or not it's worth having my K-9 Poppy search," Diego explained.

"Got it. But the police search teams have already used their K-9s in the area where the hiker disappeared," Gabriella advised.

"I understand, but Poppy has exceptional skills. I'm also wondering about something," Diego said. He stood and approached the map.

Circling the area bounded by the locations of the three missing hikers, he said, "I don't know much about serial killers, but I know they sometimes keep all their victims in the same general area. They sometimes visit them also, right?"

Gabriella nodded and met Diego's dark gaze. "They do, but I believe that the serial killer is taking them to another location to kill them. If he does that, he may place them in an area far removed from where he took them."

An exasperated sigh escaped the K-9 agent, and he jammed his hands on his hips and examined the map again. After long seconds, he ran his finger along a main highway that circled the base of each of the trails. Glancing at Sophie and Robbie, he said, "Is there any possibility that CCTV cameras may have picked up any vehicles near these trailheads?"

"Possibly for the latest victim," Robbie replied.

"We're trying to get feeds from any traffic cameras in those areas," Ryder advised, and Gabriella confirmed.

"We should have them by later today."

"Great. Would you mind reviewing the trail photos and maps with me so we can decide whether to visit any of the locations before we get the bad weather that's coming in a few days?" Diego asked, and met her gaze, his intelligent and understanding.

"Sure, and after, we can meet with the possible persons of interest once Ryder and I decide who to take," she said.

"Great. I guess we should get going," he said with a glance at a large, military-style watch on his wrist.

"I have detailed maps and photos back in my office," she said, and then skipped her glance to those left at the table. "I guess we'll connect here later."

"Call us with an ETA and we'll bring in some dinner," Robbie said.

Sophie playfully elbowed him. "Ignore him. His belly is a bottomless pit that always needs filling."

"I'll be sure to keep that in mind," Gabriella said with a smile before returning her attention to Diego.

He did a small hand command and the large German shepherd, who had been peacefully lying by Diego's chair, head pillowed on big paws, rose and went to Diego's side.

Motioning to the door of the conference room with his hand, he said, "Lead the way."

IT WAS A short drive from the new offices of Crooked Pass Security in downtown Denver to the CBI offices in nearby Lakewood. After clearing security, Diego followed Gabriella to the elevators and then to her spacious office.

The office immediately said a lot about her.

Everything was neat and orderly, including the murder board at one end of the room that was virtually a replica of the one they'd set up back at the Crooked Pass Security offices.

Her desktop had a black blotter edged with a very feminine floral pattern. A few desk accessories matched the blotter. Beside them, a picture frame held a photo that he couldn't see from his position in front of the desk. An expensive-looking silver-and-gold pen set sat at the top of the blotter. A file with papers occupied the middle of the blotter.

Gabriella went to her chair, removed her suit jacket and draped it over the back of her chair.

The action drew attention to the shoulder holster and Glock tucked within as well as the way the fine cotton of her blouse cradled generous breasts.

That dichotomy of femininity and power was a heady aphrodisiac, and he had to drag his attention away from her. His focus had to be on the case and proving himself, and not the very attractive CBI agent with the shadows of sadness in her eyes.

He rubbed Poppy's head in reward and gestured for her to sit, which she did with a bored sigh. His K-9 was used to more activity, and he'd have to take her for a long walk later to let her stretch her legs.

Gabriella swung around her desk, picked up the file crammed with a large stack of papers and tucked it against her chest.

She laid the file on top of a small nearby table and with a wave of a hand, invited him to sit.

He did, and she joined him, sitting beside him so they could both look at the materials as she spread them out and identified each of them.

"You asked to see photos of the trails. These are from the most recent disappearance," she said, and pointed out a big boulder. "We suspect Roberts was nearly at the summit when she stopped to appreciate the view and have a snack."

"And he grabbed her there? Is that what you think?" Diego asked, wanting to understand what CBI thought about the hiker's movements.

Gabriella ran a long, elegant finger with a bright red nail along the image of the boulder in the photo. "There were scattered remnants of trail mix here. That would support that hypothesis."

"And he—I assume it's a he—" he said, and met her gaze, awaiting her confirmation.

"Most serial killers are male, white, and between the ages of twenty-five and thirty-four," she advised.

That represented a large swath of the population of Denver, he thought. Motioning to the photos of the trail, he said, "He grabs her and forcefully takes her back down the mountain. No one sees them."

"No one, although we had a couple of callers say that they saw Roberts's car in the parking lot for the trailhead but didn't see her. There weren't that many people on the trail, possibly due to the unseasonable snow we recently had," she explained.

"This trail goes higher than others in the area, so there might still be snow there. I saw it myself when I hiked it," he said, and tacked on, "How did he know she was doing the hike?"

Gabriella's full lips tightened into a thin line, and she did a little shrug. "Serial killers generally go through phases. One of them is trolling, where they seek out a victim. Usually, they do it in an area where they are likely to meet the kind of person that attracts them, like the university."

"Why wouldn't he grab her there?" he wondered aloud, and shifted away the photos from the Roberts trail to those from one of the earlier disappearances.

He noticed right away that the trails looked very similar, so maybe hiking them was where the serial killer might meet his victim. If it even was a serial killer, he thought, recalling Ryder's reticence about that theory.

"The university might be too public a place for a grab. He might woo them there, though. That's another phase. The serial killer tries to ingratiate himself to his victim to create a level of comfort or confidence with them," Gabriella explained, and handed him the photos from the very first disappearance.

"There wasn't much evidence from the first two trails, either because they didn't see them as a crime scene or because the killer was careful," she explained, and sat back in her chair with a heavy sigh.

He understood her dejection. If she was right, two women had already lost their lives, and the third...

"I wish I could say these other trails are dogworthy, but it's been nearly two years since the women were on these trails," he said, and gathered up the photos of those areas, but as he did so, he noticed another set of pictures in her file.

He reached for them, but she stayed his hand with hers. He noticed her hand tremble as she did so and heard her say in a soft tone, "That one's not pertinent right now."

He wondered at her reticence about that location but honored her request. For the moment, at least.

"Ryder isn't on board with your theory because of the gap between these disappearances. Why do you think they're connected?" he pressed, wanting to know her mind and how it worked.

"As I mentioned earlier, there have been gaps before. It happens because the killer almost always takes a trophy from the victim and uses that to relive the experience. But as the adrenaline wears off, that phase fades. The killer then becomes depressed. That depression can last for a long time until he starts to fantasize again and then starts trolling once more," she explained.

"And that trophy and depression phase could account for the two-year gap?" he asked.

She nodded. "It could explain it according to all my research."

"Would you mind sharing any of the research so I can get up to speed on your theory?" he asked, wanting to be as helpful as possible during their investigation.

"I don't mind. I'll have my assistant make copies of my notes so you can review them," she said, and gathered up the photos into her file.

Before he could say anything else, she shot to her feet, marched to her murder board and rapped her knuckles against its surface. "The clock is ticking, and I worry that once he murders her, we'll lose his trail until he takes another victim. That's why we need to interview these people as soon as possible."

Her gaze gleamed with determination but also that sadness he had seen earlier that day. He understood the determination. As for the sadness, he hoped he'd one day understand what had put it there.

Pushing to his feet, he said, "Whatever you need to do, I'm ready to help."

Chapter Five

Gabriella shot a quick look at Diego as he sat beside her in the SUV. His K-9 Poppy was harnessed in the back seat, peacefully sitting there.

They'd let Poppy scent a dirty T-shirt that Roberts's mother had provided from the missing woman's apartment after the police had released the area as a crime scene. Diego now had the plastic bag that held the T-shirt so that Poppy could take another sniff before they met up with each of the three suspects they were visiting. In the meantime, Gabriella's partner Ryder would speak to the witnesses from each of the disappearances.

She'd seen what scent dogs could do on other cases with the CBI but wondered if Poppy could help them on this case.

"Do you think she can pick up Roberts's scent if one of these men is responsible for her disappearance?" Gabriella asked, and watched Diego's reaction from the corner of her eye.

He did a little side-to-side bobble of his head, as if uncertain, and then said, "Possibly. Poppy has a strong sense of smell and if one of them has been near Roberts recently, she might pick it up."

If she did, they could focus on that suspect and maybe even find Roberts before she was murdered.

Gabriella was sure that Roberts was still alive.

But not for long.

While the killer was likely enjoying his time with her, he also had to know that he couldn't keep her for much longer.

Gabriella was convinced that was his MO. Abduct, hold, murder and then dump them far removed from the original location. That explained why the bodies of the first two women had yet to be found.

But what about Isabella? the little voice in her head challenged. If Isabella was the first, was his MO the same or different? Was it possible her sister lay somewhere not far from the missing women?

"How long does a cadaver's scent linger?" she asked aloud, wondering if Poppy could pick up the smell of a body that was nearly eight years old.

With a shrug of his broad shoulders, Diego said, "Dogs have been known to pick up scents that have been in the ground for decades. Sometimes even millennia."

"Millennia?" Gabriella pressed, dubious of the claim.

Diego nodded without hesitation. "Archaeologists have used dogs to find remains at various dig sites."

So it wasn't so far-fetched that they might be able to find her little sister after nearly a decade. But only if they could make some headway on this case.

"Our victims are more recent, so hopefully we can identify a possible killing field," she said, and checked her rearview mirror before pulling into the parking lot for the office building for Cornerstone's former boyfriend, Maxwell Baxter.

"Cornerstone disappeared about six months after graduation. Baxter and she had been dating for over a year. They were both business majors, which was how they'd met," Gabriella advised as she parked in front of the nondescript glass-and-cement building in the small corporate center.

Diego turned slightly in his seat to face her and said, "I

only got a quick look at the file, but it seemed to me that the police and CBI ruled him out as a person of interest fairly quickly."

Gabriella met his gaze and nodded. "They did. He had an alibi, but I'm not convinced," she said, and wrinkled her nose.

"I guess you don't think it passes the smell test," he gathered from her gesture.

"His alibi is another woman. He was cheating on Cornerstone with her and as far as I'm concerned, that's as good as lying," she said with a determined bob of her head.

DIEGO DIDN'T DISAGREE. "Once a liar, always a liar."

"Definitely. Not to mention that I didn't interview him, and I'd like to get my own take on him."

"And Poppy's take if she can pick up Roberts's scent," Diego added.

"That's right. If you're ready, let's go interview Cornerstone's cheating boyfriend," Gabriella said, and slipped out of the car.

Diego stepped out and then opened the back door to release Poppy. The German shepherd hopped out, and Diego grabbed her leash. Together they followed Gabriella along the path to the front door of the office of a well-known accounting firm.

As they entered the lobby, the receptionist, a young, pretty twentysomething, greeted them with a warm smile. "How may we help you today?"

Gabriella pulled her CBI badge from a leather cross-body bag, held it up for the receptionist to see and said, "We'd like to speak with Maxwell Baxter."

The warm smile faded instantly. "I'll see if he's available."

Diego knew that Baxter would be available whether or not he wanted to be, but didn't say it, certain Gabriella could handle the situation if Baxter refused to cooperate.

The receptionist dialed Baxter and in a whisper into her headset, explained the situation. Barely a second later, she ended the call and said, "Through those double doors. Mr. Baxter's office is the third one to the right."

"Thank you," Gabriella said, and he trailed behind her, Poppy leashed tight to his leg.

They walked in together to find Baxter standing just outside the door to his office.

He hadn't aged much in the nearly three years since Cornerstone's disappearance, Diego thought, recalling the photo from Gabriella's file.

His blond hair was cut in a similar fade, but the T-shirt and jeans were gone, replaced by a bespoke suit befitting someone in an upscale accounting firm. He had a preppy, pretty-boy look that immediately set Diego's teeth on edge. He'd had too many of those types look down their noses at someone like him, a working-class kid who'd paid his way through college as a marine ROTC.

"Please come in," Baxter said, and held his hand out in invitation, a forced smile on his features.

As soon as they had stepped in, he closed the door behind them and hurried to his desk. He sat down and, in a tone as icy as his light blue gaze, he said, "What can I do for you?"

"We're investigating Missy Cornerstone's disappearance," Gabriella said.

Baxter's gaze narrowed and drifted from Gabriella to him and then to Poppy.

"I thought Missy's case was closed," he said.

"The case will only be closed once we find Missy and know what happened to her," Gabriella said.

"I had nothing to do with that," Baxter immediately countered.

"Great. Then you won't mind answering a few questions for me," Gabriella said and began rattling off a standard series of questions about his relationship with Missy and the events on the day she disappeared.

As she did so, Diego watched Baxter closely, trying to pick up any signs of deception. But he failed to notice anything.

Baxter's gaze stayed glued to Gabriella for the most part, except for a look in Diego's direction when she mentioned his cheating. It was almost as if Baxter was hoping for some kind of kinship since Diego was another man and might condone his actions.

When he didn't get the intended response, Baxter focused on Gabriella again, answering without hesitation or any of the little tells Diego had learned over the years as an investigator and K-9 handler.

After about a half hour of Gabriella's questioning, Baxter grew frustrated. Especially as she grilled him for yet another time with a similar question to one he had already answered, hoping to elicit a different, and possibly deceptive, response.

Baxter sat up straighter and splayed his hands on his desktop. "Agent Ruiz, I've already answered that question, and if you don't mind, I have to end this. I have a client coming in shortly and need to prepare for that meeting."

Gabriella hesitated but then rose, reached into her bag and handed him her business card. "I appreciate you taking the time to chat with us. If you can think of anything else, please call."

Baxter slipped it into his desk drawer. "I will. Believe me, I want to find Missy as much as you do. I want that sword to stop hanging over my head," he said, rose and walked to the door of his office.

When he opened it, Gabriella walked there and glanced in his direction, her meaning clear.

He stood and urged Poppy to heel with a slight tug at her leash, but at the door, he gave Poppy a hand signal to scent Baxter.

Cold Case K-9

She did, sniffing all around him for long seconds until Baxter stepped away and swiped at his pants leg as if Poppy had left something nasty behind. Baxter was clearly not a fan of dogs.

"I need to get to work," Baxter reiterated, and Diego repeated Gabriella's earlier thanks.

"We appreciate you answering our questions," he said as Gabriella and he walked out the door, Poppy just slightly behind them.

Gabriella leaned close as they walked. In heels, she was about a head shorter than him, and her silky hair brushed the underside of his jaw as she whispered, "Did Poppy pick up on anything?"

"Nothing," he said, and battled the physical response to her proximity and the smell of her, a flowery and citrusy perfume mixed with the slight odor of leather from her holster.

He willed away the attraction, and if she noticed, he didn't pick up on it as they walked to her car and he secured Poppy in the back seat once again.

"What was your read of Baxter?" she asked as she slipped behind the wheel and started the car.

"Besides his being a cheating prick who still doesn't get why that was wrong?" he said, recalling how the man had looked at him during the interview.

"Besides that," Gabriella said with a half smile and chuckle as she pulled out of the parking spot.

"He wasn't lying, and I do think he'd love for us to figure out what happened to Missy. Not for her or her family, but because it lets him off the hook. That's all that matters to people like him," he said with some bite in his tone.

She immediately picked up on it and peeked in his direction. "You've had your run-ins with the Baxters of the world?"

"You might say that, but you probably have as well," he

said, deflecting because he wasn't ready to share more about himself. At least not until he knew more about her.

"I have. People who are born on third base sometimes tend to think the world should revolve around them," she said, dragging a chuckle from him.

"Third base people. I like that and yes, Baxter is definitely self-centered, but does that make him a killer?"

Gabriella gripped the steering wheel tightly and shrugged, her lips in a tight slash. "Serial killers can be egotistical. Just look at Bundy thinking he could represent himself at his murder trial."

Even he knew that about Bundy, although he still had to read through the notes she had provided.

"I guess Baxter stays on the list of suspects for now," he said, just to be sure they were on the same page.

"He does. Next up is Nations's old boyfriend, and then we're off to see Roberts's current partner."

"Did you notice that Baxter didn't seem to like Poppy too much?" he asked.

"I did. Why?" she asked with a glance in his direction.

With a laugh he replied, "I think Bill Murray said that he was suspicious of people who didn't like dogs, but trusted when a dog didn't like a person."

Laughter exploded from Gabriella, and she looked at Poppy. "I like that. I can't wait to see what Poppy thinks of the next two suspects."

"I can't either," he said, and settled in for the short drive to their next destination.

Chapter Six

The interview with Ben Kinston went much like the one with Maxwell Baxter.

Kinston clearly hadn't been happy to see them on the doorstep of his small veterinary practice, especially since he seemed to be having a very busy day with an assortment of sick and injured pets.

Despite that, he took the time to chat about his former girlfriend Alyssa Nations. When he was shown pictures of Cornerstone, Nations and Roberts, he indicated he had no knowledge of them and had never seen them in his classes.

That made sense to Diego, since all three of the women had been business majors while Kinston had taken biology. As they were leaving, it was obvious Poppy hadn't picked up Roberts's scent on Kinston and that she liked the vet, especially when he asked permission to rub her head and give her a treat.

Diego appreciated that he understood that working dogs weren't pets.

Since the vet had a nice dog park adjacent to his office building, Diego said, "Do you mind if I let Poppy relieve herself and have some downtime?"

"Not at all. It would be nice to stretch my legs and get some fresh air," she said as they exited the vet's office.

He nodded and walked with Poppy to the dog park. The area was empty as most of the dogs were inside, awaiting treatment. He removed the leash from Poppy's harness and with a hand command, set her free to relieve herself.

The German shepherd took off, racing to the far end of the dog park to do her duty. When she was done, she raced around the park, speeding up and down some of the ramps playfully.

"It's good to see her acting like a regular dog," Gabriella said as he grabbed a waste bag from a nearby holder, and strolled with him to pick up Poppy's mess.

"It is. I feel for her when we're caught up in some investigation and she's trapped in a room."

GABRIELLA PEERED IN his direction, sensing that he also didn't like being trapped for hours. Which made her wonder aloud, "How did you become a K-9 handler?"

With a shrug, he said, "It just happened."

He also wasn't someone who liked to share about himself, but Gabriella was determined to know more because he intrigued her.

"How did you end up working with Crooked Pass Security?" she asked as they reached the back of the dog park, and he bent to pick up Poppy's waste.

He didn't face her as he said, "I knew Sophie and Robbie from some other cases we worked together. A friend knew they were hiring and suggested I meet with them."

"You worked with Ryder as well, didn't you?" she asked as he straightened and closed the waste bag.

"I did. How long have you known Ryder?" he asked, and since he'd opened up a little about himself, she did the same.

"For about six years. I interned with CBI while I was in college and once I graduated, I was offered a position with them."

"He seems like a good guy and from what I can see, Sophie and he are a good match," Diego said.

"They are. It's not easy to find that when you work in law enforcement. The demands of the job put a strain on relationships."

"Is that why you're single?" he said, and glanced at her from the corner of his eye as they walked back toward the dog park entrance.

"Who said I'm single?" she teased. She loved the flash of disappointment across his face before she put him out of his misery.

"I'm single. Not looking at the moment but if it were to happen—"

She didn't get to finish as he let out an earsplitting whistle and Poppy came running over.

The whistle was payback, she surmised from the boyish grin on his face as he rubbed Poppy's head and body before slipping her a treat.

As he leashed Poppy, he schooled his features as he said, "On to our last suspect?"

"On to Peter Konijn. Poppy is likely going to scent Roberts on him since they're currently involved," she said as they walked back to the car to visit the last suspect.

"Does he have an alibi for the day Roberts went missing?" Diego asked, brow furrowed as he waited for her answer.

"He claims he was visiting his parents, and they confirm it," she advised, and unlocked the car doors.

Once they were seated, he said, "But you don't believe that."

"Parents protect their children. That might include lying for them," she answered without hesitation.

"Even if they know he's lying and could be a killer?" Diego challenged.

Gabriella tapped her forehead in emphasis. "They might

suspect it up here, but don't want to believe it. Maybe with the right proof they would come clean."

Diego was silent for a long moment before he said, "If their son did take Roberts, their lies could be endangering her life."

She couldn't argue with that. "I know Ryder is interviewing the parents, but I may want to talk to them myself depending on the read I get from Konijn today."

"I don't blame you. Especially since the clock is ticking," he said, and captured her gaze for a hot second before she had to return her attention to the road.

The clock was ticking, so she wasted no time in getting to the Konijn family offices, which were luckily not far from Sixteenth Street and the CPS location.

"Another third-baser," Diego said as he took in the fancy brass plaque at the door that said Konijn Wealth Management.

A wry smile drifted across Gabriella's lips, and it hit him that she was even more beautiful when she smiled, lighting up her dark brown eyes. As she thanked him for opening the door and their gazes connected, he felt gobsmacked again and as her eyes widened slightly, she was obviously feeling that connection as well.

The lobby for the Konijn family business screamed money, from the gleaming mahogany wood of the receptionist's desk to the artwork on the walls. He wasn't an expert, but it didn't take one to identify a signed Warhol print on one wall and what looked like a Jackson Pollock behind the receptionist's desk.

As she had before, Gabriella approached the desk and was met with the same resistance as at Baxter's location. But the badge made things happen again and within seconds, a young man emerged from the office area.

"Mr. Konijn asked that I show you to our conference room," he said, and motioned to a door just to the left and behind the receptionist's area. Clearly, Konijn didn't want anyone to see them.

They followed him into the conference room where with an obsequious smile and clutch of his hands, the man said, "Is there anything I can get you? Water? Coffee, perhaps?"

"Just Mr. Konijn," Gabriella said, her tone making it clear she wasn't pleased with the wait.

The man's smile faded. He nodded and replied, "He'll be right with you."

He hurried from the room and barely a minute later, Peter Konijn walked in by an older man who had to be his father. They had a similar build and facial features. The older Konijn's hair had gone mostly white, but here and there were remnants of his son's sandy-colored hair.

Peter walked over, a grim look on his face. "Peter Konijn. My father, Ralph Konijn," he said as he first shook Gabriella's hand and then his.

It's not parent-teacher night, Gabriella thought as father and son sat at the conference room table. The elder Konijn took the head of the table with his son to the right.

"There's no need for your father to be present," she said, and sat across from Peter, wanting to see every reaction to her questions.

"Actually, there is. I'm also an attorney and here to make sure my son's rights are protected," the older man said with an imperial arch of a silvery brow.

"Then you'll appreciate that your son is not in custody and as such, anything he says right now can and will be used against him. If he chooses not to answer my questions, I'll take him in for a formal interview. Would you prefer that?" she said, not about to be steamrolled by Peter's father.

The older man sputtered and was about to reply when Peter laid a warning hand on his jacket sleeve.

"I've got nothing to hide, Father. Ask away, Agent Ruiz," he said, and offered her an apologetic smile.

"Great," she said, and ran through his statement about his whereabouts on the day his partner disappeared.

His response didn't deviate from the earlier facts that she'd received, even when she pressed him a second and third time about what he'd done that day.

"My son has already answered repeatedly, and my wife and I can confirm his whereabouts," Ralph Konijn chimed in, words clipped with anger.

Gabriella silenced him with a glare, and a red flush of rage swept across his features.

Satisfied with Peter's answers, she shot a quick look at Diego, who whipped out the photos of the two other missing women. He placed them in front of Peter.

Peter narrowed his eyes and examined the photos.

"I don't understand," he said, and met her gaze, puzzlement on his.

"Do you recognize either of these women?" she asked.

He dipped his head from side to side, considering her question, and after a slight hesitation, he tapped one photo. "She looks familiar. Maybe from DU?" he said, the doubt obvious from his tone.

"Her name is Alyssa Nations. She disappeared two years ago from a trail not far from where Jeannie disappeared. The other woman is Missy Cornerstone. She likewise disappeared from a hiking trail," she advised.

The blood fled from both father's and son's faces. A second later, Peter waved his hands in denial. "I know nothing about these two women."

"They were both business majors at DU. Alyssa was the same year as you and Jeannie. Missy was two years behind you, but maybe you took similar classes," Gabriella advised, and after another nod at Diego, he placed more photos of the women in front of Peter.

Peter didn't look at them. He just waved his hands again and said, "There are hundreds if not thousands of business majors. We may have crossed paths at DU, but that's about it. I don't know anything about them."

She was tempted to press him about the disappearance dates for the two women but decided to switch back to Roberts.

"Do you and Jeannie have a good relationship?" she asked as she swept up the photos of the other missing women.

"We do. We've been dating since junior year and moved in together about six months ago," Peter advised, and relaxed slightly.

"Moving in together is a big life change. How's that going?" she asked, making her tone almost friendly to lull him into a false sense of security.

"Well. We have many shared interests and friends. Jeannie was very detail oriented, and so am I," he said.

She didn't fail to miss the "was" instead of "is."

"I gather hiking wasn't one of those 'shared interests'?" she pressed.

"It is, only… I had promised my parents I'd visit that weekend," he said, and shot a nervous look at his father as if needing reassurance.

"A visit without Jeannie?" she questioned, wondering why Roberts wouldn't have gone with him.

Peter swallowed awkwardly and nervously glanced at his father yet again.

Ralph answered for his son, his tone glacial. "My wife and I didn't always see eye to eye with Ms. Roberts."

NOW THIS WAS getting interesting, Diego thought as he glanced from the Konijns to Gabriella.

"What about?" she pressed.

"It's a family matter I'd rather not discuss in front of strangers," Ralph advised, his face as stony as granite.

"Would you rather discuss it at CBI offices?" she threatened again.

After a strangled cough, Peter said, "Jeannie thought I should spread my wings and work with another firm before settling for working with the family."

"Settling is not what I would call working for a top wealth management firm," his father immediately challenged.

"I know, Father. But maybe—"

"There's no maybes here, and this is not something to discuss in front of strangers," his father said to shut down the discussion.

Interesting, he thought. Dad likely had more reason for Roberts to disappear than the son.

A pained silence followed until Gabriella said, "I think that's all we need for now."

She rose and as she did so, she met his gaze and dipped her head in the direction of both father and son.

When the Konijns stood, Diego shot to his feet and motioned to Poppy, who eagerly responded, ready to act.

Gabriella waited as he slipped behind her and positioned himself and Poppy at the door. He gestured for the Konijns to exit, and they hesitated, but he insisted. "Please, you go first."

Ralph Konijn moved toward them and as he neared, Diego instructed Poppy to scent him.

The dog sniffed the father's legs, and he shied away, as if afraid of the dog.

"I'm sorry, I don't care for dogs," he said, and hurried past. Poppy lay down, signaling that she'd scented Roberts.

A second later, Peter walked by and Poppy rose, sniffed him and lay down again. Not surprising considering that Peter and Jeannie lived together.

But Poppy's reaction to Ralph was a different thing, and Gabriella had picked up on it.

As they walked into the lobby, she asked the elder Konijn, "When was the last time you saw Ms. Roberts?"

The older man glanced at his son, clearly discomfited, and said, "I can't say. Several weeks ago, I think."

"Weeks? Are you sure about that?" Diego said, certain from Poppy's reaction that it had to be more recent.

The two men shared a look, and this time Peter answered. "Weeks. As you might have guessed, Jeannie didn't visit with my parents often."

"If you could recall when that might be, I'd appreciate knowing the date," Gabriella said, and handed Peter her business card.

Peter fingered the card and then nodded. "I'll check my calendar and let you know."

"Great. Thanks," she said, whirled on a high-heeled foot and strode toward the door, Diego following her.

There was a pep in her step that said she was pleased with the outcome of the interview.

As they settled in the car, Poppy harnessed in the back seat, she met his gaze and said, "What did you think?"

"I think you have another suspect to add to your list."

She smiled and nodded. "I agree."

Chapter Seven

He'd been surprised at the arrival of the CBI agent and her K-9 sidekick.

He didn't like surprises.

He tapped the business card on his tabletop, wondering how she had connected the disappearances of the three women.

Granted, a good cop should have made the connections between Cornerstone and Nations sooner. But they hadn't.

Most cops were idiots, which was why he'd felt safe grabbing Roberts.

But somehow this CBI agent had put two and two together.

He peered at the business card again.

Gabriella Ruiz. The Ruiz name popped out at him like a big flashing warning sign.

He hadn't known her name when he'd first taken her.

But in the days after her disappearance, her name had been plastered all over the news.

Isabella Ruiz.

Ruiz, just like the beautiful CBI agent who had visited today.

He closed his eyes and pictured the twelve-year-old who'd awakened him to his true calling.

She'd had dark hair and eyes as well, but then again, many Latinas had similar coloring.

He screwed his eyes closed tighter, trying to remember more, but the memories had grown slightly fuzzy over the years. He couldn't remember if her nose had been as pert and straight as that of the CBI agent. Or if she'd had that small-ish dimple in her chin.

He should have taken a photo of her, but her kill had been too new and exciting, and he'd been too inexperienced.

He'd been better prepared for the others. Their photos were carefully tucked away with the small mementos he'd taken from them.

But he had a few mementos from Isabella. A small gold crucifix. A lock of her dark hair. The childish bracelet, like something out of a Cracker Jack box, that said, "Best friends."

There was no way the CBI agent was related to Isabella. No way. Ruiz had to be a common name.

But just in case, he intended to find out more about the attractive CBI agent.

And if she was related to Isabella…

That would only make things even more interesting.

GABRIELLA PARKED THE car a few doors down from the building for the Crooked Pass Security offices, but Diego wasn't ready to head upstairs to meet just yet.

"I'll meet you at the offices in about fifteen minutes. I need to walk Poppy," he said as he freed the German shepherd from the back seat.

"I could use a little fresh air as well," Gabriella said, and arched her back in a stretch that had him looking at all the wrong places.

He dragged his gaze away and muttered, "Suit yourself."

She gave him a side-eyed glance, puzzled by his almost snarky tone, and he apologized. After all, it wasn't her fault he was finding her way too attractive.

"I'm sorry. I mean, don't feel obligated to stay with us. I know you probably have a lot of work to do."

"I do, but if we're going to work together, I thought it would be good to get to know each other," she said, and joined him on the sidewalk.

"Sure," he said as he leashed Poppy and leisurely walked to the end of the block and onto the pedestrian Sixteenth Street Mall.

Gabriella matched his pace as she said, "You said you just kinda became a K-9 handler. Was it in the…did I hear you used to be a marine?"

"I *am* a marine. Once a marine, always a marine," he said with a smile and shake of his head.

A ghost of a smile drifted across her face, but it was tinged with that hint of sadness again. "I should have remembered that. My dad was…is…a marine."

"You said 'was.' Did he pass?" Diego wondered, deciding to use the walk to learn more about her as well.

She shook her head. "No, he's still alive. It's just that… things are a little weird between us," she admitted.

He didn't press, certain that the weirdness might be the source of her sadness. Before he could ask her another question, she said, "Why the Marines?"

"My grandfather was a marine in Vietnam, and I wanted to follow in his footsteps and help protect my country. It also helped pay for college."

She glanced at him from the corner of her eye. "It's not easy to get one of those ROTC scholarships."

Bragging wasn't his thing so with a shrug, he said, "It just kinda—"

"Happened," she finished for him and then tacked on, "Why not stay in the Marines? Didn't you finish ROTC as an officer?"

He nodded. "Second lieutenant. I shipped overseas to Afghanistan. Did my two years there."

"Just the two? No marine career for you?" she pressed just as Poppy relieved herself, letting him break from a discussion that might be too revealing. The last thing he wanted to do was share how PTSD had derailed his military career and defined his civilian life for way too long.

He pulled a waste bag from his jacket pocket, cleaned it up and deposited it in a nearby garbage can.

When he faced her, her gaze had narrowed, and he realized she was still expecting a response from him.

"No career for me. We should head back to CPS. They're probably wondering where we are, and Robbie is probably gnawing the conference room table," he said, and gestured in the direction of the Crooked Pass Security building.

GABRIELLA DIDN'T MISS that Diego didn't want to talk about his stint as a marine. For the moment, she left that alone, much like he didn't push when she'd mentioned her rift with her father.

A rift caused by the turmoil that had followed her sister's disappearance.

"Sure," she said, and they walked back to the CPS offices. They reached the doors at the same time as a deliveryman from a local Mexican restaurant.

When the man entered the elevator with them and hit the button for the CPS offices, Diego said, "We can take that up for you."

"No thanks, mano. That Robbie is a great tipper," the man said, and rode up to the offices with them.

Diego badged them in and a second later, apparently hearing the thunk of the front door lock, Robbie poked his head out of the conference room.

"Jamie, mano," Robbie said.

Jamie, the delivery man, passed Robbie one of the bags and waited for Robbie to tip him before handing the second bag to Diego.

"See you soon," Jamie said and hit the door button to exit the offices.

"I guess Jamie's a regular?" Gabriella said with a chuckle.

"Robbie's half-Cuban but has a thing for Mexican food," Diego said as they followed Robbie into the conference room where Ryder and Sophie were clearing the surface of the table.

"I get it. I always love it when my mami makes Mexican food," she said with a smile, recalling the tamales, menudo and pozole her mother had cooked just a few months ago for their Christmas Eve meal.

"Hopefully you won't be disappointed," he said, and removed the take-out dishes from the bag.

"We didn't know what you would want, so we ordered a lot of different things," Sophie said as she walked over with plates, cutlery and napkins while Robbie laid out an assortment of drinks on a credenza off to one side of the room.

In no time they were serving themselves from the dishes filled with hearty rice and black beans, assorted tacos, and the tamales, which were always one of her favorites.

Diego had grabbed one as well and at her questioning glance, since many people didn't like the cornmeal consistency, he said, "They're a lot like our Cuban tamales."

Plate loaded with food, but not enough to make her sleepy since they had a night of work ahead, she sat at the table, and Diego placed his plate by hers. A second later, he returned with two sodas, and she thanked him.

Silence reigned around the table for only a few minutes before Sophie glanced between them and Ryder and said, "How did your interviews go?"

Gabriella motioned to Ryder, wanting to defer their discussion since the addition of Ralph Konijn to their suspect list would likely be a surprise.

"Witness statements haven't changed much except for one thing. Alyssa Nations's former roommate remembered that Alyssa had been a little spooked in the days just before her disappearance."

Gabriella paused with her fork halfway to her mouth and straightened in her seat. "Did she know why Alyssa was spooked?"

"She said that Alyssa mentioned that she thought someone was following her," Ryder advised.

His comment was almost like a punch to her gut, because one of Isabella's scout mates had told her something similar years after her sister's disappearance. She laid the food-laden fork down with a shaky hand.

"Did her roommate see anyone around that was suspicious?" she asked.

Ryder shook his head. "She says that she wished she'd paid more attention when Alyssa said it, but she didn't recall anything out of the ordinary."

"Nothing similar from Missy's witnesses?" Diego asked, and forked up some tamale.

"No. I've hit everyone on the current list, and I'm hoping that the Miami SBS branch can help with Wilson's program," Ryder advised.

"We just got the SBS reports a few minutes ago. We can take a look when you're ready," Robbie said around a mouthful of food.

His plate was piled high, and it made Gabriella remember what Diego had said about Robbie being a bottomless pit.

Beside Robbie, Sophie and Ryder sat side by side, shoulders brushing occasionally, clearly now a couple. In the few weeks since they'd met, she'd seen a decided change in her colleague. He seemed happier and often left the office with a smile, eager to go home.

Which for some reason had her shooting a glance at Diego.

There was no doubt he was handsome. Troubled, she thought, recognizing a kindred spirit that way. Maybe that was the reason for the instant connection she'd felt.

"How did your interviews go?" Ryder asked, his gaze drifting between her and Diego.

Diego did a little shrug and deferred to her, peering in her direction.

"Kinston's clear in my book," she said, and Diego nodded in agreement.

"Baxter's not the nicest guy, but I'd drop him down on the list. That leaves Konijn," she said, and again got a nod from Diego.

"There's something in your tone that says you're not eliminating him just yet," Sophie said.

Diego and she shared a quick look before she said, "Actually, it looks like we may be adding a new suspect."

Chapter Eight

Jeannie tugged and pulled at the one metal shackle, trying to free herself. Her skin was almost raw from trying to slip her hand through the band, but she had to keep on trying.

She understood now why some animals would gnaw off a leg to escape a hunter's trap.

Try as she might, she couldn't work her hand past the metal cuff around her wrist.

What was the sense anyway? she asked herself with a frustrated sob. Even if she freed her hand, there were still three other restraints keeping her prisoner.

A cellar with only one way out that was right past her captor.

Footsteps sounded above her.

He was home.

Cold filled her gut, and she drew her arms and legs tight, fearing his arrival.

A second later, a sliver of light warned he was opening a trapdoor at the top of the stairs.

The light grew brighter as he lifted it ever higher and then stepped down into the cellar.

There was something different about his pace. It was slower. More deliberate.

Would this be her last day? she wondered.

As he reached the bottom of the stairs, he flipped on the lights, nearly blinding her after a day spent in the darkness of the cellar.

"Good evening, Jeannie," he said, surprising her. She hadn't thought that he knew her name.

At her continued silence, he slipped out the knife and said, "It's usually polite to say 'Good evening' back."

Since she'd learned he liked a little fight, she tilted her chin up a defiant inch and said, "Good evening, back."

He laughed, a loud, hearty laugh, and sheathed the knife.

"I see you're learning. That's a good little toy, Jeannie," he said, and whipped up the camera.

"Look at me," he said, and when she did, he snapped off a few photos.

She waited for his next command, waited for him to undress and take her, and when he didn't, she held her breath, wondering yet again if this would be her last day of life.

Instead, he sniffed the air and said, "I can smell your fear. It's intoxicating."

He walked over then, fully dressed, bent, and buried his face against the side of her neck.

As he did so, she realized the Bowie knife was within easy reach.

She shot out her hand to grab it, but he was faster and snared her hand before she could grab it and plunge it into his heart.

He twisted her wrist, making her cry out from the pain.

He only laughed and said, "See how easy it is to want to kill someone?"

With another rough twist, her wrist snapped, and pain exploded through her body.

She moaned, but he only laughed and stepped away.

Cradling her broken wrist to her chest, she watched as he backed away toward the stairs.

"I like your fight, Jeannie. But tonight, I have something more important to do," he said. He whirled, shut off the bright lights and hurried up the steps.

Tears of pain and joy spilled down her face.

She was broken, but she was still alive.

That was all that mattered.

ROBBIE AND SOPHIE had sent Ralph Konijn's name to their Miami counterparts to get whatever information they could about the older man.

In the meantime, Diego, Ryder and Gabriella cleared off the table of their dinner remnants and tackled the information that John Wilson had sent.

Diego glanced at the reports, trying to absorb the wealth of details gathered about not only their three possible suspects but several other individuals that the three victims might have in common.

It was almost too much information, and Diego worried that it might delay them rather than help.

"This is a lot to take in," he said as he flipped through all the reports.

"It is, but let's go through each suspect and see if the analysis agrees with our initial observations," Sophie said as she turned on a monitor on one wall of the room and brought up Wilson's report.

As she did so, Gabriella rose and walked to their murder board to transfer any pertinent information there.

"Wilson's predictive program has assigned a low probability score to both Baxter and Kinston. Do you both agree with that?" Sophie said, and skipped her glance from him to Gabriella.

At Gabriella's nod, he said, "We agree."

"Konijn was slightly higher at 65 percent but in my mind,

that's still a failing grade," Ryder said as he, too, skimmed through the papers.

"And how does Wilson even get to these numbers?" Diego wondered aloud.

"Sophie can show you," Robbie said. With that, his sister scrolled through a few screens to bring up one that had a breakdown of various factors that Wilson's program had considered.

"As we mentioned earlier, John's program is like a giant internet vacuum, sucking up whatever information it can from various sources and analyzing it," Sophie explained, and using a laser pointer, she circled one reference point on the screen.

"The program looked at location data where Roberts disappeared but couldn't determine if Konijn had been in that area," she said, and then moved on to another reference point.

"A review of text and other messages got a very high rank, which tells me not all was right in the world between Konijn and Roberts," Sophie said.

"There are issues between Roberts and Konijn's father. That was obvious from our interview, and it's why we added him as a suspect," Gabriella advised. She added a note beneath Ralph Konijn's name on their murder board.

Sophie drilled down another level in the data about the text messages, and Diego didn't fail to miss the line item about violent tendencies. Pointing to that, he said, "Am I reading that right? The program is predicting possible violent behavior? How does it know?"

Robbie jumped in with an explanation. "Wilson has recently been working on adding more artificial intelligence to his program. The AI has been trained to pick up on certain patterns and actions to predict human behavior."

"For real?" Diego said, both dubious and worried about the implications of programs with such power.

"For real. Researchers at MIT have created similar algorithms, and there are already programs that can review materials to diagnose schizophrenia," Sophie advised.

"If they can do that, can they predict if someone can become a serial killer?" Gabriella asked.

"Possibly. And on that note…" Sophie flipped through several screens to display one that drew a gasp and surprise from Gabriella.

"The program says there's a 95 percent probability all three disappearances are the work of a serial killer," she said, reading aloud the program's prediction.

"Looks like you were right about this, Gabby. I should have trusted your gut," Ryder said, apology alive in his tone.

A second later, Sophie hauled up another screen that elicited shocked silence from all until Sophie said, "According to the program, there's a high probability these three other cases are also connected to the serial killer."

Diego scanned the names on the screen, and one jumped out at him.

"Isabella Ruiz? Is she a relation?" he said, and glanced at Gabriella.

Her face had paled to a sickly green and in a tremulous voice, she said, "I was hoping my sister might still be alive somewhere."

A second later, she plopped heavily into the chair next to him, body shaking as she buried her head in her hands and sobbed.

He muttered a curse and wrapped an arm around Gabriella, hauling her close as he glared at Sophie and said, "You could have given her some warning."

"I didn't read the details to see the names. I'm so sorry, Gabriella," she said, and hurried over to embrace her.

Gabriella raised her head and shakily swiped tears from

her face. "It's okay," she said. But Diego didn't know how that was possible.

She'd just discovered that her sister was the likely victim of a serial killer.

And he'd just learned the reason for that sadness he'd seen in her eyes.

"Maybe we should take a break. Give Gabriella a moment," he said as he squeezed her upper arm again, offering comfort.

"No. Every minute we waste is a minute less for Jeannie Roberts."

"Are you sure?" Sophie asked, gaze narrowed with worry.

"I'm sure," she said. Beneath his arm, strength flooded her body. She straightened her shoulders and grabbed a nearby pen as if to take notes on her pad.

He didn't miss the slight tremble in her hand that said she was fighting to keep it together.

"Do we have full details on those other victims' cases?" Ryder said, trying to move past the difficult moment.

Sophie shook her head. "We don't. The connections for these cases likely came from assorted police reports and possibly even true crime websites."

"It may take time to get the reports from local police," Gabriella said with a disappointed sigh.

Robbie mimicked typing with his fingers. "I could speed that up."

"Meaning?" Diego said with an arch of a dark brow.

Ryder held his hand up to stop Robbie from answering. "You don't want to know, Diego. But like Gabriella said, every minute counts."

"I should go to my office to get that info for you," Robbie said, shot to his feet and hurried from the room.

"Better we don't know how he gets it?" Diego asked, peering from Ryder to Sophie.

"He won't do anything to compromise the case. Trust us," Sophie said.

Diego hadn't worked long enough with them to trust them, but if his old friend Jackson did, he had to temper his concerns. Especially if it meant finding Jeannie Roberts and closure for Gabriella and her family.

"I trust you," Gabriella said, and he echoed her comment.

"Okay, let's dive through all this other info," Sophie said.

Gabriella forced her mind from the moment Isabella's name had appeared on the screen, and her reaction, to the data that Wilson's program had snared from various sources on the internet.

There was so much data that Ryder had slipped from the room to bring in another whiteboard for the new victims and their information.

As they reviewed the details and listed the relevant points connecting the women, one thing was clear: Isabella didn't fit in.

She hadn't gone to the University of Denver. She hadn't been a hiker. She wasn't in the age range.

"Isabella was the first, and he probably hadn't intended to kill her," she whispered as Ryder jotted down the last bit of information from Wilson's reports.

Ryder stepped back from the board, jammed his hands on his hips and reviewed the information again before he finally said, "Yes. That's the most likely reasoning."

"Like Dahmer's first kill. That might also explain the gap until the next murder," Gabriella said, stood and walked to the murder board.

"Something made him take Isabella. He accidentally killed her, but he liked it. As for the gap, he didn't have the right opportunity to take another woman," she said, and tapped on a name on the murder board. "The opportunity came twice over the next two years. But his method was different, and judging from the gap, he didn't like something about those kills."

"They were too fast," Diego tossed out for consideration.

Gabriella couldn't disagree. She walked back to her sister's name on the board and said, "When Isabella disappeared, the area was thoroughly searched. We never found her. Same for Cornerstone and Nations. Now we have Roberts. He likes to take time with his victims."

"Time he didn't have with those two other kills," Ryder said as he stood beside her, examining the board.

"If time is what he wants, Roberts may still be alive," Sophie said, and displayed another screen from Wilson's report.

She used the laser pointer to highlight the names of the current suspects. "We have these three. And now we've added Ralph Konijn. But according to Wilson, there are at least six other men with possible connections to our victims."

A tap came at the door a second before Robbie rushed in, laptop in hand. He paused to glance at the board before he said, "I've got info for you. I'm printing copies of all the reports for you also, but I see you have some of the names up on that list."

Which had Gabriella sighing with disgust. "So many names."

Robbie approached the monitor with the list and circled three of the names. "You can take these off the list. All these men were interviewed and had solid alibis."

"So that adds only two other names to our list," Diego said, and shuffled around some papers to read the profiles of the two new suspects. After a quick look, he said, "Both of the men are white and twenty-five. That would make them, or any of these others, only a teen at the time of Isabella's murder."

With a wave of her hand, Gabriella gestured to the file she had provided to Diego earlier that day. "When you get a chance, look at my research. In the US, our youngest serial killer was thirteen. Murdered four women including two young girls. The next oldest was seventeen. He killed three women that he stalked and murdered during home invasions."

A stunned silence filled the room, and Gabriella understood. She'd been hard-pressed to understand how someone so young could commit such heinous crimes.

"Hard to imagine, but many serial killers experience abuse at an early age," she said, and waved her hands to shut down their expected comments. "It doesn't excuse what they do, but it could explain it."

"How does it account for either of the Konijn men? I don't see either of them as being abused," Diego said.

"The father was rather domineering. Mother is likely emotionally absent. That could create the kind of environment which produces a serial killer." Gabriella paused, glanced at the board and added, "We should interview the mom."

"I agree, and if you don't mind, before we get to those police reports, I need to take Poppy for a walk," Diego said, slowly rose and stretched out a kink.

Gabriella nodded. "I think a break makes sense. I could use some fresh air as well. Do you mind if I come with?"

Chapter Nine

"Not at all," he said, grabbed his jacket from the back of his chair and slipped it on. Bending, he rubbed Poppy's head and snagged her leash. "Come on, Poppy."

He waited until Gabriella retrieved her coat and together they walked to the elevator. As they stood there, he peered at her from the corner of his eye, wondering how she was handling the fact that her missing sister might have been the victim of a serial killer.

Her arms were wrapped around herself and her face was downturned, as if she was deep in thought.

Poppy, apparently picking up on her distress, surprised him by rubbing her head against Gabriella's thigh.

With a startled jump, Gabriella came out of her thoughts. It seemed like she was about to rub Poppy's head but stopped and looked up at him.

"Is it okay?" she asked, dark eyes wide with surprise and sadness. Now he knew the reason for it.

While it wasn't normally okay to treat Poppy as if she were a pet, Gabriella seemed to need the emotional support and she was, for the moment, his partner in this investigation.

"Sure."

She rubbed Poppy's head, a shadow of a smile on her face. A second later, the elevator arrived, they boarded and stood there in silence for a moment before Gabriella said, "Thank you."

He met her gaze, puzzled, but before he could speak, she said, "For not asking. I'm not ready to talk about it."

Nodding, he said, "I'm here when you're ready."

With a tight smile, she dipped her head in acknowledgment but remained silent.

The doors opened, and they hurried outside into the chill of the early April night.

It had grown late and the area in front of the new Crooked Pass Security office was fairly empty. But a few feet away, there was still a good amount of foot traffic in the Sixteenth Street Mall. People frequented the various hotels and restaurants that would still be open despite it being well past ten o'clock.

Diego had barely taken a step when Poppy barked and veered in the direction of the corner where someone leaned against the building close to Sixteenth Street, hood pulled low across their face. Average height. A big puffer jacket made it difficult to tell if it was a man or woman.

As the individual noticed they'd been spotted, the pair pushed off and rushed around the corner.

Poppy yanked at her leash and Diego said, "She's scented something. Let's go!"

He raced to the corner, Gabriella running beside him, and turned onto Sixteenth Street, but there was no sign of the individual.

"*Such*," he said in German, instructing Poppy to track them.

Head slightly down, as if searching for the scent, the German shepherd pulled at the leash, leading them halfway down the block and toward the doors of a nearby fast-food chain.

He jerked open the door but as they entered, there was no sign of anyone in a black hoodie and puffer jacket.

Poppy yanked him in the direction of the counter where

he asked the young girl, "Did you see someone in a hoodie and puffer jacket come in?"

"Bathroom," she said, and pointed to the far side of the space.

Since Poppy was pulling them toward that area, he and Gabriella followed. At the unisex bathroom, he tried the door, but it was locked. Gabriella raced back out to the counter and returned with a key barely a minute later.

"*Setz*," he instructed Poppy, and the dog immediately sat just behind him.

He glanced at Gabriella to confirm she was ready in case the individual tried to race past them, and at her nod, he unlocked the door with the key and threw it open.

A blast of chilly air greeted them a second before they walked into the empty bathroom stall.

The individual, now a potential suspect, had climbed out the window.

They both muttered a curse at the same time and hurried back to the counter.

"Is there an entrance at the back?" Gabriella asked.

"Through the kitchen," the young woman said, and as they raced there, she called out after them, "You can't go in there!"

They pushed past teenagers assembling sandwiches to a large steel door at the back of the kitchen area.

Diego shouldered the door open and instructed Poppy to track once again. But the smells of garbage and cooking from the fast-food restaurant as well as another nearby eatery had Poppy stopping short in the narrow alley.

Too many scents and smells, he thought as he peered down the alley, trying to figure out which way their suspect might have gone.

"He could have gone in either direction," Gabriella said as she too scoped out the alley.

Gesturing to one end, he said, "That leads to Sixteenth

Street. If he went that way, we might have eyes on him from any of the CCTVs in the area."

Glancing in the other direction, Gabriella said, "My money's on him going to Fifteenth and the park. Maybe doubling back to the Civic Center Station. He could hop on a bus to anywhere there."

"I agree. Let's see if Poppy can pick up the scent again," he said.

They ran to the end of the alley and popped out on Fifteenth Street.

Diego commanded Poppy to track, but after sniffing around the alley exit and then back and forth several yards in either direction, it was apparent that it would do no good.

With a frustrated sigh and shake of his head, he said, "We can head to the station, but I suspect he'll be long gone."

"I agree. Let's head back to the CPS offices and see if they can find something on him from the CCTVs."

Turning toward the Civic Center Station, they returned to the offices and as they walked, Diego said, "How do you know it's a he?"

"Most serial killers are male," she answered without hesitation.

"Isn't it dangerous to make that kind of assumption?" he said as they stopped to let Poppy relieve herself, the original reason for their walk.

She nodded. "It is. The assumption that serial killers are usually white is what delayed the capture of the Atlanta child murderer. But we have to start somewhere."

It was as good a place as any to start, he thought as he picked up after Poppy and they returned to the CPS offices.

GABRIELLA ENTERED THE conference room and found that in their absence, Sophie, Robbie and Ryder had added information beneath the photos of their original suspects and the two new names.

But her gut was telling her it had to be one of the three original suspects. Walking up to the board, she tapped on their names and said, "Diego and I just chased down someone downstairs. Someone who Poppy recognized as having Roberts's scent. Neither of these two men even know we exist."

"Are you sure?" Sophie asked.

"Neither Gabriella nor I have spoken publicly about the case, and I don't believe our names were made available to the press, but I can check on that," Ryder said, picked up his cell phone and stepped out of the room to make the necessary calls.

"Is it possible for you to get video feeds from the area adjacent to this building on Fifteenth and Sixteenth?" Gabriella asked.

Sophie nodded. "We can check for CCTV and other feeds. What are we looking for?"

"Black puffer jacket, hoodie and jeans. Hiking boots, I think. Between five feet eight and six feet," Diego said.

"We'll get on it," Robbie confirmed, and started tapping away on his laptop.

"Great, and thanks. Which leaves us with the original three, and my gut is on the Konijn men," she said, and circled some new info that seemed rather damning. "No cell phone records at the time of Roberts's disappearance."

"We think that's suspicious as well. It warrants checking with their carriers again," Robbie said, picked up a report from the table and walked over to her with it. "These are the records the carriers gave to local law enforcement."

"It's either a glitch or intentional. My money is on intentional," Diego said as he looked at his copy of the report.

"Mine, too. The odds seem low that both of them went radio silent at the same time due to a glitch," Gabriella said, and rapped on the board with her knuckle again. "Plus, Poppy picked up a scent on Ralph. Not likely a transfer of a scent, right?" she said, and peered at Diego.

"Unlikely," he confirmed with a dip of his head.

Ryder marched back into the room, his face mottled with red and white, and set into a glower.

"Not good news, I gather," Sophie said even though it was apparent from her boyfriend's features.

"Our names were provided to local law enforcement. Crooked Pass Security was also mentioned," he said, and approached the board.

He pointed to one of the new names on the board. "Sam Hughes. He's a paramedic with the new Support Team Assisted Response program that sends a paramedic and social worker with Denver PD in cases involving either mental health or substance abuse issues. As part of law enforcement, he got info," Ryder explained, picked up a marker and jotted the information beneath Hughes' name.

"He's back on the list then, but in the meantime…" she said, and glanced at her watch. "It's nearly eleven. We should probably call it a night and reconvene in the morning."

"I think that makes sense," Ryder agreed, and walked over to Sophie, who appeared hesitant to leave her computer.

"I know you and Robbie too well, mi amor. You can work when we get home. Same for you, Robbie. I'm sure Selene is waiting for you," Ryder said, and urged Sophie to her feet.

She closed her laptop and tucked it under her arm. "You're right. We'll pick this up in the morning."

Robbie did the same and echoed Ryder's comment. "Selene will be waiting. She's probably home from the recording studio by now."

Gabriella had almost forgotten that Robbie was now involved with Selene Reilly, a rising star who had been signed by one of the country's hottest record producers and a personal favorite.

"I can't wait to hear her new album," she said with a bit of fangirl in her voice.

Robbie smiled and said, "When we find Roberts, we'll celebrate by going to her next show."

"I'd like that," she said, pleased he'd said "when" and not "if."

The crew headed down to the street where Robbie peeled off to walk to the nearby condo where he lived with Selene.

She walked with Ryder, Sophie and Diego into the underground parking lot for the building. After Ryder and Sophie said their goodbyes by one car, Diego continued walking with her.

"Is your car nearby?" she asked, and stopped next to her vehicle.

He jerked a thumb back in the direction of where Ryder and Sophie were pulling out of the parking garage. "It's in a tenant spot. I couldn't let you walk to your car alone now that we know the killer may have eyes on you."

She narrowed her gaze and considered him. "I can take care of myself," she warned.

"I have a feeling Jeannie Roberts thought the same thing, and since you fit his profile of athletic, brunette and beautiful, there's no sense taking a chance."

A rush of heat swept to her face, and she tried to tell herself that it wasn't because this very handsome man thought she was attractive. Forcing herself to ignore his comment, she said, "I'll see you in the morning."

He grinned, started to walk away, but then turned to say, "Don't stay up too late working."

She had noticed him gathering up all the reports as well and didn't doubt he'd be burning the midnight oil as well. Who wouldn't be when a woman's life was on the line?

Which had her suddenly and unexpectedly asking, "Do you want to go over the materials together?"

Chapter Ten

Stupid, stupid, stupid.

He should have been more careful.

He should have made sure not to be seen.

As it was, he'd barely been able to get away but not without a price, he thought, and grimaced. He had wrenched his back when he'd had to wriggle through the bathroom window of the fast-food chain.

But he knew just what would make him feel better.

He shifted away the chair and then the rug that hid the trapdoor into the root cellar, ignoring the pain as he lifted the door.

Taking a step down the stairs, he hit a switch, and the lights snapped on, bathing her body in glorious, cleansing brightness.

She jumped awake, that delightful fear in her eyes followed by the even more delicious eruption of courage. Her spine straightened, and she lifted her chin in challenge.

His body awoke powerfully at that, but another need rose even more powerfully.

He had to drive that spirit out of her. That was the only way to make himself whole.

He had to have control over her. Control he lacked in his own life.

As he reached the cellar floor, he looked toward the shelf

where he kept his camera. Beside it was a riding crop he'd had since the first day he'd gotten up on a horse.

His father had taught him how to use it. When to use it.

His father had also used it on him to keep him in line. To make sure he did what he was told when he was told.

Just like she would stay in line tonight, he thought, and reached for the crop.

DIEGO HAD SLEPT on far more uncomfortable surfaces during his time in the military.

Despite that, he'd probably slept better on those hard dirt and rocks than on the bed in Gabriella's guest room.

They'd stopped going over her research notes and Wilson's assorted reports at close to three in the morning. They'd forced themselves to stop only because they knew they needed rest to be sharp during that day's investigations.

She'd offered to drive him home or back to the office, but he hadn't wanted her driving around alone. Especially so late at night. Plus, he kept a spare set of clothes in his Jeep, and there was a small but serviceable washroom at the office.

His gut told him that the man who had been watching them earlier was likely the killer. And the fact that he'd been there, watching for her, worried him.

Diego didn't know what serial killer phase that might fall into. But he suspected the killer had set his sights on Gabriella. After all, what could be more tempting than to grab the sister of the girl who had been your first kill?

Those thoughts had plagued his sleep along with so many questions, chief among them: Where had the killer left the bodies of the three original missing women?

Based on what little information he'd gotten from Gabriella's research, he was sure they were all buried close together. And if they could narrow the list of locations where that might be, maybe Poppy, with her excellent sense of smell, could find them.

The whoosh of water through pipes warned that she was awake and in the shower.

Which led to the second reason for his troubled sleep.

Gabriella.

She'd been on his mind off and on during his restless night, and it wasn't just because of the investigation. He found her way too attractive, and that could only lead to problems if he lost his objectivity.

It was already difficult for him to keep from the emotional connection because of her loss.

He, possibly more than many, understood loss.

He'd suffered it way too often during his time in the military and regrettably, after.

PTSD had nearly taken his life in the many months after he'd left the Marines. With the help of friends like Jackson, he'd managed to gain the control necessary to put his life back on track. The therapy dog he'd had before Poppy had opened a new world to him, leading to his work with other veterans and a new career as a dog handler.

Poppy, he thought, and sat up to find his K-9 partner snoring peacefully by the side of the bed. Sensing his movement, Poppy awoke with a big yawn.

"Good girl," he said, and rubbed her head. Reaching for his backpack, he hauled out the emergency rations kit he always carried with him.

With a hand command, he instructed Poppy to follow him to the spacious kitchen just off the guest bedroom where he'd slept.

Uncollapsing two silicone bowls, he emptied a small plastic bag of kibble into one and filled the other with water.

Poppy immediately buried her head in the kibble bowl and

wolfed down the food in record time before taking several big gulps of water.

He always wondered how she could eat so fast without any apparent signs of stomach upset.

But as Poppy glanced up at him with a happy dog grin, he shrugged and playfully rubbed her around the head and neck, which she loved. After, he cleaned the portable bowls and packed them up.

The rushing sound of water stopped and snared his attention. He forced himself not to think about Gabriella drying off in the bathroom.

Epic fail, he thought as his body responded.

Muttering a curse, he decided to make coffee to take his mind off the attractive CBI agent.

Much like her office, Gabriella's kitchen was organized with the coffeepot and coffee-making materials neatly laid out on the counter. Canisters beside the coffee pot held ground coffee and filters. A smaller canister had packets of sugar and artificial sweetener.

She was a sugar girl, he recalled from a coffee she'd made herself the night before.

Was the artificial sweetener for a boyfriend or just regular visitors? he wondered as he prepped the drip coffee maker and then pushed the button to start the brewing.

The snick of a door opening dragged his attention and Poppy's to the area behind the kitchen.

Gabriella exited her bedroom, dressed in the apparently requisite white shirt and a black pantsuit with faint gray pin-stripes. Serviceable penny loafers had replaced the sexy heels she'd been wearing the day before.

It made sense, especially considering last night's chase. He'd been surprised that she'd been able to keep up with him in those heels, but somehow she had.

"Good morning," she said as she walked over and smiled

at the sight of coffee dripping into the carafe. "Thanks. I think we're going to need the caffeine today."

"Good morning, and yes, we're going to need the boost after our late night," he said, and wondered why that sounded way more intimate than it had been.

She grabbed a to-go cup from a nearby cabinet and faced him with a puzzled look, possibly picking up on that.

"It was a productive night. Your research gave me a lot of insights," he said as she handed him another takeaway mug.

"I'm glad I could help," she said as she pulled off the coffee and poured it into their cups. She handed him his cup, and he waited while she prepped hers. Once she was done, she said, "Can I make you something to eat? I only usually grab something at the deli by the office."

"No, thanks. Robbie and Sophie usually bring in pastries and other goodies," he explained as he sipped his black coffee.

"I guess we should get going then. We'll have a lot to do today if we want to find Roberts alive," she said, and bolted for her front door.

He followed, but as they neared the door, he swung his arm out to keep her back. At her questioning glance, he said, "He knew where you were last night. I don't think you were followed, but we can't take a chance."

GABRIELLA HATED THAT he was right.

She was used to being her own woman, but if the serial killer had turned his attention to her, it would be dangerous to work with Diego and the rest of the team.

Diego, she thought as he slipped past her with Poppy and scoped out the grounds in front of her home.

She didn't know what to make of the handsome marine.

There was a connection between them. Attraction, possibly only physical. She couldn't deny that.

She wrote it off, chalking it up to the fact that she'd been so busy with her career and her single-minded quest to find her sister that she hadn't dated in way too long.

That was why he intrigued her, she told herself. Only as she followed his broad-shouldered and muscular body out the door and to her car at the curb, she knew it was a lie.

It was way more than that. Emotional, for sure. He seemed to understand her sense of loss more than anyone else before. Maybe because as a marine who'd been deployed to some of the world's worst war zones, he'd known loss.

When they reached her car, he did a sweep around it, letting Poppy sniff all around before declaring they were good to go.

She didn't know what he'd expected to find. A bomb maybe? Although she didn't think Poppy was trained for that.

As he sat beside her after harnessing Poppy, he said, "We should have either Robbie or Sophie check to see if anyone put a tracker on the car."

"Got it. If he's fixating on me now, we need to know what he'll do," she said as she pulled away for the trip from her home to the CPS offices in downtown Denver.

She remained on high alert as she drove, vigilant for signs that they were being followed.

With a glance in Diego's direction, he was doing the same, his gaze skipping all around to make sure they were safe.

They were about halfway to the CPS offices when she noticed a gray Range Rover in her rearview mirror. She'd spotted it at least twice before, once as they turned Wadsworth Boulevard onto Sixth Avenue and then again when she'd made the left onto North Lincoln.

"A Range Rover is giving me some worry. I'm going to let them pass," she said.

"I'll check out the driver and get the plate number," Diego said, shifting slightly in his seat to get a better look.

Gabriella slipped into the right lane and slowed, making believe she was looking for parking. The Range Rover blew past her and kept traveling up North Lincoln.

"Did you see the driver? Get the plate number?" she asked, and increased her speed for the last few turns to reach the CPS offices.

"Windows were too tinted, but I got a photo of the plate. He had one of those stealth license plate covers on," Diego said, and swiped his phone. "Robbie or Sophie may be able to work their magic on the photo."

"Good. It's probably nothing but—"

"Better safe than sorry," he finished for her.

She smiled and nodded. "Better safe than sorry."

A little over a mile later, she turned into the underground garage at the CPS offices. Since it was early, there was a spot not far from the spaces reserved for the CPS staff members.

"Is this your car?" she asked as she pulled next to a late-model khaki-colored Jeep Wrangler.

"It is. I just need to get some things from the back," he said, pulled out his keys and unlocked the Jeep.

She slipped out of the car and reached into the back seat for her briefcase with all the case materials while Diego unharnessed Poppy, grabbed his knapsack and hurried to his car.

As she walked around to the back of the Jeep, he grabbed a large black backpack with his name emblazoned on the face of it. A metal water bottle was tucked into a side pouch.

He slung that backpack over one shoulder and the smaller knapsack from the night before over the other. Leash in hand, he did a soft click with his tongue, and Poppy came to her feet for the walk to the offices.

"Robbie doesn't drive to work, I assume?" she said as they boarded the elevator.

"The condo he shares with Selene is about two blocks away. He parks a car here, but usually walks," he explained.

The elevator stopped, and the doors opened onto the floor that CPS shared with a boutique law firm.

The reception desk was empty, much as it had been the day before. "Do you have a receptionist? I didn't notice one yesterday."

"Not yet. The agency only opened its doors about a month ago and is still working on staffing," Diego said as he badged them in.

"And clients, I assume?" she asked, wondering if that was why CPS was so willing to help on this case. Besides the obvious relationship between Sophie and her partner Ryder.

"Clients, too. They'll come in time, I suppose," he said with a nonchalant shrug.

At her questioning glance, he explained. "I'm told that they're well funded. Personal money and the backing of the Miami cousins from South Beach Security."

"They're doing this pro bono?" she asked as they walked into the conference room. She opened her briefcase to extract her files and research.

With another shrug of those wide shoulders, he said, "You might say that. But I suspect that it would help their reputation if they help you find and stop this serial killer."

She did not doubt that. For the moment, the press only knew that the CBI was investigating Roberts's disappearance. If word got out about a possible serial killer, the press would be all over it and anyone involved, including Crooked Pass Security.

The sound of the office entrance lock and footsteps drew her attention to the conference room door.

Seconds later, Sophie and Ryder strolled in arm in arm. Sophie carried a big bag from a nearby bakery, and the aroma of yeasty bread escaped into the air.

Robbie slipped in behind them carrying a large take-out jug of coffee and a smaller bag.

The siblings immediately got to work laying out an assortment of pastries and the fixings for coffee.

Gabriella's stomach growled noisily from the delicious smells, and she instantly covered it with her hand. "Sorry," she said with a laugh.

"I guess I'm not the only bottomless pit," Robbie kidded, and winked at her playfully as he loaded a croissant and Danish onto his plate.

"Leave some for the rest of us," Diego teased, walked over and laid a hand on the small of her back.

The feel of his hand roused a mix of emotions as he often did. But her focus had to be on the case and only the case.

The clock was ticking, and she worried that time was running out for Jeannie Roberts.

Because of that, she quickly grabbed some food, refilled her coffee mug and returned to the table.

The others did as well, sensing as she did that time wasn't on their side.

"We think someone followed us this morning in a gray Range Rover. Diego got a photo of the plate that we're hoping you can enhance," she said to start the discussion.

"Send it over and we'll track it down," Sophie said.

"Great. I'd love to know if the Konijns own anything like that," Diego added.

"Easy enough to do. I'll reach out to DMV for a list of any vehicles registered to them either personally or through their company," Ryder said, and jotted down a note on a pad.

"Great. I'd like to visit the Konijns again this morning and question them about their cell phones," she said, but Ryder immediately nixed that idea.

"I'd like to see what Sophie and Robbie can find out from the carriers first. Plus, I'd like to get a read on them myself."

She hesitated, unsure, but then dipped her head in agreement. "It would be good to get your opinion on their behavior. Which I guess means it's Sam Hughes for me."

"For us. I'm not letting you go anywhere without me," Ryder said, his tone brooking no disagreement.

His assertion of control angered her. "I'm a big girl. I can take care of myself," she repeated.

"I DON'T DOUBT THAT, but I'd feel better if you had backup. Especially since someone might be tracking you. Speaking of that…" Diego paused and glanced in Sophie and Robbie's direction.

"I assume you can check if there's a tracker on Gabriella's car."

"If someone wants to follow her, they're most likely using a GPS tracker that transmits her position in real time. We have a device that can pick up that signal," Robbie said without hesitation.

"And that means they're paying for a service to carry those GPS signals. Once we locate the tracker and get its make and serial number, we should be able to find a carrier. But we'll need a warrant to find out who's paying for the service," Sophie advised.

Ryder's gaze skipped across everyone at the table as he said, "Given that they're tracking a CBI agent during an open investigation, I'm pretty sure a judge would grant that warrant."

"Can you check before we go our separate ways?" Diego asked.

Sophie nodded but with a quick few taps of her keys, she brought up some images on the monitor on the wall. "I found CCTV footage from last night. I isolated images of the individual you chased and ran programs to get basic info."

"Like what?" Gabriella asked, dark brows narrowed in question.

"Our unsub is between five feet ten and six foot. Approximate weight is hard because of the puffer jacket, but adjusting for that, between one hundred fifty and one hundred seventy-five pounds. The average height and weight for an American man," Sophie advised with an exasperated sigh.

"Which fits either of the Konijn men," Gabriella tossed out, her frustration obvious.

"Or Sam Hughes. He's six feet tall," Diego added as he flipped through a police report that included DMV records for their possible suspect.

"*If* any of them is our unsub and *if* this is a serial killer, I'm worried about getting tunnel vision and missing the bigger picture," Ryder said, and spread some of the papers across the surface of the table. "We have three other possible suspects. We can't ignore them."

"No, we can't," Gabriella urged.

Diego could tell that this argument was one the partners had been having for some time. And he understood Ryder's reticence, since there were such differences in the way the five women identified had been either killed or taken. But he'd also picked up something from Gabriella's research and the reading he'd done the night before.

"You're concerned that the three missing women and Roberts's disappearance aren't connected. Same for those two other women. Am I right?" Diego pressed Ryder.

"Yes. The methods and opportunities are all different," Ryder said, and flipped through the papers on the desk to read out the information.

"Isabella was twelve when she was taken. The other women are all older. These two were raped and killed in their own homes," Ryder pointed out, furiously flipping through the papers in his file.

"The Night Stalker repeatedly changed MOs. He raped some. Raped and murdered others. Burglaries only in some cases. Different methods of killing for many of the victims," Diego pointed out.

Ryder leaned back in his chair, ran a hand through his hair, and glanced between him and Gabriella. "You've read Gabby's research and you're right. Different MOs don't mean it's not the same person."

"I understand your concerns, Ryder. You're right that we can't let ourselves focus on one theory so hard that we ignore other clues and suspects," Diego said, acknowledging the other man's worries.

"We'll revisit the possibility that someone besides the Konijns is responsible," Gabriella said, also trying to defuse the situation.

With a relieved sigh, Ryder nodded. "That's all I'm asking, that we keep open minds. Because we're running out of time."

"Great. Our first step is to find out if there is a tracker and start running that info," Sophie said, laying a hand on Ryder's and giving a reassuring squeeze.

"Let's go," Ryder said, and shot to his feet.

Diego rose more slowly and said, "If you don't mind, I'm going to grab a quick shower and change while you're checking Gabriella's car."

"You go ahead, Diego. The four of us can handle this for now," Robbie said.

"I won't be long," he said, stood and with a quick hand command to Poppy, who had been patiently lying by his feet, he grabbed his larger black knapsack and hurried from the room.

GABRIELLA WATCHED HIM GO, grateful for his support as well as his ability to defuse the situation with her partner. Alphas like Ryder, and Diego as well, could sometimes butt heads like two rams in heat.

But Ryder was right, as much as she might not want to admit it.

She could not let tunnel vision prevent her from saving Jeannie Roberts.

That had to be the primary objective at this moment. And if it turned out that her hunch about the serial killer and Wilson's confirmation of that was accurate, and somehow connected to Roberts's disappearance, they'd deal with that.

But first, the possible tracker, she thought as she followed Sophie, Ryder and Robbie from the room.

As they walked down the hall, Robbie ducked into his office and then returned with a small handheld device, not much bigger than a walkie-talkie. It had what looked like one fixed antenna and a longer, more flexible one.

"Is that the GPS detector?" she asked, and he nodded.

"It's nothing fancy. It just picks up RF, wireless, Bluetooth or other similar signals," he explained as they walked out of the office and to the elevators.

"If there is a tracker on the car, how would he know which one was mine unless…" She paused, recalling all the locations she'd been the day before and whether anyone had had the time to plant the device.

"Unless it was one of the people you visited yesterday," Ryder finished for her.

"Seems unlikely, but I'm keeping all possibilities open. If Sam Hughes got word early in the day about us and CPS, he could have been here watching," she said, wanting Ryder to know that she had taken his concerns to heart.

Ryder offered her a half smile and dipped his head as they exited the elevators on the parking level and walked toward Gabriella's car.

When they were standing beside it, Robbie flipped on the GPS detector and as if to prove to her how it worked, he said, "Hold out your phone."

She did as he asked, and he ran the fixed antenna over it.

A meter on the device jumped to life, the lights zipping upward into the red level.

"That's what it'll look like if we get a hit," he said, and then unraveled the flexible antenna that had a small LED light at the end.

"Most likely place is the wheel well," he said, and ran the hard antenna all around before inserting the flexible end beneath her driver-side rear wheel well.

"The flexible one detects if a magnet is holding the GPS tracker in the well," he said as he scanned, but nothing registered.

He repeated those actions at the front wheel well and then walked around to the other side.

No hits on either of those, but as he approached the back passenger wheel, the first little blip sounded at one spot, and the lights and bleeping went off the chart.

"We've got a hit," he said, and flipped some kind of switch on the device. He inserted the flexible antenna and as he ran it across one area, the lights and sound jumped high.

He reached underneath, scrabbled beneath the edge and then pulled out a small black box.

Both Sophie and he muttered a curse as they looked at the tracker.

"What's wrong?" she asked.

"It's a cheap tracker you can buy at several stores. The user has to insert their own SIM card to get it to operate," Sophie explained.

Robbie tacked on, "We'll have to open it and inspect the SIM to find the carrier. The signal will be interrupted, which may tip them to the fact that we found it."

Gabriella shook her head and glanced all around the parking lot. "How accurate is it? I mean, does someone know if the tracker is here or up in your offices?"

With a shrug, Robbie said, "One like this might not know the difference."

"I'll take another car to see Hughes while the two of you try to find out more," Gabriella said.

"That sounds like a plan. Call me as soon as you know the carrier and I'll reach out for that warrant," Ryder said, bent and dropped a kiss on Sophie's temple. "I'll interview the Konijns, father and son. If I have time, I'll also fit in Baxter and Kinston just to be sure I'm getting the same read as you did."

"We'll meet back here to see what other info Robbie and Sophie have, plus anything else that Wilson may have come up with about the connections between all our suspects," Gabriella said.

"Agreed," Ryder said, and peeled away to go his car while she went with Sophie and Robbie to return to their office and reunite with Diego.

Diego, she thought, and ignored that little race of her heartbeat as she anticipated seeing him again.

When they entered the CPS office, she noticed Poppy lying by a door at the end of the hall and walked toward the German shepherd.

The dog raised her head at her approach and gave her what she interpreted as a happy doggy grin. She went to rub the dog's head but then pulled her hand back, conscious of Poppy's role as a working dog.

A second later, Diego jerked open the door while pulling down a black T-shirt. For a hot second, she caught a glimpse of his hard body and a network of scars along his ribs.

His chocolate-colored hair was damp and bore evidence of being finger-combed. The slight stubble that had been on his face that morning had been shaved clean, exposing the sculpted lines of his face. She noticed then another set of fine lines by his jaw, close to his earlobe.

"Everything okay?" he asked at her too-long perusal.

"N-n-no. Robbie found a tracker. We're leaving my car here so they can examine the SIM card without alerting whoever is tracking us," she said with a slight stammer and the heat of an embarrassed flush.

With a boyish grin, Diego finished tugging his T-shirt into place and said, "Whenever you want to go."

"Right now would be good," she said, and whirled away to hide her reaction.

DIEGO TOLD HIMSELF not to feel satisfaction that the attraction wasn't one-sided. He told himself it was only physical. Except it wasn't.

He admired her intelligence and her determination. He understood her loss, which roused all kinds of emotions deep in his gut. He'd learned how to deal with his own pain, although it hadn't been an easy path to find a small measure of peace.

He hoped that besides finding out the truth about what had happened to her sister, she could heal as well.

As she walked down the hall, he commanded Poppy to follow and detoured to his office to pick up the smaller knapsack that he'd restocked in case Poppy needed food or water while they were on the road. Slipping on his jacket, he grabbed the knapsack and met Gabriella, who was waiting by the elevator.

She hit the call button as he approached and since it was early, the elevator reached them quickly.

They stood beside each other silently, avoiding the obvious attraction between them.

Down in the parking garage, they exited only to find that Robbie was running the GPS tracking device over Diego's car.

As they approached, he said, "Didn't want to take any chances. It's clean…for now. Sophie is working on the SIM to find out who's the carrier."

"Thanks. We'll keep you posted if we need anything else after we talk to Hughes," Diego said, and unlocked his Jeep.

He let Gabriella pass first and then opened the rear door to let Poppy hop up. Once she was seated, he harnessed her to keep her safe as they drove and then hurried over to the driver's seat.

He started the car, tapped on the navigation button, and Gabriella read off Hughes's address, which he entered into the system. Hughes's home address in the Denver suburb of Centennial was only about twenty minutes away. He chuckled because it seemed like everywhere he ever wanted to go took only twenty minutes.

"What's so funny?" she asked as he pulled onto West Colfax to access the entrance to the highway.

"It seems like everything in the suburbs is always twenty minutes away. I'm still not used to that," he said with a shake of his head as he hit the accelerator to reach highway speed.

"Why is that? Where did you grow up?" she asked with a side-eyed glance.

"My parents raised exotic plants and orchids on a farm on the edges of the Everglades. Nothing was ever just twenty minutes away," he said with another chuckle.

"That must have been a very different experience growing up."

"It was. I learned to be self-sufficient. And there were rough spots at times when weather damaged the greenhouses and plants. It's why I went the ROTC route," he explained as they sped along the highway.

"Where did you grow up?" he said, and peeked in her direction.

With a full-lipped, happy smile, she said, "About twenty minutes outside Denver. My dad was an accountant. My mom taught at our local elementary school. It was a fairly normal life until…"

He didn't need to hear what the until was, and another quick look in her direction confirmed that sadness had filled her features yet again.

He also didn't need to hear why she'd gone into law enforcement. That was obvious.

Gabriella wanted justice for Isabella and all the other victims like her.

"My life was fairly normal, too, until I got deployed to Afghanistan. I'd never experienced anything like that. The heat. Cold. Dust everywhere always," he said, hoping that by sharing they could both heal a little more.

"That must have been very different from the Everglades," she said in commiseration.

"It was. And then there was the violence. The people hurt by terrorists who didn't care if it was us they killed or their own," he said, emotion choking his throat.

She skimmed a hand down his arm, offering comfort. "I can't imagine what that must have been like. It changes you."

"It does," he said, and shook his head before he continued, hands tight on the steering wheel as so many memories cascaded through his brain.

"It weighed on me, even after I left the Marines. And it sometimes got to be too much to handle. Thankfully I had friends like Jackson—"

"Sophie and Robbie's cousin? The police chief?" she asked.

He nodded. "He's a good friend. He helped me get into a group to deal with my PTSD. Some of the therapy was with dogs, and that led to my visiting another vet out in Idaho who was training canines."

He glanced to where Poppy was harnessed in the back seat. "It changed my life."

That comforting touch came on his arm again, and softly she said, "Thank you for sharing."

With an offhand shrug that wasn't even close to what he was feeling, he said, "Partners need to understand each other."

Chapter Eleven

Partners.

She didn't know why she liked the sound of that more than she should.

"Partners," she repeated. "But I take the lead in questioning Hughes."

"Of course. You're the cop, after all. I'm just the muscle with the dog," he said with that grin that did all kinds of things to her insides.

She suspected humor was one of the ways that he dealt with difficult situations. Many of her colleagues at the CBI did the same. It wasn't her coping mechanism. She wasn't sure she had one, come to think of it.

For too long she'd been single-mindedly doing what she needed to advance at CBI and to find out what had happened to Isabella. That hadn't left a lot of time for personal interactions other than Ryder and her other CBI colleagues.

Maybe now it was time to expand that tight circle. She got the sense that Sophie and Robbie would make good friends and allies.

As for Diego, she didn't know where that might go, she thought. She took a quick look at him as he maneuvered off the highway and onto the side streets that would take them to Hughes's home.

She had checked his schedule the night before, and he wasn't due to start an afternoon shift for several hours.

Hughes's house was in what most would consider a typical suburban housing development. Trees with the first buds of green lined the street beside nicely manicured lawns that were also beginning to show the signs of spring after last week's unseasonable snow.

She immediately noticed there were two cars in the driveway.

A Jeep like Diego's, but all black except for the bright red rims and brakes on the wheels.

Next to it was a silver-gray Range Rover.

Too much coincidence. But as they drove past the driveway to park in front of the next house, she noticed that the license plate on this car was completely legible, unlike the darkened plate on the vehicle that had followed them. It was easy enough to change out plates, she reasoned.

Diego must have read her mind. "Different plates, but that doesn't rule it out. But I think these windows aren't as tinted."

"I didn't get a good enough look at the windows to judge." She'd been too worried about the possibility that someone would either take a shot at them or try to drive them off the road. Although she'd taken defensive driving courses, there were never any guarantees if someone was truly trying to do harm.

"Let's see what Sam Hughes has to say," she said, and shut off the car.

I'M ALIVE, SHE THOUGHT as she woke to a world of hurt.

Jeannie forced herself to ignore the punishment he'd inflicted the night before.

She had no doubt that's what it was and very different from what he'd done the other two nights.

The change worried her.

He struck her as a spoiled child who would kick and scream to get what he wanted but would also lose interest quickly once he had it.

Had he lost interest in her already?

Was her time running short because of that?

Don't think about it, Jeannie. Focus, she told herself as she pulled the blanket up to her chin against the chill.

She was still alive, and he was gone for the day.

Even though it was dark in the cellar, she knew it was day because she'd heard him walking around. The noise said that he was getting ready to leave for the day.

Which meant she had hours before he would return.

Hours before he'd torture her again.

She wanted the torture, twisted as that was.

The torture meant she might live to see another day.

But she wasn't going to huddle there, praying that someone would save her.

She had to find a way to save herself.

Yanking on the chains, it seemed to her that they weren't as secure as they had been.

In the dark, she worked her fingers up the chain to where it was secured. Feeling around the eyebolt buried deep in the wall, it seemed as if the wall was crumbling.

She worked at it with her fingernail. She made more of a dent in the area around the bolt.

Was it possible? Could she scrape away enough of the wall to work the bolt loose?

But what then? There were still three other bolts.

But if she could do it with one, maybe she could do it with the others.

A fingernail wouldn't be enough to do it quickly, though, she thought.

He'd left her some food after punishing her. A tray with

soft foods she could eat with the plastic spoon he thought she couldn't turn into a weapon against him.

Reaching out, she grabbed the spoon.

The bowl was too thin and fragile, but the handle was thicker. Stronger.

It would have to do, she thought as she attacked the crumbling cement.

DIEGO STOOD JUST behind Gabriella with Poppy in a position where, if necessary, he could give the attack command.

But as the door opened after Gabriella's knock, it didn't appear that would be necessary.

A petite twentysomething woman wearing the latest in yoga clothing and dabbing her sweat-damp forehead with a towel answered the door.

"May I help you?" she asked, question clouding her clear blue gaze.

Gabriella held up her CBI badge. "Is Sam Hughes available?"

"What's this about?" she said, and remained in the doorway, blocking their entry, but as she stood there, a mountain of a man came from the back of the house, a baby balanced on his hip.

"Who is it?" he called out, and walked toward the door.

The young woman finally stepped aside and as Sam Hughes neared the door, she took the baby from him and walked to one side of the living area of the home.

Sam glanced at the CBI badge as Gabriella held it up again and said, "I'm CBI Agent Gabriella Ruiz and this is my civilian consultant, Diego Rodriguez. Do you mind if we have a word with you about the disappearance of Jeannie Roberts?"

He shrugged impossibly huge shoulders that topped a heavily muscled bodybuilder's body. "Sure, but I don't know how I can help. I don't know the woman," he said, and motioned for them to enter.

As they did so, he scanned the room for any threats and to also get a feel for who Sam Hughes was.

The house screamed average, normal, middle-class family. Not what he'd expected, since Wilson's info hadn't mentioned anything about Hughes being a father and husband.

"You were both at DU together. Both business majors," Gabriella said, but he knew that wasn't accurate and she was baiting him. Hughes had been a science major.

He immediately corrected her. "I was premed, and DU has thousands of students. Like I said before, I don't know her."

"What about Missy Cornerstone or Alyssa Nations?" she asked. At that, Hughes's body did a little twitch, and his lips thinned into a tight line.

"I was in a frat, and I'm pretty sure Missy was in a sister sorority. We might have partied together. Done some of the charity events that happen as part of Greek life," he admitted, and then quickly added, "I don't get it. What does this have to do with me?"

"Do you know Missy disappeared almost three years ago?" Gabriella pressed.

All color fled from beneath the tan on Hughes's skin. "No, I didn't. We weren't close and didn't keep in touch after college."

"Where were you on Sunday?" she asked, and Hughes glanced back at his wife, who hurried and wrapped an arm around his waist.

"He was with us. We were home watching the Rockies play the Reds. It was an afternoon game," his wife said.

"Who won?" Diego blurted out.

There was no hesitation as the duo said, almost in unison, "Rockies. Six to one."

"Is that your Range Rover in the driveway, Sam?" she asked, once again trying to elicit a deceptive response.

"No. The Jeep is mine. The Range Rover is Sara's," he said, and dipped his gaze to his wife.

"If you don't believe him, check the back seat. There's a baby seat there," Sara said, challenge and defensiveness in her voice.

"We will," Gabriella said, ice in her tone.

She reached into her jacket pocket, took out a business card and handed it to Sam. "If you can think of anything, or anyone, who might have connections to Missy and the two other women, I'd appreciate a call."

Hughes peered at the card and then nodded. "Sure. Of course. Anything to help."

"Great," she said, and Sam reached past her to open the door and let them out.

As they walked down the path to their car, Gabriella said, "What do you think?"

"Doesn't strike me as a serial killer, but then again, BTK. Family man, right?" he said, and as they walked past the Range Rover, he stopped to peer into the back. "Car seat is right where she said it would be."

Gabriella looked in as well. "Definitely a car seat. But let's note the plate number so we can get the vehicle identification number from the registration. If we need to, we'll get a warrant and ask the manufacturer to provide location data. Same with the Jeep."

Diego snapped off photos of the plates and said, "Do you mind if I walk Poppy? She needs to go, and she's not used to all this inactivity."

"Not a problem. It'll help clear my brain as well," she said and walked beside him as they strolled down the block.

The neighborhood was quiet. People were just starting to wake and get ready for school and work.

"Nice. Was your neighborhood like this growing up?" he said as he scrutinized the houses along the street. They seemed like the kind of suburban homes you'd see in movies and television shows.

Gabriella looked around and nodded. "Kind of like this. Different from the Everglades, I suspect."

"There are some small developments here and there, but it is way different from my family's home and business," he said, and stopped to pick up Poppy's waste. When he was done, he backtracked to where his Jeep was parked by Hughes's home.

There was activity in the Hughes household. Passing shadows cast on the window blinds said the couple were still inside.

"Wilson's program picked him for a reason, but I'm not feeling it," Diego said as he did a last look at the house while he harnessed Poppy into the back seat.

"Connections, I assume. The program may have picked up on their associations in college. I think I remember seeing in the report that Hughes used to be a rock climber. He might do that in the same areas as the trails where the women disappeared."

"He seems kind of muscle-bound for a rock climber," Diego said as he slipped into the driver's seat and Gabriella sat beside him.

"He does. And the man watching us last night was leaner. I'm guessing Hughes is well over two hundred pounds."

"Easily," Diego confirmed, and glanced at her. "Where do we go now? Back to CPS?"

She nodded. "Back to CPS to wait for Ryder. Hopefully, Sophie and Robbie will have more for us, and you and I can go over all this data again. See if we missed anything."

There was so much data with the information Gabriella

and Ryder had gathered plus all that Wilson had provided. Maybe too much data.

He was used to being a boots-on-the-ground kind of investigator. What they were doing now felt too much like being an armchair quarterback, and he'd rather be out on the field.

Shooting a glance at his watch, he said, "I've got a better idea."

Chapter Twelve

Gabriella wasn't sure that visiting the site of her sister's disappearance was a "better idea."

She hadn't been there in a long time, and in the years since her sister had been taken, the scout camp had shut down. She suspected that what had happened to Isabella had been one of the reasons for the closure, since it was too hard to secure the area if anyone wanted to do harm.

It saddened her because she had attended the same camp years earlier and enjoyed her time there.

She slipped from the Jeep as Diego freed Poppy and then stood in the abandoned parking lot, examining the remaining trail that led into the woods and eventually, what had once been the scout camp.

He whirled on one heel and faced her. "Is this area similar to where Roberts disappeared?"

She shook her head. "No. This is a beginner trail. I know because I stayed at this camp a few years before Isabella when I was a Cadette."

"Would you mind taking me to the camp?" he asked, brow furrowed with worry since it might be difficult for her.

She sucked in a breath and held it, trying to calm the way her gut was twisting at being at the camp again. But with a resigned nod, she said, "Sure. I think I remember the way."

Liar. The way to the camp was tattooed on her brain. She'd walked it dozens of times in the weeks and months after her sister's disappearance, hoping to find something that might tell her what had happened to Isabella.

She took a halting step toward the trailhead and had to take another bracing breath. The air was colder here at the slightly higher elevation and scented with pine.

The gentle touch of his hand came at her shoulder. He squeezed reassuringly and whispered against the side of her face, "You don't have to do this if it's too hard."

It *was* too hard, but that wasn't about to stop her.

"I'm okay. I can do this," she said, but it was more to convince herself than him.

She took the first step up the trail. The ground was still hard beneath her feet but once it warmed up, it would become a slushy mess until it dried out in the warmer months.

In happier times that's when the scouts would descend on the camp to enjoy the forest and a nearby lake whose waters were fed by nearby mountain streams.

She could still remember the shocking cold after jumping in after a hot summer hike.

Diego walked a few feet behind her while Poppy sniffed the trail edges here and there, seemingly happy to be outdoors and moving around.

All around, the first signs of spring were visible, from the bright green buds on the trees to the first hints of bluebells and some errant and belated snowdrops poking their heads up from beneath the underbrush and remnants of fall leaves.

It didn't take long to reach the camp. It was a beginner's trail, after all.

There was still a clearing amid half a dozen or so wooden platforms where large canvas tents had once risen to provide shelter.

She stood in the middle of the clearing and did a slow pirouette, taking it in while Diego and Poppy walked the edges of the platforms.

Pointing to another smaller trail, she said, "There are two other platforms a little farther uphill. They're on the way to an outhouse and some shower stalls. That's where Isabella was bunking for the night."

"She wasn't alone, right?" he asked, and joined her in the center.

"No. There were three other girls in the tent. No one remembered hearing anything, but one of the girls thought that Isabella might have gone to use the bathroom," she said, recalling the witness statements that had been provided by her fellow scouts and camp counselors.

Diego walked up the narrower trail leading to the two other platforms and slightly farther away, the ramshackle remains of what must have been the toilets and showers. The wood was silvery gray from age and cracked in spots. Part of the structure had fallen in at one end, and broken wooden slats littered the ground around the building.

He let Poppy nose around the space, not that he expected the dog to get any hits. There was nothing to indicate Roberts had been here.

But something niggled at him again as it had during their discussion in the offices the day before.

Turning, he realized that Gabriella was still standing in the central clearing, arms wrapped around herself.

He returned there and raised the issue again. "I know this area was searched, as were the others, but if he keeps them for a few days, as you believe, he'd dump them after the searches were done."

Gabriella did a slow dip of her head in agreement. "I get what you're saying. But he could be dumping them anywhere."

"Bundy called his killing fields 'sacred ground,'" he said,

recalling a statement he'd read while doing some research on his own.

Gabriella's nod was more emphatic this time. "Yes, he did. The sicko even wanted his ashes scattered there after his execution."

Diego muttered a curse at the depravity of that wish but then pushed on. "What makes them special? Why does he choose that area?"

"Usually, it's a remote area. Like Gilgo Beach for LISK, but not always. Sometimes they just dump them where it's convenient and they're unlikely to be discovered."

Diego held his hands out wide. "This is a remote area. And if Isabella was his first, wouldn't this be a special area for him?"

GABRIELLA DID A slow pivot, examining the woods around them. The area was remote and since the camp had closed down a few years after Isabella's disappearance, it wasn't a commonly visited location as far as she knew. The trails were too short and easy for any hiker to want to use them.

"Possibly. But this area was used for years after Isabella was taken. If he left her here, she might have been discovered by other scouts," she said.

Diego motioned to the large hillside beyond the clearing for the tents and washroom facilities. "When you stayed here, did you ever go up to that higher ground?"

Gabriella shook her head. "Not to the top. The trails only go about halfway up the mountain, and we rarely went beyond a lake that's about one hundred yards away. We'd swim there."

Diego jammed his hands on his hips and peered up the mountainside. "That leaves a lot of ground that was possibly never searched. And the Cornerstone and Nations disappearances occurred after the camp was being used, right?"

"Right. They stopped using the camp about three years after…and it was another two years before Cornerstone disappeared," she said. She peered up the mountainside beyond the camp area.

A loud snap and crunch suddenly pulled their attention back toward the parking lot area. They stood there, vigilant, and a minute later, a softer thud, like someone carefully closing a car door, sent them into action.

They raced down the trail at a run, hoping to see who had come to the location.

Diego stumbled on an exposed tree root and went down hard. Gabriella offered him a hand up and he scrambled to his feet, Poppy loping beside him.

As they hit the ground at the trailhead, the only car visible in the area was his Jeep.

He muttered a curse. "I'm sorry. If I hadn't fallen, we might have caught whoever that was," he said with a shake of his head.

"Don't blame yourself. We were too far away," she said, and looked his way. "You're bleeding."

He swiped at his chin, and his hand came away wet with blood. "I have a first aid kit in the back of the Jeep," he said, and used the key fob to open the hatch.

They walked there together, and he pulled up the floor to reveal a spare tire, a road kit, and beside it, a bright red first aid kit.

Gabriella grabbed the kit and once the floor was back in place, urged him to sit on the tailgate. She opened the kit and removed alcohol pads, antiseptic and a bandage to cover the cut just beneath his chin. Ripping open the alcohol pad, she said, "This is going to sting."

"I've had worse," he said, and she didn't doubt it. She'd seen the evidence that morning when she'd caught a glimpse of his scars.

Delicately she wiped the dirt away from the cut and the area around it. Luckily it was more like bad road rash than a deeper cut. "It's not that bad."

"It's not your face," he teased with that boyish grin again that made dimples erupt.

"It's not my face because I'm not clumsy," she teased right back as she dabbed on some antiseptic and then covered the injury with a bandage.

But as she finished, something made her cup his cheek and tenderly run her thumb across the slight indent in his chin. "Thank you."

His brows narrowed in question as he said, "What for?"

"Believing in my theory. Being willing to take the extra step to find out what happened to Isabella and all those women."

A half smile ghosted across his lips before he cradled her cheek. "I want you to have closure. To see some of that sadness drift out of those beautiful eyes," he said, voice deep with emotion.

His caring stirred her. "I wish I could do the same for you. I know you've been hurt. That you still hurt and… I'm here for you if you ever want to share more," she said because he'd already told her a part of his story, but not enough for her to understand what had made him the man he was.

The smile broadened into a crooked grin. "Someday, maybe."

He slapped his hands on his thighs and said, "We should head back to CPS. I want to ask Sophie and Robbie if we can somehow use one of their fancy tech things to scope out this mountainside."

"I agree," she said, and handed him the first aid kit. He lifted the floor and returned it to its place and then followed her so he could harness Poppy in the back seat.

But as she neared the passenger door, she noticed what looked like an envelope tucked beneath the windshield wiper.

She was about to reach for it but then pulled her hand back. She stopped Diego as he also went to grab it.

"It could be evidence," she said, her gut tightening with the realization that whoever had been in the parking lot had been there for them.

She reached into her coat pocket, pulled out nitrile gloves and slipped them on.

Gently she lifted the windshield wiper and removed the small envelope.

It had her name on it in block letters and contained something small.

Hands shaking, she spilled the envelope contents into the palm of her gloved hand.

Chapter Thirteen

All color fled her face, and her body swayed, like a tower about to topple.

Diego reached out just as her knees buckled and offered support by wrapping an arm around her waist.

"What's wrong?" he asked, but then he noticed the thin gold chain and crucifix in her palm.

He didn't need to hear her say it, but her words confirmed his worst suspicions. "This was Isabella's. He left it beneath the windshield wiper," she said in a shaky voice.

"Okay. Let's get inside the Jeep where it's warmer," he said. He was worried she was in shock.

He bundled Gabriella inside the vehicle, sick with worry and guilt. If he hadn't fallen, they might have seen who had been in the parking lot.

Muttering a curse, he stepped away from the Jeep to examine the ground by the front of the Jeep where their serial killer may have stood as he placed the envelope on the windshield. He let Poppy nose around and she stopped at one spot and laid down by one of the tires.

Sure enough, there was a boot print by the front tire. He took a glove out of his pocket and placed it by the boot print to mark the evidence.

Walking to the back of the Jeep, he examined the dirt and

leaves in the parking lot, Poppy walking beside him. The ground was mostly frozen, but there were patches here and there where the sun had warmed it enough to defrost. And in two of those spots were the imprints of tire treads.

He took a quick look at them and then at his tires. They weren't his, and he marked them with gloves as well.

Based on those two tire tracks, he imagined where the car might have traveled and slowly walked that area to look for any other signs of the serial killer, but there were none.

Satisfied he had preserved as much evidence as he could, he returned to the Jeep and Gabriella. With a hand command, he instructed Poppy to sit.

She was still seated there, almost zombie-like, but at least some color had returned to her face. As she noticed him, she lowered the window and mouthed, "I'm sorry."

He cradled her cheek and said, "No worries. Poppy and I have identified a boot print and some tire tracks. I'll call Ryder and see if CBI's CSI can come and make casts of them for identification."

She shook her head and whispered a strained, "No. No, I'll do it. I can't let him get into my head."

He understood. She couldn't let the serial killer be the one in control.

"Got it. I'm going to start the car so we have some heat," he said as she carefully slipped the envelope and necklace into an evidence bag.

He opened the back door and clicked his tongue so that Poppy would hop in. Once she was harnessed, he carefully walked around to make sure there were no other boot prints and climbed into the driver's seat.

Gabriella had made the call and was chatting with Ryder as he started the Jeep.

"Diego found some evidence. We need to get casts of the

boot prints and tire tracks," she said, and glanced in his direction.

A mumbled response drifted across the line to which Gabriella responded, "We can't move the Jeep. It'll compromise the evidence. We'll wait for you."

She ended the call, dropped her phone into one of the cup holders, and then stared at the envelope and cross she had placed into an evidence bag. "He didn't just put a tracker on my car. He's watching us. Me."

Diego couldn't argue with that. "You're right. We need to up your protection."

She vehemently shook her head. "No. We need to let him play his game. Let him make a mistake that leads us to him."

"That'll put you in danger, and that's not acceptable," he said, but she just shook her head again and met his gaze.

"It wouldn't be the first time. And it may keep Jeannie Roberts alive longer," she said, and nervously fingered the bagged envelope and cross once again.

He reached over and stayed the anxious motion. "What if it does the opposite? What if he decides he's done with her?"

"That's a possibility," she said. She couldn't deny Diego might be right. "I just hope that by distracting him with me, he'll forget about her for a little bit. Enough for us to find her."

Or at least that's what she hoped as she set the bag with her sister's necklace and crucifix on the dashboard to keep from handling it and possibly damaging any evidence.

But with it sitting up there, the bright spring sunlight making the gold glint with life, pain jabbed her middle like a gut punch.

It was like losing her sister all over again, and she sucked in a breath and held it, trying to dam up the emotions threatening to overwhelm her.

The gentle touch of his hand on her cheek undid her, and

she buried her face in her hands and let the tears come. The
sobs racked her body until his arms awkwardly wrapped
around her, offering comfort. He soothed her by rubbing his
hands up and down her arms and murmuring words whose
meaning was lost in the sea of emotions flooding her.

Slowly calm returned, and she said, "I'm okay. Really,
I'm okay."

He released her, and she sat up straighter and wiped away
the remnants of tears from her face. "When we're done here,
I need to tell my parents."

"Whatever you need. The team can handle whatever evidence we have until you're ready," he said, and did one final
stroke down her arm in sympathy.

She nodded and met his concerned gaze. "I'm ready. I
have to be."

The honk of a car horn dragged her attention from Diego
to Ryder's SUV as it stopped on the road leading into the
parking lot. A CBI CSI van had already pulled up in front
of him, and CSI techs streamed out of the car and donned
jumpsuits and other protective clothing to keep them from
contaminating the crime scene.

Ryder remained by his SUV, keeping free of the scene.

"We should brief him," Gabriella said, and stepped out,
careful not to tread on the boot print Diego had marked.

She mindfully walked away from Diego's Jeep and to
Ryder.

"You okay?" Ryder asked, concern etched onto his features as he stroked a hand down her arm.

"As well as can be expected," she said as Diego joined
them.

Ryder looked at the other man and winced as he glanced
at his chin. "Did he attack you?"

"No such luck. I'm just clumsy and fell as I ran down
the trail and no, we didn't get a look at whoever left the…

the…" he said, stumbling as he tried to describe what the killer had left.

"Evidence. His trophy," Gabriella said. As close as she was to this case, she had to remain clinical if they were going to catch him.

Ryder's dark brows shot up in question. "He left his trophy? Isn't that unusual?"

"It is but… Isabella also had half of a 'Best Friends' bracelet we got out of a cereal box. I suspect he still has that," she said, throat choking up as she thought about how she and Isabella had laughed while they'd slipped on the bracelets and vowed to never remove them. Hers was carefully tucked away in a jewelry box.

Diego's soft touch came at her shoulder, providing comfort again, and she looked up at him and offered a forced smile in thanks.

"It may be another hour or so to make the casts and dust for fingerprints," Ryder said, and peered at where the CSI agents were working in the parking lot.

"Gabriella needs to see her parents. Do you mind if we take your car? I can leave you the keys for mine," Diego said, and held his keys up to Ryder.

Ryder swiped the keys from Diego's hand and held out his keys, but as Diego took them, he met Gabriella's gaze. "Are you good with that? Would you rather I went with you?" he said, likely because they had been partners for far longer than she had known Diego.

But despite that, the connection with Diego was strong and he understood the loss she might be feeling. Again. As fresh as it had been the day Isabella had disappeared.

"I'm good with that. More than good," she said, and risked a glance at Diego, who forced a smile and squeezed her shoulder once more.

"Okay. We'll meet back at the office once you're done,"

he said, and didn't wait for her reply to join the CSI agents at work.

Gabriella watched him walk off and then met Diego's gaze.

"Are you sure?" he asked, clearly needing reassurance of her decision.

She smiled and cupped his cheek. "I've never been more sure."

He nodded. "Let's go then."

Chapter Fourteen

Idiot, idiot, idiot, he said to himself and cursed.

It had been impossible to stay and see her reaction to his little gift. He should have realized that and waited until the car had been somewhere else.

Somewhere he could have watched the doubt at what she was seeing become pain with the realization.

Idiot, he chastised again and opened his phone to check the location of the tracker.

Still at the Crooked Pass Security offices, which didn't surprise him since they'd used a different vehicle to go to the scout camp.

But was it just coincidental that they'd done that, or had they found the tracker?

He drove away that worry and fantasized about how she had handled his little gift. Had she cried or had she put on her tough-cop persona?

He grew hard at the thought of the latter. He loved strong women, because he loved seeing them break.

Just like Jeannie Roberts, he thought.

But then a knock came at the door, jolting him from those thoughts.

"Come in," he called out, voice gruff with lust.

"Your 2:00 p.m. meeting canceled. They said they'd reschedule," his secretary said, rousing anger at her interruption.

"You couldn't just call to tell me that," he snapped.

"I'm sorry. I just thought—"

"Well, think better next time," he said, and waved his hand in dismissal.

His secretary backed away quickly and closed the door.

He opened his computer and scanned his calendar. With his 2:00 p.m. canceled, he had the rest of the afternoon free.

He knew just what to do with all that free time.

GABRIELLA PARKED THE car in front of a brightly painted Victorian home just a block or so from Highlands Square.

"Is this where you grew up?" he asked, taking in the quaint tree-lined street populated by many other well-kept Victorians as well as some smaller bungalows and cottages.

She nodded and peered toward the home. "It is. The neighborhood has changed a little. A lot of the homes have been renovated, and the town center is more upscale than I remember. But it was a great place to grow up until…"

She didn't need to finish. It would have been great until Isabella's disappearance.

"People mean well, but it must have been hard with everyone's sympathy and helpfulness," he said, his tone a little more bitter than he intended.

She whirled to face him, eyes narrowed to examine him. "It *was* hard. You sound like you know what it's like."

He didn't normally share, but since her life and grief had been laid bare before him, he shrugged and revealed what he normally kept private.

"I lost most of my team during our last deployment. We had been sent in to raid a house where insurgents had taken several marines hostage. As we approached in the helicopter, we were hit by a rocket. The copter had to make a crash landing and many of my team members were instantly killed. Those of us that survived found ourselves under attack from the Taliban, and we lost another three people to enemy fire," he said.

Gabriella didn't say a thing. She just reached over and ran the back of her hand across his cheek before dropping it down to rest over his heart.

He covered her hand with his and braved a smile. "Thanks. If anyone understands, it's you."

She nodded and sucked in a deep breath. Her words exploded from her mouth as she said, "I don't know how to tell them."

"Do you want me to do it?" he asked, willing to shoulder the burden if it would ease her suffering.

She vehemently shook her head. "No, I need to do it. I know they were still hoping…" She stopped, muttered a curse and looked away, shaking her head again. "I can't lie. Even though I knew better, I was hoping Isabella would come home as well."

He stroked his hand over hers and said, "I get it. I can't tell you how many times I replayed that raid in my head, wondering how I could have changed what happened."

A strangled laugh escaped her. "Me, too. I ask myself why I didn't go on the overnight also. As a student counselor, I could have. But I had something else to do and I thought, 'What could happen?'"

Twining his fingers with hers, he squeezed her hand. "Maybe it's time we both stop trying to change the past and work on building a different future."

She nodded in agreement and offered him a small smile. "I'd like that but for now…"

Looking away, she said, "I have to deal with the present."

He offered another reassuring squeeze before releasing her hand so she could exit the car.

She waited for him at the curb and slipped her hand into his as they walked up the path toward the front door. Along the edges of the path, daffodils and tulips had pushed their way from the dark soil, providing bright spots of yellow, white, pink and red.

Joyful colors. Not that there would be much joy in this house today, Diego thought.

As they neared the front door, it opened, and a woman came to the door.

Gabriella's mother, he was sure. If he wanted to know what the CBI agent would look like in thirty years, all he had to do was look at the woman now standing on the front porch, arms wrapped around herself. Her gaze puzzled at first until it met her daughter's and realized this was not a happy visit.

"Javier," she called out, looking back over her shoulder. "Gabriella is here with…a friend," she said but didn't move from her spot on the front porch.

When Gabriella reached her, she laid a hand on her forearm and said, "We should go inside, Mami. I have something to tell you."

The woman's lips tightened and her face went pale, but she did as Gabriella asked, and they followed her into a large sunny parlor. A fire burned in a nearby fireplace, providing welcome warmth against the chill of the spring afternoon.

A man who had been seated at a leather recliner near the fireplace rose as they entered.

"Gabby? Mija? Qué pasa?" he asked.

"Papi. Mami. You should sit down for this."

In her role as a CBI agent, Gabriella had visited families more than once with bad news.

But nothing could have prepared her for this, she thought as she sat across from her parents who sat beside each other on the sofa. Diego took a seat in an adjacent chair.

She wrung her hands together, seeking calm she wasn't feeling. She forced herself to face them as she said, "This is my civilian partner, Diego Rodriguez, and his K-9, Poppy. They're helping me on the case of the missing hiker."

"The young teacher, right? But what does that have to do with us?" her mother asked, gaze darting between her and Diego.

With a sharp dip of her head, she said, "I'm assisting on the investigation, and I believed it was connected to some cold cases I'd been reviewing."

"Cold cases? Like Isabella's?" her father asked, immediately realizing where she was going.

"Yes, like Isabella's. I know we've all been hoping—"

"Of course, we've all been hoping, mija," her mother said in an anguished cry.

Her father laid a hand on her mother's arm to quiet her. "Mi amor. Let Gabby finish. Por favor."

It was like ripping off a bandage, she thought. The faster she did it, the less it would hurt.

"My investigations led me to believe that Isabella was the first victim of a serial killer."

Her mother shouted "no," but Gabriella pushed on. "Today that killer left me Isabella's crucifix."

"No, no, no," her mother wailed, and covered her face with her hands.

"I'm sorry, Mami. Papi. I'd hoped for so long it was just a kidnapping—"

"Just a kidnapping, mija," her father challenged as he wrapped his wife into his arms to offer comfort.

"Yes, Papi. Just a kidnapping, because at least then she'd still be alive," Gabriella said, and jumped to her feet. "We have to go. Whoever did this to Isabella has another woman, and we have to find her. Stop him."

Her father's face was set in stone, all hard edges that deepened the lines of worry and sadness that had been etched onto his features by Isabella's disappearance.

"Go, mija. Do your job. Your mami and I will be here when you can talk more," he said with a slow, respectful dip of his head.

"Thank you, Papi. I'll be back as soon as I can," she said, and hurried to the door.

"I'm very sorry for your loss," Diego said, and chased after her as she dashed outside and almost ran back to Ryder's SUV.

He opened the back door, harnessed Poppy and then popped into the passenger seat. "Are you okay?"

With a heavy sigh, she said, "As well as can be expected. We need to find this guy. We can't let him kill another woman."

"He won't. We'll stop him. Let's get back to CPS and see what additional info they've found so far."

"Agreed," she said, and pulled away from the curb.

He slipped into the bushes of the house across the street from the Ruiz home.

He'd gone straight there after leaving the office, certain that Gabriella—what a beautiful name for a beautiful woman—would head straight to her parents' home once they left the scout camp.

He hadn't been wrong, but then again, he rarely was.

It was why he was always steps ahead of the police.

Like now, he thought as the black SUV drove away and he slipped onto the sidewalk to watch it drive away. They'd be headed back to the CPS offices, but he was going to linger here for a little bit and enjoy the show inside the family home.

Her parents were visible through the front windows, huddling close together. The pain was visible on their faces as they relived their daughter's death all over again.

Delicious, he thought, feeding on their grief. But not for too long, he reminded himself and buried his head deeper beneath the hoodie he'd slipped on after he'd left the office.

Pivoting on one well-soled heel, he hurried up the block to where he'd parked the Range Rover. The tires and sides of the car were dirty from his earlier trip to the scout camp. He should have cleaned the car before returning to the office, but he hadn't had time, thinking that he had that two o'clock appointment.

He couldn't leave the car dirty, with all that potential evidence on it.

A quick trip to the car wash and then home. To her.

He'd been ignoring Roberts the past day, too seduced by the deliciousness of the older Ruiz sister.

But he couldn't keep her for much longer. So tonight, he'd play with her some more. Maybe tomorrow, too, but after that…

It would be time to get rid of his little toy and think about taking another.

Gabriella came to mind then.

How enticing it was to think about making two sisters his.

Yes, he would have to think about watching her. Wait for the right time.

And when he struck, she wouldn't know what had hit her.

Chapter Fifteen

Jeannie heard footsteps above and carefully eased the two bolts back into the wall. With a sweep of the flimsy blanket he had given her, she tried her best to hide the dust from the plaster she had worked away from the bolts.

It was hard to tell how successful she'd been in the non-existent light in the cellar.

As he snapped on the stage lights, they stunned her again with their intensity, and she worried they'd display the remnants of her handiwork.

He stepped down the rest of the stairs and stood before her, camera in hand.

She took a quick look at the floor and fear filled her as she saw the telltale white of the wall dust.

"That's it. I love seeing that fear," he said, not realizing the reason for the fear.

She used that opportunity to push the blanket off and over the dust, and tilted her chin defiantly, knowing he liked that too.

"I'm not afraid of you. You're nothing but a loser who has to tie up women to have them," she said, and raised her hands to prove her point, careful not to dislodge the bolt she had worked free.

"Feisty today, aren't you?" he said with a laugh, raised the camera and snapped off some photos.

She cursed him, but he only laughed and set aside the camera.

"I'll miss you, Jeannie. You've been one of the better ones," he said as he approached.

Time was running out, she realized. She sensed it in his mood. But she wasn't going to go out without a fight. She'd make sure that she was going to be the last woman he took.

MUCH LIKE GABRIELLA, Diego hated that the killer was always two steps ahead of them.

The tracker.

Following them to the scout camp.

And now this.

"Yes, Papi. I understand. Thanks for letting us know," she said as she disconnected the call she had just put on speaker.

"How did he know where your parents live?" Diego asked as Gabriella settled into the seat beside him.

With a shake of her head, she said, "It wouldn't be hard. They've lived there forever, and when Isabella disappeared, the house was all over the news."

"We can go back and look for cameras along the street. See what they've recorded," Diego said, and peered around the table at everyone gathered there.

"Definitely, but first, let's go over what we've got so far," Sophie said, and with a quick look at Ryder, urged him to proceed.

"CSI techs say they found DNA on Isabella's crucifix. They're processing it right now, and we should have something in a few hours," he advised.

"They'll run it through CODIS. But what if Konijn isn't already in there?" Gabriella said, and nervously tapped the table with her hand.

"Then we'll check it against any genealogy sites we can access. If we're lucky—" Robbie began, but Gabriella cut him off.

"We haven't been lucky so far."

Diego laid a hand on hers to quiet the nervous motion. "I haven't known you long, but I know you probably have more than luck going on, right, Robbie?" he said to take down the temperature in the room.

"We got the VIN for Hughes's wife's Range Rover, but we didn't have to go to the vehicle manufacturer for location info. She works at the hospital, and CCTV puts the car at the hospital the morning you were followed."

"Do we take him off the list then?" Diego asked.

"Not off, but he's lower with the info we gathered," Ryder said, and prompted Sophie for her report.

"We were able to get the carrier from the SIM card on the tracker. Which is back on Gabriella's car—but more on that later," Sophie said.

"I got a warrant, and the carrier provided the name of the account holder. It's an LLC that looks to be a shell company," Ryder advised.

"We checked the Secretary of State records and got a name and street address for the Registered Agent. It turns out he's an attorney who represents Konijn's wealth management firm," Robbie said, pulled some papers from a file, and passed them across the table to Diego and Gabriella.

Diego took a look at the business record and then held up the papers as he asked, "Is this enough to bring in father and son?"

"No. Not yet, but soon," Gabriella said with a tired sigh.

Diego was sure there was more the two tech geniuses had found. "Any luck on the partial plates or the CCTV feeds?"

"We were able to get a better read on the plate from one of the CCTV feeds, and we gave that info to Ryder," Robbie said, and glanced at the CBI agent.

"Plate came back to a gray Range Rover registered to a different shell company," Ryder said.

"Let me guess. Same Registered Agent?" Gabriella said, and Ryder nodded.

"Just how many shell companies do the Konijns have?" Diego wondered aloud.

"Glad you asked," Sophie said and pulled out a sheath of papers she handed over. "Sorry, it's only one copy, but I didn't want to kill more trees."

The report was nearly an inch thick. Together they skimmed through all the pages of business records as Sophie said, "These are all companies the lawyer acting as the Registered Agent has set up, which may include people other than the Konijns."

"How do we limit it to just them?" Diego said.

"You don't need much to register a company. Fill out a simple form and pay, that's it," Sophie said, but Robbie immediately jumped in with more.

"We assumed that their offices and homes might be held in the names of one or more of the LLCs. Bingo, we connected the office and homes to three of these shell companies."

"I think that with this info we have enough to at least bring in the Konijns for additional questioning," Ryder said.

"I want to be there when you do the interviews," Gabriella said, fresh determination in her voice.

"I'll call and set it up for first thing in the morning," he said.

"You know they're going to lawyer up, right?" she pressed.

"Of course, but they'll be rattled," Ryder said with a smile.

Gabriella likewise smiled and said, "And when they're rattled, they may make a mistake."

"I guess that in the meantime, Gabriella and I will go back to Highlands Square and check for cameras that might have gotten video of our killer," Diego said with a glance at her.

"We will, but you mentioned not removing the tracker. Why?" she asked the team at the table.

"Don't want to tip him off until we exhaust all possibilities at the carrier. We've also put another tracker on the car so that we can follow you as well in case he removes his. The most important thing is to keep you safe. We all think his leaving you Isabella's crucifix is an escalation that says you're next," Ryder said.

Gabriella nodded. "I agree. Maybe that's another way to draw him out. Using me as bait."

Diego slashed his hands through the air. "No way. That's too dangerous."

Gabriella took hold of one of his hands and said, "If we have to do it to get Jeannie Roberts back, I'm willing to take that risk."

Diego inhaled deeply, held it and then released it with a rush of words. "I'm going to be on you like white on rice," he said.

GABRIELLA WANTED TO ASSERT, as she had before, that she could take care of herself.

But in the short time they'd gotten to know each other, she knew he respected her and what she could do.

Because of that, she didn't challenge him over his protectiveness.

Instead, she pushed ahead with an idea that Diego had proposed earlier that day while they were at the scout camp.

"While Diego and I go back to my parents', do you think you could check on something?"

"Of course. What is it?" Sophie said as she gathered the papers they had reviewed during the meeting.

Gabriella did a quick look at Diego. "While we were at the scout camp, Diego raised the possibility that the killer may have brought back Isabella to the area after the searches were completed."

Ryder dipped his head from side to side as he considered it. "Possible but risky."

"It was his first. He probably wasn't as…regimented," Diego pointed out, and immediately fixed his attention on Sophie and Ryder. "You've used lidar in the past to find ground anomalies, right?"

"We have. On multiple occasions," Robbie confirmed with a dip of his head.

"Do you think you can do it in the area around the scout camp?" Gabriella asked.

"Possibly. We'll reach out to our contacts in the area," Sophie confirmed.

"Great. Do you think you could do one other thing?" Diego asked with another glance at the report from the company register.

"Sure. What is it?" Sophie asked, gaze intense as she looked at the thick pile of paper.

"Can you see what other properties those LLCs own? See if any are in the general area of either the scout camp or the trails where those women were taken?"

"We can work on that. We can also have Wilson see what other info he can get for those shell companies," Robbie replied, and slapped his hands on the table. "I don't know about you all, but I need a break and—"

"Food. You always need food," Sophie said with a laugh and shake of her head.

"Yes, I do. And it'll give us a break to think over everything we've discussed and make sure we didn't miss anything," he said, rose and walked over to the credenza where he picked up one of the many menus sitting there.

"Chinese, anyone?" he asked.

As she drove her car toward her parents', she recalled a joke that a comedian had told about Chinese food and how it seemed they could make it even faster than you could order it.

The food had come quickly, but they'd still managed to

walk Poppy so she could relieve herself and fed her while Sophie and Robbie had laid out the dishes they'd ordered.

Hunger and the need to move the investigation along had made for a quick dinner.

"Do you think we'll find anything?" Gabriella asked, and looked at him as they returned to Highlands Square. The lights from the passing streetlamps cast patterns on his handsome face as they drove.

"We will. Too many people have those doorbells now, capturing everything that goes on," he said, and it was impossible to miss his tone.

"Too many? I guess you're not a fan?"

With a shrug, he said, "People complain about invasions of privacy all the time and yet they put out so much info willingly. Social media. Doorbell cameras. Cell phones. Virtual assistants that turn on our lights or answer our questions. They all create breaks in our privacy."

She understood that more than most. They regularly used that kind of info and more, like toll payment devices, to track and catch criminals.

"It's not always a bad thing," she said, earning a rough laugh from him.

"No, it isn't. It makes our lives easier at times. But I wonder if people know just how much they're giving up."

"Probably not," she said as she pulled up in front of her parents' home. Before she left the car, she looked around. "My father thought he spotted someone watching from across the street. Near those bushes," she said, and pointed in the direction of the home opposite her parents.

"Let's see if Poppy can pick up a scent," he said, and slipped from the passenger seat.

She left the car and then waited for Diego to swing around with Poppy. Together they crossed the street, and he commanded Poppy to search.

"*Such*," he said.

Poppy nosed around the bushes and then took off along the sidewalk, head down as she seemingly followed a scent.

The home with the bushes didn't have a doorbell camera, but the next one did. If the killer had passed this way, he would have been seen.

But they didn't stop to check. They let Poppy continue along, searching, until she stopped in front of one home, went to the curb, and then nosed around some more before lying down.

"The scent stopped here. This is where he must have had his car," Diego said, and glanced back in the direction in which they had come. Motioning with his hand, he said, "At least two doorbell cameras on this side."

Turning, he scrutinized the homes on the opposite side of the street. "One more there," he said, and pointed in the direction of a home.

"Great. Let's start on this side and see if the owners have video and if so, if they're willing to share it," she said.

Diego nodded, and they backtracked to the first house with a doorbell camera.

A young father with a toddler on his hip answered. His gaze narrowed in puzzlement as Gabriella held up her badge.

"How can I help you?" he asked, and then called for his wife to come and take the toddler.

She hurried over and took the boy away, but not before shooting her husband a worried look.

"There's nothing to worry about, Mr.—"

"Evans. Chris Evans like the actor," he said with a smile.

"CBI Agent Ruiz and this is my civilian consultant, Agent Rodriguez. We see that you have a doorbell camera, and we're wondering if you might have recorded something earlier this afternoon. Around four o'clock?"

He shrugged. "It's possible. People on the sidewalk trip

the motion detector. Honestly, it's frustrating at times," he said and wiped a hand across his short-cropped hair, which rasped with the motion.

Gabriella handed him her business card. "If you wouldn't mind checking, we would appreciate you sending it to my email."

"Sure, no problem," he said, whipped out his phone and swiped the screen. With a nod, he said, "I do have it. Some guy in a hoodie walking by. I'll send it."

"Great, and thank you," she said.

"Anything we should worry about?" the young father said.

Gabriella and Diego shared a look. "Make sure to keep your doors locked, and if you have an alarm system, set it. Just as a precaution. We're working on the case involving the missing hiker."

He nodded. "Thanks for that advice. I'll let my wife know as well," he said, and closed the door.

They repeated that visit at the two other homes they had identified earlier and luckily, each of the homes had video of the hooded man and promised to send it. The one home had even captured him climbing into a gray Range Rover, confirming that it had likely been the killer watching Gabriella and her parents.

When they returned to their car, Diego said, "You should send those videos to Sophie and Robbie. They may be able to clean them up."

She nodded, whipped out her phone and did as he'd suggested. "Done. Should we go back to CPS?"

Diego shook his head. "Not yet. My place is on the way back. I'd like to stop there and pick up some things."

"Why?" she asked.

"Because you're not going anywhere without me, and that includes tonight."

Chapter Sixteen

Diego didn't know what she would make of the furnished studio apartment he'd rented until he could find something more permanent once he was sure Crooked Pass Security was the place he was meant to be.

For weeks he'd thought he'd found that place with Jackson in Regina, but fate clearly had another plan for him.

Which made him wonder if it included Gabriella, he thought as she stood by his door, waiting for him to grab some clothes and his toilet kit.

"It's not much, but I wanted to save money while I found the right place," he explained as he set his duffel by the door and then went in search of another bag to pack up what he might need for Poppy.

"It's nice," she said, but he didn't buy it.

"It'll do. I want to volunteer at a local church that hosts a group for veterans with PTSD and also be closer to CPS once I know…once it's more settled," he said.

He hadn't said it outright, but Gabriella had picked up on his uncertainty.

"It's not easy to know where you belong."

He stopped riffling through a cabinet that held Poppy's food and treats. Meeting her gaze from across the room, he said, "It's not."

Grabbing a smaller bag of food and another of treats, he tossed them into a reusable shopping bag.

She was waiting for him by the door still, her gaze fixed on him as he walked over to grab his duffel and did a hand command for Poppy to heel. Poppy immediately came to his side, and he said, "I'm ready when you are."

GABRIELLA WASN'T SURE she would ever be ready for this intriguing and complex man.

And although her home wasn't as small as his studio, she wasn't sure it was big enough. She wasn't sure what could be big enough to help her avoid the maelstrom of emotions she felt around him.

But she lied and said, "I'm ready."

With a slight shift of his head, he invited her to open the door, and she did. But then he stopped her and said, "Let me check it out first."

Given that the killer could now be tracking them, she deferred to his request.

He pushed through the door, bags in hand and Poppy at his side.

His studio apartment was ground floor and not far from a private parking lot. Quiet since it was well past dinner hour, and most people were probably getting ready to settle in for the night.

No one was on the grounds or in the parking area. No sign of motion anywhere except for Diego ahead of her with Poppy at his side.

He reached the car and turned, waiting for her.

Like white on rice, she remembered, and realized he meant it.

She hit the fob to unlock all the doors, and when she got to the driver's side, she said, "I appreciate the concern, Diego. I do, but—"

"You can take care of yourself," he said with a crooked grin, dropped one bag and reached up to cup her cheek. "Sometimes it's okay to lean on others."

As she had done the day before, she laid her hand against his chest, directly over his heart, and said, "I'm here if you want to lean sometime, too."

His grin broadened into a wide smile, and he nodded. "I'll remember that."

He opened the door for her. She slipped in, waiting for him to drop his bags onto the floor, harness Poppy and settle into the seat beside her.

Diego's apartment was a short ten-minute ride to the Crooked Pass Security offices, so she understood why he had chosen it. If this investigation was indicative of their workload, he might regularly put in late nights at work. A short commute would make his life easier.

She pulled into the parking lot and a CPS spot that was empty. In no time, she, Diego and Poppy were headed to the elevator bank.

But as they neared, the loud screech of tires snared their attention.

Before she could react, Diego had wrapped her in his arms and dragged her behind the protection of a parked car as a barrage of gunfire peppered the wall behind them and smashed into the parked car. Bits of concrete and shattered glass rained down.

Another loud screech sounded, and then there was nothing but silence.

"Are you okay?" Diego asked as they crouched by the car.

She faced him. His hair was littered with small pieces of concrete and glass. Brushing them away, she said, "I'm fine. You? Poppy?"

He rubbed Poppy's fur, brushing away the debris from the shooting, and then said, "We're okay."

With that, he helped her to her feet. They were about to look for any evidence when a loud pounding from the stairwell stopped them.

Ryder, Robbie and Sophie surged out of the stairwell, faces etched with fear and worry.

"Are you okay?" Ryder asked, and skipped his gaze over all of them.

"We are. Someone's car, not so much," Gabriella said and gestured to the vehicle that had taken the brunt of the damage during the drive-by. Shattered rear windows and pockmarked metal memorialized the violence.

"I'll call CSI and get them working on this, but did you see the car? Shooter?" Ryder asked.

She shook her head and peered at Diego, who had been the one to react before she had realized there was any danger.

"Not a gray Range Rover. Black pickup, I think. Tinted windows. I saw a muzzle. Dark face, maybe a mask," he said, and circled a hand around his face in explanation.

"Let's get upstairs and see what video we can grab from the parking lot cameras," Sophie said, and laid a gentle and comforting hand against her shoulder.

She nodded, and they walked to the elevator bank. As she saw the dings caused by the bullets in the elevator door, it finally sank in.

Someone had tried to kill them.

Her gut chilled and a rough shudder racked her body, but she controlled it. She couldn't let the killer distract her from her primary goal: saving Jeannie Roberts.

If it had been the killer, she thought, baffled by a very different way of attack.

In the CPS conference room, Sophie and Robbie immediately got to work, pulling up video from the parking lot CCTVs.

As they ran the video, it confirmed Diego's initial impressions.

A large black pickup, a Ford F-150, raced from the bowels of the parking lot and screeched to a halt. The tinted window drifted down to reveal the muzzle but not much else.

Muzzle flashes repeated over and over as bullets flew.

A brief silence followed by another screech as the pickup roared out of the parking lot.

Robbie tapped on the keys and rewound the video to the spot where the pickup first appeared. The plates had been obscured, but with another few taps, Robbie was able to reveal the faint outlines of the plate numbers beneath the license plate screen.

"I'll send this to Ryder so he can have DMV give us the owner info," Sophie said as her fingers flew over across her phone screen.

"Chances are it's another fake LLC connected to the Konijns," Diego said, and tossed his pen on the tabletop in frustration.

"Maybe, but I'm not so sure," Gabriella said, and laid a hand over his to offer support.

Puzzled, Diego looked at her as he cupped her hand in his. "Why do you say that?"

"I know serial killers can change how they operate, but this kind of attack won't give them satisfaction. It's not personal enough," she said.

"He can't get his jollies from the pain he inflicts," Robbie said, ever the one to hit the nail on the head.

"That's right," Gabriella said and plowed on. "He wouldn't get any pleasure from something like a drive-by."

"What about the DC sniper attacks?" Sophie asked.

"I see you've been doing some homework," Gabriella said with a nod to the other woman's insightfulness. "When you think about it, they were able to see what that shot did through the scope. See the kill. It wasn't some wild shoot-'em-up like what just happened."

"Makes sense," Diego said, and squeezed her hand before releasing it.

"That leaves us with the evidence we have so far and also, anything you've come up with since we sent over that doorbell camera footage," Gabriella said, and glanced across the table to the two tech geniuses.

Robbie nodded and quickly pulled up some images onto the monitor on the wall. "We were able to snag these images of our unsub from that footage. Similar height, weight and build to the suspect from the other night. Big difference: the pants," he said and zoomed in on that element in two different sets of photos. "The other night he was wearing jeans. Tonight, they look like dress pants. The kind you might wear at a fancy office."

"Like Konijn's wealth management firm," Diego said.

"Like that. Given the timing, he may have left the office and not had time to change. He just tossed the hoodie and jacket over what he was wearing," Sophie replied.

Diego and Gabriella shared a look before she said, "And this height, weight and build are similar to the younger Konijn, right?"

Sophie nodded and displayed a copy of Peter Konijn's driver's license. "He matches the height and weight we guesstimated from the videos. You've seen him in person, so you'd be a better judge as to the build."

"Definitely in the range," Diego confirmed.

Satisfied with that, Gabriella pushed on with what they had discussed earlier that day. "Any luck on the properties owned by the LLCs or the possible lidar imaging?"

"Too much luck," Sophie said with a tired sigh, and a second later, a map with at least three dozen red dots filled the monitor. "These are all the properties we suspect are owned by possible Konijn LLCs."

"We eliminated any locations that were multiuser dwellings. Figured it would be too much of a risk for him to transport women," Robbie said, and with a few taps of his keyboard, about two dozen of the marked locations dropped off the map.

"That's a logical assumption, but it still leaves almost a dozen places," Gabriella said as she scrutinized the map.

"It does. So we asked Wilson to overlay these sites with the locations for our victims and provide a probability as to where the killer might be," Sophie said as her fingers flew across her keyboard. When she was finished, six places were now shown with bright green dots and a number.

"Does that number reflect the probability of it being the killer's location?" Diego said, beating her to the question.

"Yes. So for this location, the probability is 75 percent that it's where our unsub and hopefully Roberts will be," Sophie said, and used a laser pointer to highlight that spot on the map.

"And that's based on what?" Gabriella pressed, trying to understand how Wilson and his program could pinpoint the locations.

Sophie nodded and with a grim smile, passed a report across the table. "This report shows the variables considered to reach this conclusion. Things like proximity to the attacks and disappearances. Also, the nature of the house. For example, ranch or colonial—"

"Because who wants to lug a body up and down stairs," Diego said as he flipped through the pages of the report.

"Possible but harder to do. But also, did they own it at the time of each attack or kidnap," Robbie explained.

So MANY VARIABLES that would have taken them many workhours, if not days, to gather and Wilson's program had done it in only a few hours.

"Pretty amazing but also pretty scary," he said.

"AI and programs like this can be intimidating, but they won't ever replace human intuition," Sophie said.

Diego nodded and closed the report. "Do you mind if I take this for a deeper look?"

"Not at all. You might spot something the program didn't. It's not foolproof," Sophie said and motioned for him to keep it.

Maybe not foolproof, but he could see how it could make an investigator feel foolish at not making the connections as quickly as the program, he thought.

Gabriella moved on with, "What about the lidar imaging?"

Robbie's lips thinned into a knife-sharp slash, and he shook his head. "There are only a couple of people in our area who can help us with that and unfortunately, they are all out of town to work on a gig investigating Mayan ruins."

"We reached out to others, but they can't make it for a few days. By then it might be too late," Sophie said, but as she had done before, she worked the keys and brought up another map.

"We do have this," she said.

"Let me guess. Wilson's program," Diego said as he scrutinized the map. Rising, he walked to the monitor and pointed to one area on the map. "This is the scout camp, right?"

Sophie nodded. "It is. Just like Wilson used certain parameters to select those properties, he did the same here. Things like where the attacks and disappearances occurred and also, height and weight of the individuals and how far someone might be able to carry them."

As Diego watched, a transparent purple circle appeared in an area just above the location of the scout camp. "This is the possible killing field?" he asked.

Robbie nodded. "That's the area where he's likely to have

brought his victims. We relied on your theory that since this was the site of his first kill, it would be special to him."

He turned to examine Gabriella, who was studying the map intently. "You're familiar with the area. Does that seem plausible?"

She did a little sway of her head and then nodded. "Like I mentioned earlier, the trails only go partly up the mountain and the area Wilson's identified is past that. But it doesn't preclude that it's possible."

Ryder came to the door of the conference room, his face set in hard lines. He held up his smartphone and said, "We've got a hit on the license plate number on that Ford F-150."

Chapter Seventeen

"Great. Is it to one of the LLCs or Konijn?" Gabriella asked.

Ryder shook his head and walked over to the table. "It's not. I just sent you the info, Sophie. Can you pull it up?"

She did, replacing the map image with copies of a driver's license and a rap sheet.

"Jack Hayes. Petty criminal. Arrested several times for drug dealing and assault and burglary. Currently free because of our new no-bail policies," Ryder said with an angry sigh. "I've put a BOLO out for him."

"Seems like someone hired to intimidate us?" Diego said.

Ryder did a sharp bob of his head. "Definitely. That drive-by was a warning. We're getting close."

That wasn't sitting right with Gabriella. She slashed her hand through the air and said, "Our killer has been extremely careful until now. Why would he hire someone like Hayes to take potshots at us?"

"People have done stupider things," Diego offered in explanation.

She wasn't buying it. "This just seems like a diversion to pull us away from what's important."

"I can't disagree. Hopefully, an officer will spot him and bring him in. In the meantime, what have you been up to while I was gone?" Ryder asked.

They quickly filled him in on the prospective locations identified and for review, Sophie pulled up the two maps side by side.

Ryder surveyed them and said, "Six is still a lot of places to visit."

"I agree. I think we should visit the Konijns and see how they react to questions about the LLCs and these particular properties," Gabriella said.

"Agreed. We can do that first thing in the morning," Ryder said, then glanced at Sophie. "Can you print out a list of those six properties—maybe even a photo?"

"I can have that for you first thing in the a.m.," she confirmed.

Gabriella peered at Diego and said, "If the weather's good tomorrow, do you think we could take Poppy into that area identified by Wilson and search for…" She couldn't finish as the possibility of finally finding her sister nearly overwhelmed her.

Diego skimmed the back of his hand across her cheek and said, "We can go find Isabella."

"Great," she said with a strangled sigh, and then glanced at the others. "Unless we get something overnight, I guess I'll see you at the Konijns' at 9:00 a.m."

"I'll be there," Ryder confirmed with a dip of his head.

"Sophie and I will keep working on some leads. Maybe see if there are any connections between Hayes and the Konijns," Robbie said.

"Thank you. Diego and I will be at my place if you need us," she said and slowly rose, exhaustion pulling at her after the long and emotional day.

"Get some rest," Ryder called out as they walked out of the room.

She felt guilty because she suspected that her colleagues would be at work long after Diego and she had gone home.

Diego. Home, she thought, and spared a glance at the man standing beside her with Poppy at his side.

She couldn't remember the last time a man other than her father had been in her home, mostly because she wasn't the kind for one-night stands or long relationships for that matter. She'd been too consumed by work and by her search for the truth behind her sister's disappearance.

Having him there again, in her space, was going to be a challenge on multiple levels. But if the killer had turned his attention to her with his little gift, it made sense to have added protection.

He must have sensed her turmoil, because he slipped an arm around her waist and drew her into a comforting embrace.

"I know it's been rough for you today," he whispered, and hugged her.

"That's an understatement," she said with a rough laugh.

"Some rest may help," he said as the elevator arrived and they stepped onboard.

Silence reigned on the way down to the parking lot.

He stepped in front of her as the doors opened, providing protection, but the CSI team was still there and finishing up.

It was safe for now, she thought as he gently touched the small of her back and they hurried to her car. In steps that were becoming familiar, he loaded Poppy into the back, harnessed her and then joined her in the front seat.

He faced her then and skimmed the back of his hand down her cheek. "Let's get home and get some rest. Tomorrow may be a rough day."

She nodded and tried to force tomorrow from her mind, especially if Diego's theory was supported by Wilson's program, finally leading them to Isabella.

"If I remember correctly, your home isn't far?" he said as she pulled out of the parking lot.

She chuckled and was about to reply when he beat her to it.

"Twenty minutes, right," he said with a laugh.

"About that," she confirmed with a slight smile as she made the few turns to access the highway.

She was grateful that Diego remained silent during the ride. She was too busy processing all that had happened that day and what it meant not only about her sister but more importantly how to save Jeannie Roberts.

Her gut told her Jeannie was still alive.

No program or AI could ever do that, she thought, recalling all the info that Wilson had provided in just a few short hours.

As she pulled up in front of her modest Craftsman-style home, it occurred to her that she'd been on autopilot as she drove. But as it did every time she got there, a sense of peace enveloped her.

Until she realized that the handsome and complex man sitting beside her would again be passing through the doors into what she considered her fortress of solitude.

"We're home," she said with a forced smile.

"Good. Let's get you settled inside and then I'll take Poppy for a walk around the grounds to make sure it's all secure," he said, and once again skimmed the back of his hand across her cheek, offering comfort.

"Okay."

DIEGO HAD HER back as they walked to the front door of the beautiful but simple home. As it had the first time, it brought a feeling of comfort.

An open gable marked the edges of a large front porch. At one end was a wooden bench with some pillows and on the other, two comfortable-looking Adirondack chairs bracketing a small table with a metal lantern.

He could picture her sitting there, in this quiet neighborhood, watching the world go by and in more ways than one.

Much like he had lost a portion of his life to the PTSD that had chased him after his service, she had let her determination to find her sister steal part of her life.

The pillars holding up the porch and part of the siding were done in a white-and-gray stone that matched the dark charcoal color of the board-and-batten siding. All those neutral colors made the natural color of large double wooden doors pop, even at night.

Two modern black-and-white sconces cast a welcoming glow, and she unlocked the door and they stepped into an open living room/dining/kitchen area. Directly above the kitchen was a loft to her office area.

"You can use the guest bedroom again," she said with a wave of her hand toward the room.

"If you don't mind, I'd like to make sure the area is clear," he said, and at her nod, he walked Poppy through her home.

In front and to the right there was a utility room and what could have been a third bedroom, only she was using it as a home gym.

A bathroom separated that bedroom from the one in the back she wanted him to use, although he'd likely take the couch this time because it gave him a better vantage point on most of the entrances into her home.

On the left-hand side in the back was her bedroom and he entered that area mindfully, moving to the French doors by her bed to make sure they were locked. The doors faced a fenced-in yard. Moonlight silvered the green of the grass and the bushes and spring bulbs blooming along the edges.

He pushed past the bed to a spacious bathroom, again in neutral colors and stone.

Behind the bathroom was a nice-sized walk-in closet.

All clear, he thought, and as he walked back out, it hit him.

Her rooms smelled like her, fresh and flowery, and his body responded to her scent.

He sucked in a breath to quell the desire. What a mistake. Her scent only wrapped around him deeper, making him ache.

"Everything okay?" she asked as he returned to the main living area, mistaking the reason for his worry.

"We're good here. I'm going to take Poppy for a walk around the grounds and then feed her if that's okay," he said, and Poppy sat beside him, waiting for another command.

"Mi casa es su casa," she said, hands wide in invitation.

It would be easy to see this as a home with her. The space was welcoming. Homey.

But as quickly as he thought that, guilt nearly swamped him as he remembered his fallen brothers who would never see home again.

Forcing a smile, he said, "Gracias. I won't be long."

He dashed out the front door and walked with Poppy all around the front of the home, seeing if she would pick up any scents the way she had on the sidewalk earlier.

Nothing on the front porch.

The house didn't have a garage, so he led Poppy around the side and to the gate for the white vinyl fence that encircled the yard.

Inside the backyard, he walked Poppy all around and to the far end, but again she didn't pick up on anything. He unleashed her and let her run free for a few minutes while he again checked the French doors to Gabriella's bedroom. They were locked, and she had drawn the curtains to close off the space.

His bedroom also had French doors, and he checked them. Locked as well.

Satisfied, he watched as Poppy relieved herself. Quickly he cleaned up, leashed her and walked back to the front of the house. Entering, he found Gabriella sitting at the kitchen table with the report that Sophie had handed him and a large black mug.

"I made some coffee," she said. Not that she needed to tell him—the earthy and comfy scent of it spiced the air.

"Thanks. I could use something warm," he said, and rubbed his hands together before freeing Poppy of her leash and harness.

With a hand command, he led her to the kitchen where he filled collapsible bowls with water and kibble and set them off to one side on the floor.

Gabriella had left him a mug on the counter, and he prepped his coffee, joined her at the table and sat kitty-corner to her.

Poppy gobbled down her kibble and meandered over to sit at their feet.

"There's a lot of info in that report," he said, and flipped a hand in the direction of the inch-thick pile of paper in front of Gabriella.

She had opened to the first page and tapped it. "Like Sophie said, these are the six locations with the highest probability based on a lot of variables."

"You have doubts about the criteria he used?" Diego said, and leaned in to watch her expressive face. The doubt was apparent as she picked up her mug, leaned back and scrutinized the page.

"Certain kinds of homes scored lower for various reasons, including apartment buildings. But several serial killers did their work in apartment buildings. Jeffrey Dahmer, for example," she said.

"So you would add more locations to investigate?" he asked, worried that with the clock ticking, such a task would be impossible.

With a hesitant shake of her head, she said, "That would add too many, because the Konijns have tons of rental properties. And yes, it makes sense to flag single-family homes first. Many serial killers used their properties to bury their victims."

"Should we look for remains there first instead of the scout camp?" he asked, although his gut told him that the killer might have a stronger connection to that site.

Shrugging, she said, "I agree with you that if Isabella was his first victim, that might make the scout camp special."

She jabbed a finger between two locations identified by Wilson's program. "These are ranked as lower probability. We'd have to dig through all this to find out why," she said, and riffled through the pages of the report. "But I think these should be higher on our list. They're closer to the scout camp, for starters. Single-family with larger properties. No neighbors to hear or see what's happening."

"We can start with those after we interview the Konijns," he said and bent to rub Poppy's head.

"I'm calling it a night," she said, although he suspected that she'd be thinking about the case as she lay in bed, much like he'd be running through all the info that had been dumped on them.

He rose as well, a little slower as she stood there, waiting for him. For what he wondered until she leaned toward him, cupped his cheek and dropped a kiss on his lips.

"Thank you for all that you're doing," she whispered against his lips.

Her lips were warm and oh so sweet and when she didn't immediately pull away, he cradled the back of her skull with his hand and said, "I want to help you find peace, Gabriella."

She kissed him again, a slow, leisurely kiss that held the promise of more until she reluctantly took a step back. "We should get some rest. I'll set the house alarm from my room."

Before he could say a word, she hurried away and closed the door.

A little whine from Poppy had him looking at his dog, who

was peering at him with a look that seemed to say, "Are you just going to let her go?"

"Yes, Poppy, I am. It's not the right time," he said, and with a wave of his hand, he commanded Poppy to follow him to the guest bedroom.

As he entered, he heard a loud beep warning that she'd set the alarm. Because of that, he didn't open the French doors to check the backyard once again. But with the bright moonlight, he could see that all was quiet there.

He undressed and showered, feeling as if he had to wash off all that had happened that day, from the tumble at the scout camp to the drive-by that had his back aching from protecting Gabriella.

Gabriella, he thought as he ran soapy hands across the assorted bruises and scars on his body.

Stellar-shaped scars from when he'd been shot on deployment. The harder, pronounced ridges along his ribs and lower from the shrapnel created by the rocket that had brought down his helicopter and killed so many of his brothers.

He was damaged goods, and his wounds were the least of it. Not the kind of man for someone like Gabriella.

He finished the shower, toweled off, slipped on sweatpants and climbed into bed, wincing as his back once again protested the movement.

Resting his head on his hands, he inhaled deeply. The pillows and sheets smelled like her. He closed his eyes, picturing her. Imagined what it would be like to have a wife and kids. He hadn't thought about that in years. He'd been too busy rebuilding himself. Trying to put the pieces of who he had been back together and helping others do the same.

But as he drifted off to sleep, imagining that new beginning, the darkness came again, clawing at him. Pulling him back into an abyss that he'd thought he'd escaped years earlier.

"No, no, no," he called out, and flailed as bullets ripped into his body and the sound of gunshots echoed in his brain.

The scent of sulfur attacked his senses until another achingly familiar aroma wafted in.

Gabriella, he thought, and suddenly she was there in his arms. Warm, but it was a wet warmth, and he realized she was bleeding.

"No, no, no," he wailed in anguish. *This is just a dream*, he told himself as he tried to get a grip on ground that seemed to disintegrate beneath his fingertips until they dug into something warm and solid and real.

Chapter Eighteen

A noise had dragged Gabriella from a troubled sleep.

She couldn't identify it at first but then realized it was Diego, shouting out.

Grabbing her Glock, she raced from her room into his, expecting a fight.

The fight she found was Diego still asleep, wrestling his demons.

Poppy was at the foot of the bed, whining in sympathy.

As he flailed and called out again, she laid her gun on a nearby dresser and carefully approached him. Kneeling on the bed, she caught his muscled arms as he raised them as if to ward off an attack.

"No, no, no," he cried out, the pain of his dreams all too real.

"Diego, wake up, Diego," she said softly as she ran her hands down his arms to his shoulders to comfort him.

His eyes opened, dark and full of agony, but as he painfully dug his fingers into her upper arms, it was obvious he was still lost in that private hell.

"Diego, por favor. Wake up," she pleaded, and winced at the strength of his grip.

Like a light snapping to life, his eyes suddenly lost their glazed look. As he focused on her and realized he had a death grip on her arms, he loosened his hold and muttered a curse.

"I'm sorry. I'm so sorry," he said, and tenderly ran his hands across the marks on her arms that said she'd have bruises by the morning.

She brushed her fingers through the longer locks of his hair and murmured, "It's okay. You were having a nightmare."

And now that it was over, she realized how compromising her position was, straddling his hips, hands pinning his shoulders to the mattress as she'd struggled to keep him from hurting himself.

"I should go," she said, but he raised his hands, which had drifted to her hips, and cradled her back, drawing her down to rest along the length of his body.

"I don't want to be alone anymore," he said softly and with such anguish, she couldn't leave.

She pulled up the disheveled bedsheets and comforter and snuggled into his chest.

He wrapped his arms around her, kissed her temple and whispered, "Thank you."

Running her hand down his arm, she grasped his hand, and said, "Sometimes it's easier if you share."

His rough laugh vibrated against her core. "I'm not sure it could ever be easy."

"Try," she said, and rose slightly to watch his face as he answered.

TRY. HOW MANY times had he told himself to try to forget as he'd battled to overcome the traumas of war that had followed him into civilian life?

"I told you I struggled with PTSD. It's not the kind of thing that just goes away," he said, and plowed on. "Things can trigger it, like today's gunfire. It was in my dream. You were in my dream," he said, and cradled her cheek.

"You were shot. I felt your blood on my hands just like I

felt the blood of my brothers," he said, hand trembling against her soft skin. He stroked his thumb across her cheek and in his mind, it left a smear of blood there.

"I'M OKAY, DIEGO. It was just a dream," she said as she realized his nightmare was taking hold again. To draw him back, she cupped his face in both hands and nuzzled his nose with hers.

"It's okay," she crooned, and brushed her lips against his over and over, trying to soothe. Little by little, the stiffness that had been in his body seconds earlier relaxed, and his choppy breaths slowed and lengthened.

He brushed back a lock of her hair that had fallen forward and gently tucked it behind her ear. "Thank you."

"Anything for my partner," she said, offered him a small smile and stroked her thumbs across his cheeks. His skin was smooth there but beneath her palms, there was the rasp of his evening beard.

The edge of his lips tipped up in a precursor to his boyish grin and he slipped his thumb across her smiling lips, his chocolate-colored eyes dark, almost bottomless.

She could lose herself in those eyes, she thought as another emotion slowly crept in.

He skimmed her lips again with his finger and tracked that motion with his gaze. "This could be a big mistake," he said, voice in low tones and husky.

"It could. But there's only one way to find out," she said, and before he could protest, she covered his lips with hers in a kiss that invited him to join her.

SHE'D DRAGGED HIM from his hell just moments before and now she was promising him a heaven he hadn't thought possible.

He groaned and opened his mouth to her, accepting that

promise. Kissing her over and over until Poppy's whine registered to his ears. She had heard his groan and misinterpreted.

"*Aus*," he said, and with a wave of his hand, instructed her to leave the room.

"It's like having a child," she said with a laugh and then kissed him again.

He joined her in that happiness, chuckling as he wrapped his arms around her, rolled and pressed her into the mattress.

She drifted her hands to his back, holding him close as they kissed until desire roused, and kissing alone wasn't enough.

He rolled again and she straddled him, and waited, her midnight-dark eyes suddenly questioning, as if asking, "Are we sure?"

For the first time in forever, he could say he'd never been more sure of anything in his life.

"WE'RE SURE."

Those two words loosed the last of the bonds keeping them from fulfilling the attraction that had been building between them for days.

She grabbed the hem of her nightshirt, jerked it over her head and tossed it aside.

He skimmed his hands up her sides to cup her breasts, and her body shook with need.

"You're so beautiful," he said as he caressed her.

She mimicked his actions, running her hands down his arms to his broad shoulders, and then down to rest on his chest. She couldn't miss the damage on his warrior's body that marred his physical perfection.

He was all lean, sculpted muscle beneath tanned skin that was smooth except for the scars of war. Scars that weren't limited to his body.

Scars like those she carried in her heart.

For what remained of this night, she wanted peace for both of them and released herself to the pleasure of his touch.

Bending, she kissed him, opening her mouth to his. Inviting him to join her in that peace and satisfaction.

He slipped his hands around to her back and urged her beneath the bedcovers and his naked body. Warmth filled her as skin met skin, and she sighed as that warmth slipped into her.

"You feel amazing," he said as he ran his hands up and down her back, and then guided them to her hips, where her center cradled his hard length.

She moved, and they both moaned as passion rose.

He kissed and caressed her breasts, urging her on until the shift of her hips nearly undid them both.

"Protection," she whispered urgently, seeking completion.

"Wallet. Nightstand," he said, and she leaned over, grabbed it and fumbled to remove a condom.

She hurriedly sheathed him in the protection, and he rolled, trapping her beneath him, but then hesitated, his dark gaze questioning.

She answered that question by rising, kissing his lips and then whispering, "Por favor, Diego."

IT HAD BEEN so long since he'd been with a woman. Maybe never with a woman like Gabriella.

She deserved better than him, but for now, he wanted to be her man.

He found her center and tenderly eased within her. Waited for her to accept his possession, and as she moaned against his lips, pleading for more, he answered that plea.

He moved, driving them both ever higher to the peak of passion. When it came, he groaned with the pleasure of it and stilled inside her to savor her release and his, kissing her deeply. Wanting their union to last forever.

As their climax ebbed, he lowered himself onto her, shifting to one side slightly to keep his weight off.

He stroked back her hair and dropped a kiss on her cheek. Struggling to find the words to share what he felt, the simple touch of her index finger against his lips spared him that.

"We should get some rest," she said, and then snuggled into his side.

Wrapping his arms around her, he held her close, and her warmth bathed his body.

He savored that warmth and the feel of her, so soft and yielding against him.

It had been too long and never like this. Never with a woman like her, he thought again as the image of her beside him blurred as sleep slowly pulled him away.

When the dreams came this time, he wasn't at war. He was with her, hiking along a bright, sunny mountain trail. She was in front of him, looked over her shoulder at him and smiled.

He smiled back and tugged her hand to haul her close only…

A baby tucked into a carrier. Dark-haired and dark-eyed like the two of them.

Gently he ran a hand over the baby's wisps of brown-black hair, and his heart filled with joy.

"He's beautiful, Gabriella."

She rose on tiptoes and kissed him, lips warm against his.

But something slowly pulled him from the dream to reality. Her lips, shifting against his.

As he opened his eyes, he realized she was straddling him again and kissing him, a welcoming smile on her face.

"You were grinning in your sleep. I can't resist that grin," she said, and ran a hand through his hair to tame the longer locks.

"You can't?" he said, and grinned for real.

"I can't," she said, and pressed him back against the mattress.

GABRIELLA RAN SOAPY hands across her body and fought the desire that instantly rose after a night and early morning of making love with him.

She rinsed off the soap but couldn't leave the shower just yet. She needed time alone to process all the info Crooked Pass Security had provided and what was happening with Diego.

Diego, she thought as she finally shut off the warm water and grabbed a towel.

There were lots of things she hadn't expected during this investigation. But the biggest thing she hadn't expected was him.

She didn't regret what had happened. On the contrary.

She would do it again. Oh, how she would happily do it again.

There was the pleasure factor, of course, but it was more than that.

She didn't know how that was possible in only a few short days, but she knew it.

With a self-deprecating laugh, she recalled how her parents had said that they knew from the very first they were meant to be together.

While thinking it romantic, she'd pooh-poohed it to herself, not wanting to rain on her parents' parade.

As she finished drying off, she thought that maybe she'd been too quick to doubt them.

She exited her bathroom and quickly dressed, donning a pale blue blouse and one of the many dark blue pantsuits that screamed cop.

Opening her bedroom door, she was greeted by the enticing smells of bacon and toast, and the sight of Diego cooking at her stove.

He half turned and grinned, and her heart did that little stutter it did whenever he gifted her that boyish grin.

"I hope you don't mind, but I thought we might need to fuel up for today," he said, and dipped his head in the direction of the breakfast bar.

He'd set the table and laid out dishes with bacon slices and a high pile of toast.

As he finished at the stove, she realized he'd made scrambled eggs.

"Thanks," she said, accepted the plate he handed her and followed him to the breakfast bar.

"There's coffee, too," he said, and gestured to the mugs he'd set on the table.

"I'll get us some," she said.

In no time she was back at the breakfast bar and sitting beside him, eating. She hadn't realized how hungry she was until the first fork of creamy scrambled eggs had her almost shoveling them into her mouth.

"You're a good cook," she said as she took a break to sip her coffee and grab a slice of perfectly crispy bacon.

"My mami taught us. She thought all the boys should learn to cook," he said with a smile that reached into his dark eyes.

"She did a good job," she said, and snared a piece of buttered toast. "Delicious."

"Thanks. Are you ready for today?" he asked with a side-eyed glance.

Was she? she wondered. She hoped today would put them one step closer to arresting either one or both of the Konijns and after...

She wouldn't think about the after and possibly finding Isabella and the other women.

"I'm as ready as I'll ever be," she said with a determined nod.

Chapter Nineteen

Diego stood by Ryder and Gabriella as they asked to see the Konijns at the front desk.

The receptionist, the same young woman from the other day, hesitated until the two agents pulled out their badges and held them up for her to see.

With shaky hands, she tapped out a number on her console and as someone answered, she said, "There are two CBI agents here to see you and your father."

The headset kept them from hearing his response, but then the young woman ended the call, rose and walked to the door of the conference room. "They'll be with you shortly."

Barely a minute later, the two Konijns hurried from the far side of the office, their features set in hard, implacable lines.

"If you wouldn't mind stepping inside," she said, and motioned for them to enter.

Before they could, the Konijns stormed up to them.

As Poppy had done the other day, she instantly lay down to notify him that she had scented something. He suspected it was Roberts's scent again.

"This is harassment," Ralph Konijn warned as he pushed past them into the conference room.

The son was slightly more welcoming. "Apologies, but we

had to reschedule an important call," Peter said, and swept his hand in the direction of the conference room door.

Gabriella and Ryder walked there, but he hesitated, wondering if he'd pick up on Roberts's scent anywhere else in the office.

At Gabriella's inquiring glance, he pointed to the reception area. "I'll wait out here."

She nodded, hurried into the room and closed the door.

The flustered receptionist wrung her hands nervously. "Is there anything I can get you? Coffee? Tea?" she said, relying on her past training to restore calm.

"Coffee, black, and the men's room would be great," he said with a smile to defuse the awkward situation.

"Restroom is down that corridor and to the right. I'll bring your coffee in a minute," she said, and hurried away from the reception area.

He walked to the end of the corridor, but as he glanced toward the restroom, which he didn't need to use, Poppy jerked him in the opposite direction.

Poppy pulled him along until he reached the large corner office. A plaque identified the space as belonging to Ralph Konijn. She lay down again, confirming she had a scent there.

He clicked his tongue to command her to continue searching and Poppy rose, nosed along the floor until she reached the next office and lay down. Peter's.

He clicked again and Poppy kept going, passing two other offices before she sat down in front of a third. Raul Guarino.

The man came to the door of his office. "May I help you?" he said with an arch of a sandy-colored brow.

"I think I took a wrong turn. I was looking for the restroom," he said, playing dumb.

The man hesitated as if trying to judge if he was telling the truth, but then the receptionist appeared, cradling a cup of coffee.

"I was looking for you. The restrooms are the other way," she said, and shot a worried look at the other man. "I'm so sorry, Mr. Guarino. I should have walked him there."

"Yes, you should have. Make sure it doesn't happen again," he said, chill icicles dripping from his tone.

The receptionist gave him a pleading look. "I'm sorry. I'll just take that coffee and head back to reception to wait for my colleagues," he said, sorry but not sorry that he'd gotten the young woman in trouble.

Poppy had definitely had a hit on Raul Guarino, and he intended to find out why.

GABRIELLA AND RYDER sat opposite the unhappy Konijns.

"As I said before, I consider this police harassment. You have no reason to keep on coming here with all these questions," Ralph said with a dismissive wave of his hand.

"Actually, we have many reasons, but chief among them is finding Jeannie Roberts. And then, arresting a serial killer responsible for the murder of five women," Gabriella said in as calm a tone as she could muster.

Both men jumped a bit, clearly startled.

"Ridiculous," said the elder Konijn.

Peter waved both hands to stop any further questions while at the same time saying, "We have nothing to hide. We've done nothing wrong."

"Both your cellphones were dead around the time of Jeannie's disappearance. How do you explain that?" Ryder pressed.

Father and son shared a look. Peter dipped his head as if pleading with his father to respond and a second later, Ralph said, "We have a secure area at our home for important business discussions. You never know who's listening."

"It's extreme, I know. But we had an important deal go south last year and we suspected that we had been hacked, so we take precautions whenever we can," Peter explained.

Gabriella glanced toward Ryder, thinking it was way too convenient. "And no one can confirm that's where you were at that time?"

"Just my mother. The housekeeper is off on the weekends, and goes home," Peter said.

She suspected she could keep asking questions that wouldn't give them any more information. Because of that, she pushed on to the most important reason they'd come that morning.

"We have DNA evidence that identifies our suspect," she said even though the CSI people were still running the DNA samples through the last of their tests. The initial report had been sent to her just a couple of hours ago.

Both men appeared startled again, and she continued. "We're hoping you'll willingly provide DNA samples so we can eliminate you as suspects," she said as Ryder reached into his jacket pocket to slip on gloves and remove two DNA test kits and evidence bags.

"This is insane," Ralph blustered, but Peter laid a hand on his father's arm to calm him.

"If we do this, will you stop harassing us?" Peter asked.

"No, absolutely not," Ralph interrupted, but once again Peter silenced him with a gentle squeeze of his arm.

"If you have nothing to hide, this is the best way to prove it," Ryder said.

Peter immediately nodded to confirm his acceptance, but Ralph hesitated. At his delay, Peter said, "This is the best way to end this, Father."

With a loud harrumph, Ralph finally relented.

Ryder efficiently opened the first tube, removed the swab and took a sample from Ralph first, obviously worried he'd change his mind.

When he was done, he placed the tube in an evidence bag and marked it with Ralph's name.

He repeated the same procedure with Peter, and once he was done, he tucked the evidence bags into his suit jacket pocket.

"Thank you for your cooperation," Gabriella said, and stood to signal their interview was over.

"We'll keep you advised of any developments," she said, and walked out of the conference room and into the reception area where Diego was sitting, Poppy at his feet.

As soon as he spotted her, he surged to his feet, walked over and leaned close to whisper, "We need to talk."

UPSTAIRS HAD BEEN quiet for hours.

Jeannie assumed he had gone to work much as he had the last few days.

That meant this was her last chance for freedom.

She furiously scraped at the last bolt, trying to remove enough of the crumbling wall to free it as she had the other three bolts.

He hadn't noticed that the night before when he'd come to torment her. She'd been careful to hide the evidence, and he'd seemed distracted as he punished her. Almost as if he was already thinking about the next woman he'd take.

But not if she had anything to say about it.

Today wasn't just about freeing herself. It was about protecting whoever was next.

The plastic spoon snapped from the pressure as she dug it in hard against the wall.

She muttered a curse, but there was no way she'd stop now.

Jerking on the shackles, she felt a little give.

She jerked on it again with just her hands, but it held.

In her brain, she suddenly heard the voice of a former trainer reminding her that her strongest muscles were in her legs.

Lying on her back, she firmly planted her feet on the wall, grabbed the chain with both hands and pulled.

DIEGO WAITED UNTIL they were out the door of the wealth management firm and almost by Gabriella's car to say, "Poppy got a hit on someone else in that office."

She stopped short and whirled to face him. "A hit? Roberts's scent?"

He nodded. "Raul Guarino. He's a few doors down from the Konijns' offices. It could be because of that, but it's worth checking out," he said, sure that it had been more than just possible contamination from the Konijns.

"I'll run him and see what we can find. I'll also share his name with Sophie and Robbie. See what they can come up with," Ryder said, and glanced back toward the office building. "My money is on them being involved in this. I'm hoping the DNA connects them to Isabella's crucifix and that small amount of touch DNA from the first rape/murder."

"I agree. In the meantime, I want to check out some of the locations identified by Wilson's program," Gabriella said, and walked toward her car.

"I'll go with you," Diego said, alert to any possible dangers as he strolled beside her.

As she neared her car, she slowed and then stopped.

Diego wondered why, but then he noticed the envelope tucked beneath the windshield wiper. Again.

Muttering a curse, he shielded her body with his and scrutinized the parking lot. Mostly empty since people had already entered the various buildings since it was past nine o'clock.

"Let me get that," Ryder said, and brushed past them, gloves on and an evidence bag ready to preserve the evidence.

He slipped the envelope from beneath the wiper, opened it and pulled out the single piece of paper within.

A photo of a naked Jeannie Roberts slumped on the ground. Hands and feet shackled to a wall. Above her image in bold black letters: "You're next!"

"Not if I can help it," Diego said, wrapped an arm around Gabriella's waist and tenderly squeezed to offer reassurance.

"If he used a color laser, there may be some hidden metadata in the photo. At a minimum, it should tell us when it was printed," Gabriella said in total investigator mode despite the personal threat.

"Wall and floor look old. It may help us limit which places to visit," Diego said as he scrutinized the other elements in the photo, avoiding the disturbing image of the young woman.

"Let's review the list and start with those older locations," Gabriella said, and glanced at Ryder. "Hopefully CSI can get some prints or touch DNA off the envelope or photo. Compare that to the other samples we have."

"I'll take it straight there. Keep me posted on anything you find at the locations," Ryder said, and marched to his car for the trip to the CBI offices and then Crooked Pass Security.

"Will do," Gabriella said, but her body was tense beneath his hand, a testament to the fact she had been affected by the killer's threat.

Once Ryder was out of earshot, he leaned close and whispered against the side of her face, "Are you okay?"

Chapter Twenty

Am I okay? Gabriella wondered as she battled the visceral reaction to the photo and threat.

"Gabriella?" he pressed at her hesitation.

She set aside her fear and disgust, and strength flooded through her body. Nodding, she said, "I'm more than okay. I'm more determined than ever to stop this guy."

Diego blew out a sigh of relief. "Good. Which location do you want to hit first?"

She opened her car so they could slip inside to review the list.

But as she took a spot behind the wheel as Diego harnessed Poppy and then slipped beside her, she said, "He was here at the same time as us but so were the Konijns. Is it possible that it's not one or both of them?"

"We're letting him track you since you're the bait and it worked. Too well," Diego said.

"The Konijns knew we were here. They may have had time to exit the building, leave this gift for me and still sit for an interview," she said aloud, running through all the possibilities.

"The buildings and parking lot have CCTV. I'll text Sophie and Robbie and have them track that down," Diego said, whipped out his phone and messaged the rest of the CPS team.

While he did that, she reached into the back seat for her briefcase and pulled out the report on the various locations. She opened it on the console so they could review the ages of the sites and visit those that seemed old enough based on what they'd seen in the photo.

They flipped through the pages, identifying likely candidates and once they had those, they mapped out an efficient way to visit them to not waste time.

She just hoped time hadn't run out for Jeannie Roberts.

HIS TRACKER APP beeped to let him know they were on the move.

The tracker had kept him advised so far except for one short blip. He'd worried at the time that it had been found, but since then, it had been working flawlessly.

As he watched where they were going, he breathed a sigh of relief that it wasn't in the direction of his home.

But the fact that they'd come back for another interview warned that he couldn't hold on to Roberts any longer.

He jumped up from his chair, slipped on his winter coat and rushed out a side door much as he had earlier to leave his little gift for Gabriella.

At his car, he hopped in and sped away, eager for those final moments with her. They always brought such satisfaction, as did keeping the right trophy so he could relive the experience until it was time for another woman.

No, not just another woman.

Gabriella.

It would be tough to take her, he thought as he drove.

She always had that muscle-bound gorilla and his dog with her.

Could he take them out first? he wondered, pushing the speed along the mountain roads in his haste to reach Roberts.

His mind raced with all the possibilities, zipping from

the pleasure of killing Roberts to how he might get Gabriella alone.

He almost passed the turnoff for his home.

He screeched to a stop and backed up to make the turn.

Loose gravel kicked up as he sped along the road leading to his home.

But when he neared the house, a slight motion in the woods snagged his attention.

Roberts. Running through the underbrush.

He cursed, jammed on the brakes and threw his door open to chase after her.

FEAR STOPPED HER cold as she heard a car gunning up the drive.

Jeannie hadn't expected him home so soon.

She'd thought she'd have hours to find a way back to a main road and hopefully salvation.

Past the underbrush and trees with their first blasts of spring green, she detected a silver-gray Range Rover racing up the road.

She should have moved deep into the woods and away from the driveway, but it had been the only guide to finding civilization. The home where she was being held was fairly remote and although she'd spotted a house farther up the mountain, she'd decided heading down to a main road might be better than a house that might be a vacation home.

As he flung his door open and flew out, intending to recapture her, she caught her first glimpse of his face.

Handsome. Sandy-haired. Familiar, she realized, but couldn't place him.

She memorized that face, because when she made it to freedom, he'd pay for what he'd done.

Armed with that thought, she raced through the underbrush as he came after her.

GABRIELLA PUT AN X through the third location on their list and sighed.

It had been nearly two hours since they'd left the Konijns' offices to visit the homes they'd identified based on the photo the killer had left behind.

The photo with the "You're next" had rattled through her brain over and over as they'd inspected each of the locations.

There had been cooperative residents at two locations who had let them walk Poppy around and were only too willing to help.

But that kind of help didn't eliminate them immediately. It wasn't unusual for criminals to appear eager as a ruse.

No one had been home at the third location, but Diego had walked Poppy around the front porch area and door. She hadn't scented anything, and so they'd decided to move on.

"This home is farther than I thought," she said as she drove to the mountainside location.

"It'll take at least twenty minutes," he said with a wry grin.

She chuckled and shook her head. "At least."

A second later, her cell phone rang with an incoming call. Ryder.

She hoped he had good news for them.

"What do you have?" she asked as she turned onto the highway for the ride to the fourth location.

"They've finished processing the DNA test kits and are working to compare them to the DNA we have from Isabella's crucifix, the touch DNA and CODIS. That may take another hour or so," he advised. In the background, there was suddenly loud talking and the sounds of activity.

"Hold on," Ryder said, and appeared to be speaking to someone before coming back on the line.

"We just heard from a local police department that they have Jack Hayes in custody. It was a routine traffic stop and when the officer checked, he realized there was a BOLO."

"Great. Text me their address and we'll head there after our next stop," she said, and did a side-eyed glance at Diego who nodded to confirm that course of action.

"I'll head there now and wait for you," Ryder said, and ended the call.

"What do you think Hayes will add to this investigation?" Diego asked, eyes narrowed as he examined her.

She did a little shrug. "I don't know. It almost feels like a diversion."

"I agree," he said with a nod.

"A diversion that's costing us time," she lamented, reminded yet again of the clock that was ticking.

"Do you think his threats are a diversion also?" Diego wondered aloud.

"Bringing Isabella into the mix is a bigger distraction. He has to know how much it means to me to find her," she said, and hesitated, dipping her head from side to side before tacking on, "I'm not sure I take the threats seriously."

"I take them seriously. Very seriously," he said, and brushed the back of his hand along her cheek.

She smiled, appreciating his concerns. "Thank you, but think about it. He has to get past you and Poppy. Not an easy task," she said, and pulled over for the exit to a smaller road that ran along the base of the mountain.

"Not an easy task," he admitted as she glanced at Poppy, who was perched on the back seat, watching the world go by.

A world that wasn't going by fast enough, she thought and increased her speed in her haste to reach the next location and then head to the local police station to interview Hayes.

Luckily, there was little traffic on the side road, and in no time, she was traveling up the mountainside. She was about halfway when she had to slow to search for the turnoff for the location.

"Seems remote," she said as she turned onto a gravel driveway.

"Remote is good for lots of reasons, but especially for a serial killer. But it's a pricey location for someone who we think is what? Twentysomething?" he said as he glanced around the area.

"Not if you're born with a silver spoon like Peter Konijn or his father," she said, and did a final turn to pull in front of a large contemporary home with soaring windows that provided views of the nearby mountains as well as the city of Denver.

They exited the car and approached the front door. She rang the doorbell, but no one answered. She had expected as much since there was no car in the driveway, although one could have been parked in the nearby three-car garage.

Shaking her head, she said, "This is so wrong. This is not the kind of home we expected. It's not old at all."

"No, but maybe it's been renovated and sits on the foundation of an older home," Diego said as he stepped back off the porch to examine the structure.

His perusal was interrupted by the crunch of gravel as a vehicle came up the path.

A delivery truck.

The driver pulled behind them, got out and then walked up with a package.

"Are you Peter Konijn?" he asked, and even before Diego answered, he was handing the package to him.

"THANKS, BUT I'M NOT. Do you do regular deliveries here?" Diego asked.

The driver nodded. "He does a lot of online shopping."

The driver's eyes narrowed then, and he skipped his gaze from him to Poppy, and then to Gabriella. "You cops?"

Gabriella flashed her badge. "Yes, why?"

With a big shift of his shoulders, he said, "No reason, except, it's just weird I've never seen him in the four years I've been on this route. Even when I ring and know that someone's home, he never comes to the door. Never leaves a holiday tip either, when he has the money to build this big fancy house." He tossed his hand in the direction of the home with a harrumph.

"Were you on the route before he built this house?" Gabriella asked.

The driver nodded. "I was. It used to be an old cabin. They tore it down."

And built the big fancy home over an old foundation and possibly a cellar, Diego thought.

"Do you remember when he did that?" Gabriella asked, and Diego immediately knew where she was going.

The driver pursed his lips and looked upward as he considered when that might have happened. "About two years ago. It took them a while to finish the new place. Just completed it a couple of months ago."

"Thanks. I'm going to give you my business card in case you think of anything else," Gabriella said.

The driver took the card, did a jaunty little salute and then returned to his truck to resume his delivery route.

Diego held the package in his hands and glanced at the name again just to confirm. With a dip of his head, he said, "This isn't the address we have for Peter, but he could use this as a vacation home. Plus, there's this: two years to build. Two years with no kidnappings, right?"

"Two years between the Nations and Cornerstone kidnappings and Roberts's disappearance. That's just too much coincidence. Let's have Poppy scent the front door," she said.

Diego followed as she walked to the door, Poppy at his side. At the door, he instructed her to scent all around, but she didn't indicate that she had a scent. He pondered that for a moment, and then said, "If Roberts was wrapped up in something, like a blanket, and carried…"

He hesitated because even with that, Poppy should have picked up on a scent unless…

Bending low and close to the ground, where large slabs of slate sat close to the home, he inhaled deeply.

A perfumy fragrance mixed with the stronger aroma of a bleachy substance.

Standing once again, he pointed along the edge of the home and said, "It's been cleaned with something that might be throwing off Poppy. Let me walk her around the house and see if she picks up on anything."

She nodded, and he forged ahead, brushing through some decorative bushes by the side of the house. They had just been planted judging from the fresh earth and stakes a landscaper had put to hold them in place until they rooted.

At his command, Poppy sniffed along the edges of the home, nose to the ground.

Nothing happened until they reached the back corner of the home. At that point, Poppy lay down to confirm she had a scent.

"Good girl," Diego said and fed her a treat. "*Such*," he said, instructing Poppy to continue her search.

Poppy immediately shot to her feet, but seemed conflicted as to which direction to go, almost as if she was catching a scent in either direction. "*Such*," he said, and guided her toward the back of the home.

Poppy eagerly took off in that direction, stopped by a sliding glass door and lay down.

He was about to reach for the door when Gabriella laid a hand on his arm to stop him. "We don't have a warrant and probably not enough probable cause at this point. If we go in, we risk jeopardizing evidence."

He muttered a silent curse, worried that Roberts might

still be inside. But then it occurred to him that Poppy had a hit away from the house as well.

Gesturing back toward the corner of the home, he said, "Poppy picked up a scent there also. If Roberts was able to escape…"

"Let's see what's there," she said, and they walked back in that direction. As they neared the corner, Gabriella gestured to the imprint of a boot print.

Diego bent slightly to examine it. "Looks familiar. Like what we found at the scout camp."

Gabriella nodded. "Definitely. If Roberts escaped, Peter might have been right on her trail."

He muttered a curse, straightened and instructed Poppy to continue her search.

His canine pushed on, nose to the ground, and they followed, careful to look for more boot prints.

They were about fifteen yards from the house and halfway to the road when they noticed an area where the leaves and underbrush had been disturbed. Carefully they made their way toward it. Poppy yanked to go to the area where a scuffle had clearly occurred.

The German shepherd lay down and Diego rewarded her with a head rub. "Good girl," he said as he stood to examine the ground.

"If she escaped, she didn't get far," he said, and glanced back to the house.

Gabriella peered down the mountainside. "Just a little farther and she would have gotten to the road. Someone might have seen her there."

He didn't doubt it, but based on the disturbance before them, Roberts had been taken again.

"My gut says she's not here anymore," he said, doing a slow turn on his heel to scrutinize the area all around them.

"I agree, but if she's not here, she's likely dead," Gabriella said with a disgusted sigh, and jammed her hands on her hips as she also did a slow perusal of the location.

But then she was in action, whipping out her cell phone and calling Ryder. When he answered, she said, "We need to bring in Peter Konijn and we need a warrant."

Chapter Twenty-One

To avoid wasting time, Ryder brought Peter Konijn and his blustering father to the same police station where Jack Hayes was being held.

When Gabriella arrived with Diego and Poppy, Ryder guided them to a conference room. Once they were inside, he said, "Peter Konijn has lawyered up. We're waiting for the lawyer to arrive, so I thought we'd start with Jack Hayes. See what we get from him."

Gabriella nodded. "Any news on the DNA matches or the warrant?"

"The request for the warrant was prepared and I have an agent going to a friendly judge to sign it. As for the DNA matches, I'm told any minute now," he advised.

"Great. Progress," she said although in her heart she worried it was possibly too late for Jeannie Roberts.

Ryder held his hand out in the direction of a nearby interrogation room.

"I'm going to hang back. I want to reach out to Sophie and Robbie and see if they have anything. Plus, I should walk Poppy," Diego said.

Ryder nodded. "Just ask the officers to let you in when you're done."

Gabriella walked to the door and waited for Ryder, and then the two of them entered the interview room.

As soon as she did, she knew Hayes was not the man who had been lurking around the CPS offices. He was too tall and as heavily muscled as a professional wrestler. Also, he had very obvious tattoos on his hands and fingers, and as she dug up her memories from the video feeds they had, she didn't recall any such visible markings.

But as those seconds in the parking garage flashed through her mind, she could picture him as the man at the wheel. She hadn't seen much past the tinted window and the muzzle fire, but she had seen that he was tall.

"Jack Hayes. I'm CBI Agent Gabriella Ruiz and this is CBI Agent Ryder Hunt," she said as she sat down, and Ryder handed her a file.

She opened the file and skimmed through the long rap sheet. "Drug dealing, assault, burglary, and now we can add attempted murder and federal gun violations."

He sat there sullenly, powerful hands clasped before him. Head downturned to look at the hands shackled to the table.

"I don't think you did this on your own," Gabriella began. "I think someone paid you to shoot us. I think Peter Konijn paid you."

A burst of laughter escaped him. "Rabbit? You think I'd tell you if Rabbit paid me?" he said with another laugh and abrupt shake of his head.

"Rabbit? You call him 'Rabbit'?" Ryder pressed.

Hayes finally looked up, obviously amused. "Yeah. That's what we used to call him in college."

"Why?" Gabriella asked, wondering why anyone would give him a nickname that made him sound like a child's storybook character.

With a lift of his heavily muscled shoulders, he explained. "We had a Dutch exchange student who told us Konijn meant 'rabbit.' And boy was he that in college with the girls," he said and made a crude hand gesture.

Gabriella shared a look of disgust with Ryder before proceeding. "You obviously know Rabbit quite well. So maybe you know that he's possibly murdered some women. Women you might know," she said, pulled some photos from her file and placed them in front of Hayes.

She tapped the first photo. "Alyssa Nations. She went to college with you, too. She's been missing for over two years."

She did the same with the second photo, tapping Cornerstone's photo. "Missy's been missing about the same time. We assume that both of them are dead and that your friend Rabbit is responsible."

Without missing a beat, she removed Roberts's photo and laid it before him. "We also think he took this woman and is about to murder her."

That shrug came again, along with a negligent toss of his head. "What's that got to do with me?"

"Are you familiar with the felony murder rule?" she asked.

"Do I look like a lawyer?" Hayes blurted out with a sarcastic laugh and jerk of his body.

It was as good a time as any for the good cop, bad cop routine. Looking at Ryder, she said, "I'll let my colleague explain."

Ryder nodded. "We don't like accomplices in Colorado. We think they're as responsible for a death as much as the person who pulled the trigger," he began, but Hayes didn't respond so he continued.

"Being an accomplice means not just taking part in the murder. It also means in the furtherance of the act. Do you know what that means? In the furtherance of?" Ryder pressed.

He was met with silence again, so he explained. "That means helping him in any way. That includes trying to kill Gabriella and our civilian consultant in that parking lot to keep us from investigating those murders and the kidnapping."

"I have nothing to do with any of that," Hayes said as it finally registered that he might be in deep trouble.

"Once we prove Rabbit is responsible, you'll go down with him, which could get you anywhere from sixteen to forty-eight years in prison. I'm going to ask the judge to give you that for each of these women," Ryder said, and jabbed a finger on the women's photos.

Hayes jumped to life, surging up in his chair and slamming his hands on the tabletop. "I have nothing to do with this."

"But you do according to the felony murder rule, Jack. Your good friend Rabbit just ended your life unless you cooperate," Gabriella said in a soothing tone, wanting to cajole Hayes into assisting them.

"Cooperate? How?" he asked, his earlier sullen behavior fading.

"Admit that Rabbit hired you and why. Tell us what you know about these women," Gabriella said, and held her hand palm upward in an invitation for him to speak.

"You'll go to bat for me?" he asked, his blue-eyed gaze almost pleading.

"We'll speak to the district attorney about your cooperation," Gabriella said.

Hayes hesitated, but with a rush of breath, he said, "Rabbit came to me. Said some people were hassling him and he needed someone to warn them off."

"He asked you to shoot at us?" Gabriella asked, just to make sure she understood what Peter Konijn had asked him to do.

Hayes shook his head. "He didn't tell me how. He just wanted me to scare you off. I figured a drive-by might do it, but I only meant to scare you."

He had accomplished that, not that she would admit it.

"He thought scaring us would stop our investigation?" Ryder asked with an abrupt laugh.

"You'd have to ask him," Hayes said, and shrugged those powerful shoulders again.

"We will, Jack. We have Rabbit in a room just a few doors down," Gabriella said, and stood.

Ryder did the same and said, "An officer will be in to take you back to the jail."

Without another word, they exited and met for a second in the hall before entering the second interview room where the Konijns waited.

"Not the sharpest tack," Ryder said.

Gabriella couldn't disagree. "Peter isn't either if he thought he could scare us off."

"Stupid move," Ryder said.

They were about to walk to the other interview room a few doors down when an officer entered the area followed by an older man in an expensive three-piece pin-striped suit and shiny black oxford shoes.

The Konijns' lawyer, she supposed, which was confirmed as he walked past them and into the interview room, briefcase in hand.

"Looks expensive," Ryder said.

"Looks like we'll have a tough time, but I'm good to go," Gabriella said, and Ryder echoed it.

"I'm good. Let's go," she said, and walked into the interview room.

DIEGO KNEW HE had no place in the interview room. He wasn't a cop, after all.

But he also couldn't just sit there being useless.

He called Sophie and Robbie, hoping they had been able to get additional information.

When Sophie answered, he said, "Tell me you have something."

"We do. We were able to clean up the license on that Range

Rover enough to get a hit and no surprise, it's part of a fleet rented out to one of the shell companies we believe are owned by the Konijns. We're sending you the info," Robbie said, and a second later, the whoosh of his phone confirmed he'd gotten a message.

Sophie continued with their report. "We couldn't get any help on the lidar front, so we tried another route. Wilson was able to get satellite images of the area over several years in and around the disappearance of Nations and Cornerstone."

"The images were that clear?" he asked, wondering what they could see from thousands of miles in space.

"He reached out to a friend in NASA. They have the World-view website, which is a real-time satellite map, but its resolution isn't very sharp. But they have other images that are high-res, and he was able to process them," Sophie advised.

The whoosh said Sophie had sent those images.

"Wilson has identified some spots above the scout camp that warrant investigation," Sophie added.

"Great. That's a lot of useful information," he said.

"We've got more," Robbie said, excitement in his voice.

"Hit me with it," he said, also growing excited that they finally had more to work with.

"We have this morning's CCTV video from the Konijns' parking lot. The good news is that we have video of some-one approaching Gabriella's car. Based on the time stamp, it could be Peter Konijn. The bad news is that the video is very poor quality. But we were able to enhance it," Robbie said, and the whoosh that followed had him glancing at the image of their suspect.

Even enhanced the image was grainy. "It could be Peter Konijn," he said, but wondered if that was being influenced by all the other evidence they'd gathered so far.

"We ran Peter's photo to compare and got a match, but then

again, with an image this grainy it could just be someone who looks similar," Sophie said, the earlier excitement fading.

"It's something, though," he said to offer his team encouragement.

"We'll keep pushing and see what else we can find," Sophie said.

"Thank you. This is all good."

He took a quick look at the information they'd sent, but since he'd always been better on his feet, he decided to take another walk with Poppy, who was always grateful for the activity.

Heading out of the precinct again, he let Poppy take the lead, strolling along the street as he considered the information CPS had provided, especially the comparisons of the satellite images of the scout camp area.

There had been more than just three areas flagged on that mountainside.

Did that mean that in addition to Isabella, Cornerstone and Nations there were others?

And what about the two other women who didn't fit the MO of the serial killer but had been identified by Wilson's program?

They had yet to do an in-depth review of those cases, but he suspected that if they were able to prove Konijn was their man, they could pull all the evidence from those crimes and tie him to those rapes and murders as well. Especially since they'd found some touch DNA at the first scene that hadn't been noticed before.

Which had him wondering what was going on in those interrogation rooms.

Turning, he gave Poppy one last chance to relieve herself, cleaned and then hurried back to the precinct.

THE KONIJNS SAT at the interview table flanked by their high-priced attorney, who handed them a business card as soon as they entered.

Before they were even in their seats, the attorney said, "I strenuously object to your treatment of my clients."

"Mr. Bruce. To be clear, your clients are implicated in the disappearance, and likely murder, of three women, and the rape and murder of two other women," Gabriella said.

Ryder immediately jumped in. "And the kidnapping and imminent murder of Jeannie Roberts."

"My clients strongly deny those allegations," Bruce said, his tone as unctuous as the gel keeping every strand of hair in place.

"We also have proof that Rabbit," she began and looked in Peter's direction. "That is your nickname, isn't it, Peter? Rabbit?" she repeated just to embarrass him some more.

It worked as his face flushed and he angrily tapped the tabletop with his fingers as he slouched in his seat.

"Your friend, Jack Hayes, who's in a room just a few doors down, shot at me and a civilian consultant. He's indicated that you hired him to scare us off," Gabriella said.

Ralph Konijn surprised them by looking at his son and blurting out, "Jack Hayes. That idiot friend?"

The color on Peter's face deepened to almost maroon, and that nervous tap grew ever faster.

"Peter? Answer me," Ralph said, and at that, his attorney laid a hand on his arm to silence him.

"My clients need a moment. Alone," Bruce said.

"Not a problem but while you're at it, you may want to explain to Ralph about the felony murder rule," she said as a parting shot.

When she exited the room, Ryder at her back, she realized Diego was standing just a few feet away, head buried in his phone, and Poppy at his feet.

As he noticed them, he looked up and smiled. It warmed her inside and awoke a wealth of emotions.

"How's it going?" he asked.

"Ralph Konijn is being as overbearing as usual but that might work to our advantage. Jack Hayes fingered Peter as the person who hired him to shoot at us. No pun intended, but that gives us a lot of ammunition," Gabriella said.

"Big pun," he said with a grin.

She pointed to his phone. "Do you have anything?"

He held up a photo for them to see. "This was taken from the Konijns' parking lot. Based on the time stamp, Peter could have gone to your car before he joined you in the conference room."

"Fuzzy. It could be Peter or someone who looks like him," Ryder said as he bent slightly to examine the photo.

"CPS is going to use facial recognition software to see if it helps at all," he said and quickly added, "But there's more."

Gabriella watched as he pulled up another image of a mountainside marked with an assortment of circles. "Is that the scout camp area?" she asked.

"It is, and those circles are changes in the topography based on comparisons of satellite imagery over the years," he explained.

Ryder narrowed his gaze and asked, "Changes? Natural or—"

"Likely man-made. We'll have to take Poppy there to see what she can find," he said, and swiped his phone closed.

"That's all we have so far," he said with an almost disappointed tone.

She cupped his jaw and stroked her thumb along his chin. "It's all helpful."

The door to the interview room opened then, and the attorney poked his head out and said, "My client wishes to speak to you."

Chapter Twenty-Two

Gabriella and Ryder reentered the interview room and sat but before they could say a word, the attorney raised his hand.

"Before we proceed, we need to discuss what you can do for my clients in exchange for their cooperation," Bruce said.

"That depends on the information that your clients are willing to provide," Gabriella advised, hopeful that Peter would confess where he had taken Jeannie Roberts.

"We'd want a reduced sentence for cooperation," Bruce said with a nervous glance at his clients.

Ryder, still in bad cop mode, jumped in. "You want a reduced sentence for no less than three murders, possibly five, and the latest kidnapping?"

Peter waved his hands in the air in denial and said, "I have nothing to do with what happened to those women."

Gabriella gave the attorney a laser-like stare. "Doesn't sound like cooperation to me."

"As Mr. Konijn has said, he has nothing to do with those murders or the kidnapping," Bruce said calmly.

Her gut told her something wasn't adding up. As Ryder started to say something, she stuck out her hand to ask him to wait. "If Peter isn't going to confess to these murders and the kidnapping—"

"I'm not. I have nothing to do with them," Peter insisted yet again.

Gabriella and Ryder shared a glance, and then she faced the attorney and asked, "What is your client willing to plead to?"

"In connection with the shooting that took place, my client is willing to plead guilty to misdemeanor menacing—"

"Menacing with a deadly weapon is a felony demanding jail time and fines," Gabriella countered.

"No jail time, but we're willing to pay a reasonable fine," Bruce advised after a quick look at Ralph Konijns, who had sat there, stone-faced, ever since they had reentered. His usual bluster was gone, replaced by simmering anger.

It was apparent in the flush across his face, the tight lines of his body and how his hands were clasped so tightly before him that his fingers were white from the pressure.

She was angry as well that Bruce and the Konijns thought they could get away with the murders thanks to their money.

That anger made her shoot to her feet. "Peter Konijn. We're arresting you for the murder of Isabella Ruiz and the attempted murders of myself and civilian consultant Diego Rodriguez," she said since so far, they only had DNA for Isabella's murder and Hayes's confession about the shooting.

Peter and his attorney immediately protested, but she ignored the protest as Ryder stood, handcuffs in hand, and approached Peter. "Please rise, hands behind your back."

Grudgingly, Peter complied, still protesting as Gabriella read him his Miranda rights and asked him if he understood those rights.

"Of course I do. I'm not an idiot," he said but lost some of that confidence as Ryder walked him to the door.

"Dad, do something," Peter pleaded, and looked back at his father.

Ralph Konijn only shook his head, looked away and mumbled, "My sons are idiots."

She should have been shocked by his lack of care, but then again, he struck her as the kind of man who only cared about himself and how people would perceive him.

The attorney jumped to his feet. "We will get you out of here, Peter. I'll speak to a judge immediately."

Gabriella followed Ryder and Peter out of the room and walked with them to the jail portion of the precinct where Jack Hayes was sitting in one of the cells. The last thing they wanted was to put Peter nearby so the two men could cook up some kind of lie, so Ryder walked him to a cell at the far end and secured him there, ignoring him as he continued to protest his innocence.

As they were walking to where Diego waited for them with Poppy, Ryder said, "Methinks he doth protest too much."

"He does, but something is bothering me," she said, and stopped as Diego and Poppy joined them.

"What's wrong?" Diego said, and stroked a hand down her arm, mindful of not having a big PDA in front of Ryder and all the police officers in the area.

"My gut tells me we're missing something," she said, shook her head and then said, "Did you hear what Ralph said as we were walking out?"

Ryder frowned and shrugged. "About his son being an idiot?"

"Sons. I think he said 'sons' but as far as we know, he has only one," Gabriella advised, and glanced toward the cell where Peter was now pacing back and forth nervously.

The whoosh of an incoming message erupted from Ryder's phone, delaying discussion.

He glanced at the message, muttered a curse and then jerked his head in the direction of a nearby conference room.

Once they were inside, he handed the phone to Gabriella.

"The DNA doesn't belong to either Peter or Ralph Konijns. But it does belong to a close family member. Plus, it's a match to the new touch DNA evidence found at the home of one of the other murder victims," she said.

"A family member?" Diego pressed.

Gabriella nodded. "Yes, a family member. I'm sure he said 'sons.'"

"Let's replay the tape and confirm," Ryder said, and hurried from the room to obtain a copy of the recording, leaving Gabriella and Diego alone in the room.

GABRIELLA'S UPSET WAS obvious and with Ryder gone, Diego didn't hesitate to cup her cheek and offer comfort.

"We were so sure it was Peter and now this," she said, distressed.

"But you were on the right trail. It is a Konijn. Just not one we know about," Diego reassured her.

"Ralph could be an illegitimate son. Why doesn't that surprise me? He's so…arrogant. He thinks rules don't apply to him, even the rules about being faithful to your spouse," she said angrily.

Ryder returned a second later, a USB drive in hand that he placed into a nearby computer to bring up the recording. He fast-forwarded to the moment just before Gabriella had indicated that they would be arresting Peter.

The video played and Ralph's words echoed in the room.

"My sons are idiots."

For good measure, Ryder rewound the tape and played it a second time.

"My sons are idiots."

"We need to bring Ralph back in," Gabriella said, pulled out the attorney's business card and dialed the number.

There was an angry burst from the man that even Diego could hear. "This is harassment. We've only just left the station."

"Then we'll expect you to come in soon," she said, and ended the call.

"Gutsy," Diego said in approval.

Gabriella smiled. "I don't expect Ralph is going to be forthcoming about any of his affairs. Do you think Crooked Pass Security can do anything with these DNA results?"

"Possibly. Genetic genealogy can trace ancestry and relationships between people, but that can take time," he said.

"Whatever you can do would be appreciated," Ryder said, and immediately sent the DNA results to Sophie.

Almost instantly another whoosh sounded, and Ryder said, "Bruce and Ralph Konijn are back. An officer is taking them back to the interview room."

"We should go," she said but then faced Diego. "I just hate wasting your time by having you just sit here."

"If you don't mind, I'd like to watch the interview. I'm a pretty good judge of character and after, I'd like to go to the scout camp and check out the anomalies on those satellite images," Diego said.

"I'll arrange for that," Ryder said, and left the room.

"You should go. We can meet you there," she said, worry darkening her gaze.

He should, but he was worried about what they might find, and as difficult as it might be, Gabriella should be there if he found Isabella.

"I thought you might want to be there in case..."

He didn't need to finish. With a nod, she said, "I want to be there."

Since they were in the conference room, he didn't hesitate to bring her close and hug her hard, offering comfort.

When she pulled away, she swiped at the tears on her face and with a deep inhale, prepared herself for the upcoming interview.

A knock at the door came only a second before Ryder walked in. "We're ready."

They walked out of the room, and Ryder directed Diego to an observation area behind the interview room. As he entered, he noted that Ralph Konijn and the attorney were seated at the table, heads bent close, whispering to each other until Gabriella and Ryder walked in.

Immediately they sat up and became silent.

Gabriella and Ryder sat across from them, and Gabriella said, "We now have DNA results that confirm your son committed the abduction and murder of Isabella Ruiz and the rape and murder of Sadie Lyons."

A bit of a stretch since all they knew was that it was a family member, but based on Konijn's earlier words, logical.

"Peter did not do that," Ralph calmly said.

"You're right. It wasn't Peter. It was your other son. Would you care to share more info about him?" she asked.

Ralph would be good at poker, Diego thought, since the man had no response to Gabriella's words other than to deny it.

"Peter is my only son."

"Not true. DNA doesn't lie, and I can understand why you'd deny it. I'm sure your wife and colleagues would be appalled to find out you have an illegitimate son. Especially one who's a serial killer," Gabriella said, and then reached into the file before her.

She withdrew a photo. The contemporary home they had visited about two hours earlier.

"Nice house, right? Replaced an old cabin that used to be there," she said, and at that, a slight tic jumped along Ralph's jaw.

"We expect to have a warrant any minute now to search that home. I think what we'll find is more DNA and enough evidence to connect your son to five—" she held up one hand in the air, fingers spread "—that's five murders that could become six if you don't help us."

"I have no other son," he said, but his voice this time was a little shaky and that tic in his jaw only grew jumpier.

Gabriella sighed and leaned back in her chair. "Mr. Bruce," she said, and faced the attorney. "I hope you did what I asked and explained the felony murder rule to your client."

"I did, Agent Ruiz. By the way, is it a coincidence you have the same name as the first alleged victim or do you have a connection and conflict?" he asked smoothly.

"Isabella was—is—my little sister. You might think that's a conflict, maybe because it makes me even more determined," she said.

The attorney glanced at Ryder and said, "Highly irregular, wouldn't you say? This kind of connection could bias this agent against my client."

Diego held his breath, knowing that Ryder hadn't necessarily agreed with Gabriella's theories about the cases, even though they'd proven to be accurate. For all Diego knew, Ryder had also had qualms about Gabriella being too personally involved.

"My colleague has been totally professional in her handling of this case. I have no doubt anyone reviewing it will confirm that. I also do not doubt that we will prove your client's illegitimate son is responsible for these horrible crimes," he said, and then flipped a hand in the direction of Ralph Konijn.

"Your client, on the other hand, has done nothing but obstruct the investigation. He knows who owns this house," he said, and pointedly jabbed a finger at the photo.

"He knows his illegitimate son owns it. He may even know what his son has been doing, which makes him responsible for these murders," Ryder said, and opened his copy of the file and yanked out photos of the murdered women.

For emphasis, he pointed a finger at Isabella's photo and said, "Isabella was only twelve. Twelve."

A change came over Ralph Konijn then as he glanced from Isabella's photo to Gabriella. It was almost like watching the Grinch develop a heart, something he hadn't thought possible with the arrogant and uncaring Konijn.

"I'm sorry this happened to your family," he said, and then bent and whispered something in his attorney's ear.

"We need a few minutes," Bruce said.

Gabriella and Ryder immediately left the room, and Diego joined them in the hallway.

"He's going to talk," he said, having witnessed what he thought was a transformation of the older Konijn.

"I think so. That'll give us a name, probably faster than we would have had with genetic genealogy. But it's just a name," Gabriella said in a tone that was part exhausted and part disappointed.

Barely a minute later, Bruce opened the door to the interview room and called out, "My client wishes to speak to you."

Chapter Twenty-Three

The air vibrated around him, alive with the signs of spring and something else.

Danger.

As wide-open as the spaces were around him as he carried Jeannie's limp body up the trail, the world felt like it was closing in around him.

The agents were close. Through the video cameras he'd set up in and around his home, he'd seen them poking around. And a couple of hours later, he'd seen the CSI truck pull up.

He did not doubt they'd gotten a warrant and would be ransacking his home for evidence. It might take them a little time to find the entrance to the cellar, but they'd find it. And when they did...

He had thought about running, and as he trudged up to the scout camp, he thought about it again.

It wasn't too late to empty the rest of the money in his bank accounts into a Swiss account he'd opened years earlier. It was enough money to sustain him for years. Certainly enough to buy him a fake identity.

But running struck him as the coward's way out.

It felt wrong.

What felt right was vengeance. Retribution for ruining the life he had built for himself.

All would still be great if it wasn't for that persistent CBI agent.

That beautiful CBI agent, he thought, recalling what he'd seen of her when she'd come to interview his father and half brother.

Isabella had been beautiful as well. And innocent. So innocent.

His first in so many ways. He realized Roberts wasn't meant to be his last.

No, Gabriella had to be his last.

Jeannie moaned as he dumped her in a corner of the room in one of the last remaining structures at the scout camp. This shower room was farther up the mountain, well removed from where he had taken Isabella, and not as well-known. It was from an earlier embodiment of the camp that had been abandoned for the location lower down the mountain.

Jeannie moved and moaned again as she lay against the wooden wall.

Good. The ketamine was wearing off.

He squatted there, watching her awaken. Watching that lovely fear in her eyes and then the determination.

Standing, he took out the knife and held it up for her to see.

Her eyes opened wide, and she struggled against the bindings at her hands and feet, not that she'd be able to escape.

Lifting his cell phone, he recorded her struggles, pleased by them. Growing aroused as well, but he fought back desire.

He had to stay clearheaded if he was going to exact precious vengeance.

Satisfied he had enough video, he slipped his knife into a sheath at his waist and walked out of the shower stalls.

Cell service was weak here. He'd have to climb farther up the mountainside, which was fine.

It would be the perfect spot for all this to end.

But first, he had to leave his little surprise for whoever

might find Roberts. He'd been working on it for a week or so from plans on the internet, but he hadn't had a chance to test it yet. Still, he did not doubt he had done it right and would accomplish the job.

Hiking up the mountain, he found the perfect spot and took a moment to appreciate the views of the valley below and then his killing fields, recalling the spots where he had placed Isabella and the others. So many others.

Smiling, he brought up the video and edited it to a perfect section. Then he typed out a message, marked his location with a pin and sent the video.

Then he sat down to wait for her.

RAUL GUARINO.

Gabriella was familiar with the name since Diego had mentioned Poppy getting a hit on the man at the Konijns' wealth management firm.

"Raul is Ralph in Italian. His mother must have named him that to either honor or goad Konijn," Gabriella said.

"He lived in that cabin with his mother. Konijn said he paid for it and that he would visit off and on until Raul became a teen and his mother died. Then things got tense between them," Gabriella said, recalling Konijn's earlier testimony.

"He may have felt abandoned when she died and angry when his father tried to keep him under his thumb the way he does Peter," Diego said.

"But he brought him into the firm," Ryder said, head slightly downturned as he considered all that Konijn had revealed during the interrogation.

"Possibly to keep him silent about the affair," Gabriella suggested.

"That tension that he mentioned happened right around when Isabella disappeared and with his mother's death, he had that cabin all to himself," Diego said, and it made her heart ache at the thought of Isabella all alone in that cabin cellar, suffering at Guarino's hands.

Diego picked up on her upset since he stroked a hand down her arm, tenderly held her hand and offered a reassuring squeeze.

"Don't think about it," he said, aware that she was hurting.

"Tough to do," she admitted with a strangled sigh.

A sudden whoosh of a message intruded.

Ryder slipped his phone from his pocket and smiled as he read the message. "They're executing the warrant. They'll keep me posted on any developments."

"Great," she said, and was about to discuss their next steps when her phone made the familiar doorbell chime that said she also had a message.

It was from an unknown number with no preview to hint at the content.

She almost deleted it, thinking it might be spam, but with everything going on, she didn't want to miss any message that might help with the investigation.

But as the video played, it took all her strength to stay on her feet as her blood ran cold and her heart seemed to stop beating in her chest.

Diego laid a hand on her arm as she wavered and with a shaky hand, she shared the message with them.

THE HEAT OF anger tangled with fear in his gut as he viewed Jeannie Roberts, tied up like a hog for slaughter, with the bright red word "Trade?" across the top of the video. As he tamed his anger, he realized there was also a pin location in the message text.

"Trade? Does he seriously think we'd trade you for Roberts?" he said, disbelief in his tone.

"We need to see where this is," Gabriella said, and tapped the pin to reveal the location.

Diego immediately recognized the area. It was high up on the mountain where the scout camp was located.

"He's gone to his killing fields," he said, worried about what that might mean for both Roberts and Gabriella.

"I don't think this pin is for Roberts," Ryder said as he also examined the location revealed by the pin.

"I agree. This is where he is. Where he wants to meet me," Gabriella said.

Diego's gut tightened again at the thought of her offering herself for their victim. "No way. You can't do that. He's too dangerous."

"We've been having a cold snap. It's barely past forty and Roberts can't last for long, even if she is in some kind of shelter," Gabriella warned, and glanced at the video again. "Do you think this is one of the buildings at the scout camp?"

Diego examined the dingy wood in the video. "Possibly," he said, and worried about the gaps between the wooden planks on the floor and walls, which would let cold into the space.

"We need to see how to approach this location," Gabriella said, and then hurried back into the nearby conference room.

Ryder and Diego followed, Poppy at his side.

Gabriella grabbed her laptop from her knapsack and a second later, broadcast the image of the location on a nearby monitor.

"I've never been up in this area when I was a scout. It's challenging to reach the summit," she said, rose and gestured to the area identified by the pin.

"But Roberts is not there. He's trying to distract from where he's hidden Roberts," Diego said.

"Do you think that you and Poppy can follow Roberts's scent and find her?" she said.

He didn't doubt it, but it might take time, especially if this building was farther up the mountain.

"Can you overlay those satellite images that Sophie and Robbie got for us?" he said, hoping they'd help limit the search area.

"I might not be a tech genius, but I think I can manage that," she said, and a few minutes later, she had dropped the image over the pin, sized it, and increased the transparency so they could see the location of the pin as well as the anomalies identified by Sophie and Robbie's analysis.

Diego walked to the monitor, jammed his hands on his hips and examined the images. Ryder joined him there, also scrutinizing the area.

"Guarino is almost at the summit. You said you've never been there before?" Ryder said with a questioning glance.

Gabriella nodded. "Never. I'm sure that's not a popular trail so it might be overgrown. Hard to get up there and there is only one way up. He'll know I'm headed there."

"You can't surprise him," Diego said, worried that she'd be a sitting duck.

Gabriella pursed her lips and did a little shrug of delicate shoulders. "There might be another way. I can go up and around and come down from above him. I'd have the element of surprise that way."

"*We*, Gabriella. There's no way you're doing this alone," Ryder said, and quickly tacked on, "Along with a few other agents on the trail and with Diego."

Diego nodded and circled an area on the map that had snared his attention. "There are some man-made structures. Do you know of any other scout camp structures other than those we visited?"

Gabriella dipped her head, considering it, and then shook her head. "Not that I remember. But maybe Sophie and Robbie can find an older map of the camp?"

"I'll get them working on it. In the meantime, I'll start at the original camp and work my way to this area," Diego said, and trailed his finger along the monitor, showing the route Poppy and he would take.

"I'll arrange for other agents to meet us there as backup," Ryder said, and walked away to make the necessary calls and plans for the additional CBI agents.

"I've got a change of clothes in my trunk that are better suited for a hike. I can change once we're there," she said, and was about to walk away when he gently grasped her arm.

"You do not have to do this," he said, worried about what surprises the killer might have in store.

Her lips firmed into a thin slash, warning she wouldn't budge. Her next words confirmed it.

"I have to do this for me, but more importantly, those families deserve closure and those women deserve justice. Nothing else matters."

Chapter Twenty-Four

Jeannie Roberts huddled into a tight ball, fighting the shivers racking her body.

Cold, so cold, she thought.

A brisk wind whistled in through the gaps in the walls and swept up through the floorboards of the old shower stall.

She knew it was a shower stall from the rusty showerhead across from her.

That explained the gaps in the floorboards. They let water run off.

The other breaks in the wall were from where the wood had rotted out here and there, or shrunk from years of exposure.

He had tied her to one set of boards, and she'd tried for over an hour to break them, hoping that the weather had weakened them.

They'd given a little but held. If anything, it had made it harder for her since pulling them off the support beams had only created greater gaps that allowed the unseasonably cold spring air to stream through, chilling her.

She would die if she didn't get out of here soon.

The signs of hypothermia were already registering. The shivering and drowsiness. Slight confusion and cold on her skin.

She had to move. Stay alert. Giving in meant death.

She wasn't ready to die.

IT TOOK THEM well over half an hour to prep any materials they might need and make it to the old scout camp.

Another half an hour or more until the extra CBI agents arrived, including a sniper armed with an M40 rifle Diego recognized from his time in the Marines.

With all the agents gathered around, Gabriella laid out who would be going where on copies of the maps they had worked on earlier, which she passed out at their arrival.

"Diego will have Poppy search for Roberts along with you. We have identified this area as a possible killing field, so keep an eye out for anything unusual and mark it for our CSI team," she said, and pointed to two of the agents.

Running a finger along her map, she showed the remaining four agents their plan to flank Guarino. "We'll go up the trail together until we split up here. At that point, we should use extreme caution because we don't know what this killer has planned."

Gesturing to the sniper, she said, "Do you think you can get eyes on him from that area?"

The sniper looked at the map, then peered up the mountain toward the summit. "It may be possible."

"Good. Once you have eyes on him, let us know so we can assess if we need to change our plan," she said, glanced around the team gathered there and nodded.

"Let's go," she said. The agents immediately went into action, following the instructions they'd been given.

He hesitated, hating the thought of Gabriella being in danger, then reminded himself that this was the life she'd chosen. He had to support that in any way he could.

Because of that, he buried his fear deep and gave Poppy the track command.

"*Such*," he said, and doubled down with the hand command as well.

Poppy immediately took off, nosing the ground in front of them.

She didn't pick up on any scent immediately, so Diego guided her onto the trail for the scout camp.

It didn't take long to reach the buildings they'd already searched.

He didn't expect Poppy to get a hit, but he let her nose around anyway. They were looking for any possible trail that might lead to the areas they'd identified on the map.

Sure enough, as they reached the farthermost shower stalls, close to the area from which Isabella had disappeared, there seemed to be a path away from the camp and up the mountain.

The path had not been used in a long time, but there was still enough of a break in the underbrush and trees for them to follow.

They had only gone along that trail for about one hundred yards when Poppy suddenly stopped cold and raised her head. Instead of continuing up the trail, she pulled him through thicker underbrush and trees for several yards before nosing in a mound of leaves, old pine needles and vines.

She scented the area and then sat to signal she smelled something.

"What is it?" asked one of the agents who had been following behind him.

As he carefully examined the mound, he realized what it was.

"A grave," he said, and as sad as he was, he was also grateful.

Someone would be going home soon.

GABRIELLA GLANCED UP the trail.

No sign of Guarino, which was good.

If they couldn't see the killer, he probably couldn't see

them. That was essential for being able to surprise and apprehend him.

The spot she'd picked for them to break apart was hopefully not a place where Guarino might detect their approach.

The doorbell chime of her phone erupted, shockingly loud against the silence of the mountain.

She whipped her phone out and silenced the sound.

Another message from that same unidentified number.

Another video, different from the first, of Roberts struggling to break free. The words in bloodred across this video said, "Time's running out."

She didn't need him to tell her that.

But worse, he was watching Roberts. If Diego found her before they did, Guarino might bolt from his location.

She texted a warning to Diego not to enter the building when they located Roberts.

A when and not an if. She had total faith in Diego and Poppy.

Once Diego acknowledged her warning, they proceeded up the trail, mindful that Guarino might also have trail cams to warn of their approach.

Luckily there was nothing, so they proceeded to the spot she had designated for them to separate.

She faced Ryder, wanting to be sure he was in support of this plan, and at his nod, she faced the sniper and another agent and said, "Hold here until we advise that we're in position to apprehend Guarino."

"Copy that," the two agents confirmed.

She was about to head up the trail when Ryder swept his arm out to stop her. "It's pretty overgrown," he said, and pulled out a small machete from a knapsack he'd brought with him.

"Okay, but we need to be careful. Sound travels far on

mountainsides like this," she said, and as if to support her, Poppy's bark drifted up from below.

"Got it," he said, and carefully moved along the trail, both cutting and shoving aside brush to clear their way.

DIEGO HAD HOPED to reach the areas identified on the map much more quickly. Definitely before Gabriella and her team reached the summit and had a possible confrontation with the killer.

But along the way, Poppy had pulled him away from the trail and to suspect areas multiple times. They had identified at least four other mounds that were possible grave sites and marked them for the CSI team.

Eventually, they returned to the trail and were halfway to Roberts's possible location when the sudden snap of a branch was followed by a shout of pain.

He whirled to find one of the agents had been speared in the leg by a booby trap.

Muttering a curse, he stopped the man as he tried to pull it out.

"Leave it in. We don't know if it's hit anything important," he said, afraid that if it had hit a large vessel, the agent would bleed out before they could get him back down the trail.

Facing the uninjured agent, he said, "Call for an ambulance and help him back down. Carefully."

"Got it," the man said, helped the injured agent to his feet and together they hobbled down to the trailhead.

Using the communications equipment they'd donned before heading up the trail, he called Gabriella.

"We've got a problem," he said.

Chapter Twenty-Five

Gabriella listened as Diego explained about the booby trap and ahead of her, Ryder paused, likewise hearing the conversation.

"How bad was he injured?" she asked, worried about her fellow agent.

"I don't think it was life-threatening, but we need to be alert," he said.

"Roger that. Be careful," she whispered, worried that Diego was heading to the other location on his own.

Ryder faced her, worry etched on his features. "Do you think he could have booby-trapped this trail?"

Uneasily, she shook her head. "I'm not sure. He thinks he can outsmart us and maybe he has. For now. We need to have eyes on every inch of ground."

He nodded. "Got it," he said, and this time, moved along the trail more slowly, vigilant for signs of any traps or snares.

It delayed them, way too much, much as it had delayed Diego, Gabriella worried.

With the wind on the mountain and unseasonable cold, Roberts had to quickly be losing body temperature. It could already be at fatally low levels.

As they broke free of the tree line above the location Guarino had pinned, it struck her that it was an absolutely glorious spring day.

No one should die on a day like today, she thought as they pushed ahead and reached the peak above Guarino's position.

Sure enough, he was exactly where he said he'd be, sitting on the ground in a lotus position, eyes closed as if he were in deep meditation. His hands rested peacefully on his knees but as she looked more closely, she noticed something in one hand.

Her gut tightened and in a whisper, she reached out to the sniper positioned below them.

"Do you have eyes on him?"

"I got him," the agent confirmed.

"What does he have in his right hand?" she asked.

What seemed like a painfully long time passed before he said, "A cell phone."

DIEGO STOPPED SHORT as he heard the chatter between Gabriella and the sniper.

A cell phone? To talk to them or for something else? Like a bomb maybe?

Rushing ahead while aware of the danger, he reached a series of rickety buildings that resembled those in the scout camp located lower on the mountainside.

Gingerly he picked his way around them and as he did so, a soul-wrenching cry stopped him cold.

He listened again, trying to pinpoint where it had come from, and seconds later, the rattle of wood boards guided him toward the backmost hut.

"*Such*," he said to Poppy. She immediately moved in the direction of the sound and laid down next to one of the dilapidated shower stalls.

Roberts was visible between the gaps in the wall, naked skin pale against the darker wood of the building.

"Jeannie," he called out softly, and a soft whimper answered him before the tips of her fingers, nails broken and bloody from trying to escape, slipped through the gaps in the wood.

"I'm with CBI, Jeannie. We're here to help," he said.

"Don't leave me," she cried, and frantically yanked at the wood boards.

"I won't. I won't, Jeannie, but you need to help me. Do you see anything inside that looks like a booby trap or bomb?" he asked as he worked his way around the shower stall, searching for signs of any kind of danger whether a booby trap or bomb.

He had thought about training Poppy for explosives once but hadn't done it. Now he regretted it.

There were no visible signs of any booby traps or IEDs.

He approached the door of the stall, ready to open it, but as he did, a ray of sunlight, almost like a message from the heavens, illuminated the latch.

He saw it then.

A black wire, running from the latch and down to the ground.

He splayed on the ground and peered beneath the floor of the shower stall.

The wire from the latch connected to a black box a little bigger than a shoebox.

"Gabriella, I see what looks like a bomb. Opening the door will trip it," he advised, and then hopped to his feet.

"We need to defuse the situation and that bomb, Diego. Stay back," she said.

GABRIELLA TOOK A step toward Guarino to speak to him, but Ryder grabbed hold of her arm to keep her back.

"What do you think you're doing?" he said in an urgent whisper.

"He said 'trade.' That can't happen if he doesn't see me," she said.

"It's too dangerous. We don't know if he hasn't booby-trapped himself as well," Ryder said, and peered down the slope, scrutinizing Guarino as he calmly sat there.

As if sensing his perusal, Guarino's eyes slowly drifted open, and a cruel smile slipped onto his lips.

He lifted the hand that held the cell phone, finger poised on the screen, and called out, "I wanted a trade, Gabriella. It doesn't seem as if you understood what I meant."

"Don't, Raul. Please," she said, and slowly approached him, hands help up in apology and to ask him to stop.

"Don't? Please? Is that all you have, Gabriella?" he said with a harsh laugh.

"What I have is enough evidence to put you away for a long time, Raul. Hard time unless you cooperate," Gabriella warned and continued her approach.

"Cooperate. I hate cooperation," he said with another, almost exasperated laugh. "You know what I did with women who tried to cooperate to get free?"

She didn't want to know, but the longer she kept him talking, the higher the possibility that Diego might be able to free Roberts.

"Why don't you tell me what you did? I bet you'd like to relive that," she said, and finally moved within several feet of him. That let her see the almost manic look in his gaze. A look that said that not all of them would leave this mountainside alive.

"I killed them slowly. Inch by inch you might say. A finger. A toe. Not the eyes, though. I wanted them to see what I was doing," he said gleefully.

"What about the others? The ones who fought back?" she asked, just to keep him talking.

"Ah, they were the best. It's why I keep them longer. A gift for their spirit," he said with a wistful smile.

"Is that why you kept Isabella?" she asked, preparing herself for his answer.

Guarino tsked and shook his head. "My little Isabella. She was my first, you know."

"I know. Why? Why did you take her?" she asked.

"She was so pretty. She would have been as beautiful as you if I hadn't..." He stopped then, as if surprised by what he had planned to say next but then continued.

"I didn't mean to kill her," he said, his gaze pleading, as if seeking forgiveness.

But then darkness slipped into that gaze, as if another person was taking control.

"But I liked it. A lot. I knew it was wrong. I tried for a long time not to do it again, but it was too hard to fight the need," he admitted, and again, forgiveness and darkness twisted into a sick singsong in his tone.

"We can help you understand that need, Raul. There are therapists—"

"My father sent me to therapists! They know nothing," he screamed and wildly waved the hand with the cell phone.

She pumped her hands in the air, trying to urge calm, and once again said, "Please, Raul."

IT WAS A race against time, and Diego didn't intend to lose the race.

With one last swing around the shower stall to make sure there weren't other traps or bombs besides the one at the door, he examined the various slats.

Cheap, untreated pine that had suffered after years of exposure.

One wall seemed to have received the brunt of the exposure.

He found a larger gap where he could slip his finger in to grasp the side of the panel. Putting all his strength and weight into it, he yanked, trying to pull it free.

It snapped, sending him flying backward onto the ground.

He tossed aside the rotten slat and returned to the wall, breaking off another piece of wall and then another.

Bending, he looked inside to where Roberts was curled into a fetal position at the far side of the shower stall.

"I'm here, Jeannie. I'll have you out in a second."

Jerking against another slat, he snapped it and tossed it aside. Repeated it with yet another slat, creating enough space for him to slip through.

He jerked off his knapsack, tossed it away and gave Poppy a command to sit.

Bending, he eased through the gap and over to Roberts, who was barely conscious. He touched her arm. Her skin was ice-cold.

Too cold, he worried.

He ripped off his jacket and wrapped it around her.

She stirred then and opened her eyes, her gaze slightly unfocused first, and then fearful.

"I'm here to help, Jeannie. I'm with CBI," he repeated since it was clear that hypothermia was making her confused.

He pulled out a knife to cut the zip ties at her ankles and wrists, and she cried out "No" and kicked out at him.

"I'm with the police. I'm here to help," he said again, and it seemed as if it finally registered.

She stilled and he slipped the knife beneath the zip ties, cut them off and said, "Can you walk?"

"Maybe," she said hesitantly.

He nodded, eased an arm around her waist and helped her rise. Together they hobbled over to the hole he'd made in the wall.

Easing through the gap first, he then helped her exit, but she stumbled badly, falling into his arms.

"We have to move away from here, Jeannie," he said, bent and hauled her into his arms.

"PLEASE PUT THAT DOWN," Gabriella said with hands upraised, urging Guarino yet again to calm down.

"Please! You disappoint me, Gabriella. You deserve to suffer like the others," he said, his face almost purple with rage.

"We have to take him out, Gabriella," Ryder said across her earpiece.

She shook her head, and whispered back, "No. Hold your fire."

"You're suffering, just in a different way, Raul. You didn't want to hurt them. You just can't control yourself," she said, and took a step closer, hoping to grab the cell phone before he could trigger the bomb Diego had found.

A bomb that might kill Roberts as well as Diego and Poppy if they were still there with her.

"I don't need to control myself. I just need to control them. The women and you," he said, and calmed a little.

But that calm was more frightening than his earlier maniacal state.

He met her gaze, clear-eyed and determined. "I'm in control here, Gabriella. And I'm going to make you suffer," he said, and pressed his finger to the cell phone screen.

Chapter Twenty-Six

A blast of pressure pummeled him while sharp splinters pierced his back.

The force of the explosion sent him flying and as he fell, he protected Roberts and Poppy as best he could, hauling them beneath him as pieces of debris rained down.

Several of the pieces were on fire, and he bolted to his feet quickly to keep them away from Roberts and Poppy, and to put them out before they could ignite a blaze.

On the ground, Roberts shivered despite his jacket. Poppy nosed around her, sensing her discomfort.

He called Poppy over, quickly examined her for injuries, and satisfied she was unharmed, he directed her to lie down beside Roberts. "*Platz*," he said, and once she had, he urged Roberts close to Poppy, hoping the warmth of the dog's body would help.

Then he went in search of his knapsack where he had an assortment of supplies, including survival blankets that would help.

The knapsack had been tossed several feet away and he grabbed it and rummaged through it to remove two survival blankets. Ripping open the bags, he wrapped Roberts in the blankets and massaged her legs and arms, trying to get warmth to return.

As he did that, he called out to the team. "Can anyone hear me?" he asked, and realized he could barely hear himself past the ringing in his ears caused by the blast and the dislodgment of his earpiece.

He jammed it back in place in time to hear the worried chatter across the line.

"Diego, copy. We hear you. Are you okay?" Gabriella asked.

"I am, but Roberts needs medical attention. I'm going to carry her down."

"Ambulance should already be there for the wounded agent," she said.

"What about Guarino?" he asked as he gently lifted Roberts into his arms, careful to keep the blankets and jackets tight around her to try and conserve what little body heat she had left.

"Dead. Sniper took him out after he triggered the bomb," she advised, and it was impossible to miss the frustration in her voice.

As he walked along the trail to the parking lot, he said, "It may not be the justice you wanted for Isabella, but...he can't hurt anyone ever again."

"No, he can't. But how will we ever get closure now for all those families and Isabella?" she asked, pain alive in her voice.

He hadn't wanted to tell her while they were trying to reach the summit, worried it would be a distraction. But there was no reason to delay any longer.

"We found possible burial sites. I marked them and can lead CSI back to the locations," he advised, stumbled on an exposed root he couldn't see because of his burden, and managed to catch himself before they went rolling down the trail.

Muttering a curse, he said, "I'll be waiting for you in the parking lot."

"Coming down as soon as I can," she said. He gave his attention to picking his way along the trail.

His arms and back ached from the weight of her, but she still hadn't roused enough to assist, and that worried him.

Had her body temperature dropped to fatal levels? he wondered and increased his pace as much as he could, Poppy loping just ahead of him. He was grateful to see that the dog seemed unaffected and unharmed by the explosion.

He lost track of time, plodding along, sweat running down his face and back from the exertion of carrying her.

With only yards to go, a pair of EMTs came running up the trail hauling a stretcher.

They quickly bundled Roberts onto the stretcher and hurried away with her, leaving him to trudge down the last little bit of the trail.

As he reached the parking lot, black circles danced in his vision, and his knees grew rubbery. He reached for a nearby tree trunk to steady himself and grasped it, the bark rough against his palm.

Focusing on that, he held on to consciousness. He wasn't ready to rest. Not until he'd led the CSI team to the five graves they'd found above the campgrounds.

As he sat there on the cold ground, another EMT walked over to him.

"Agent Rodriguez? Maybe we should take a look at you, too," he said, and offered a hand to help him to his feet.

He rose unsteadily, and Poppy was immediately at his side, giving him another anchor to reality.

Haltingly, he walked with the EMT to the back of a second ambulance that had answered their call for help. The EMT seated him there and immediately went to work, checking his vitals.

"Your blood pressure is a little low. We need to rehydrate you," he said, wrapped an emergency blanket around him and prepped an IV.

"Thanks," he said, and a second later, Poppy hopped up

beside him. He wrapped an arm around her and checked her yet again for signs of any injury.

"You're okay, girl," he said.

"But you're not. We should go to the hospital to remove those splinters in your back," the EMT said.

"Can you take them out now?" he asked, not wanting to leave the area until he had led CSI to the graves and was there to help Gabriella if one of them was Isabella's.

The EMT lifted the blanket and examined his back. "Yes, but it'll hurt like a—"

"Do it," Diego asked, and met the EMT's dubious gaze. "Please. I'm not done here."

With an uneasy dip of his head, the EMT relented, got an IV into him and shifted the blanket so that he could pull out the splinters in his back.

The cold of scissors, cutting away his shirt, registered only seconds before a sharp pull sent pain radiating through his back. His muscles jumped and the EMT muttered, "Sorry, man. I'm trying to do it as painlessly as I can."

"It's fine," he mumbled behind his gritted teeth, and fought off the black circles again, closing his eyes to ignore them.

He had to stay strong. It wouldn't be the first time he'd been wounded and still had to work.

Burying his head against Poppy's soft fur, he focused on that to keep from jumping every time the fire erupted across his back.

"All are out. I'll just get them clean and bandaged, but when was the last time you had a tetanus shot?" the EMT said, his touch gentle as he swabbed disinfectant across the assorted wounds.

Diego flinched and said, "I'm up to date on shots."

The sound of sirens and crunch of gravel dragged his attention to the second ambulance that was pulling out of the parking lot.

"How is she doing?" he asked the EMT who had worked on him.

"Core body temperature was only eighty-two, so she had severe hypothermia. She's lucky you found her when you did," the EMT said, and offered Diego a sweatshirt from a cubby in the ambulance.

"It's a spare I keep. They said to give you this back," he said and handed him the jacket he had wrapped around Roberts.

Diego pulled on the sweatshirt and after, his jacket, which he'd have to toss after today. Feathery white down poked from several large tears, and blood marred various spots.

He jerked his arm through one sleeve and then stopped as he realized the IV was still in his other arm.

"Can you take that out?" he asked, and earned an eye roll from the EMT.

"It's against medical advice, but I know you won't listen anyway," he said, carefully extracted the IV and then quickly slapped an adhesive bandage to stop any bleeding.

GABRIELLA HIT THE ground of the parking lot almost at a run.

She stopped short as she caught sight of Diego with the EMT, Poppy at his side.

Racing over, she wrapped her arms around him, uncaring of how unprofessional it might look.

"I was so worried," she said.

"I'm okay," he said, which earned a guffaw from the nearby EMT and a muttered, "No, he's not."

Gabriella released her hold, stepped back and examined him. Streaks of dirt and a little blood marred his handsome face. Bits of twigs and some leaves were tangled in the longer strands of his hair. Beneath the dirt and blood, his tanned face was paler than usual.

She brushed her hand through those locks to get rid of the debris and said, "We should get you to the hospital."

He vehemently shook his head. "Not until the CSI team is here and I take them around."

She knew better than to argue. "Stubborn."

"Says the pot," he kidded.

"How is Roberts? CBI Agent Blake?" she asked, and looked around for another ambulance just as Ryder and the other agents came to join them.

"Roberts was suffering from extreme hypothermia. The agent was lucky that the stake didn't hit anything important. Both are on their way to the hospital," the EMT advised as he worked to clean up his rig.

"I'm going to send Agent McIntosh to the hospital to check on Roberts and Blake. Hopefully, we were able to get to Roberts in time," Ryder said, and scrutinized Diego.

"Looks like we should get you there also," he said.

"I'm good. Just a few cuts and scrapes," Diego replied, and slipped off the back of the ambulance to stand as if to prove he was truly fine. With a hand command, Poppy hopped down and heeled at his side.

The sound of a vehicle drew their attention to the entrance of the parking lot, where three CSI vans were pulling in along with a duo of vans from the medical examiner's office.

Ryder looked at them and said, "Do you want me to take one of the CSI teams to the summit where Agent Samuels is securing the scene, and you go with Diego to the graves?"

There was an unspoken question there also: Are you ready to possibly find your sister after so many years?

"Yes, please do that. I'll go with Diego, Poppy and the CSI team," she said, and slipped her hand into Diego's, needing that connection.

She'd always thought of herself as tough and independent, but when finally faced with knowing what had happened to Isabella, she suddenly didn't want to be so independent.

A gentle squeeze on her hand reassured her that he would be there for her.

In a flurry of activity, Diego was identifying on the map what Poppy had confirmed with her searches while Ryder returned to the summit with one of the CSI teams.

As a final confirmation of Guarino's evil, they realized that the graves were arranged in the shape of a cross with one grave in the center of the formation.

"Do you think…" she began but couldn't finish, overwhelmed with emotion.

"I think the center grave, the heart of the cross, may be Isabella," he said, confirming what she had been thinking.

"Do you want us to start there, Agent Ruiz?" one of the CSI techs asked.

Gabriella shook her head. "Start where you think is the best place to preserve evidence. I won't let my connection possibly damage the case."

With a solemn nod, the agent faced Diego. "We're ready when you are."

DIEGO EXAMINED GABRIELLA'S face, trying to gauge if she had prepared herself for what the investigations might reveal.

Her face was all severe lines, and all life had left her normally warm and engaging gaze. She had her game face on, but from the trembling of her hand in his, it was clear she was struggling to hold it together.

But they had a job to do. Gabriella knew that more than most.

He nodded and said, "I'll lead you up to the killing fields."

With a soft click under his tongue to Poppy and a gentle tug on Gabriella's hand, he pushed off in the direction of the trailhead.

His legs felt slightly unsteady, as if he was on a ship at sea instead of on land, but he ignored that. Just like Gabriella had to stay strong, he had to as well. He could rest once those up on that mountainside finally found their peace.

He pushed on, carefully watching for exposed roots and anything else that might trip him up. He didn't think he could handle another fall. He already had enough aches blossoming all across his body.

It took nearly half an hour before they hit what might be the first grave and just to confirm that they hadn't been wrong, he once again instructed Poppy to search.

"*Such*," he said, and much as she had done earlier, Poppy nosed around the area and then lay down near the spot they had identified earlier.

The lead CSI agent directed one of his team to work on the first grave.

Diego and Poppy repeated the process for the other four graves.

Once they had done that, the CSI agents swarmed the area, beginning the work of gathering evidence and recovering Guarino's victims.

The lead agent stood before them and said, "I'm going to request more agents and lights since it'll be dark in another hour or so. But it's going to take time. Maybe you should return to Denver to wait. We'll let you know once we have anything."

Chapter Twenty-Seven

Gabriella had thought she was ready to know what had happened to Isabella.

But as she took note of all the activity at the scene and then peered at Diego, who was bravely standing there despite his injuries, she realized that it was time to step away and let others do what they did best.

She had already done all she could to get them here, as had Diego and Poppy.

"Let's go back to CPS and fill them in on what's happening," she said with a firm squeeze on Diego's hand.

His gaze skipped over her features. "Are you sure?"

"I am. We all need some rest and…separation from this," she said, and with a gentle tug on his hand, they hurried to her car.

As she drove, Diego called Sophie and Robbie with his report and after he ended the call, he said, "Do you mind if I just close my eyes for a moment?"

"No, go ahead," she said, but was worried that he was hurt far worse than he had let on.

She kept an eye on the road but did the same with Diego to make sure he was fine.

His soft even breaths said he slept, and as she tenderly touched his hand as it rested on his leg, the cold was gone, replaced by a warmth that lessened some of her worry.

He roused as she made the last turn off the highway and onto the street for the CPS offices.

"How are you feeling?" she said as she turned into the parking lot and then pulled into one of the spots reserved for CPS.

"Achy. Some pain on my back," he admitted, and blew out a tired sigh. "Why don't I feel satisfaction that Guarino is dead?"

"Because his victims and their families won't get justice?" she said, shut off the car and faced him.

With a shrug and toss of his hands, he said, "Some might think justice was served by the sniper, but I think the families might have wanted to know why. Right?"

He nailed her with his gaze because she was one of those families. "Does the why matter? Isabella is gone. Taken too soon, but hopefully she'll be home now."

Nodding, he cradled her cheek. "I know I'm sorry doesn't cut it, but I'm sorry."

She cupped his hand, stroked it and offered him a weak smile. "Thank you."

The beep of his phone shattered the moment. He glanced at it and said, "Sophie and Robbie. They have dinner waiting for us."

"That Robbie is a bottomless pit," she said with a chuckle, but deep down, she recognized it was their way of offering comfort at a difficult time. Her Mexican mother would have done the same.

She exited the car while Diego got out, unharnessed Poppy and grabbed his knapsack from the back.

"I'll have to feed her, too, while we eat and then walk her," he said as they strolled over to the elevator bank.

Since it was after normal business hours, the elevator arrived quickly and in no time they were in the Crooked Pass Security offices. The heavenly smells of food filled the space as they walked in, and Gabriella's stomach growled in response.

She covered her midsection with her hand as Diego smiled and said, "I'm starving, too. We never got lunch."

No, they hadn't, because too much had been happening too quickly.

But no longer. Now it was time to sit and wait for the CSI experts to do their work.

Sophie rushed from the conference room, concern etched on her features.

"Are you okay?" she asked, and examined Diego from head to toe.

Diego pointed to a washroom at the end of the hall. "I'm going to clean up before we sit to eat," he said, and didn't wait for a reply to walk off, Poppy obediently at his side.

Sophie peered at her and said, "I wish I could help more somehow."

Gabriella closed the distance between them and hugged the other woman. "Sophie, if it wasn't for you, Robbie and the rest of your team, I don't think we would have saved Jeannie Roberts and found the others."

Sophie tightened the embrace and said, "I wish we could have helped more."

"You've done what seemed impossible," Gabriella said, grateful for all their help.

Robbie popped out of the conference room and took in the scene. She waited for his usual quips, but he only offered a sad smile and went back in.

Sophie and she followed him and when Diego entered, they sat and ate, fairly silent as hunger and the realization that the case was almost done hung over them.

When they finished, Diego fed Poppy her kibble although he had been sneaking her tidbits from the Cuban food that the siblings had ordered from Diego's favorite restaurant.

"I've got to take her for a walk," he said once Poppy had gobbled down her food.

"I'll go with you," she said. They went to street level, strolling in silence for a few blocks, letting the German shepherd relieve herself and get some air before returning to the office.

As Diego turned at one point, she noticed the damage to the jacket and realized that each tear and bloodstain on the fabric meant he was wounded beneath them.

She gently stroked her hand across his back and said, "Are you sure you don't need to go to the hospital?"

He waved her off. "I'm okay. The EMT took care of it."

Since he wasn't going to give in at that moment, she let it go, although she intended to press him later and tend to the injuries.

As they returned to the conference room, Ryder was sitting there, eating some food that Sophie had set aside for him.

He smiled stiffly, worrying her.

"How was it going at the scout camp?" she asked.

"Good, but it's going to take time. CSI agent said he'll update us in the morning," Ryder said.

She'd been waiting nearly eight years to find Isabella. Several more hours wasn't going to make a difference, and the time away from the case might let her prepare for finally finding her sister.

"That sounds good," she said, earning a raised eyebrow from Ryder, as if he didn't believe she was giving in so quickly.

"Time to go then. Selene is waiting for me," Robbie said, and rose.

"We'll meet back here at nine," Sophie said, and ran a loving hand across Ryder's shoulders.

"Nine. That's good," Gabriella said, and glanced at Diego, who nodded.

"I'm good with that. I'll walk you to your car."

It sounded to her like he'd be going his own way tonight, which roused disappointment. Even though she no longer needed his protection with Guarino gone, she'd hoped for...

What had you hoped for? the little voice in her head challenged. *Love in just a few days?*

Surprisingly, that's just what she felt for him in an incredibly short time.

When they reached her car, she stopped and faced him. "I want to thank you for all that you, Poppy and the team have done," she said, and rubbed Poppy's head, earning an appreciative lick of her hand.

"She likes you," Diego said with a happy laugh, and then his gaze locked with hers. "I like you, too. A lot."

Relief flooded through her, and she smiled. "The feeling is mutual. Actually, it's more than just like, Diego. Ridiculous as it sounds, I love you."

A rough breath escaped him, and a broad grin erupted on his face. He cradled her cheek, stepped closer and whispered against her lips, "I love you, too, Gabriella."

"I hope that means you'll come home with me tonight. I don't want to be alone," she said.

GOING HOME WITH GABRIELLA. It had been so long since he'd felt that he had a home, but that's how he felt with her. As if he was finally where he belonged.

"Let's go home," he said, and in a rush, they packed Poppy into the car and were on their way to her home.

When they entered and got Poppy settled for the night, Gabriella said, "Let's take a look at your back, and I won't take no for an answer."

"Yes, ma'am," Diego said with a little salute, aware she wouldn't give up.

She grabbed his hand and led him to her en suite bathroom where he sat on the toilet, his back to her.

He jerked off his shirt, biting back a groan at the pain that erupted across his back from the movement. But then her gentle touch drifted across his skin, offering comfort.

Comfort he hadn't felt in so long with anyone else.

Quickly and efficiently, she applied more antibiotic ointment on the wounds and fresh bandages. As he stood and faced her, she offered him some over-the-counter painkillers.

"I wish I had something stronger," she said.

He shook his head. "These are fine. I want to keep sharp," he said, but not because he was worried about an attack. Instead, it was because he didn't want to miss a minute of being with her.

She nodded, slipped her hand into his and led him toward her bed, stopping at the edge.

Turning, she faced him, her gaze questioning. "Are we foolish to feel like this?"

He shook his head. "Foolish is never being able to feel like this. I know that because for too long I couldn't feel anything."

Smiling, she splayed a hand over his heart. "I want to feel everything with you," she said, freeing the last of his restraint.

They rushed to bed, clothes tossed in their haste to be together. As he joined with her, it was like coming home after being lost in the desert for far too long. They moved together, seeking release but also completion of a different kind.

As they finally fell over together, he cuddled her close and said again, "I love you."

She stroked a hand across his chest and kissed the underside of his jaw. "I love you, too," she said, and pillowed her head on his chest.

He held her close, offering her comfort in the aftermath

of their loving. She'd need that and more in the morning, he suspected.

He didn't doubt that one of the graves was Isabella's. Probably the one in the center, as if she was the heart of Guarino's hideous crimes.

It was with those thoughts skipping through his brain that he drifted off to an uneasy sleep that seemed too short when the first rays of sunlight drifted in through the French doors of her bedroom.

They had just finished showering when Gabriella's cell phone rang.

She answered, and her body stiffened instantly. With curt replies, she answered whoever was on the other end of the line.

"Yes, I get it. I'll be there," she said, and ended the call.

GABRIELLA FACED DIEGO, who stood there with question in his gaze. "That was the lead CSI agent. They've removed one of the victims to the ME's office and want me to come in for a possible identification."

"Isabella?" he said, dark brows rising in emphasis.

"They believe so from what they have. I mean, it's not possible to ID her face, but…we should go," she said, unable to voice what she'd see when she got to the ME. Unable to process what would remain of her loving, inquisitive and amazing baby sister.

She took a step away, but he tenderly wrapped her in his embrace. "I'm here for you. For whatever," he said.

Choking back a sob, she said, "I know."

They hurriedly dressed, delaying only to feed Poppy and then let her relieve herself outside.

The German shepherd seemed to sense their haste since she gobbled the food quickly and wasted little time in the yard.

It wasn't a long drive to the ME's office, but it seemed interminable that morning.

As they parked and walked to the front door, she realized Sophie, Ryder and Robbie were there to offer support.

"I appreciate you being here," she said, and together they walked in. Once Gabriella and Ryder had checked in, one of the medical examiners came out from the back and led them to a waiting area for victims' families.

"This may be difficult, Agent Ruiz," the ME said, and nervously fingered a clipboard between his hands.

"I understand. What do you have?" she asked, trying to keep her voice as neutral and professional as possible.

"We have dental records from your sister's case. Also her medical records. You may not remember all the details from them—"

"Her wisdom teeth were impacted, and she had them removed. She also had one slightly crooked front tooth. Her central incisor," she said and pointed out that tooth in her mouth before continuing. "She'd fallen off her bike the summer before and broke her arm. Her radius about midway," she said, and once again demonstrated it on her body.

The ME nodded. "That's consistent with what we have in our records, and also with the victim we removed from the central grave at the location. I'm so sorry, Agent Ruiz."

"I want to see her," Gabriella said with purpose.

"Agent Ruiz, this will be difficult—"

"I want to see her," she repeated, her tone leaving no doubt that she wouldn't waver from that request.

With another nod, the ME held the clipboard out in the direction of the door.

Diego laid his hand on her back, offering comfort and support as she stepped into the hallway and then followed the ME as he walked to the morgue door.

He opened the door, and they stepped inside. Three tables had sheets draped over their occupants.

He walked her to one and slowly pulled away the sheet

to reveal a skeleton that had been reassembled on the shiny steel table.

"We don't have all of Isabella as the grave was subject to some scavenging—" he began, but Gabriella raised a hand to stop him.

She was well familiar with what happened to bodies buried in areas frequented by animals. She didn't want to imagine that with her sister.

And it was Isabella. She did not doubt that.

The dental and medical details were there for her to see. As was her general height.

Diego squeezed her shoulder, offering reassurance, and she nodded, shakily said, "Thank you. I appreciate all that you're doing."

With that, they left the morgue and rejoined the CPS team in the waiting room.

Sorrow filled her, but so did something else. Determination.

"This shouldn't have happened to Isabella. But it also shouldn't have happened to those other women. We had evidence that might have helped. They shouldn't have been cold cases for so long," she said as she recalled the finding that there had been touch DNA on one of the victims that hadn't been found during the first investigation.

Ryder nodded in agreement. "We can do more. Working with Crooked Pass Security has proved that," he said, and glanced at Sophie and Robbie.

"We're in," Robbie said without hesitation.

"Good. These aren't going to be the only cold cases we solve," she said, and together, they all walked back to their cars, but as they neared hers, she faced Diego.

"I want you to be a part of more than just what Crooked Pass Security does, Diego. I want you to be a part of my life," she said, cupped his cheek and ran her thumb across his lips.

His smile beneath her thumb registered a second before he said, "I want to be a part of your life, Gabriella. I love you."

She went on tiptoes to kiss him and wrapped her arms around his waist, mindful of his injuries.

He enveloped her in his embrace and at his side, Poppy barked and hopped happily.

She laughed and bent to rub the dog's head, earning several doggy kisses as she said, "I want you, too, Poppy."

Her phone chirped to warn of a message, and she glanced at it.

The lead CSI agent wanted them back at the scout camp.

She showed it to Diego, and he nodded. "I'm ready whenever you are."

She slipped her hand into his and said, "I'm ready. For everything."

* * * * *

HIGH COUNTRY ESCAPE

CINDI MYERS

Chapter One

Roxanne Byrne had a lot of practice starting over. Some might say she specialized in picking up the pieces and building a new life. New job, new home, new people who didn't know her history—she had the routine down pat by now.

But this time was going to be different. This fresh start would be the one that led to the comfortable rut she was looking for—the place where she finally fit. First of all, she had chosen the perfect setting, she thought, as she turned onto the postcard-cute main street of Eagle Mountain, Colorado. The town's main drag was lined with shops and restaurants, all decorated with pumpkins and baskets of crimson and gold mums and notices of fall sales. Mountains rose up beyond the town, the peaks already dusted with a sifting of snow. The small town had a good mix of locals and newcomers, tourists and residents. A recent upgrade in internet services made it possible for her to work remotely, and the mountains and forests offered the contact with nature Roxanne found healing. She was going to be happy here.

She parked her slate-gray Toyota RAV4—another new addition to her life—in front of Java Moose Coffee and sighed. This was it. Day one of the new Roxanne.

She glanced over as a black Volkswagen Beetle slid into the parking space next to her and a woman emerged from the driver's seat, her long, straight hair the same deep maroon as the flowers filling a half whiskey barrel beside the door of the shop. She smiled at Roxanne as their eyes met, revealing slightly crooked front teeth. A nervous flutter ran through Roxanne and she looked away, then hurried into the shop.

The woman followed. Suddenly self-conscious, Roxanne avoided looking at her and joined the queue at the counter. When it was her turn, the barista, a curvy blonde wearing a purple sweaterdress and black boots, greeted her with a dazzling smile. "What would you like today?" the woman asked.

"A London Fog, please," Roxanne said.

"Anything else?"

"No thank you."

"Name?"

Roxanne hesitated. Most of the time she made up something. She didn't like people knowing who she was. But this was her new home, and she hoped to visit this coffee shop often. "Roxanne," she said, then added, "I just moved to town."

"Welcome to Eagle Mountain, Roxanne. I'm May. I'll have that tea right to you."

Roxanne moved aside to allow the redhead to order. She asked for hot chocolate, then made her way to a table in the corner. Roxanne relaxed a little. She couldn't say why the redhead had put her on edge so. There was nothing familiar about the woman. And it wasn't a female she was worried about, anyway. She inhaled slowly, counting to four, held the breath for four, then let it out, counting to six. She didn't have anything to worry about. She was safe here. She needed to remember that.

"Here's that London Fog." A few seconds later, May handed the drink over the counter. "Enjoy."

Roxanne carried her cup to a small table by the window. At the first sip of the creamy, sweet combination of Earl Grey tea, vanilla syrup and steamed milk, she smiled. She looked out the window at people passing on the street, in sweaters and jeans, fleece jackets and boots. The September air held a clean crispness that hinted at new school years, upcoming ski seasons and the holidays lurking just ahead. All kinds of reasons to celebrate.

To new beginnings, she thought, and sipped the tea again.

"Excuse me. I don't mean to intrude, but are you Cheryl Roxanne Bingham?"

Ice speared Roxanne and she hastily set down her cup before she dropped it. She stared up at the redhead, who now stood beside her table, a question in her blue eyes. "I was sure it was you," the woman continued. "Then I heard you tell the barista your name was Roxanne and I mean—it's not that common a name, is it?"

"Who are you?" Roxanne demanded.

"I'm not a reporter or anything, if that's what you're worried about." Uninvited, the woman slid into the chair opposite Roxanne. "My name is Debra Percy. I just want to talk to you for a minute. I think you can help me."

"Help you with what?" As soon as she asked the question, she realized the trap she had fallen into. She should have sent the woman on her way or gotten up and left. She didn't know this person and she didn't want to be drawn into whatever she was about. But it was too late now. She sat frozen in place, unable to make herself get up and leave.

Debra leaned across the table, her voice low and confiding. "I'm looking for my sister, Bettina. Bettina Percy. She was three years older than me. She disappeared when I was ten and she was thirteen. We think William Ledger took her."

Roxanne closed her eyes and swallowed the bile that rose in her throat at the name. Debra didn't say anything in the long silence that followed, but when Roxanne opened her eyes, Debra was watching her, blue eyes bright and alert.

"You know the name, I can tell," Debra said. "You are Cheryl Bingham, aren't you?"

"I don't use that name anymore," Roxanne said. "I changed it. How did you find me?"

"It wasn't easy." Debra sipped her hot chocolate and licked the foam from her upper lip. "It helped that you kept your middle name—Roxanne. But more importantly, I was determined. I'll do anything to find out what happened to my sister."

"I don't know your sister," Roxanne said. "I can't help you. I'm sorry."

She had wasted the words. Debra plunged on, determined to tell her story. "Her name was Bettina, but we always called her Betty. But maybe Ledger called her something else. He did that, didn't he? Gave new names to the girls he kept?"

Roxanne clenched her teeth, feeling sick. Still, she said nothing. But her thoughts were screaming in her head. *You have no right to do this. You have no right to make me remember.*

"I read in the papers that he called you Mary. And there was another girl found with you—Alice. Only that wasn't her real name, either, was it?"

Roxanne's eyes widened. "Was your sister Alice?" She had always wondered what happened to Alice, but had never heard anything more about the other girl Ledger had kidnapped. The one he had taken before her.

Debra shook her head. "No. I think Betty must have been before either of you. I was hoping he said something about her. Or you found something that belonged to her. Anything to hint at what happened to her. Did he ever talk about another little girl, with strawberry blond hair and blue eyes?"

"No." Roxanne shook her head. "No. There was no other girl." She pushed back her chair and hurried away, stumbling on the threshold. She groped her way into the driver's seat of the car and hit the starter button. Only then did she look toward the coffee shop again. But Debra hadn't followed her. She could still see the woman in profile, sipping her hot chocolate at the table by the window.

Roxanne took a deep breath, counting. Holding it. Releasing slowly. She closed her eyes against the tears that stung and waited while the panic subsided. *Leave it*, she told herself. *Leave it in the past. Ledger can't hurt you now. You're safe here.*

She wanted to believe the words. Some of the time she did. She wanted to believe them all of the time, but she wondered if she ever would.

"OKAY, I THINK I've fixed the problem." Dalton Ames nodded toward the computer screen in front of him. "Now you can access the calendar from the protocols section, so if you want to know when you last treated a case of hypothermia, you can pull it up with a couple of keystrokes."

"I don't know how often we'd use a feature like that, but it's amazing you can do that." Fellow search and rescue volunteer Caleb Garrison leaned over Dalton's shoulder and studied the screen. The two men were at Eagle Mountain Search and Rescue headquarters, installing the new software Dalton had designed for the organization.

"The whole idea is that everything cross-references to everything else," Dalton said. "You can search our history of callouts by the type of injuries treated, time of year or even time of day. If you want to know how many children were treated in a given time period, you can create a report for that. And I thought it might be handy to know the types of calls we see most often at different times of year. Maybe we can do some public education to try to reduce particular calls in a particular area, or even work with the highway department to identify places with the most accidents that we end up responding to."

Caleb nodded. "That's a great idea. Of course, you can't educate for everything. Some people are always going to take unnecessary risks, and the weather is always going to be unpredictable."

"If nothing else, knowing that we see more sprains in July could help when it came to maintaining our inventory of supplies," Dalton said.

"It could," Caleb agreed. "And it could help us plan training sessions for the kinds of incidents we most need to be prepared for at various times of year. And track that everyone is up-to-date on all their certifications."

"We do a good job of that already, I think," Dalton said. "And some of the veterans, like Tony Meisner, can probably tell you off the top of their heads that August is the biggest month for broken bones while in January we see more accidents on Dixon Pass."

"Yes, but everyone doesn't know that stuff," Caleb said. "Anything we can do to automate information to take a burden off volunteers is going to be helpful."

Dalton nodded. He had already put in more than a hundred hours on this software, though it was a labor of love. Of course, if it worked out well, he hoped to sell the program to other emergency responders. He'd already had success selling the reservation software he had designed for his parents' Jeep rental business. That software, along with a few apps he had created in his spare time, was already bringing in tidy sums.

Still, it wasn't all about the money. He wanted to give back to the organization that had welcomed him and given him a focus beyond his computer. He figured most of the volunteers felt the same. The work demanded so much of them all, but it also challenged them and allowed them to make a real difference in people's lives.

"Are we good to go, then?" Caleb asked.

"I think so." Dalton returned to the computer's home page, the Eagle Mountain Search and Rescue logo filling the screen. "I'm sure more bugs will pop up as we use the software more, but I should be able to fix them."

"Thanks." Caleb shouldered his backpack. "I need to get going. Danielle has a new contract and she needs me to watch the baby. Now that Lily is crawling, Danielle has a hard time getting anything done in her studio with her around. Lily thinks all the clay and stuff are toys."

Dalton tried not to imagine what "stuff" baby Lily might want to play with in Danielle's studio. Caleb's wife worked as a forensic reconstructionist, using the skulls of the dead to re-create how they would have looked in life.

After Caleb left, Dalton shut down the computer, locked up the building and drove back into town. He had just enough time to grab coffee before his afternoon tour at Alpine Jeep. Coming into the shop, he almost collided with a woman with long purple-red hair. "Sorry about that," he said, reaching out to steady her.

She smiled. "It's okay." She looked him up and down. "You can run into me anytime."

He stepped back, not sure how to respond. His brother Carter would have come up with something smart and flirty to say in return, but Dalton had always been better at typing than talking. "Uh, see you around," he stammered and went inside.

As he moved toward the front counter, he looked back over his shoulder in time to see the woman get into the driver's seat of a black Volkswagen Beetle. "Her name is Debra. She's single, but she's doesn't know how long she'll stay in town."

He turned to find the barista, May Delgado, grinning at him. "Why are you telling me about her?" he asked.

May shrugged. "I thought you might be interested."

He glanced toward the Beetle, which was backing out of the parking spot. Was he interested? He only had a fleeting impression of the woman—not an unpleasant one, but not particularly memorable, either. "I don't even know her," he said.

"That's how most relationships start, isn't it?" May asked. "Two people who don't know each other—then they do."

He shook his head and leaned on the front counter. "Just the usual, May."

"Double mocha, coming up." She turned to the coffee machine. "If Debra doesn't interest you, you just missed a pretty brunette who said she's new to town. I think she's renting one of Robbie Lusk's tiny houses. Her name is Roxanne."

"Are you playing matchmaker or something?" he asked.

"Not me. But single people are going to match up with other single people. And I'm in a position to know about most people in town—at least the tea and coffee drinkers." She turned and slid a cup toward him. "Roxanne is a tea drinker," she added.

He tapped his debit card on the machine to pay and dropped a dollar in May's tip jar. Was he so obviously bad at meeting women on his own that May had taken pity and decided to match him up? If so, he ought to welcome her efforts. He wasn't like Carter. Though they were identical twins, they didn't have identical personalities. Carter had been born with good looks and a golden tongue, while Dalton was more quiet and awkward. The perfect image of a computer geek, right down to the dark-rimmed glasses.

May leaned across the counter, providing a distracting view of her cleavage, but he knew she wasn't flirting. She and Eldon Ramsey, another search and rescue volunteer, were definitely a couple. Sometimes Dalton felt as if he was the only person he knew who wasn't paired off.

"I like the glasses," she said.

Dalton put one hand to the black-framed eyeglasses he had recently taken to wearing. "I've had contacts for years, but the dry air here really bothers me," he said. "I decided to go back to these for a while."

"Gives you a sexy geek vibe," May said.

Right. Whatever.

"Are you going to the Fall Festival tomorrow?" she asked.

"I have to be there," he said. "Search and rescue has a booth." The festival was a combination beer-tasting and fundraiser for local charities, one of several held throughout the year. Search and rescue volunteers ran a booth to sell T-shirts and collect donations. "I think Eldon and I are working the same shift."

"Then I'll see you. Though I'm working my own booth. Or rather, Chris Mercer and I are splitting a booth to sell my jewelry and her art."

"Good luck," Dalton said. "I hope you sell out." If he did have a girlfriend, he would buy her a pair of the earrings May made, intricate creations fashioned out of semiprecious stones and silver and copper wire.

"I'll send all the single women who stop by my booth to see you," May said. "Maybe you can interest them in more than a T-shirt."

"I thought you weren't going to play matchmaker," he said.

She smirked. "But now you've given me ideas."

Chapter Two

Eagle Mountain's Fall Festival was exactly the way Roxanne had always pictured small-town celebrations—lots of cute stalls spread out in a picturesque park, vendors selling locally themed and handmade items, charities hosting bake sales and local restaurants catering roasted corn, barbecue sandwiches and ice cream. Laughing children chased each other through the pumpkin and corn shuck decorations, and families and groups of friends tried their hands at games of skill or sipped drinks in the beer garden.

Roxanne wandered the grounds, determined to get to know her new home. She was going to smile and mingle and fight the urge to hide in her house. This was New Roxanne—the friendlier, more outgoing version. "Hey, Roxanne!"

Startled, she looked over to see the barista, May, waving to her from a booth that advertised Fine Art Jewelry and Paintings. Roxanne hurried over. "Hi, May," she said. She glanced at a display of intricately sculpted bracelets, necklaces and earrings. "Is this your work?"

"It is," May said. "And the paintings are by my friend Chris. Chris, come meet Roxanne. She's new in town."

A woman with cobalt blue hair and full sleeve tattoos turned toward them. "Hi, Roxanne," she said. "Welcome to Eagle Mountain."

"Your work is so beautiful." Roxanne touched the edge of a canvas that depicted a fairylike figure stepping into a mountain stream.

"Thanks," Chris said. "What kind of work do you do?"

"Nothing like this," she said. "Just computer stuff. IT."

"Oh my gosh. You have to meet our friend Dalton," May said. "He's another computer genius."

"Oh. I'm not a genius." Roxanne took a step back, but May was already leaning out of the booth and calling to someone across the way. "Dalton, come over here!" She motioned him toward them.

And then Roxanne was face-to-face with a sandy-haired man with black-framed glasses and a tentative smile. "Hello," he said, and the word touched Roxanne like a caress.

"This is Roxanne," May said. "She's new in town. And she's a computer geek like you. Roxanne, this is my friend Dalton Ames."

Dalton looked sideways at May, who was grinning at them. Then he shifted his gaze to Roxanne once more. "It's nice to meet you," he said. "What brings you to Eagle Mountain?"

Roxanne had planned an answer for this question. She was going to say she had always loved the mountains and now that she had a job where she could live anywhere, she had decided to make Eagle Mountain home. But that rehearsed speech vanished and what came out instead was, "I wanted to make a fresh start. This seemed like a good place to do it."

"Ooh, I bet there's a story there," May said.

"Mom!" A slender girl with long, dark brown hair barreled across the park toward them and skidded to a stop beside Chris. "Hey, Dalton," she said. "Hey, May." She looked at Roxanne. "Hello."

"Roxanne, this is my daughter, Serena." Chris hugged the little girl against her. "Serena, this is Roxanne."

"I like your name," Serena said.

"Thank you," Roxanne said. "I like your name, too."

"What do you need, sweetheart?" Chris asked.

"Can I have money for a snow cone?" Serena asked. "Please?"

"Didn't your dad give you money for the carnival this morning?" Chris asked.

"But I spent that already," Serena said. "And I haven't had a snow cone yet."

"Here." Dalton reached into his pocket and pulled out a piece of colored paper. "I have an extra ticket I'm not going to use."

"Dalton, you don't have to do that," Chris protested.

"It's okay," he said.

"Thank you," Serena said. She took the ticket and skipped away.

"That was sweet of you," Chris said. "Thank you."

He waved away her words, then turned back to Roxanne. "I hope you like it here," he said. "I have to get back to the search and rescue booth. I hope I see you around." He nodded, a gesture that seemed old-fashioned and courtly, and made her heart skip a beat.

"He's cute, isn't he?" May leaned close and kept her voice low. "Some people think his twin, Carter, has more charisma, but I think Dalton has that quiet smolder going on."

Chris laughed. "Don't let Eldon hear you say that."

"Eldon Ramsey has my heart." May clasped her hands to her chest. "But that doesn't mean the rest of me doesn't notice a cute guy with a smolder."

Roxanne wouldn't have said Dalton Ames was exactly smoldering, but she had definitely felt some heat there.

She shook herself. It didn't matter. Starting over did not mean diving right into a relationship. She needed to get the rest of her life in order first. She could change some things about herself, but not that. She would never stop being careful.

"Who was the brunette you were talking to?" Eldon asked as soon as Dalton returned to the search and rescue booth. "I don't think I've seen her around before."

"Her name is Roxanne. Apparently she's new in town." He cut his eyes at his fellow SAR volunteer. At six-four and over two hundred pounds, Eldon Ramsey was an imposing figure, but he also had a reputation as a jokester. "I think your girlfriend was trying to set me up," Dalton said.

Eldon laughed, a booming sound. "May is a romantic. If you're not interested, just tell her to back off."

Dalton busied himself refolding a stack of T-shirts shoppers had pawed through. It wasn't that he wanted to remain single, but he didn't like people thinking he was desperate.

"Hey, there. I was hoping I'd run into you again."

The redhead from the coffee shop leaned over and put a hand on his shoulder. She shaped her lips into a pout. "Don't tell me you don't remember me."

"I remember you," he said. "It's Debra, right?"

She beamed. "And how did you know my name? Were you asking about me?"

"Um, May, the barista, told me."

"I'm flattered. Now it's only fair you tell me your name."

"Um, Dalton." She was obviously flirting, but he couldn't think of anything clever to say. Why was he so bad at this?

"I saw you talking to the brunette over there." She gestured to May and Chris's booth, across the way. "Is she your girlfriend?"

"No! I mean, I don't even know her."

"I thought the two of you looked very friendly."

"I only talked with her a few seconds."

Debra shrugged. "I don't really know her, either. We ran into each other at the coffee shop. I try to be friendly with everyone but she was downright rude."

The woman he had met hadn't been rude. Just…reserved.

Like him. Though come to think of it, he had been accused before of being rude also. Too quiet. Standoffish. "Not everyone has an easy time talking to strangers," he said. "I think she's new in town."

"So am I." She leaned across the counter, flashing a bit of cleavage. He forced his gaze up. "Care to show me around?" she asked.

"Um, I have to work the booth right now."

She laughed, a musical sound. "I didn't mean right now, silly." She picked up one of the shirts he had just folded and shook it out. "Eagle Mountain Search and Rescue," she said, reading the logo on the front. "I take it you're part of the group."

"Yeah. We both are." He gestured to Eldon, who was busy making change for a customer on the other side of the booth.

"That's so heroic," she said.

"No," he said. "I'm just trying to help."

"You'll have to tell me about it some time."

Again, he couldn't think of a thing to say. Whereas men like his brother were always able to come up with a glib remark, it took Dalton a while to organize his thoughts. By the time he found the right words, it was often too late.

An older couple approached and he turned to greet them. They asked about search and rescue and ended up making a donation. When Dalton turned back, Debra was gone.

Eldon moved over to join him when the older couple had left. "Who was the redhead?" he asked.

"Her name is Debra." He refolded the shirt she had left lying on the counter.

"I overheard some of what she said. She was really into you."

"I don't know why. She's doesn't even know me."

"She doesn't have to know you to be attracted to you. May and I didn't know each other when I asked her out."

May and Eldon seemed like such a good couple. Really in sync. "Why did you ask her out?"

"Because she's hot." He laughed. "Hey, if you like a woman, ask her out. Maybe it doesn't work out, but maybe it will."

Why was everyone after him to go out with someone? Was his mother bribing his friends to talk to him about his monk-like existence?

The arrival of Ryan Welch and his partner, Deni Traynor, interrupted his thoughts. "We're here to take over," Deni—her light brown hair in two short braids—announced. She propped her sunglasses on top of her head, revealing blue-green eyes. "Anything we need to know?"

"Did you sell any shirts?" Ryan, with the lean, muscular build of a dedicated rock climber and short brown hair just peeking from beneath an EMSAR ball cap, asked.

"It's been kind of slow," Eldon said. "We sold three T-shirts and collected forty dollars in donations."

"Deni and I will see if we can do better than that," Ryan said.

"Looks like Carter and Caleb pulled in the most money today," Deni said as she scanned the day's log.

"No surprise there," Dalton said. "We always said Carter could sell sand in the Sahara."

"You two are twins," Ryan said. "Shouldn't you have the same gift for gab?"

"We have different personalities," Dalton said. He smirked. "Carter got all the charm, but I got the smarts."

"Go, boy genius." Deni made a shooing motion.

Dalton and Eldon left—Eldon to join May in her booth and Dalton to the parking lot. His big plans for the evening included video games, then a little work on an update on the reservation program he had designed.

Nothing wrong with spending a Saturday night in, he told

himself. It wasn't the image most people had of a single twentysomething. But he liked his own company. He preferred it even, much of the time. He could go out anytime he liked. Debra would have accepted his invitation.

But he didn't want to go out with Debra. Roxanne, on the other hand... She was even prettier than Debra, but quiet, like him. She had struck Dalton as a little sad. Maybe he could cheer her up, or at least listen while she talked. He was good at listening. But if she didn't want that, maybe they could just be with each other, without a lot of expectations.

Once the idea was planted, he couldn't shake it. He wanted to go out with Roxanne.

It figured. The first woman who had interested him in, well, a long time, and he didn't even know her last name or how to find her.

ROXANNE ENDED UP buying the fairy painting and a pair of earrings from May and Chris's booth. From there she had moved on to purchase a mug from a local potter, homemade jelly from the 4-H club, herbal tea from someone else and cookies from the high school cheerleaders. Satisfied that she had done her part to support local causes, she carried her purchases to her car and set out for home.

In keeping with her goal of making a fresh start, the place she had rented was unlike anywhere else she had lived. It was small—a genuine tiny home—and resembled a cross between an old-fashioned train caboose and a child's playhouse. It had dark green siding and cream-colored trim, and a cupola bedroom with a stained glass window. The front porch was large enough to hold a single chair and a doormat, and the whole thing was parked in a clearing in the woods seven miles from town. The rental agent had described the place as "remote and quirky"—two adjectives Roxanne couldn't help noting could also be applied to her.

The road to the house was narrow and winding, with a steep drop-off on one side. Roxanne didn't look forward to trying to negotiate the route in the dark, but she hoped by the time she had to do so, she would be so familiar with the route she didn't have to worry about driving off over the side.

She was about five miles from home, half lost in thoughts of what she might make for dinner, when she became aware of a vehicle behind her. It was approaching fast and had on its bright lights, despite the fact that it was still full daylight. There must be some kind of emergency. She searched for a place to pull over to let the other driver pass, but there was none. Thick trees closed her in on the left, and the steep canyon dropped off less than three feet from the right side of her car.

She tapped her brakes. Maybe the other driver didn't realize how close they were to her. But the vehicle—a truck, she decided—kept coming. She flinched as its horn blared, the raucous sound insisting she move out of the way. But there was nowhere for her to go. She gripped the wheel so tightly her arms ached and sped up as much as she dared. But no matter how fast she drove, the truck behind her kept gaining.

Roxanne's car skidded around a curve and she struggled to get back on the road. "Slow down!" she shouted, though she knew the other driver couldn't hear her. Her back right tire dropped onto the gravel shoulder again and she fought the steering wheel. Then a terrible jolt shook her as the truck collided with her car, and she lost control entirely, her windshield shattering and the seat belt biting painfully into her upper body, a silent scream ripping through her, along with a sudden, blinding pain.

Chapter Three

Dalton didn't know if this was the most foolish thing he had ever done, but it had to rank up there. Carter probably would have laughed him out of the room, and his sister, Bethany, would have given him that pitying look he had seen other women give men who did useless things. His oldest brother, Aaron, would have probably cited some law he was breaking—harassment, or stalking maybe. But Eldon had told him if he liked a woman he should go ahead and ask her out, so that's what he was doing.

Except first he had to find Roxanne. He remembered May had mentioned Roxanne was renting one of the tiny houses on Robbie Lusk's ranch. Hannah Gwynn, a search and rescue volunteer whose day job was as a paramedic, had mentioned going on a call to that neighborhood a few weeks ago. "There's six of these houses, each one a different color, one after the other out on County Road 3," Hannah had said. All he had to do was knock on doors until he found the right one.

He drove slowly along the winding, narrow road. Through the trees lining the road, he caught glimpses of the drop-off on the right. There were probably some spectacular views, maybe even some good climbing, in that canyon. But he couldn't take his eyes off the road long enough to scout things out. He had no idea how far out the tiny houses were and didn't want to miss them. How tiny were they, exactly? Big enough for a grown person to live in, but what if they were hidden from the road behind all these trees?

He should probably turn around, he thought, even as he kept driving. What was Roxanne going to say when he showed up at her house? That was stalker behavior, right? She would probably call the sheriff. Who could blame her? He really needed to turn around now.

Lights up ahead distracted him. He leaned forward, straining for a better look. There were two cars. One of them was tilted at an odd angle, way over to the right. The other wasn't a car, but a truck. The kind with a lifted body, oversize tires and big welded bumpers.

Dalton slowed, then stopped in the road next to the scene. The car was on its side, balanced on the edge of the road, caught by a sturdy pine rooted in the side of the canyon. The truck was still running, the driver's door open. He spotted a man up on the side of the car, trying to wrench open the driver's door.

Dalton moved his Jeep over and parked, then got out and jogged toward the wreck. "Wait!" he called out to the driver of the truck. "I'm calling for help." As he ran, he pulled out his phone and punched in 911. He thought he heard someone answer, but the call immediately dropped. A check of the phone showed a very weak signal. He thumbed open his search and rescue app and typed in a message, asking for help and reporting a motor vehicle accident and his location.

Meanwhile, the man from the truck had ceased pulling at the door of the car. "Who are you?" he demanded.

"I'm with Eagle Mountain Search and Rescue," Dalton said. "Let me help."

He started toward the man and the car, but the man jumped down and barreled into him, knocking him to the ground.

"Hey!" Dalton struggled to rise. The man raced past him, jumped in the truck and sped away.

"Help! Is someone there? Please help."

The woman's voice was weak, but clear. Dalton stood and made his way to stand beside the car. "Help is on the way," he said. "Where are you hurt?"

"My head," she said. "And my shoulder. I'm caught in the seat belt. Please help me."

"Try not to move too much," he said. "We need to secure your vehicle before we can get you out of there." Though the RAV4 rested against the trunk of the pine tree, movement the wrong way could send it plummeting into the canyon. Dalton needed to wait for more help to arrive. They would assess the situation and work together to secure the vehicle, free the woman and get her to treatment for her injuries. But meanwhile, he needed to keep her calm.

"Are you by yourself?" she called.

"There was another man here, but he left," Dalton said. "But more help will be here soon."

"The other man…do you know who he was?"

"No, I didn't recognize him."

She fell silent and he wondered if she had lost consciousness. "Are you still with me?" he called.

"Yes, I'm here."

"What's your name?" he asked.

"Roxanne. Roxanne Byrne."

The name jolted him. "Roxanne! It's Dalton Ames! May introduced us this afternoon. What happened?"

"I don't know. I was driving home, then this car came up behind me. It was going really fast, not stopping at all. And it just hit me. Just slammed into me…" Her voice faded and he wondered if she had lost consciousness.

"Stay with me, Roxanne," he said.

"Did you see what happened?" she asked.

"No, I came up right after it happened, I think," he said. "There was a truck here when I arrived. And a man. He was trying to open your door. But when I approached, he ran away."

She moaned, a sound of such pain he had to fight not to climb onto the car and go to her. "Roxanne, what is it?" he called. "What's wrong?"

She said nothing, but he could hear her sobbing. The sound tore at him. "Roxanne, talk to me. Are you in pain? Is that why you're crying?"

"I… I'm not in pain," she managed between sobs. "Not much. Just…afraid."

"Don't be afraid," he said. "You're safe now. I promise I'll stay with you."

"Thank you." She fell silent, no longer crying, but not saying anything, either. Dalton tried to think how to soothe her, or at least distract her. Carter would have known what to say. He would have told a funny story or asked her to tell one to him. But Dalton couldn't carry off that kind of charm.

"I'm still here," he said. "I promise I won't leave you alone."

"Okay."

She didn't seem to want to say more, so he didn't force a conversation. Long minutes passed with only the ticking of their cooling vehicle engines breaking the silence. Then he heard a siren, the wail growing louder and louder as it approached. "Help is here!" he called to Roxanne. "We'll have you out soon."

Then he jogged to the road to meet them.

Search and rescue captain Danny Irwin was first out of the specially outfitted search and rescue Jeep. Eldon, Ryan and Deni climbed out after him. A second car disgorged Carter, Caleb, Sheri Stevens and Harper Vernon. Sheri was a veteran volunteer, known for her climbing prowess, while

Harper was a newer volunteer, like Dalton and his siblings. "Who's manning the SAR booth at the fair?" Dalton asked.

"May and Hannah are taking care of it," Danny said. Hannah had taken temporary leave from SAR until after her baby was born.

Danny surveyed the RAV4 balanced against the tree. "What happened?" he asked.

"She says someone ran her off the road. When I got here there was a truck parked—lifted, with oversize tires and big welded bumpers. A man was trying to open the driver's door, but when he saw me, he jumped down, shoved me to the ground and ran away."

"Maybe he was trying to help, but when you showed up, he was afraid of being arrested," Caleb said.

"Have you talked to the driver of the Toyota?" Danny asked.

"Her name is Roxanne Byrne," Dalton said. "She just moved to town. I think she lives in one of the tiny houses out here somewhere. She said her head and her shoulder hurt. I hated not being able to help her, but I thought I should wait for you guys."

"Good thing you did," Eldon said. "That car needs to be secured before anyone goes near it." He hefted a heavy chain he had already pulled from the rescue Jeep. "Ryan and I will take care of that."

"You can help me with the litter," Caleb said to Dalton.

In the midst of a rescue, Dalton seldom thought about the roles everyone played but later, when he was reviewing all that had happened, he was struck by how they all worked together to do the many small jobs that needed to be done to make a rescue go as smoothly as possible. As soon as Ryan and Eldon had set anchors and fastened chains to hold the RAV4 in place, someone else took a chain saw and cut away branches of the pine tree that blocked access to the side doors.

Other people gathered medical equipment and Danny, a registered nurse, climbed up to make the initial assessment of the driver.

"She hit her head," he reported a few moments later. "There's some bleeding, maybe a concussion. Sounds like she wrenched her shoulder in the crash, possibly due to the seat belt or the airbag. Some minor scratches and bruising. She says there's no spinal or lower body injury, but we'll want to be sure. Let's see if we can get the door open and get her into a neck brace."

Eldon, with the aid of a pry bar, was able to wrench the door open. Rescuers swarmed in and around, applying protective gear and helping to ease Roxanne out of the driver's seat and onto a waiting litter, which was carefully lowered to the ground. Dalton handled one end of the litter, watching her pale face against her dark hair. She looked frightened but alert. Not in extreme pain. Then Danny moved in to complete his examination and Dalton stepped back to make room.

"I'm not finding any other injuries," Danny said after a moment. "Would you like to sit up?"

"Yes, please."

He took her hand and helped her sit. She looked around at all of them, until her gaze came to rest on Dalton. She relaxed a little bit then. "I'm so glad you came along when you did," she said.

"Can you tell us what happened?" Danny asked.

She turned her attention to him. "I was driving home when a vehicle came up behind me, very fast. It plowed into me and ran me off the road."

"Should we get a sheriff's deputy out here?" Dalton asked. He had moved closer, wanting Roxanne to know he was keeping his promise to stay near her.

"Ryker radioed he's on his way," Sheri said. "If he doesn't

get here before the ambulance, he can interview her at the hospital."

Ryker Vernon was a Rayford County sheriff's deputy—and Harper's husband.

He arrived just ahead of the ambulance, and Roxanne repeated her story for him. Her voice was steadier this time.

"Do you know who the other driver was?" Ryker asked.

She hesitated, and Dalton saw the pain cross her face. "I… I'm not sure," she said.

"But you thought you recognized him?" Ryker prompted.

"I did. But it can't possibly be him." She shook her head. "It must be my imagination."

"Who do you think it might be?" Ryker asked.

Roxanne ran her tongue over her swollen bottom lip. "This man has been in prison almost fifteen years."

Dalton blinked. Roxanne knew someone in prison? Someone who would do something like run her off the road?

"Maybe he got out of prison," Ryker said. "We can check."

She looked at Ryker, eyes wide with alarm. "That's impossible," she said. "I was told he'd never be free again."

Ryker studied her a moment. "What was your relationship to this man?" he asked, his tone more gentle.

She looked down at her lap. "His name is William Ledger," she said.

Dalton had to strain to hear the words. Even then, he wasn't sure he heard her right. The name didn't mean anything to him.

Ryker's expression grew grim. He closed his notebook and stood. "I'll check on Ledger for you and we'll talk more later," he said. "In the meantime, let's get you the medical care you need."

The ambulance pulled up and Roxanne was loaded in. While the others began packing gear, Dalton found Ryker. "Who is William Ledger?" he asked.

"I'm not sure," Ryker said. "If he's who I think he is, she's right—he went to prison a long time ago and shouldn't be out."

"What did he do?"

"I don't want to say until I know for sure. You were first on scene, right?"

"Yes. And there was a man here. An older man with short, graying blond hair and a mustache. He drove a lifted pickup truck with oversize tires and welded iron bumpers front and rear."

"How old was he?"

"I don't know. I'm not good at guessing ages. Maybe late forties. Early fifties?"

"How tall?"

"Shorter than me. Stocky—with broad shoulders. Maybe five-eight or five-nine."

"Can you tell me his eye color? Any distinguishing characteristics?"

Dalton shook his head. "No. I didn't see him that long."

"Did he have an accent? What did he sound like?"

"He asked me who I was—or rather, he demanded to know. But I didn't hear any particular accent. I told him I was with search and rescue and he glared at me, shoved me over, ran to his truck and drove away." Dalton looked in the direction of the retreating ambulance. "What is this all about?"

"Roxanne may be the only one who can answer that question."

He wanted to see Roxanne again, but after today, would she want to see him? Maybe she would associate him with an upsetting incident. Once again, he had no idea what to say. Computers were so much easier to figure out than other people.

"YOU DON'T HAVE a concussion. That's good news." The emergency room doctor, a young Hispanic woman with a braid of

black hair and kind eyes, smiled at Roxanne. "You're probably going to be pretty sore, but rest, ice and anti-inflammato-
ries should help your shoulder feel better in a couple of weeks.
See your regular doctor if you have any further problems."

"I don't have a regular doctor," Roxanne said. "I just
moved here."

"Then make an appointment with the clinic in Eagle
Mountain. They should be able to help you." The doctor
stood, preparing to leave. "Do you have someone who can
pick you up and take you home?"

No. She had no one. Knew no one. "I'll find someone,"
she said. A taxi or an Uber, maybe? Did they have those in
Eagle Mountain?

The doctor left. Roxanne sat on the side of the gurney,
wondering what to do. She ached all over, but worse was
the fear that made her heart gallop every time she closed her
eyes and remembered William Ledger's face. He had been
smiling—the way he used to smile. Pretending to be so caring, but he had never cared about anything but making her
do what he wanted. She would never forget that smile, even
if it was set in an older face.

"Ms. Byrne? There's someone here to see you." She
opened her eyes and saw a slight man in scrubs looking at
her curiously. She looked past him and recognized Dalton
Ames. He wasn't wearing the black-framed glasses he had
on when she had first met him, but was otherwise the same.
"Dalton?" She stood. "What are you doing here?"

"Danny told me you probably wouldn't be kept at the hospital," he said. "So I came to see how you were doing. I
thought you might need a ride home."

"Yes, I need a ride. That…that's so thoughtful. How did
you…?" She frowned and shook her head. "I remember now.
You were there. By my car. Talking to me."

"I'm sorry I couldn't climb up there and get you out right

away," he said. "But it wouldn't have been safe for either of us."

She shuddered, thinking how precarious her position must have been. "Just knowing someone was there, and that help was on the way, was good," she said. "Thank you."

"How are you doing?" he asked.

"I'm sore, but the doctor says I don't have a concussion."

"Still, something like that must have shaken you up," he said. When she didn't reply right away, he added, "But you don't have to talk about it if you don't want to."

She nodded. "Thanks for understanding." Of course he was curious. People always were. But once they knew what had happened to her, they always saw her differently. She didn't want that with this man. Not yet.

"When you're ready, we can go," he said.

He waited while she gathered her belongings, then an aide with a wheelchair transported her to the hospital's front door, where she was allowed to stand and walk on her own. Dalton hovered at her side. He didn't touch her, but she sensed he was prepared to catch her if she started to fall. It was comforting, having him standing there.

She felt a little unsteady, but she didn't fall, and soon they were standing beside a bright red Jeep with *Alpine Jeep Tours* stenciled in the back window. "My parents own a Jeep tour and rental business," he said when he noticed her reading the sign. "I guide for them and usually drive one of our fleet when I'm not working."

"So, you give guided tours?" she asked.

"Yeah." He offered a shy smile. "Maybe I can give you a tour sometime, since you're new to the area. We take people into the mountains, show them the scenery, visit ghost towns and old mines and share some of the history of the area."

"I thought you worked in IT," she said. Wasn't that what May had said?

"I handle all the computer stuff for the Jeep business." He held the passenger door open for her and she slid in, then he walked around to the driver's seat. "And I design software. I designed the reservation system my parents use, and the via ferrata across town is using it now. Of course, my sister is marrying the owner of that place, so it's not like it was a hard sell. But I've got other businesses interested in it. And right now I'm working on software for first responders. Eagle Mountain Search and Rescue is beta testing the program."

She heard the excitement about his work in his voice and the touch of pride. "That's great that you're able to take your experience with search and rescue and Jeep rentals and use it to tailor software to the needs of those endeavors," she said. "It's technical, but it's also really creative."

"Well, sure," he said. "People who think tech isn't creative don't know anything about it."

"People I know never understand why I find writing code interesting," she said. "I try to tell them it's all about finding ways to solve real problems, but they don't see it."

"Oh, I get that, too," Dalton said. "Everybody cares about the results of what we do, but their eyes glaze over if I try to explain how it's done."

For the rest of the drive to Eagle Mountain, they discussed the ins and outs of software development, testing and troubleshooting. Roxanne began to relax. Work was the one area in her life where she rarely second-guessed herself. Coding was logical and predictable, unlike other people.

But she fell silent as they neared the scene of her accident, her body tensing as her mind replayed the moments before the collision. Dalton glanced over at her. "That must have been terrifying," he said. "Being run off the road."

"Yes." She had a hard time getting the word out, the muscles of her throat had clenched so tightly.

"But you survived it," he said. "You're going to be okay."

She closed her eyes, the words the same ones she had told herself so many times, especially in the early days, after she had escaped from Ledger. "You're right," she whispered. "I'm a survivor."

He didn't ask what she had survived beyond the accident. He didn't ask about the man who had driven the truck, or why the sight of him had shook her so. He didn't tell her why she shouldn't be afraid or how she needed to put the past behind her. He merely listened and…accepted.

She directed him to her house. When he turned into the driveway she indicated, they had to maneuver around a large moving van. "What's going on?" she asked, alarm clear in her voice.

"Is that your house?" he asked, indicating a blue-and-white building about the size of a garden shed.

"No, mine is the green house over there." She pointed across the drive. "I guess I have a new neighbor."

A petite woman with bright red hair emerged from the blue house. She looked their way, then started toward them. Dalton rolled down the window. "Sorry about the moving truck," she said. "They should be gone in half an hour or so." She glanced from Dalton to Roxanne. "Are you my neighbors?"

"I am." Roxanne leaned forward. "I'm Roxanne."

"I'm Kara. Kara Lee." Kara's smile was tentative. "I'm glad there's someone else out here," she said. "I've been a little nervous about living somewhere so remote."

"I've only been here a few days myself," Roxanne said. "But it's very peaceful."

"That's good to hear." Kara glanced over her shoulder. "I'd better help get the rest of my things unloaded. But I'll see you around a lot, I'm sure."

"It was good to meet you," Roxanne said.

Dalton continued up the driveway and pulled the Jeep close to the door. "She seemed nice," he said.

"She did." Roxanne sighed. "It's kind of a relief to have someone in that house now. Like she said, it doesn't feel so isolated."

Dalton turned his attention to her house. "This is a cute place," he said.

"I like it." She put her hand on the door to open it, but didn't move right away. "Thanks for the ride," she said. "I wasn't sure how I was going to get home."

"I was actually on my way to see you when I came upon the wreck," he said. "I mean, I was looking for your place, hoping to find you."

She frowned. "Why?"

"Because I wanted to ask you out."

He couldn't have surprised her more if he had told her he was from another planet. Not that men hadn't asked her out before, but Dalton didn't even know her. "Oh."

He shifted to face her more. "So, maybe my timing is terrible, but do you want to go out sometime? Get dinner or something?"

She opened her mouth. Closed it again. She was tempted to say yes, but she knew very little about him. And he knew even less about her. Once he heard her whole story, he was liable to run in the opposite direction. It had happened before. Best to save them both the trouble. "I need to hold off on dating anyone right now," she said. "Until I get some things settled in my life."

What was she thinking, inviting more questions? She braced herself to come up with an explanation of what she needed to settle. *Everything* didn't seem an appropriate answer.

"Yeah, I get it. Bad timing." He shoved his hands in his pockets. "Forget I asked."

His awkwardness charmed her. "I won't forget," she said. "And I hope I'll see you again."

His eyes brightened and she felt that look in the pit of her stomach. Smolder, May had called it. Was that what this feeling was? Not burning, but an unfamiliar warmth.

"Yeah," he said. "I'd like that."

"Yes." She opened the car door, but still didn't get out.

"Will you be okay?" he asked. "Here by yourself?"

"Yes." She had good locks, and she knew how to defend herself. She would be all right. Ledger was devious and even dangerous, but she also knew something else about him. The man was a coward.

But Roxanne—when it really mattered, Roxanne was brave. She was a survivor.

Chapter Four

William "Billy" Ledger is an American convicted sex of-
fender, child rapist and kidnapper infamously known for com-
mitting the abductions of a nine-year-old girl he renamed
"Alice" in 2006 in San Antonio, Texas, and a ten-year-old girl
he called "Mary" in 2009 in Corpus Christi, Texas. He was
discovered and apprehended when "Mary" escaped and ran
to a store where she called police. She led law enforcement
to the house where she and "Alice" had been held captive.
He was convicted in 2010 and sentenced to life in prison.

The Monday after Roxanne's accident, Dalton sat on his
sofa, researching William Ledger, the man Roxanne thought
had run her off the road. He read through the Wikipedia
entry twice, a pain in the pit of his stomach and anger tightening his chest. How did Roxanne know a man like William
Ledger? Was she Alice? Or Mary? How had such a horrible
thing happened to her?

He closed the screen and sat back. No wonder Roxanne
had been so upset, if she thought her former kidnapper was
the man who had run her off the road. But that couldn't be
right, could it? The article said William Ledger had been
sentenced to prison for life.

He leaned forward and began searching further, but could
find nothing more about William Ledger. Maybe he could

have dug deeper and eventually found what he wanted, but he had a faster way of getting information. He pulled out his phone and punched in a number.

"I'm working, Dalton. What do you want?" His oldest brother picked up, his voice clipped and no-nonsense, but that was Aaron every day of the week.

"Do you know who William Ledger is?" Dalton asked.

A pause, then Aaron's tone was sharper. "Why are you asking about him?"

"I was first on the scene at Roxanne Byrne's accident yesterday," Dalton said. "I heard her say she thought the person who ran her off the road might have been William Ledger. I just finished reading the Wikipedia entry about him."

"Then why are you calling me?"

"Because you're a sheriff's deputy and you can tell me how a man who was sentenced to life in prison could possibly be running around free."

Aaron blew out a breath. "Ledger was paroled two weeks ago. But you didn't hear that from me. We don't want word to get out that we're looking for him."

"How is that possible? I read what he did to those girls." The article had been mercifully short on details, but Dalton could imagine, and anything he thought of probably wasn't as bad as what had really happened.

"His attorney appealed and his sentence was lowered due to some legal technicality and he was credited for time served and released," Aaron said.

"So it could have been him who went after Roxanne?"

"Doubtful. He was in prison in Texas. Roxanne is here. She's changed her name and kept a low profile."

Dalton swallowed. He didn't want to ask, but he wanted to know. "Was she one of the girls he kidnapped—Alice or Mary?"

"If you want to know that, you should ask her."

"I'm asking you. Was she?"

Another sigh. "She was. Her lawyers and the court did a good job of keeping the girls' real names out of the press and Roxanne has never done an interview about it. I don't know how Ledger would have found her."

"But what if he did find her?" Dalton asked. "What does he want with her?"

"Who knows what a person like that is thinking? Look—don't go telling this to anyone. Not only is it nobody's business, but the more people who know Roxanne's story, the more danger she might be in."

"What kind of jerk do you take me for?"

"You're not a jerk. It's just a touchy situation. I only told you because you're the only person other than Roxanne who saw the guy. We don't know how he feels about that, so watch your back."

Dalton swallowed. It hadn't crossed his mind that he might be in danger.

"I read your statement, but is there anything about this guy you left out?" Aaron asked.

"No." He closed his eyes, trying to replay those few minutes by the side of the road. "He was yanking on the door pretty hard. I thought it was because he was in a hurry to get the driver out of the car."

"Maybe he was," Aaron said. "But not necessarily for a good reason. That is, if it even was Ledger. Has the sheriff contacted you yet?"

"No."

"He wants you to come by the office and look at some photos. See if you recognize the man."

"Sure. I can do that. I have a tour this afternoon."

"Let Carter or Dad do it. This is more important."

"What am I supposed to tell Mom?" Dalton asked. "She'll freak if I tell her I have to be at the sheriff's office."

"Tell her it's search and rescue business."

"Bethany and Carter are with SAR, too."

"I'll call her and tell her I need your help with something," Aaron said. "Official business."

"That will make her even more curious."

"You know how to evade Mom's and Dad's questions by now. Just get over here."

"All right."

Instead of phoning his parents, Dalton called Clayton Kinneson, a retiree who filled in giving tours during their busiest season. "Clayton, can you take my one o'clock tour today?" he asked. "Something came up."

"Sure, I can do that," Clayton said. "Is everything all right?"

"It's fine. I just had an appointment I forgot about. I really appreciate it."

"No problem. I'm always happy for the extra money."

That difficulty handled, Dalton drove to the sheriff's department. As he turned into the alley leading to the parking lot, he passed a white sedan. The woman behind the wheel looked like Roxanne, but she didn't see him wave. He parked and went inside.

An older woman with short, spiky hair, red-framed glasses and dangling earrings greeted him. "You must be Dalton," she said. "All of you Ames brothers are like peas in a pod."

"You really think so?" he asked. He and Carter might be identical, but Aaron definitely took after their father.

"You all have that same look in your eyes," she said. "Like you're plotting something."

"Dalton isn't plotting anything." Aaron spoke from a doorway to their left. He motioned to Dalton. "Come on back."

He followed Aaron to a small, gray room. Before Dalton had a chance to take a seat at the table there, the sheriff entered. Sheriff Travis Walker was tall and lean, with dark hair and chiseled features. He had a reputation for being firm but fair. "Hello, Dalton," he said and shook Dalton's hand. "Thanks for coming in. Have a seat."

Dalton sat, and the sheriff opened the file folder he had been carrying. "We're recording this," he said, and nodded to the overhead camera. He recited the date and time and the names of everyone present, then turned his attention back to Dalton. "I'm going to lay out a group of photographs. I want you to look at them all carefully and decide if any of them are the man you saw beside Roxanne Byrne's car yesterday. The suspect we're looking for may or may not be in this group of photos, so don't feel like you have to select one of them. Only tell us if you're sure the man you saw is one of the faces I'm going to show you. Do you have any questions?"

"No, sir." Dalton wiped his hands on the thighs of his jeans, suddenly nervous.

Travis laid out six black-and-white photos on the table. Dalton leaned forward and studied each of them. He had expected to feel something if he recognized the man he had seen yesterday—some *zing* of recognition. Instead, he felt nothing.

"Do you see the man?" Aaron asked after a moment.

Dalton sat back and shook his head. "I don't recognize any of them. I only saw his face for a few seconds. He was wearing a hat. And he had a mustache." The men in the photos were all clean-shaven. Still, he ought to be able to recognize him, shouldn't he?

Travis gave no indication that he was disappointed. He began gathering up the photos. "Thank you for coming in," he said again.

"Was William Ledger's photo one of those?" Dalton asked. "Does that mean I didn't see him?"

"He might have been wearing a disguise," Aaron said. "Or Roxanne could have been attacked by someone else."

"Do you remember any part of the license plate number

of the vehicle?" Travis asked. "Or anything else about the vehicle?"

"No. It was just a big pickup truck with after-market welded bumpers."

"We're looking for trucks like that with any front-end damage, but it's possible with a bumper like that there isn't any," Aaron said.

"I wish I remembered more," Dalton said. "But I was focused on the accident. I thought this guy was just a bystander trying to help."

"Come on," Aaron said. "I'll walk you out."

They headed back down the hallway. "Does Roxanne know Ledger is out of prison?" Dalton asked.

"We told her this morning."

"How did she take it?"

"She was pretty upset." Aaron stopped at the door leading to the lobby. "Why are you so interested in Roxanne?" he asked. "I didn't know you two knew each other."

"We don't. May Delgado introduced us at the fair Saturday morning, then I was first on scene at the accident Saturday afternoon."

"You were the one who made the 911 call," Aaron said. "How did that happen?"

"I was driving in that area and saw the wreck."

"What were you doing out on County Road 3?"

Dalton scowled. "Do they teach you how to grill people at the law enforcement academy?"

"Just answer the question."

He shoved his hands in his pockets. "I was looking for Roxanne. I'd heard she lived in one of those tiny houses and thought I'd look her up, maybe ask her out."

Aaron grinned. "I'm betting that's a first."

"What do you mean by that?"

"You're not exactly a Don Juan. Not that there's anything wrong with that. This woman must have really got to you."

"Yeah, well, now this has happened and she's here in a place where she knows hardly anyone. I feel for her."

Aaron put a hand on his shoulder. "She could probably use a friend. Just…go slow. She's been through a lot."

He shook off his brother's hand. "Just because I'm not dating every woman I see doesn't mean I don't know how to behave."

"Still, I think Roxanne is a special case," Aaron said. But he relented and opened the door.

Dalton mulled over Aaron's words as he drove to his apartment. He thought he knew what Aaron had been trying to say. Roxanne had suffered a lot at a young age. That had to have affected her. But she had come here to make a fresh start. Because of what happened all those years ago or because of something else? He wanted to know. He felt drawn to her. She was quiet, like him, and reserved. Debra had called her rude, but he didn't think that was true. Roxanne struggled with people, the way he did. Maybe he could help her with that—and she could help him.

ROXANNE PACED. TEN STEPS to one end of her tiny home, ten steps back. She nibbled at her thumbnail and replayed the conversation she had had with Sheriff Walker that morning over and over. William Ledger was free—his life sentence shortened to only fifteen years. Because of some clerical error? No one seemed clear on that part but it didn't really matter: The end result was the same—William Ledger was a free man. Free to hurt other children. Free to hurt her.

The sheriff had been gentle. Sympathetic. Everyone was, once they learned her story—that of a poor child who had survived a terrible experience.

But she wasn't a child anymore. What had happened to

her would always be part of her, but she didn't want it to define her. She didn't want people thinking about it every time they looked at her.

She stopped and took a deep breath. Now that she knew Ledger was out there, she could watch for him. She had trained to defend herself—martial arts classes and long hours at a shooting range. Most of all, she had learned to be aware. To be skeptical of people's motives and to trust her instincts. Some people would argue that made her a cynic, but she preferred to believe it made her safe.

The sound of tires on the gravel of the driveway set her heart racing. She stood to one side of the window and peered out, and a wave of relief washed over her as she recognized the Jeep that pulled up beside the rental car she was driving until her RAV4 was repaired.

She waited until Dalton knocked before she opened the door. "Hello," she said and put one hand to her hair. When was the last time she brushed it? Did she look as harried as she felt?

His expression was somber, tight lines at the corners of his soft green eyes. "Could I come in?" he asked. "To talk?"

"Sure." She stepped aside and allowed him to pass.

He stopped just inside the door and looked around—at the built-in sofa, the table that extended from one wall and the two small chairs flanking it, at the L-shaped kitchen counter and gleaming, compact refrigerator and dishwasher, and at the stairs leading up to her loft bedroom. She had tried to make the place a home, with colorful blankets and potted geraniums, and a few framed pictures on the wall. "Nice place," he said.

She led the way to the sofa, a built-in with thick foam cushions, beneath a picture window. She sat and waited for him to tell her why he was here.

He remained standing, looking everywhere but at her. "I

just came from the sheriff's department," he said. "They wanted me to look at some photos, see if I recognized the man I saw trying to get into your car after the accident."

She swallowed. "They showed me photos, too," she said. "Did you recognize anyone?"

"No. I'm sorry."

"I couldn't be sure about the photos, either," she said. There had been one she thought might be Ledger but he was so much older now, and the man who had attacked her wore a mustache. It wasn't his appearance that made her think of Ledger, but the way he moved and the look in his eyes. A horrible, greedy look that formed ice in the pit of her stomach.

Dalton walked to the window and looked out, his back to her. She studied him. He was slender, but muscular, the T-shirt he wore stretched over strong shoulders and biceps. His sandy-brown hair curled up at the back of his neck, and he wore a knotted bracelet on one wrist. Something flared low within her as her gaze roamed over him. It had been a long time since she had been involved with a man. The last one had broken up with her because he said she made him too nervous. "You're so silent," he said. "I never know what you're thinking."

Why did a lover have to know what she was thinking? Wasn't she entitled to her own thoughts?

Dalton turned toward her once more, and she felt pressed back in her chair by the intensity of his gaze. "I looked up William Ledger online," he said.

Of course he would. Anyone would. "I didn't mean to pry," he rushed to add. "But the way you said his name… I was worried."

She had read the Wikipedia entry. The entries on true crime websites. She didn't let him ask the next question. "I was Mary," she said.

His expression changed. Instead of the pity she had expected, she read…admiration? "You're the one who got away and went for help," he said.

She nodded. No one had ever singled out that fact before. Not right away.

"That took a lot of courage," he said. "How old were you?"

"I was ten. I'd only been there three months." But it was long enough. Long enough to last a lifetime.

"I'm sorry you had to go through that," he said. "And I'm sorry to hear they let him out of prison."

"The sheriff told you that?"

"My brother did. He's a sheriff's deputy. Aaron Ames."

She remembered the deputy with dark curly hair and brown eyes. "I didn't realize he was your brother."

"The two of us don't look that much alike. Though the sheriff's office manager says we all look like we're plotting something." Amusement tugged at the corners of his mouth and flashed in his eyes.

She found herself almost smiling in return. "Are you? Plotting something?"

"I'd like to figure out how to find William Ledger and send him back where he belongs."

She didn't ask whether he meant prison or hell. She sighed. "You don't have to worry about him."

"I'm worried for you. And Aaron said I should watch my back. Ledger knows I saw him."

She sagged back against the sofa cushions, weak at the realization of the truth of his words. "I'm sure it was me he was interested in," she said. "If it even was Ledger I saw."

He sat beside her, then, his hand resting near hers, but not touching. "Why would he come after you, after so many years?"

"I'm not sure. Except…" She knotted her hands together, trying to find words for the jumbled thoughts that had been tumbling in her head since yesterday. "He always talked of me and Alice as belonging to him. Not as if we were his children, but his possessions. He owned us and we owed him for taking care of us."

He tensed, his fingers digging into the sofa cushion. "That's sick."

She nodded. "The one time he said anything to me after I escaped, he said, 'How could you leave me when I gave you everything?' Maybe that's what's driving him now. He thinks of me as his and he wants me back."

"He can't have you."

The declaration was so forceful it surprised her. Dalton Ames hardly knew her. But at the same time, she was touched by his protectiveness. She brushed her fingers against the back of his hand, like a child daring herself to get too close to a hot stove. Dalton's skin didn't burn her, but she felt the heat of him moving through her, the thrill of the contact awakening parts of her too-long dormant. "Thank you. I don't intend to let him have me."

He relaxed a little and turned to look at her again. "How do you think he found you? Aaron said you changed your name, and you just arrived in Eagle Mountain."

"I don't know. Maybe he was following me, but I think I would have noticed. I'm really careful about things like that. And maybe it wasn't even him. Maybe I just imagined it was him."

"You didn't imagine someone running you off the road," he said. "It would be a big coincidence to have a complete stranger do that. Do you really think it wasn't Ledger?"

She shook her head. "I knew it was him the moment our eyes met. The way he looked at me, and his smile..." She shuddered.

Dalton put his arm around her. The gesture surprised her, but it had been so natural and, well, kind. He struck her as the type who would patiently listen to lonely people talk for hours or be quick to comfort a child. She leaned against him, braced by his solid form. This was exactly what she needed, to feel that there was something strong between her and danger. But after a moment she forced herself to pull away. She couldn't afford to depend on Dalton. It wasn't fair to involve him in her problems.

He looked around the room. "How are you going to protect yourself, out here alone?" he asked.

She credited having a brother who was a cop with inspiring this question. "There are heavy-duty locks on the doors and windows," she said. She had considered installing an alarm system, but living so far from town, she wasn't sure how useful such a system would be. "I have a brown belt in jujitsu, and I have a gun. And the sheriff has promised to have deputies patrol in the area regularly."

"Okay, I'll admit I'm impressed." He grinned, and the expression was genuine. They locked eyes and she vibrated with awareness. What had May said—smolder? She felt as if she might give off sparks at any moment.

Then a sound distracted her. "Someone's coming," she said, and jumped up and hurried to check the window.

Chapter Five

A black Volkswagen Beetle trundled up the driveway. Roxanne frowned. "What is she doing here?" she asked.

The car stopped and Debra climbed out. She swept her long hair over her shoulder and assessed the home, a closed-mouth smile forming dimples in her cheeks.

"Are you two friends?" Dalton asked.

"No. We met at the coffee shop. But I don't want to talk to her." Had she come to ask about her sister again? Roxanne couldn't help her. Worse, she didn't want to help her.

Debra strode to the door and knocked.

"I'll get rid of her," Dalton said. Before Roxanne could object, he opened the door.

Debra took a step back, surprise transforming her face for a moment, making her look more vulnerable and older. But the sly expression soon returned. "What are you doing here?" she asked Dalton.

"What are *you* doing here?" he asked.

"I heard Roxanne was in an accident. I wanted to see how she's doing. Is she in there?" She looked past him. "Hi, Roxanne. Are you okay?" And then she shoved a startled Dalton out of the way and came to stand in front of Roxanne. "I figure us newcomers to town need to stick together."

"Thank you for your concern, but I'm fine," Roxanne said.

"What happened? I noticed your car isn't out front. Was it totaled? Were you hurt?"

Roxanne stepped back. "I don't want to talk about it. How did you find out where I live?" She had welcomed Dalton's sudden appearance, but now that Debra was here, she was questioning her choice of new home. True, Eagle Mountain was a small town, but she hadn't realized it would be so easy for anyone at all to track her down.

"Oh, I overheard someone say you were in one of the tiny houses," Debra said. "They weren't hard to find."

Roxanne felt sick, but tried to hide it. Debra moved farther into the house. She picked up a small ceramic vase from a table, examined it and put it down. "You have some nice things," she said.

Roxanne said nothing. Dalton cleared his throat. "Was there something you wanted?" he asked.

Debra turned to face them. "I wanted to know about Roxanne's accident," she said. "What happened?"

"It's over now," she said. "It doesn't matter."

Debra pursed her lips and sighed. Roxanne half expected the other woman to scold her for not sharing the details of her ordeal. Instead, she said, "I'm afraid I have some bad news."

Roxanne glanced at Dalton, who was frowning at Debra. "What is it?" she asked.

Debra's gaze shifted to Dalton. "It would be better if I told you when we were alone."

She didn't want to be alone with this woman. She couldn't even say why. Debra was annoying but harmless, surely. "Tell me now," Roxanne said.

"It's about Billy." Another glance at Dalton.

Dalton moved closer to Roxanne. "What about Billy?" he asked.

Debra's eyes widened. "You told him about Billy?"

"I never call him that," Roxanne said. "But yes, he knows

about William Ledger." She rarely told anyone but revealing her past to Dalton had been surprisingly easy.

"Well, well. You two certainly have gotten close quickly." Debra smirked—that really was the only way to describe the look.

Roxanne fought the urge to fidget. "What do you want to tell me?" she asked.

"They let him out of prison. Can you believe that? After what he did to you and Alice. And to Betty. Betty is my sister," she told Dalton. "I'm sure Billy Ledger kidnapped and kept her before he took Alice and Mary. Even if Roxanne won't admit to knowing anything about Betty."

"I *don't* know anything about her," Roxanne said. "I wasn't lying."

Debra shrugged. "Anyway, Billy is old now. We've all moved on. Here's hoping he has, too."

"Why do you call him Billy?" Dalton asked.

"That's what Mary and Alice called him," Debra said. "I read that in the newspaper stories about the trial."

Billy was the name Ledger had made them call him. A friendly name for a man who was not their friend.

"Anyway, I doubt you have anything to worry about," Debra continued. "He's not likely to find you, anyway, since you changed your name and moved around so much."

"You found me," Roxanne said.

Debra nodded. "I did. But I worked at it. You didn't make it easy. But I was able to find the record where you changed your name, and I have a friend who could look up driver's license records for me. Then I went to your last address and talked to people. Someone there told me you were moving here." She shrugged. "I'm really good at talking to people. And I'm smart and persistent. From everything I've read, Billy wasn't all that bright. Just mean. Dumb and mean. A nasty combination, for sure."

Roxanne shuddered.

Dalton's arm was around her again, steadying her. "Thanks for stopping by," he said. "Roxanne needs to rest now. Doctor's orders."

Anger flashed across Debra's features but was quickly masked. "I hope you're feeling better soon," she said. "See you."

Dalton walked Debra to the door. Roxanne followed more slowly. They stood together at the window and watched her get into her car and drive off. Only then did Roxanne turn away, hugging her arms across her stomach.

"What was that about Betty?" he asked. "Or would you rather not say?"

She liked that he always gave her the option of not talking. "Debra cornered me in the coffee shop last week," she said. "She knew who I was. She knew about William Ledger—he insisted we call him Billy. I didn't even know his last name until after he was arrested. Anyway, Debra's older sister disappeared when she was thirteen and the family thinks Ledger took her. Debra wanted to know if I knew anything about that, but I don't."

"Is it possible there were other children he kidnapped?" Dalton looked as if the idea pained him.

"Anything is possible. I was only with him for three months. If Debra could find Alice and talk to her, Alice might know something. She was with Ledger for three years."

"What happened to her?" Dalton asked.

"I don't know. Both of us were in the foster system, without families to worry about us. I think Ledger targeted us because of that. We went back into the system after we escaped. I was lucky enough to end up in a good situation, with caring foster parents. Not everyone is so lucky. And I never knew Alice's real name. The police and the attorneys made it a point to keep our identities secret. So even if I had wanted to, I couldn't look for her."

Not that she had tried that hard to find Alice. "After the trial, I wanted to put everything having to do with those months behind me," she said, "I wanted to forget." Though, of course, she never could. But she had worked hard to build another reality, one in which those three months with Ledger were only a small part of a much bigger, fuller life. For the most part, she had succeeded.

"That's certainly understandable," Dalton said.

"I really am tired now," she said. "I think I need a nap."

"Then I'll leave," he said. He pulled out a phone. "Let me text you so you'll have my number."

"All right." She rattled off her number and moments later, her phone pinged with a message.

"Call me anytime," he said. "I don't have a brown belt in jujitsu but I can act intimidating when I have to. And I'm a good listener."

"Thanks."

She walked with him to the door and locked it behind him, then watched him drive away. The warm feeling he had kindled in her lingered, comforting. She liked Dalton. She felt closer to him that she had anyone in years. But being with him felt dangerous. She had always been careful to not involve others in the ugly side of her life, yet here he was, ankle-deep and ready to wade in further.

AFTER THE LAST tour every afternoon, Dalton and Carter had to wash the Jeeps and get them ready for the next day's tours. After a brief lull at the beginning of September, business was picking up again as tourists signed on for drives through forests of golden aspen in the high country. Tuesday afternoon, Dalton did the work methodically, his mind on what always occupied him these days: Roxanne. Was she really safe by herself, so far from town? Had William Ledger really been the man who ran her off the road? Where was he now?

A blast of cold water hit him in the back and he jolted upright. He whirled and scowled at Carter, who held the hose, water directed off to the side now. "Watch what you're doing!" Dalton said.

"You're the one who's in la-la land today," Carter answered. "You're a thousand miles away. I asked you four times to hand me the window cleaner and you completely ignored me."

Dalton shook his head and passed over the bottle of window cleaner. "I was just thinking, sorry."

"Are you thinking up a new computer program?" Carter squirted fluid on the Jeep's windshield, then attacked it with a cloth. "Imagining how you'll spend your riches?"

Dalton began wiping down his Jeep with a chamois. "Not that."

Carter stopped and stared, eyes wide in an exaggerated imitation of shock. "Don't tell me it's a woman!" He grinned. "Has the boy genius been struck dumb by Cupid's arrow?"

"What are you blathering on about?" Dalton turned away.

"I'm just saying it's about time. And I can relate."

Dalton thought of Carter's fiancée, teacher Mira Veronica. It was true that during the early days of their relationship, most of Carter's attention had been focused on her. Maybe his brother did understand, at least a little.

"I met someone I'm interested in, but she's not really ready for a relationship," Dalton said.

"Is she on the rebound?" Carter asked. "Sick? Tell me she's not married."

"She isn't any of those things."

"Then what is it?"

She may be being pursued by her former kidnapper. But

that wasn't Dalton's story to share. "It's complicated and I don't want to talk about it."

Carter was going to do his best to wheedle the truth out of him. Dalton knew his twin. But just as his brother had straightened and started toward him, both their phones alarmed with the tone reserved for search and rescue. Simultaneously, they dug phones from pockets and checked the screens.

"Looks like a hiker with a sprained ankle in a canyon off County Road 3," Carter said.

"Roxanne lives off County Road 3," Dalton said.

"That's your crush's name—Roxanne?" Carter pocketed his phone. "If this is her, I'll get to meet her."

Dalton shut off the water while Carter coiled the hoses and tucked the rest of the cleaning supplies out of the way. Then they piled into Carter's Jeep and raced to search and rescue headquarters.

A dozen volunteers milled around the headquarters building by the time Carter and Dalton arrived, including their sister, Bethany. She hurried to join them, her dark curls pulled back in a high ponytail. Bethany had been the first to join Eagle Mountain Search and Rescue, something she didn't hesitate to remind her brothers if she thought they were being too cocky.

"Hey, Bethany," Dalton said. "How's it going?"

"Business is booming. I probably shouldn't have left Ian alone, but I hated to miss out." She glanced over her shoulder at her fellow volunteers, who were gathering around their captain, Danny Irwin.

"Nobody wants to miss out," Carter said and led his siblings to the meeting up front.

Carter was right. As tough as search and rescue work could be sometimes—both physically and mentally—it was also compelling. No one wanted to miss the dramatic moments others would talk about for years. And even something as routine as this supposed sprained ankle could turn risky if reaching the injured person required negotiating dangerous terrain.

"We have a female in the canyon with an ankle injury," Danny said. "Says she's unable to walk and get out on her own. She doesn't have any water or emergency supplies with her."

"How did she get down in there?" Ryan asked. "There aren't any hiking trails in that area, and there's no good climbing routes, either."

"Not sure," Danny said. "We'll have to figure out how to get down to her when we get there."

"What's her name?" Carter asked.

Dalton glanced at his brother. He had wanted to ask that question, but hadn't wanted to call attention to himself.

"Don't know," Danny said. "We'll find out when we get there."

They caravanned in several vehicles to County Road 3. They were several miles from Roxanne's house, Dalton decided, as Carter pulled his Jeep in behind Grace Wilcox's Subaru. Danny was already standing at the edge of the road, peering down into the canyon. "The slope isn't too bad here," he said when the others had gathered alongside him. He indicated a faint path, probably made by wildlife. "We can work our way down through there. Watch out for loose rock." He pulled out his phone and punched in a number. Moments later, a woman's voice answered. "Hello?"

"This is Captain Danny Irwin with Eagle Mountain Search and Rescue. We're on our way into the canyon right now. Can you give me an idea of your location?"

"Um, I'm by some scraggly trees with orange and brown leaves. There's a bunch of rocks."

The rescuers exchanged looks. The canyon was filled with rocks and the scrub oak she was describing.

"Look up to the canyon rim," Danny said. "Can you see any houses or any unique rock formations?"

"Let's see. There's this sort of ledge of rock sticking out from the side of the canyon. No houses. Oh, and there's a really tall pine tree."

"I think I know where she's talking about," Ryan said.

"Sit tight and we'll be there as soon as we can," Danny said. "How's the ankle?"

"It's really swollen and it really hurts."

"We're on our way."

Ryan led the volunteers into the canyon. At the bottom, he turned west and they began bushwhacking through thick oak brush, thin, vine-like branches grabbing at their clothes and rocks shifting beneath their feet. "Not exactly an easy hike," Grace commented. "What do you think she was doing down here?"

"Maybe she wanted to photograph the leaves," Deni said.

"Or she saw a cute animal and followed it in," Sheri Stevens said. "I remember a call for a lost hiker and it turned out he had decided to follow a bobcat to try to get a photo and ended up with no idea how to get back to the trail."

After twenty minutes of fending off scratching brush and maneuvering around rocks, someone at the head of the line shouted. Moments later, Dalton and his siblings joined the volunteers gathered around a woman with dark red hair. "Debra?" Dalton asked.

Debra looked over at him. "Oh, hi, Dalton. What are you doing here?"

Aware that everyone had turned to look at him, Dalton felt his ears burning. "I'm with search and rescue," he said. "Are you okay?"

"I hurt my ankle." She gestured toward her left foot, which was propped on a rock in front of her, her hiking boot on its side on the ground below.

Danny knelt in front of Debra and prepared to examine her foot, while the other volunteers began unpacking first aid supplies. Some of them, like Dalton and Carter, waited for instructions. It didn't look as if they were going to need to rig ropes or clear brush, but you never knew what might transpire during even a routine rescue.

"Do you have any water?" Debra asked. "I'm really thirsty."

"Of course." Grace handed her a bottle of water. She nodded to a pack on an adjacent rock. "Have you been down here awhile?"

Debra drained half the bottle, then paused. "Only a couple of hours. It wasn't this hot when I started out."

"Did you drink all the water in your pack?" Sheri asked.

"Oh, the pack's for my drone. There's no water in there." She yelped and scowled at Danny. "Take it easy. You're hurting me."

"Sorry about that," Danny said. "Looks like a moderate sprain. You'll need X-rays, but we'll wrap it with some cold packs and get you out of here."

"So, like, will you call a helicopter or something?" Debra asked. "I've seen that on television."

Danny managed to keep his expression neutral. Probably why he was captain, Dalton thought. "No need for a helicopter," he said. "We'll carry you out on a litter."

The volunteers who had been tasked with carrying the pieces of the wheeled litter were already assembling it nearby. Dalton began stretching, preparing to take his turn as one of the litter-bearers. Hauling a patient over this rough terrain wasn't going to be quick or easy, but they had managed worse.

"How did you end up down here?" Grace asked, as she handed Danny chemical cold packs and elastic bandages. "There's no trail that I remember."

"I came down here to fly my drone and take some pictures,

but I guess I got too close to the canyon walls and crashed the drone. I climbed up and retrieved it, but coming down I fell and hurt my ankle."

"How's the drone?" Carter asked.

"The drone's okay. It's in my pack."

"Pretty rough hiking," Danny said. "How did you get into the canyon?"

"I parked on the road and came down. There was kind of a trail."

Dalton peered up at the canyon rim. How far were they from Roxanne's house? "What were you taking pictures of?" he asked.

"Somebody told me there are petroglyphs on some of these canyon walls. I wanted to see if I could find any."

"I don't think there are any petroglyphs in this canyon," Eldon said.

"How do you know?" Debra asked. "I could have been the first to discover them." She looked down at Danny. "What are you doing? That's really cold."

"I'm putting these cold packs around your ankle to reduce the swelling and relieve the pain."

"Oh." She looked back up at Dalton. "Have you talked to Roxanne today? How's she doing?"

Dalton was conscious of Carter—and everyone else nearby—listening in to this conversation. "I haven't talked to Roxanne today," he said.

"Some boyfriend you are."

Now he was sure his face was flaming. "Roxanne and I are just friends," he said. "I met her the same day I met you."

"In that case, you and I should go out sometime," Debra said. "I promise, I'm a lot of fun. Roxanne strikes me as pretty dull." She smiled slyly and winked. Dalton's face burned. Had she actually *winked* at him?

Someone behind him made a choking sound. He turned to

see Bethany, her hand over her mouth. She sent him a sympathetic look and shook her head.

"How does your ankle feel now?" Danny asked.

Debra looked down at her wrapped foot. "Cold. Pretty numb, actually."

"We'll remove the cold packs when we get to the road and let the EMTs check you over." Danny stood. "Any other injuries?"

"No." She glanced at her pack. "Well, my drone's a little cracked, but I don't suppose you fix those."

Danny shook his head. "We're ready for the litter now."

Dalton, Carter, Eldon and Ryan brought the litter over. Grace and Sheri helped Debra onto it and deposited her pack behind her head. "You need to wear this," Danny said, and held up a helmet.

"Why do I need that?" she asked.

"In case we drop you," Eldon said.

She opened her mouth as if to protest, but Danny was already sliding on the helmet. "Now lie down and we'll strap you in."

"What if I don't want to be strapped in?" she asked.

"Unless you're planning on walking out on that injured ankle, we have to strap you in," Danny said.

She lay back then. "You'd better not drop me," she ordered.

"We haven't lost a patient yet," Eldon said and positioned himself at one corner of the litter.

Rather than spend time trying to find the trail Debra had said she had taken, they set out back the way they had come. Several volunteers moved ahead of them, clearing as many obstacles as they could. But it was a slow, bumpy ride. Debra periodically whined that they needed to be more careful. "You're safe, don't worry," Ryan said, but Debra clearly wasn't persuaded.

The ambulance was waiting up at the road. The volunteers deposited the litter next to it and the EMTs moved in. "I'm fine now, really." Debra sat up as soon as the straps holding her in were removed and stripped off the helmet. She smoothed out her hair and pushed away the blood pressure cuff one EMT was trying to apply. "I don't need that. Really. I'm fine."

"You should have your ankle x-rayed," Danny said. "You might have torn some tendons."

"If it's not better in a day or two, I promise I'll see a doctor," Debra said. "Right now, I just want to go home. Somebody help me up."

One of the EMTs offered a hand. Wincing, Debra pulled herself to her feet and balanced precariously. "You can't drive," the EMT said.

"It's my left foot that's hurt." She looked around. "My car is right there." She pointed toward a black Volkswagen Beetle, parked across the road in the shade of a piñon. She hefted the backpack to one shoulder, then hobbled over to the car. No one tried to stop her.

Danny turned to Dalton. "Friend of yours?" he asked.

He shook his head. "I've run into her a couple of times in town, but I don't really know her."

Carter moved in closer. "She's into you," he said. "You going to go out with her?"

Dalton scowled at his twin. "No."

"Who is Roxanne?" Bethany asked.

Everyone was staring, waiting for an answer. Dalton wasn't going to get away with not giving one. "Roxanne is a friend. She's new in town, too."

"I remember now!" Eldon said.

Everyone focused on him. "The woman who was run off the road." He looked around them. "Not far from here. Brunette? Drove a RAV4?"

Several of the volunteers nodded. They had either assisted

on the callout or had heard about it. "So the two of you hit it off?" Bethany asked.

"Yeah," Dalton said.

"But you're not dating," Carter added.

"No."

No one said anything. Dalton turned and began disassembling the litter. Eldon moved in to help him. The EMTs returned to the ambulance and everyone else went back to loading gear and preparing to leave.

They were back in Carter's Jeep before anyone spoke. "So I take it you asked this Roxanne woman out and she turned you down. Is that right?" Carter asked.

"No." Dalton grimaced. "Not exactly. I told you it's complicated. And none of your business."

"But you really like her, right?" Bethany said.

He didn't say anything.

"You do," Bethany said. "I can tell."

He turned to glare at his sister. "How can you tell?"

"Because you're acting the same way you did when Amanda Dietrich went to the prom with Derek Robinson. You wanted to ask her out but didn't work up the nerve soon enough and she ended up going with him instead."

"That was in tenth grade!" Dalton protested.

Bethany shrugged. "You're still just as mopey."

"You're being ridiculous," he said.

"If you like her, just be her friend," Carter said. "Give things time to develop."

"We are friends," he said. "She knows she can call me anytime."

Carter groaned.

"What? Why are you groaning?" Dalton asked.

"You are so clueless. You don't want to depend on her to call you. You call her."

"I don't want to come off as a stalker."

"You won't come off as a creep if you have a good reason to call," Bethany said.

"I can handle my relationships on my own," Dalton said. "I don't need you two managing my life."

"You're not doing such a great job so far," Carter said. "What kind of work does Roxanne do?"

"She's a programmer."

"That's perfect!" Bethany's voice rose almost to a squeal. "The two of you can geek out together."

"I've got it," Carter said. "Call her up and tell her you need help figuring out a problem with the new software you're developing."

"I don't have a problem with my new software," Dalton protested.

"Caleb said the calendar doesn't sync up like it's supposed to all the time," Carter said.

"I'm going to fix that."

"Ask Roxanne to help you," Bethany said. "It's a way for the two of you to spend time together, but not a date."

"I don't need to trick a woman into spending time with me," he said.

"You wouldn't be tricking her," Bethany said. "Isn't it a good idea to have another set of eyes look at your project? She'll help make it even better."

"I'm going to handle this my way," he said. "You two need to stay out of it."

Bethany sighed and sat back. "We're just trying to help."

"Sometimes you're too cautious for your own good," Carter said.

"I said I'll handle it." He spoke through clenched teeth. The trouble with families was that sometimes they cared too much. But his love life—or lack of it—was something he needed to figure out for himself.

Chapter Six

Roxanne kept an eye out for any sign of William Ledger, or anyone else suspicious, but saw nothing over the next week. She finished unpacking and settled into a routine of work and getting the house arranged the way she wanted. She planted chrysanthemums and flowering kale in the beds out front, and bought a pumpkin at the farmer's market to decorate the front porch. She saw her new neighbor, Kara, a few times and they talked briefly about nothing in particular. Roxanne began to relax. Maybe the sheriff's deputies had scared away whoever had run her off the road. It hadn't been Ledger— that was just her imagination conjuring up a familiar devil.

She made a point to take a break after lunch each day to walk around her little house, tending to the flowers and soaking in the peacefulness. This was home now. She was going to be happy here.

Ten days had passed since her accident when she was stooping to examine the developing chrysanthemum buds— and froze. There, in the freshly dug soil beneath her front window—was that a footprint? Heart hammering, she glanced around, as if expecting to see someone lurking. But all was still, the only sound a birdcall in the distance. She forced herself to look at the print again—to really study it.

It was small—too small for a man? It was rounded at the toe—like a tennis shoe?

Moving around the house, she found three more of the same impression, none complete or particularly distinct, but definitely shoe prints. Kara crossed the driveway to join Roxanne. "Is something wrong?" she asked. "You look upset."

"Does that look like a footprint to you?" Roxanne asked. She pointed to the impressions in the flower bed.

Kara studied the imprints. "Who would be walking in your flower bed?" she asked. She looked down at Roxanne's feet. "Are they yours? Maybe you were weeding or something?"

Roxanne shook her head. "They aren't yours, are they?" she asked.

Kara laughed. "Why would I be creeping around your house?"

"I'm sorry," Roxanne said. "Of course it wasn't you."

Kara hugged her arms across her stomach. "It's spooky, isn't it? I'm already nervous about being out here so far from town, but the rent is so reasonable and I really like the tiny house. It's so cozy."

"I think this is as safe as anywhere," Roxanne said. She turned away from the mysterious footprints. Looking at them was too upsetting. "Where did you live before?" she asked.

"Oh, I've lived all over," Kara said. "I guess I'm the restless type. I live one place for a while, then move someplace else. I was in Houston before this. This is much nicer. What about you? Where did you live before?"

"I was in San Antonio for a long time. But I wanted to make a fresh start."

"Do you work from home? I see you over here all day."

"Yes. I work for a software company." She didn't elaborate—most people weren't that interested. "What do you do?"

"Oh, I work from home, too. Project management." She

glanced back at the flower bed. "What are you going to do about those footprints?"

Roxanne pulled out her phone and took a few pictures, then dialed a number. "Mr. Lusk?" she asked when her landlord answered.

"Roxanne, how are you doing?" The old rancher had a gravelly voice. Roxanne thought she heard the growl of the ATV he frequently rode around the ranch.

"I've come upon something strange around my house." She stared down at the footprints next to her newly planted flowers.

"Strange how? What is it?"

"There are footprints in the flower beds. As if someone had been looking in the window."

"I saw you planted flowers," Lusk said. "They look really nice. Are you sure those aren't your footprints?"

"I'm sure. Would you mind coming down and taking a look and telling me what you think?"

"I'll be down in a minute."

She ended the call and continued to study the prints. "Mr. Lusk is coming down to take a look," she told Kara.

"That's good. Let me know what he says. I need to get back to work."

Kara moved away, but Roxanne scarcely noticed. She was trying to remember what size shoe William Ledger wore. Her impression had always been that he was a big man, but she had been a ten-year-old girl. All men looked big to her back then.

A few minutes later, the roar of the ATV's unmuffled motor heralded her landlord's arrival. Robbie Lusk was a third-generation rancher in his sixties, lean and weathered, dressed in worn denim jeans, a chambray shirt faded almost white and a leather vest blackened in the creases by age. He stopped the ATV a few feet from Roxanne and stiffly dismounted. "Let's have a look here," he said and peered down into the flower bed.

"Do you have any idea who it could be?" Roxanne asked.

"I have an idea, all right. Dang kids."

"Children? Who?"

"My nephews were visiting and roaming all over the ranch. I told them to stay away from the tiny houses, but you know teenagers—they don't listen. I'll give 'em a good talking-to and it won't happen again or I'll have their hides."

She supposed those prints could have been made by a teenager. Studying them again, she was sure of it. "I'm relieved it was only your nephews."

"I'm sorry they upset you like this. If you see any of them down here, you be sure and call me. I'll deal with them right away."

He returned to the ATV and settled onto the seat, but didn't start it immediately. One thing she had quickly learned was that Mr. Lusk liked to talk. "So how are you doing?" he asked. "Are you settling in all right?"

"I'm doing well," she said. "I really love it here."

"I heard about the accident with your car. Sounds like that was a close call. You have to be careful on these winding mountain roads. Especially at night. A deer or other animal jumps out in front of you, you try to avoid hitting them and the next thing you know, you're over the edge. You're lucky you weren't killed."

That wasn't what had happened, but she was relieved he had landed on this explanation for her accident. "I'll definitely be more careful," she said. "The body shop should have my car back to me in about ten days."

"You be sure you look the car over good before you sign off on the repairs." He shook his finger at her. "There are too many people around who would try to take advantage of a young lady on her own."

Let them try to take advantage of me, she thought but only nodded. "Thanks for the advice."

"Now, this one time…"

She resigned herself to listening to a long-winded story when her phone vibrated, startling her. It was probably a junk call, but she was prepared to pretend it was an important work consultation if it would move Mr. Lusk on his way. She checked the phone screen. Dalton Ames.

"That might be the biggest smile I've ever seen from you," Mr. Lusk said. "That must be a call from someone special."

"Um, just someone I need to talk to." She backed toward the house. "It was good to see you, Mr. Lusk. Thanks for stopping by." She waved, then darted inside. "Hello?"

"Hello, Roxanne. It's Dalton. I hope I'm not calling at a bad time."

"No, this is a good time."

"I think I told you I'm working on some software for search and rescue?"

"Yes. How is that going?"

"I've run into a little problem getting the calendar to sync in all the different modules. I was wondering if you'd mind taking a look and seeing if there's anything obvious I'm overlooking."

"I'd be happy to help you."

"Could you stop by my place sometime when you're free? It shouldn't take long."

"I'd love that." After a week of no contact, she had given up on seeing Dalton again. The idea had disappointed her, even though she had no one but herself to blame for his absence from her life. She had made it clear she wasn't interested in dating. He had no doubt moved on to someone else.

Except he had called her and asked for her help. She still didn't want romance, but maybe this would be the way for them to build a friendship of sorts. Another person to anchor her in her new life. "I could come this afternoon, if that works for you," she said.

"Sure. Make it after four. I should be home by then. I'll text my address."

AT FOUR FIFTEEN, Roxanne knocked on the door of Dylan's apartment. She had thought he might live in the large complex of apartments near the river. Instead, Dylan rented a garage apartment off a quiet side street a few blocks from downtown.

"Thanks for coming over," he said when he answered her knock. "Come on in."

She followed him into a small, dim room outfitted with a sofa, a well-used recliner and a very large desk with a thirty-two-inch monitor. He pulled a second chair up to the desk. "You can sit here. Would you like some water? Or, I might have a Coke somewhere."

"I'm fine, thanks." She sat, and put her purse on the floor by the desk.

He sat in the desk chair and swiveled to face her. "How have you been?" he asked.

She opened her mouth, fully intending to lie and tell him she was fine, busy unpacking, etc. Instead, she said, "The sheriff's department says they haven't found any trace of William Ledger, and I haven't seen him, either. But I had a scare when I found footprints in the flower bed under my window."

Dalton leaned toward her. "Do you think Ledger was there?"

She shook her head. "They were too small to be his. Anyway, my landlord said they belonged to his nephews. They were visiting and apparently running wild. He told them to stay away from the tiny houses, but they must have been curious." She sat back. "It was unnerving, though."

"Do you believe your landlord—that it was just his nephews?"

"Well...of course. I don't think Mr. Lusk would lie to me. And the prints weren't large enough to be a grown man's."

"What about a woman?"

"I guess... I mean they could have belonged to a woman. But what woman would be looking in my windows?"

He looked away, then back at her. "We had a search and rescue call a week ago—a hiker with a sprained ankle in the canyon that runs behind your house."

She frowned. "I didn't know there were any hiking trails down there."

"There aren't. This person says she went down there to look for petroglyphs." His eyes met hers. "I don't know if I'm supposed to tell you this or not, but it was Debra Percy."

"Oh." She sat back, trying to let this sink in. "But she was down in the canyon, right? A long way from my house."

"Yes, but she had a drone. She said it crashed and she hurt her ankle while retrieving it."

"What did she say she was doing with the drone?" Roxanne asked.

"She said she was looking for petroglyphs." He leaned forward. "But there aren't any petroglyphs in the canyon."

"So you think she wasn't actually looking for petroglyphs? Maybe she didn't know there weren't any really there."

"Or maybe she was using the drone to spy on you."

The idea of anyone spying on her was unsettling. "But why would Debra want to spy on me? I mean, she's a little too intense for me, but she's looking for information about her sister. She's decided I'm the person who can give her that information and doesn't want to accept that I don't know anything. But a drone isn't going to help her get the information she's looking for."

"I don't know. It just struck me as odd." He lifted his hands as if to type, then put them back in his lap. "She asked me if I had talked to you lately. And then she asked me out."

She what? the voice in Roxanne's head screeched. That this thought had occurred annoyed her. She hardly knew Dalton. So what she actually said was, "So, did you make a date?" Then held her breath, waiting for an answer.

"No." He held her gaze. "She doesn't interest me."

And Roxanne did. That message was clear in his eyes. She interested him, even though he knew more about her past.

She looked away, uncomfortable with his scrutiny, yet feeling his gaze still on her.

"I've been thinking," he said. "About Alice. If you wanted to find her now, I could do some digging online. I'm pretty good at that kind of thing. I helped Carter's fiancée find out about a man who was harassing her."

"Do you mean you can hack into files?"

"Well, yeah. But I don't do it to be malicious. Only to help people."

"Thanks, but I don't really want to find Alice," she said. "She's a part of my life I don't care to revisit."

"Fair enough."

She tensed, waiting for the questions she was sure would come—the questions others had asked, once they learned her story. Questions like "what did he do to you?" and "how did he capture you?"

"Take a look at this and see if you can spot where I'm going wrong." His words directed her attention to his computer screen once more. "I should be able to link the data in any part of the program with the calendar, but it's not working on every page," he continued. "I know I'm missing something, but what?"

She scooted her chair closer and leaned toward the screen to scrutinize the lines of code showing there. But even as she tried to focus on the code, she was aware of his thigh next to hers and the warmth of his skin so close to her. She inhaled a steadying breath and caught the scent of his soap or shampoo and the clean cotton of his clothing.

Normally, being too close to people—especially people she didn't know well—was uncomfortable for her. But she was drawn to Dalton. There was physical attraction, but also the comfort of being accepted just as she was. There was no burden of expectations with him. The idea had a heady novelty that kept her off-balance.

She forced herself to read the code and translate it into the functions it represented. She didn't trust herself to read people accurately, but she knew programming. The correct code produced the desired results, every time. "Tell me what this section of the program is doing," she said.

"Sure." He clicked from the code to the actual page. "This is where we log in details of the accident. There's a spot here to put the date, and that's supposed to automatically make it possible to print a report or pull up types of calls sorted by date."

"Huh." She reached past him to switch back to the string of code, then straightened. "I see your problem. You left something out." She began typing in the correct string of code, fingers lightning-fast on the keys.

"How did I miss that?" he asked.

"You know it's *supposed* to be there, so your mind fills in the blank and makes you think it is there," she said. "That's my theory, anyway." She sat back. "Is that the only place you're having a problem?"

"There are two others," he said. "I bet it's the same problem."

He navigated to the other trouble areas. One had the same problem, which he quickly corrected. The second page had a different string of corrupt code, but she spotted it and together they rewrote the correct instructions.

"Thanks," he said when the work was done.

"You'd have figured out the mistake on your own eventually," she said.

"Maybe, but you helped me solve the problem a lot faster." He turned toward her and she couldn't look away. He had such beautiful eyes—green flecked with gold, fringed with thick, dark lashes, magnified by his glasses. But the best thing about his eyes was the way he looked at her, as if she was something amazing.

Heat rose to her cheeks at the thought, and her gaze shifted to his lips. How would he react if she leaned forward and kissed him? She had never spontaneously kissed a guy before but right now, with this man, that was exactly what she wanted. Would he think she was coming on too strong? Would things get out of hand too quickly?

Was she overanalyzing this?

Yes. Just kiss him already.

She closed her eyes and leaned closer. *Here goes nothing...*

The jangle of a phone that sounded like it was coming from the narrow space between them sent her reeling back, gasping, eyes wide-open. Dalton swore fluently and groped for the pocket of his jeans and pulled out his phone. He swore again, then looked at her. "Sorry about that. It's my mom."

"That's okay." She slid her chair a little farther back. "Go ahead and answer." She had to raise her voice to be heard over the insistent chiming of the phone.

"If I don't, she'll just keep calling." He swiped at the screen. "Hi, Mom, I'm kind of busy right now."

"Too busy to eat?" The voice of the woman on the other end of the phone sounded clearly in the small room. Even though Roxanne pretended to be focused on the computer screen once more, she couldn't help overhearing. "I'm calling to invite you to dinner."

"I'll just grab something here," Dalton said.

"Don't be ridiculous. I'm making your favorite—lasagna.

And your brothers and sister are coming. You can bring whoever owns that white car that's been parked at your place all afternoon."

Roxanne let out a startled laugh.

Sorry, Dalton mouthed.

"I'll wait while you ask her to dinner. Or him. No judging."

Roxanne did laugh then. She couldn't help it. Dalton's face was red. "Sorry," he said again, out loud this time.

"It's all right," she said. "I'd love to have dinner with your family."

"I'll expect you both in half an hour," his mother said and ended the call.

Dalton laid the phone on the desk. "You don't have to go," he said. "I'll make some excuse to Mom."

"You don't want me to go?" The idea disappointed her.

"No! I mean, I'd love to spend more time with you. But my whole family—it can be a lot."

"I've already met Aaron and Bethany and Carter. Is there anyone else?"

"Just my parents. And Aaron's and Carter's fiancées and Bethany's fiancé."

"Is your mom a good cook?"

"She's a great cook."

"Lasagna is my favorite, too," she said.

He closed the program on his computer, then stood. "Are you ready to go?"

She nodded. Nothing intense about meeting his family, right? Butterflies took off in her stomach and she fought the urge to flee. Back to her solitary home. Away from people who might misunderstand or judge her.

But that wasn't happening here, she reminded herself. Dalton didn't do those things and even if his family did, she could face them, knowing he had her back.

Chapter Seven

Dalton loved his family. He loved them enough that when the rest of them decided to move from Vermont to Eagle Mountain, Colorado, he hadn't hesitated to join them. But he couldn't help thinking that at times the Ames clan could be a little…overwhelming. He thought this now as he led Roxanne up the walkway to his parents' home. From the street they had been able to hear the blare of music and cacophony of people talking, laughing and even shouting.

He gave her a weak smile. "They're not exactly a reserved bunch," he said.

"It sounds like they're having a good time," she said.

The door opened before they reached the steps and Bethany leaned out. "I thought that was your car," she said. "Hello, Roxanne. You look like you're feeling much better than the last time I saw you."

"Oh, yes," Roxanne said. "I'm fi—"

Bethany grabbed her hand and pulled her inside. "We're looking at table decorations for my wedding. Tell me what you think. I'm having a terrible time deciding."

"Well, I—" Roxanne looked back over her shoulder at Dalton.

"Bethany, don't—" he began, but the two women had already disappeared through the door.

Dalton hurried after them. He immediately collided with Carter, who shoved a cold can into his hand. "Try this," he said. "It's cider Dad picked up somewhere." He sipped from his own can. "Pretty good stuff."

"Where did Bethany take Roxanne?" Dalton asked.

"That was Roxanne?" Carter grinned. "You sly dog. Things must be moving pretty fast if you're already bringing her home to meet the family. I wouldn't let Mira anywhere near the whole crew until I was pretty sure she wasn't going to run away screaming."

"We're not that bad," Dalton protested.

"You aren't. But Mom can be a bit much sometimes. And Dad's jokes aren't really that funny most of the time."

"Dalton!" Their mother headed down the hallway toward them. "Weren't you supposed to bring someone? Where is she?"

"Hi, Mom." Dalton leaned in to hug his mother. She smelled of oregano and hair spray, a scent he probably could have used to track her in any crowd. "Roxanne is here somewhere. Bethany took her to look at table decorations."

"I already told Bethany we should go with the white candles on silver trays but she keeps dithering. The wedding is going to be here before she makes up her mind."

"She's still got a few weeks," Dalton said.

Diane Ames gave him the look moms everywhere leveled at children who refuse to see the obvious. "The wedding is in three weeks," she said. "Everything should have been decided long ago." She looked back over her shoulder. "I need to check the oven, but as soon as that's done, I want you to introduce me to your young lady."

"Mom, she's not my—" But his mother was gone.

Carter put his arm around Dalton. "Drink up, and go with the flow. Mira tells me she thinks Mom and Dad are 'darling.'"

"Your fiancée comes from a big family like ours," Dalton said. "Roxanne isn't used to all this chaos. And we're not even dating."

"So you say." Carter shrugged. "Don't stress so much. Maybe the novelty of a big family will charm her."

Dalton let Carter lead him into the large room at the back of the house. Double doors opened onto an even larger deck, where most of the party seemed to have gathered. Only Aaron was seated on one end of the sofa, scrolling through his phone. "What are you doing hiding out in here?" Dalton asked.

"Dad cornered Willa and is telling her about the camping trip we took to Yosemite the summer I was twelve," Aaron said.

"And you abandoned your future wife to that?" Carter asked.

Aaron grimaced. "I stuck around until he got to the part where I tried to rope a moose. It was too embarrassing."

"You almost got us kicked out of the park," Carter said.

"I didn't come close to getting the rope around the moose," Aaron said. "And what Dad never tells anyone is that he gave me the rope and showed me how to use it."

"Wasn't there a tin star, too?" Dalton asked. "And a toy six-shooter?"

"That's probably what made you the lawman you are today," Carter said.

The furious glare Aaron directed at them only made Carter laugh harder.

"You boys are having too much fun in here." Carter's fiancée, Mira Veronica, moved into the room. A striking brunette with large brown eyes and a heart-shaped face, Mira taught Spanish at Eagle Mountain High School. Carter moved to put his arm around her. "Did you see Dalton's girlfriend out there anywhere?" he asked. "Bethany dragged her away before she even crossed the threshold."

Dalton started to protest that Roxanne was not his girlfriend, but why waste his breath? And the truth was, he wanted to be more than friends. He was being patient, hoping she would change her mind.

"I saw a very pretty brunette with your sister." Mira smiled at Dalton. "She was holding a cocktail in one hand and a paper fan in the other and was smiling at some story Bethany was telling."

"Maybe the one where Bethany was babysitting the two of us and you took off your diaper and ran naked down the street," Carter said.

Dalton glowered at him. "How many of those ciders have you had?" he asked.

"Probably not enough for you to beat me in a fight," Carter said.

"I don't have to physically fight you," Dalton said. "Make me mad enough and I'll just mess up your phone."

Carter put a hand over the phone in his pocket. "You wouldn't dare."

"Don't try me."

Aaron stood. "I'd better go back out there and find Willa," he said.

"Maybe she's with Roxanne," Dalton said, and followed him out the door.

"Dalton!" His father hailed him from the opposite end of the deck, where he sat in a patio chair beside a petite blonde with hazel eyes. A diamond engagement ring caught the sun as she swiveled toward the new arrivals.

Reluctantly, Dalton detoured to his father's side. "Hi, Willa," he said to the woman. "Hi, Dad."

"Hello, Dalton," Willa said. "If you two will excuse me

for a minute." She stood and made her escape, joining Aaron and hurrying away.

"How are you doing, son?" George Ames was tall and dark-haired, with high cheekbones he shared with his eldest son, Aaron. The features of Bethany and the twins more closely resembled their fairer mother, though they all had their father's expressive mouth, and the habit of tilting their chins down when listening intently.

"I'm fine, Dad. I was fine when you saw me this morning." Dalton had given a morning tour at Alpine Jeep and had reported to his father afterward.

"Your mother said you were bringing a woman with you." George said this in the same tone of skepticism he might have used to announce that he had heard Dalton was bringing a live gazelle to dinner. The youngest Ames offspring had never actually brought anyone to dinner with the family before.

"Roxanne is around here somewhere." Dalton turned a full circle and caught a flash of dark curls at the corner of the garage. He set down the half-finished cider and excused himself then, not waiting for a reply, and hurried to where Roxanne stood with Bethany, Mira and his mother.

Roxanne caught his eye as he approached, a hint of a smile on her lips. She looked…content. "Roxanne was just telling us you two share an interest in computers," Diane said, waving him over. She turned back to Roxanne. "Dalton won't brag on himself, so I will. He's very talented. He's already making a name for himself with the programs and apps and other things he's created."

"So I've heard," Roxanne said. She avoided looking at Dalton, her lips pressed firmly together, as if holding back laughter.

"She also told us you two met when you rescued her after a car wreck," his mother continued. "So romantic."

"I was part of the search and rescue team," he said. "Bethany was there, too."

"But you were first on the scene," Diane said.

"Actually, we met at the Fall Festival in town," Roxanne said. "May, from the Java Moose, introduced us."

"My version is a better story," Diane said.

Carter slipped in next to their mother. "When is dinner ready?" he asked. "I'm starving."

"It's ready now," she said. "Help me get everyone to the table."

He cupped his hands to his mouth. "Dinner's ready!" he shouted, stopping all conversation.

"I promise, I raised him better than this," Diane said, as the family headed for the long dining table at the far end of the living area. "Roxanne, you sit here next to me." His mother indicated the chair to her left at one end of the table. "Dalton can sit across from you." Bethany and her fiancé, Ian Seabrook, sat next to Dalton, while Aaron and Willa took the chairs beside Roxanne. Carter and Mira flanked his father at the other end of the table.

When everyone was seated, George said grace, then Diane began passing dishes. There were two glass casseroles of lasagna, a tub of salad, another huge bowl of green beans and three baskets of garlic bread. "Is this dinner for a special occasion?" Roxanne asked.

"Only that we're all together," Diane said. "I like to get everyone together for a meal at least once a week, if possible." She speared a bite of salad and chewed, then continued. "Bethany and Ian were planning to stop by, so I called Willa and she said she and Aaron would come. I knew Carter can't say no to my lasagna, and he would bring Mira. Then it was just a matter of persuading Dalton to come." She smiled. "And it was the perfect opportunity to meet you."

"How did you know about Roxanne?" Dalton asked.

Her expression was the perfect imitation of Mona Lisa. "I make it a point to keep up with my children."

Laughter from across the table surprised him. "I'm sorry," Roxanne said. "But the expression on your face…"

"Where is your family, Roxanne?" Diane asked.

Her expression sobered. "My parents were killed in an auto accident when I was seven."

"Oh no. Did you go to live with relatives?" Diane asked.

"There were no close relatives," she said. "I went into the foster care system. I was in a group home for a while, but I eventually ended up with a lovely couple. I lived with them until I went away to college."

"That must have been difficult for you," his mother said.

"Everyone has difficult things in their life," Roxanne said. "But we can't let those things define us."

Dalton had to look away, afraid she would mistake his admiration for pity. She had been through so much, yet come through it all with such grace—or at least it seemed that way to him.

"Mom, you outdid yourself with dinner." Aaron, seated on Roxanne's other side, said. Dalton remembered that he, too, knew Roxanne's history. Was he deliberately trying to get their mom on to another topic?

Roxanne turned to Bethany. "Congratulations on your upcoming wedding. Where are you getting married?"

"At Eagle Lodge, in the mountains above town," Bethany said. "It has the most beautiful views and I think we're timing it for the best fall color."

"No one is going to be looking at the scenery when you walk down the aisle," Diane said. She leaned toward Roxanne. "She has the most beautiful dress. And her bridesmaids are all wearing a gorgeous russet silk—all the colors are fall inspired, and the flowers are maroon and dark blue. It's going to be stunning."

"It sounds beautiful," Roxanne said.

"It's exciting," Bethany said. "But really, I'm most excited to be married to Ian." The couple locked eyes, and Dalton could have sworn at least half the women in the room sighed. He was pretty sure Roxanne wasn't one of them, but she did look a little misty-eyed. What was it about weddings that always got to women? He didn't have anything against them, but he didn't see why the wedding was so important. What happened after the wedding—living life together as a couple "'til death do we part"—seemed to matter to him more than a brief ceremony.

Finally, dinner was done and everyone pushed back from the table. "Let me help you clear up," Roxanne said.

"The men will take care of that," Diane said. She put her hand on Roxanne's arm. "I love to cook, but if I'm going to do all that work, someone else has to clean."

"I like the way you think," Roxanne said.

For the next half hour, Dalton was stuck in the kitchen scraping dishes while his father and brothers loaded the dishwasher and put away leftovers. When the room was deemed spotless enough to pass his mother's inspection, he found Roxanne in the living room, leaning over a photo album his mother was paging through.

The album did not, as he had feared, contain pictures of his younger self in embarrassing positions. Rather, it was the album of photos his parents had taken on their honeymoon to Italy, three decades previously. The shots, many faded to pastel tones, featured a young woman who might have been mistaken for a fairer Bethany with curly bangs, and a version of Aaron, with long hair falling into his eyes. Roxanne smiled and oohed over the photos.

She looked up when Dalton and his brothers and father joined the women. "Willa and I have to go," Aaron said. "I have early shift tomorrow."

"We need to leave, too," Mira said. "Thank you so much for the wonderful dinner. And it was good to meet you, Roxanne."

"It was good to meet all of you." Roxanne stood.

"We should be going, too," Dalton said and moved to her side.

The round of goodbyes took ten minutes, but at last they were seated in Dalton's Jeep, headed back toward his apartment, where Roxanne had left her car. "I'm sorry about all the questions about your family," he said. "My mom can be relentless, sometimes."

"They were ordinary questions," she said. "The kind people ask when they want to know someone better. It's okay."

"Like I told you, the whole family at once can be a lot. Thanks for being such a good sport."

She said nothing else until they were standing outside his apartment. He wondered if he should ask her up. She turned toward him. "You have a wonderful family," she said. "I enjoyed meeting every one of them. They were all so nice—the kind of family I fantasized about having when I was a kid. Thank you for inviting me."

"They all liked you a lot," he said. "So do I." He wanted to kiss her. He wanted more than that, but he would settle for a kiss. Sometimes, he thought she wanted that, too. Earlier today, right before his mother called, he had thought she had been about to kiss him, but the call had broken the spell.

"I like you, too." Regret colored the words, and she looked away. "I want to be your friend, but please don't expect more from me. Not right now. It isn't fair to either of us."

"Hey, it's okay." He hated seeing her upset. "No pressure. I wouldn't do that to you. But I do want us to be friends."

She nodded, and when she looked at him again, she no longer looked sad. "Thank you again for a wonderful evening. I'd better go now."

"Yeah. Be careful."

She nodded. "I always am."

Just like that, he was reminded of what she had endured—and the threat of danger that still hung over her. Maybe the driver who had run her off the road wasn't William Ledger. But what if it was? How was Dalton going to protect her from that?

ON THE DRIVE back to her rental, Roxanne basked in the unfamiliar feeling of relaxation and happiness that enveloped her. Was this contentment? She felt as if she had spent the last few hours soaking in a spa, but instead of aromatherapy oils and warm water, she had been surrounded by the genuine warmth of the funny and expressive Ames family. The closest she had come to that feeling of being accepted was at the end of her first year with Marjie and Theo Young as her foster parents. The first Christmas in their home had been magical, surrounded by such joy and caring. She felt she had at last found home.

The Youngs had been like a real mom and dad to her, but they had never adopted her. She had never worked up the courage to ask them why, but had always assumed it was because something was wrong with her. She had told herself many times that this probably wasn't true, but once that kind of thought lodged itself in your head, it wasn't easy to shake.

And then there was Dalton, at the center of it all. He was sexy but a little nerdy, quiet and thoughtful yet sharp-witted, strong and brave, and selfless enough to give his spare time to helping strangers—who could blame her for being attracted to a man like that?

She hadn't had a best friend for many years but she was beginning to think of him that way. Truthfully, he made her think about other things, especially when he was standing close and she became so aware of him physically. It would be so easy to give in to desire and pull him further into her complicated life. But with William Ledger on the loose, his intentions toward her unknown, it would be unfair—and even dangerous—to get too close to Dalton.

On this unsettling thought, she parked in her driveway, got out and started walking toward her house. She had mounted the steps to the tiny front porch when she realized the door was standing open. She looked around, as if expecting to spot another car. Had she left the light on? Had a visitor found the door open and decided to wait for her inside?

But she knew she hadn't left the door open. She always locked her door, the same way she always jammed a chair beneath the knob of her bedroom door at night and double-checked that all the windows were locked as well. Those safety precautions were as ingrained in her as brushing her teeth every morning and night. And there was no visitor's car in her driveway.

She stared at the open door for a long moment before it registered that the lock had been broken, the wood around it gouged and raw. Shaking, she raced to her car. She scanned the back seat to make sure no one had hidden there, then jumped inside, slammed the door and locked it. She turned the car around and drove to the end of her street, then, sure no one was following her, pulled over and called 911. "Someone has been in my house," she told the operator. "I came home and the door is open and the lock has been broken." She gave her name and address, promised to wait at the end of the street for help to arrive, then hung up the phone. She stared at it in her hand for a long moment, then dialed another number. "Hello, Dalton? Could you come out to my place? Someone broke in while I was gone."

Chapter Eight

Dalton sped toward the tiny house, Roxanne's words repeating like a mantra. She had sounded calm but also tense. He didn't think she would have called him if she wasn't afraid. A sheriff's department SUV turned onto County Road 3 ahead of him and he tried to identify which deputy was driving. Not Aaron, who wasn't on duty this evening. Not the sheriff himself, who drove a truck. Who was in there didn't really matter, but trying to figure it out distracted Dalton from his fear that Roxanne was not, in fact, all right. That whoever had broken into her home was still there, determined to harm her.

They hadn't driven far before he saw headlights from a car pulled to the side of the road. As he neared, he recognized Roxanne's white rental. She got out of the car and stood beside it as first the SUV, then Dalton's Jeep, parked behind her.

Deputy Shane Ellis—tall, blond, with the muscular legs of the professional baseball pitcher he had once been, stepped out of the SUV and sent Dalton a questioning look. "Roxanne called me," Dalton said before Shane could ask why he was there. He moved past Shane to Roxanne. "Are you okay?" he asked.

"I'm fine." She hugged her arms across her chest, shoulders hunched. She didn't look fine, but he was smart enough not to say so.

"Ms. Byrne?" Shane moved toward them. "I'm Deputy Ellis."

"Thank you for coming," she said.

"I understand you believe someone broke into your house," Shane said.

"Yes. I came home and the front door was open. The lock had been broken."

"Did you go inside?"

"No. I got back in my car and called 911."

"Did you see anyone? Or any other vehicle, near the house?"

"No. But I didn't stay there long. And it was dark."

"All right. I'll go and check it out in a bit. Where were you before you came home?"

"I was having dinner." She glanced at Dalton. "With Dalton's family."

"How long were you away from home?"

She frowned. "About four hours," Dalton said.

"Yes, that sounds right," she agreed.

"You two wait here and I'll go check it out," Shane said.

When they were alone, Dalton put his arm around her. "Thanks for coming," she said. "I feel silly now, dragging you out of the house. I'm fine. It just…shook me a little bit."

"I'm glad you called," he said. "I'm happy to help any way I can." He had plenty of questions, but none of them had answers at this point—did she think this was the same person whose footprints she had seen in her flower beds? Did she think it was William Ledger? But if she wanted to talk about such things, he'd let her bring them up. He didn't want to upset her further.

"I meant to ask you, are you in the wedding party?" she asked. "For your sister's wedding, I mean."

The abrupt change of subject startled him. But she was probably trying to distract herself, so he would do his part.

"Uh, no. I think they're just having a couple of attendants each. Ian has asked a couple of climbing buddies, and Bethany has two friends she grew up with to stand up with her."

"That's nice. The wedding sounds like it's going to be beautiful. And Carter and Aaron are engaged, too? Have they set wedding dates?"

"Aaron and Willa are getting married in December but I haven't heard many details. Carter and Mira are waiting until next summer. I'm pretty sure they're going to be married in Santa Fe. That's where Mira is from."

"I've never been to Santa Fe, but I hear it's beautiful."

"Yes." It was the kind of casual conversation he could have with anyone, but maybe that was the point—to keep any kind of real emotion at bay.

They fell silent, and he was grateful to see Shane's SUV returning. "There's no one at the house now," Shane said. "Could you come with me? There's something you need to see."

They both returned to their vehicles and followed Shane back to the tiny house. Light glowed from every window of the house, and strings of white lights illuminated the trees around the dwelling. As soon as they were out of their vehicles, Roxanne's neighbor, Kara, emerged from the house across the drive and hurried over. "What is going on?" she asked. "I saw the sheriff's car over here and got really worried."

"Someone broke into my house," Roxanne said.

"Oh no!" Kara put her hand on Roxanne's shoulder. "Are you all right? Did they take anything?"

"I'm a little shook up, but physically, I'm fine," Roxanne said. "I don't know yet if anything is missing."

"Are you a neighbor?" Shane asked.

"Yes, I live over there." Kara pointed to the blue house across the drive. "I'm so sorry this happened, Roxanne. That's so upsetting."

"Did you see anyone over here this afternoon or evening?" Shane asked.

"No. I was in Junction," Kara said. "Doing some shopping."

"What time did you get home?" Shane asked.

"Maybe twenty minutes ago?" She turned to Roxanne. "I saw your car pull in, then leave again. And then the sheriff's deputy arrived."

"Thank you, ma'am," Shane said. "If you think of anything else that might be relevant, give me a call." He handed her a business card. "Right now, I need you to return to your home."

Kara leaned close to Roxanne. "We'll talk later," she said, then left.

"Let's take a look around," Shane said to Roxanne.

To Dalton, the place looked undisturbed. He had to look closely to see that the lock had been smashed. They followed Shane into the house. "Don't touch anything, but just looking around, can you tell me if anything is missing?" he said.

Roxanne turned a slow circle, eyes scanning the room. From their spot in the middle of the room, Dalton thought he could see almost every part of the structure. "There's nothing obviously missing," she said after a moment. "My laptop is still here. Someone who wanted to rob me would take that, I'd think."

Shane nodded. "I'd like you to take a look upstairs," he said. "There's something upstairs that seems out of place to me, but I'd like your take on it."

Roxanne hung back. "If it's a dead animal or something like that, I don't want to look."

"It's nothing like that," Shane said. "It's just…confusing."

She took Dalton's hand. "You come, too," she said.

"Do you want me to go first?" Dalton asked.

"No, I can do it." She straightened her shoulders and

started up the narrow staircase. He followed closely, heart pounding in anticipation.

"Don't touch anything," Shane called up after them. "Just look."

She stopped at the top of the stairs and gasped. Dalton squeezed in beside her. There, in the middle of the queen-size bed, sat a large doll with blond pigtails in a pink dress. Bethany had had a similar doll when she was little, with all kinds of clothes and accessories, and even a book that told the doll's story. But someone had painted over this doll's features with garish makeup—a slash of red lipstick outside the lines of the plastic lips, and bright blue eye shadow and heavy eyeliner and false eyelashes.

A note was propped against the doll, the bold lettering, written with a black marker, visible from the doorway: "Mary, won't you come home and play with me?"

Roxanne stared at the doll and swayed slightly. Dalton's hand on her back steadied her, but she couldn't shake the dizzying feeling of being pulled back in time. Back into a nightmare. She was breathing hard—not quite hyperventilating but close—and she bit the inside of her cheek, tasting blood. Dalton's grip on her tightened, then his breath brushed her ear as he spoke. "Let's go back downstairs," he said.

She let him guide her down the stairs, though all of her awareness was still on the threshold of the bedroom—the image of the doll, and the note with it, flashing in her head like an old film strip.

Shane was waiting by the front door. "Who is Mary?" he asked.

Roxanne walked past him, out the door. The two men followed and she led the way to a wooden picnic table situated under a tall pine tree a short distance from the tiny home, beneath the glow of a string of white lights. She sat at one end of the table and Shane sat at the other. Dalton went to stand behind Roxanne.

"You saw the doll?" Shane asked.

"Yes."

"Does the doll belong to you?"

"No."

Shane's eyes met Dalton's as if to ask if Roxanne was always this terse or this was her reaction to shock. She didn't miss the exchange, but didn't comment on it. She was in shock, but she was going to push past that. Dalton put one hand on her shoulder, a solid weight that made her feel more connected to her body, less floating on waves of fear. "Do you think whoever broke into the house left that and the note behind?" Dalton asked Shane.

"I don't—" Shane began.

"Mary was the name William Ledger gave me after he kidnapped me," Roxanne said, interrupting him. "You know who William Ledger is?"

"Yes." Shane's expression was grim. "You think he was the person who ran you off the road ten days ago?"

"Yes."

"What about the doll?" he asked. "What's the significance of that?"

She closed her eyes briefly, the image of that horrible doll imprinted there like a scene from a horror movie. She opened them again and met Shane's direct gaze. He had blue eyes, and a boyish face, though there was nothing boyish about the way he looked at her now—all serious intensity. "William Ledger gave me a doll like that when I was with him," she said.

"Did it have the makeup like that?" Shane asked.

"Yes. It's a cheap knockoff of those collector dolls with the historical costumes and books and accessories and stuff. Ledger gave it to me when I had been with him about a month.

He…he said it was a reward because I'd been so good." She looked down at her hands, knotted in her lap. "I was terrified of it. At night I would put it in a corner and pile blankets over it so I didn't have to look at it." And so the doll couldn't see her. Her ten-year-old mind had been sure something evil looked out of that doll's eyes.

"Do you think this is the same doll or just a similar one?" Shane asked.

His question pulled her back to the present, out of the pit of the nightmare past. "I don't see how it could be the same," she said. "I'm sure the one he gave me was taken as evidence after Ledger was arrested. I never saw it again."

"Who else knew about the doll—besides Ledger?"

"The police knew. And Alice."

"Alice was the other girl he kidnapped?" Shane had pulled out a notebook and was scribbling furiously in it.

"That's right."

"Where is Alice now?" he asked.

"I don't know."

"Do you know if the doll was ever written about in the papers or mentioned at Ledger's trial?"

"I don't know. I was a witness, so I wasn't there for the whole trial. But no one ever asked me about it."

Shane nodded. "Did you recognize the handwriting on the note?"

"No. But I never saw Ledger's handwriting."

"Okay." Shane tucked the notebook away once more. "Whether this was done by William Ledger or someone else, I don't think it's safe for you to stay here," he said.

"No," she said. "I'm not going to stay here." The thought of going back inside and seeing that doll again made her shudder.

"Do you have somewhere you can go?" Shane asked. "We can try to find a bed in a women's shelter for you."

"I know a place she can stay," Dalton said.

She turned to look at him. Was he suggesting she stay with him? "That's sweet of you to offer—" she began.

"You can stay with my parents," he said. "None of us kids live at home anymore, so they've got plenty of room."

"I wouldn't want to impose…" she said, hesitating.

He moved around to sit beside her on the bench. "You met my mom," he said. "She loves taking care of people. And it would be a lot better than a shelter."

It would be much better than a shelter. Walking into the Ameses' house had been like being wrapped in a warm hug. She looked at Shane. "Would that be all right, if I stayed with the Ameses?"

"It should be. I'll let the sheriff know, but don't tell anyone else you don't have to."

"You don't think I'd be putting them in danger, do you?" Nausea swamped her at the thought. "Maybe I should go to the shelter."

"Has anyone around you been threatened or menaced?" Shane asked.

"No. Not that I know of." But she could have told him she didn't have any people around her. She knew almost no one in town—except Dalton and his family, Debra Percy, her neighbor Kara, and May the barista and a few others she had met casually.

"You should be fine," Shane said. "Let us know if you see or hear anything suspicious."

He stood and she rose also. "I need to get a few things," she said.

"I'll go with you," Shane said. "Don't touch anything you don't have to. And let me know if anything else is out of place."

She had to force herself to walk upstairs to her bedroom, taking comfort from the fact that the deputy was right behind her. She avoided looking at the doll as she collected clothes and toiletries. Downstairs, she added her laptop and files she needed for work. Shane helped her carry everything to her car.

Dalton joined them. "I called Mom and she's thrilled to take you in. She's getting the guest room ready for you."

"What did you tell her?" Roxanne asked.

"I told her someone had broken into your house and you weren't comfortable staying out here by yourself until the sheriff's department figured out who was responsible."

He had told the truth, without the horrible backstory. "Thanks," she said.

Dalton led the way back to town, Roxanne behind him and the sheriff's department SUV trailing. The Ameses came out to meet them when they pulled into the driveway. "I'm so glad you're okay," Diane said, and pulled Roxanne into a hug. Roxanne froze, but as Diane's warmth seeped into her, she relaxed a little and patted the older woman's back. "Thank you," she said. "It was a shock, but I'm okay."

"What an awful thing to come home to." Diane stepped back. "When Dalton told me, I could hardly believe it. And I'm so glad you're not going to be out there by yourself while the sheriff looks for whoever did this. You're welcome to stay here as long as you like."

"Thank you," she said. "I really appreciate it."

"Come on inside and I'll show you to your room."

She picked up her computer bag and Dalton followed with her suitcase. The Ameses led the way to a bedroom at the top of the stairs. Diane pointed out the bathroom across the hall. Bedroom and bathroom were done in shades of blue and yellow, with a pile of pillows atop a patchwork coverlet and a student desk under the window. "It's not fancy, but we hope you'll be comfortable."

"It's lovely." Roxanne swallowed past a sudden lump in her throat. "Thank you."

Mrs. Ames touched her shoulder. "If you need anything at all, you let us know," she said.

She and her husband left. Dalton set the suitcase on the desk. "How are you feeling?" he asked.

"Better," she said. She looked around the room, at the plain homeyness of it. She had moved around a lot in her life—first in a series of shelters and foster homes, then to various dorms, apartments and rental houses. In each one she had tried to make a home. This simple room felt more welcoming than many of those places had. "I'm still afraid, but it feels safer here."

He moved closer, but didn't touch her. "I bet you're exhausted," he said. "Try to get some rest and I'll call you tomorrow."

"Thanks. For everything." She hesitated, then leaned in and kissed his cheek. He patted her shoulder, then left. She heard him say something to his parents, but couldn't make out what. Then a door opened and shut and she heard the Jeep start in the driveway.

She sat on the edge of the bed. Sleep felt a long way off. She didn't want to lie down and dream the old, bad dreams. She thought she had put those nightmares behind her. Leave it to Ledger to bring them all back.

Chapter Nine

"Your doll is so pretty." Alice reached out a hand to stroke one blond braid of the two-foot-tall doll Billy had presented to Roxanne that morning. Roxanne couldn't bear to look at the garish toy. Alice looked more like a doll to her, with shiny black hair and gold-flecked brown eyes set in a perfect, heart-shaped face. Alice stuck out her lower lip. "Billy never gave me a doll."

"You can have her," Roxanne said. "I don't want her."

"That's not very nice," Alice said. She slid onto the twin bed beside Roxanne. The two girls shared a bedroom in the nondescript house on a quiet suburban street. It looked like a lot of other bedrooms Roxanne had been in, with two twin beds covered in matching floral coverlets, a fluffy pink rug between the beds. Except the windows of this room were boarded up, and the door had double locks on the outside. The door was locked now, Billy gone who knew where. Roxanne sometimes wished he would never come back, except that would probably mean she and Alice would starve, locked in here.

Roxanne merely scowled at Alice. When she had first arrived here, she had thought of Alice as her friend. Alice comforted her when she cried and told her everything would be all right. She had shared food with Roxanne and encouraged her to cooperate with Billy, to keep him from getting angry.

But early on, Roxanne had realized she and Alice didn't see their situation at all the same way. From the first hour in this awful house, Roxanne had been looking for a way to escape, whereas Alice reacted with horror at the very thought. "We can't leave Billy!" she protested the first time Roxanne whispered to her about trying to escape.

And then Alice began to tattle to Billy whenever Roxanne did anything "wrong." She caught Roxanne tugging at the edge of the boards over their bedroom windows and immediately reported to Billy. Billy had responded by locking Roxanne in a closet. She didn't know how long she was in there, cowering in the dark before Billy let her out. The punishment hadn't taught her to stop trying to escape, but it had reinforced the idea of keeping any attempts to herself.

Alice was staring at the doll again. "We could undo her braids and comb out her hair," she said. Alice liked to comb hair. She often insisted on brushing Roxanne's hair, running the brush through it until Roxanne's head ached.

"You can comb her hair if you like," Roxanne said.

Alice looked at her a long moment. It was so hard for Roxanne to figure out what was going on behind those placid amber eyes of hers. Then Alice slid off the bed and fetched the hairbrush. She picked up the doll and carried it to her bed and began undoing the elastic bands at the end of each braid.

Roxanne lay down and faced the wall. She imagined busting a hole through the drywall and running away. Would she find someone to help her, or would they send her back to Billy?

She fell asleep and woke later, to Billy shaking her shoulder. He held the doll, its hair undone, a tangled mess about its shoulders. Alice stood just behind him, nibbling at one thumbnail. "Look at the mess you made," he said. It was one of his favorite admonitions. She and Alice were always making messes, whether it was failing to perfectly smooth their sheets when they made their beds or missing a spot when they washed dishes.

Roxanne sat up, rocketed from sleep to wary wakefulness. "I didn't do anything," she said.

"How did her hair get like this?" Billy demanded.

"Alice did it."

She realized her mistake immediately. Over Billy's shoulder, she could see Alice shaking her head.

Billy looked at Alice. "Did you mess up the doll's hair?"

"No." Alice shook her head. "Mary did it. She said she didn't like the doll."

Billy thrust the doll at Roxanne. "You're going to spend the rest of the evening picking out these tangles and rebraiding her hair," he said. "No supper for you until you do."

Roxanne knew pleading or crying were useless. She laid the doll on the bed. "All right."

"You must do what I tell you," Billy said, something he preached often. "The doll is yours to look after. Just like I look after you."

Roxanne said nothing. She would never treat even a doll the way Billy treated her. And one day, she would get out of here. She would escape.

ALL DAY WEDNESDAY, Dalton thought about Roxanne. He had resisted calling her or asking his mom about her. That was a sure way to focus his mom's attention on their fledgling friendship. After he was done with work, he planned to drop by the house and see for himself how Roxanne was doing.

After his last tour of the day, he washed the Jeep as usual, then drove the short distance to a gas station to fill the tank. He was standing at the pump, watching the numbers click over when a beeping horn caught his attention. He turned to see Aaron in his sheriff's department SUV gliding by. Aaron raised a single finger in salute as he rolled past the gas station.

Dalton finished filling the Jeep's tank, then headed in the direction Aaron had been traveling. He spotted his brother parked near the soccer fields and pulled in across the street.

Aaron looked up from his laptop and rolled down the window as Dalton approached. "Let me in," Dalton said.

The door unlocked and Dalton moved aside a satchel full of paperwork and books and sat. The radio crackled softly with murmured conversation. "What do you know about the break-in at Roxanne's place yesterday evening?" Dalton asked.

"The creepy doll? Nothing really."

"Do you think William Ledger broke in and put that doll there?" Dalton asked.

"Maybe. Or someone who knew him and the kidnapping story." Aaron gave him a hard look. "What has Roxanne said about it?"

"Not much. I haven't talked to her since I dropped her off at Mom and Dad's last night. But I know she thinks it was Ledger. No one else really knew about the doll."

Aaron said nothing. The chatter on the radio had ceased and the two brothers sat in silence, though Aaron kept his gaze on Dalton, who couldn't stop himself from fidgeting. Was this another interrogation technique Aaron had learned in cop college?

"You okay with Roxanne staying with Mom and Dad?" Aaron finally asked.

"It was my idea."

"It's probably as safe a place for her as any," Aaron said. "We're making regular patrols by the house. If there's any trouble, we'll move her to a safe house—as much to protect Mom and Dad as to safeguard her."

Dalton's stomach hurt. "You don't really think they're in danger, do you?"

Aaron's scowl made him look almost menacing. "I've read Ledger's file. He's not a nice guy."

Dalton nodded. Even the little he had read online made that clear. But the whole situation felt so unreal. The doll was unsettling, but its appearance hadn't felt life-threatening. "Has the department had any luck tracking down Alice?" he asked.

"The other girl who was held captive with Roxanne?" Aaron asked.

"Yeah. She knew about the doll."

"I don't think we've looked for her. Why would she threaten Roxanne?"

"I don't know." Dalton raked one hand through his hair. "I'm just trying to think of anyone else who would have done this. What about Debra Percy?"

"The woman who was flying the drone off County Road 3? What about her?"

"She's been acting strange. Almost stalking Roxanne."

Aaron nodded. "Roxanne hasn't mentioned her—that I know of. But I can do a little checking."

"Thanks." Maybe it was time for Dalton to do some digging, too.

"I know you helped us out when you dug up background info on Mira's stalker," Aaron said. "But stay out of this. We're doing everything we can to figure this out and protect Roxanne."

"I believe you," Dalton said. But the sheriff's department had a whole town full of people to protect. He only had Roxanne. Thinking about her hurt wounded him. He wasn't ready to examine those feelings too closely, but digging around on the computer didn't require a lot of emotion. He had a talent and there was no reason he shouldn't use it.

ROXANNE SPENT HER first morning with the Ameses focused on work. Concentrating on code kept her thoughts from the fear-induced spiral that had kept her tossing and turning all night. One of the many things she liked about her job was the distraction from her thoughts that it provided. What seemed tedious to some was a welcome escape to her.

But by four o'clock she was done for the day and stared aimlessly out the window at the sunny lawn and distant peaks. She kept replaying the events of yesterday evening. That horrible doll, and all the memories it had brought to the surface. Not that she would ever forget what had happened to her, but she had gotten good at not dwelling on that time. She would rather focus on the future, but whoever was tormenting her now—Ledger or someone who knew his secrets— kept dragging her back into the mire of her past.

A gentle tapping on the door interrupted her thoughts. She turned in her chair. "Come in."

Diane eased open the door. "Are you busy working?" she asked.

"No, I'm done for the day. I didn't realize you were home. I didn't hear a car."

"I walked to work today." She patted her hips. "Trying to fight the middle-aged spread."

Roxanne thought she hardly looked old enough to be the mother of four grown children, but she wasn't good at flattery, so kept silent. "Would you like to come downstairs for a bit?" Diane asked. "I could use some help in the kitchen."

"Of course." Roxanne stood. "Mrs. Ames, I'm so sorry I didn't offer."

She waved away the apology. "Call me Diane. And really, I need the company more than the help."

She led the way downstairs into a yellow-and-white kitchen. Sunlight spilled from windows on two sides across marbled tiles. Diane opened a cabinet and took out a basket of potatoes. She selected a paring knife from a block on the kitchen island, then pulled out a stool. "You can sit here and peel potatoes while I cut up chicken to grill."

Roxanne slid onto the stool and picked up the knife. This scene felt familiar—when she was a young teen she had often helped her foster mom prepare meals. She hadn't seen it then as anything more than a mostly pleasant chore, but now that she was grown she realized how many times she had poured out her heart to Mama Marjie, and how much good advice she had taken in.

"What brought you to Eagle Mountain, Roxanne?" Diane asked, as she cut open a package of chicken thighs.

"I wanted a fresh start, and this seemed like a good place for it." Roxanne cut a long spiral of potato peel. "The mountains are so beautiful."

"When young people tell me they want to make a fresh start, I always think of a broken relationship," Diane said. "Is that what happened to you?"

"No. I just wasn't happy where I was."

"Where was that?"

"San Antonio. I thought it would be easier to get to know people in a small town like Eagle Mountain." She had believed there would be safety in the anonymity of a city, but there was also loneliness.

"Small towns can be cliquish, but Eagle Mountain isn't like that," Diane said. "So many people here are from other places. Of course, it's easy for us to fit in, since we have a business where we meet so many people."

"How did you end up here?" Roxanne asked.

"Dalton didn't tell you this story? We're from Vermont originally."

She shook her head. "We've never talked about it." Probably because she was so reluctant to talk about her own past, she never asked other people about theirs.

"Oh, well, Bethany moved here first. She did have a bad

relationship and wanted to get away. And I think she wanted to be on her own for a bit. She took a job working for the very Jeep business we now own. We came to visit, fell in love with the place, learned the business was for sale and here we are."

"All of you? I mean, all your children, too?"

"The twins—Carter and Dalton—didn't really have anything keeping them in Vermont, and they liked the idea of living in Colorado. Bethany was already a member of search and rescue and they wanted to do that, too, and they came to work for us at the tour company, so it was an easy choice for them. Aaron was a bit surprising—he was already working for a sheriff's department in Vermont. But there was an opening here and he decided to take it. He's never said, but he hadn't been very lucky in love, either, so I think that was another reason for the move. And of course, once he moved here, he met Willa, so I have to think Providence had a hand in it all."

"And now three of your children are getting married," Roxanne said. "That must be exciting."

"It's a lot." Diane drizzled olive oil over the chicken. "It really hits home that they're no longer yours when they take a spouse."

"You still have Dalton."

"Yes." She smiled, a fond look that pulled at Roxanne's heart. "He's always been the quietest of the four of them. The brightest. Sometimes the most devious."

"Devious?" The adjective surprised her.

"That may not be the right word, but he's always thinking about things—doing things that surprise us. He'll find his match one day." She sent Roxanne a speculative look.

Roxanne focused on cutting the eye out of a potato. She liked Dalton. A lot. But she wasn't in a place where she could even think about a relationship.

The doorbell chimed. Diane hurried to wash her hands. "I'll get that."

She left the kitchen and Roxanne peeled the last potato and tried not to listen to the muffled voices from the front room. Moments later, Diane returned. "There's someone here to see you, Roxanne," she announced.

"Hi." Kara lifted her hand in a shy wave. She held a small box in her other hand. "This came for you this morning and I was worried you might need it," she said. "I hope you don't mind that I tracked you down."

"Oh. Thanks." Roxanne took the box and read the label, aware of the other two women watching her. "It's just some face cream I ordered," she said. "You know, after seeing one too many social media posts."

"Oh my gosh, I do that, too," Kara said. "You'll have to let me know if you end up liking it."

"Um, how did you find me?" Roxanne asked. Why had she believed she would be harder to find in a small town? Obviously, that wasn't true.

"Actually, I wasn't trying to find you," Kara said. "I was trying to find Dalton." She turned to Diane. "I figured he would know how to get in touch with Roxanne. I saw the name of your Jeep tour company on the back of his Jeep, so I went there first, but the woman at the counter told me Dalton had left for the day. She didn't know where he lived, but she gave me your address." She turned back to Roxanne. "I thought I'd leave the package here for Dalton, but then Mrs. Ames told me you were here. So this is where you're staying?"

"I'll have to speak with Ashlynn about giving out our address," Diane said. "I've got to finish getting dinner ready. But you two feel free to sit out in the living room and visit."

The women moved to the living room and Kara perched on the edge of the sofa. "I hope you don't mind me bringing the package," she said. "I'm not trying to intrude on your privacy."

"No, of course not." Roxanne sat in the chair across from her and put the package on the coffee table between them. "Thank you for going to so much trouble. Is everything okay out at the house?"

"Oh yes. I mean, I haven't seen anybody over there or anything. Mr. Lusk came over and put a new lock on the door this morning. I guess you'll need to get the key from him."

"That's good."

"Have you found out anything more about the break-in?" Kara asked. "Do they know who did it?"

"I haven't heard anything," Roxanne said.

"I haven't seen anyone except Mr. Lusk since the sheriff's deputies left." Kara smoothed her hands down her thighs. "It's freaking me out a little, being out there by myself since this happened. Did they take anything valuable?"

"Not really." Her peace of mind. Her sense of safety. Had that been the aim all along?

"It's good that you have friends to stay with," Kara said. "Does Dalton live here, too?"

"No. He has his own place."

"Oh." Kara's face was full of questions, but all she said was, "He's really cute. Have you known him long?"

"Not long."

Kara laughed. "Then you must have really made an impression, if you've already moved in with his family." She covered her mouth with her hand. "Sorry. That probably sounded really rude. I didn't mean it that way. It's great that you have such good friends." She stood. "I'd better go now. I promise I'll keep an eye on your place. Do you know when you'll be moving back in?"

"I'm not sure." Roxanne stood also, and walked with Kara

to the door. "I'll let you know. Thanks for dropping off the package."

She closed the door behind the other woman and turned the lock, then returned to the kitchen. Diane was finished dicing the potatoes. "Would you and your friend like something to drink?" she asked. "I'm sorry I didn't offer before."

"That's all right. She couldn't stay long."

"I guess Eagle Mountain was a good choice for you," Diane said. "You're already making friends."

"Kara is my neighbor at the tiny houses." A potential friend.

"It's good to have neighbors who are friends."

"She said the sheriff's department is done with the property and my landlord has installed a new lock. There's no reason I couldn't move back in." Except that Ledger—who else would have left that doll and that note?—was still at large.

"I think you should stay here for a while longer." Diane didn't look up from chopping herbs. "You know you're welcome. And my oldest son, Aaron—did you know he's a sheriff's deputy?"

"Yes." Roxanne tensed. "What about him?"

"He didn't go into any details, mind you. He takes confidentiality very seriously. But he did tell me it wasn't a good idea for you to move back to your tiny house until they had figured out who was behind the burglary and arrested them. He told my husband and me to be on the lookout for any suspicious activity in the area, and he said he and the other deputies would be making regular patrols by the house."

So much for being an unobtrusive guest. "I'm so sorry. I didn't mean to upset you."

"We're not upset," Diane said. "Though if you have any idea of who we're watching out for, that would help."

Roxanne hesitated. "Maybe a man. But I'm not sure. It… it's someone who tried to harm me once before. A long time ago. He was in prison, but now he's out. He'd be in his late forties or maybe early fifties now. Not too tall, with a mustache." She shook her head. "I'm sorry I don't know more."

Diane moved over and put her arm around Roxanne. Roxanne held her breath, surprised by her longing to lean into the hug. She couldn't speak, sure she would burst into tears if she tried to say anything.

"We want you to be safe and it sounds like you'll be safest here," Diane said. "Better to have a lot of people looking out for you."

Roxanne nodded. "Thank you," she managed to whisper.

Diane patted her shoulder. "Look in that cabinet behind you and take out the cocoa, baking powder and vanilla. I feel like making some brownies for dessert. Chocolate doesn't cure everything, but it can't hurt, right?"

It was such a simple thing—homemade brownies and hugs. But Diane would probably be shocked to know how much they meant to Roxanne.

Chapter Ten

Dalton didn't make it to his parents' house in time for dinner that evening. He had just left Aaron at the soccer fields when his phone alerted with a search and rescue summons to look for a missing camper in the mountains above town. He stopped by his apartment long enough to grab his SAR gear, then headed for headquarters.

Carter was already there when he arrived, and Bethany pulled into the lot shortly after him. "We're looking for a ten-year-old girl, Sarah Michaelson, missing from her family's campsite at the Bryson Creek National Forest campground off Forest Road 1432," Danny told them.

"That's a pretty small campground," Tony said. "Only eight campsites, if I'm remembering correctly."

"You are," Danny said. "Sarah was there with her parents and her six-year-old brother. She told her mom she was going to walk up to the entrance to the campground to take photos of some wildflowers she had seen there. When she didn't come back after forty-five minutes, the mom went to look for her. The whole family and some of the campers in the area searched for her, too, but they didn't find anything. That's when they called 911." He glanced over at Sergeant Gage Walker, who stood a few feet away. "Do you have anything to add?" he asked.

Gage, the sheriff's younger brother, moved to stand beside Danny. His expression was grim. Dalton remembered the sergeant had a young daughter of his own, probably close to Sarah's age. "The entrance to the campground is only about a hundred yards from the family's camp," Gage said. "It's right on the forest service road. No one saw Sarah around the time she went missing, and no one reported traffic on the road, though there's a lot of brush and some big boulders that block the view of the entrance from most of the campsites."

"Are we sure she walked up to the entrance?" Harper asked. "Maybe she changed her mind and went in a different direction."

"We're not sure of anything at this point," Gage said. "We'll need to search the entire area around the campsite. On foot. Most of that area is heavily wooded, making an aerial search, even with a drone, impractical." He glanced at Danny. "That's all I've got right now."

Danny nodded. "All right, everyone. Carrie has maps of the area. You'll work in teams to search your assigned sections. Anna and Jacquie will start at the family's campsite and try to determine which direction Sarah went, but as soon as she's cleared the campground itself we'll start our search."

Volunteer Anna Trent and her trained search dog, a black standard poodle named Jacquie, moved to join Gage. "We're ready when you are, Sergeant," she said.

Gage, Anna and Jacquie left and the others lined up to take a map and receive their search assignments.

The road to the campground was lined with vehicles—sheriff's department SUVs and Forest Service trucks, along with passenger cars of locals who had heard about the missing girl and showed up to help search. People milled about the campsites and clustered around the girl's family, who stood with Sheriff Travis Walker and Forest Service Ranger Nate

Hall. "Search and rescue is here," the sheriff told Sarah's parents as Dalton and the others followed Danny into the camp.

"Thank you for coming." Sarah's father, red-eyed and white-faced, greeted them.

"Is there anything you can tell us to help in our search?" Danny asked. "For instance, had Sarah seen something on an earlier hike that interested her? Something she might have tried to go back and photograph? Or is she the type of kid to get sidetracked by an animal or a bird?"

Sarah's mother shook her head. "No, she isn't like that. Sarah is very mature for her age and she wouldn't have wandered off by herself. If she said she was going to the campground entrance, that's where she would have gone."

"Is she shy or outgoing?" Danny asked. "Would she have talked to strangers?"

"She isn't shy," her mother said. "But she knows not to engage with people she doesn't know. We taught her to be careful."

"Sheriff!"

They turned to see Deputy Jamie Douglas leading a slight, older man toward them. "This is Mr. Roman," Jamie said. "He may have some information for us."

Roman wiped at his nose and looked nervously at the crowd gathered around him. About five foot six, he was dressed in a red-and-black flannel shirt that looked a size too large, khaki pants and black sandals and wore the expression of someone who wanted to be anywhere else but talking to law enforcement. "I don't know if it means anything or not, but earlier today, I thought I heard a scream. But it could have been an animal or something."

"When did you hear this?" Travis asked.

Roman sniffed. "About noon? I wasn't looking at a clock or anything, but I was just back from a hike."

"Just the one scream?"

"Yeah. Not all that loud."

"Which direction was it coming from?" Travis asked.

"I thought up toward the road." Roman looked around. "But it's hard to tell direction in these woods."

"Did you hear anything else?" Travis asked. "A car or other voices?"

"Not really. Just campground noises. People at the next campsite were packing up to leave, and they were talking back and forth, so they pretty much drowned out everything else."

"Thank you, Mr. Roman," Travis said. "Deputy Douglas will get your information, and we'll be in touch if we have more questions." He turned back to Sarah's parents. "Tell the searchers what Sarah was wearing, please."

"She had on blue cotton shorts and a T-shirt from Black Canyon of the Gunnison National Park," Mrs. Michaelson said. "And blue sandals. She was carrying a cell phone in a pink case. She was so proud of that phone. She got it for her tenth birthday. It doesn't have a lot of apps on it or anything, but she loved taking pictures with it." She put a hand to her mouth, fighting tears.

"Thank you both," Travis said. "We'll keep you updated on anything we find." He walked away from the family. Danny and some of the volunteers, including Dalton, followed. "Gage and Anna and Jacquie are at the family's campsite now," the sheriff said. "I'm hoping they'll pick up a scent. Wait to head out until we see what they find."

They didn't have to wait long. Gage soon joined them. "The dog led us right to the road," he said. "Then she lost the scent. Anna thinks that means the girl got into a vehicle. She and Jacquie are still searching, trying to pick up the scent again."

"So maybe Mr. Roman did hear a scream, when someone pulled the girl into a vehicle," Danny said.

"Or maybe it was an animal noise and the girl went willingly with someone she knew," Travis said.

"The family is from Junction, aren't they?" Gage asked.

"I'll ask them if there's anyone local Sarah would have gone with," Travis said. "In the meantime, we'll have searchers comb both sides of the road leading from the entrance. Search for the girl, but also look for any signs of a struggle."

Dalton was assigned to search with Harper and Caleb. The three searched along a half-mile section of the road and into the woods a hundred yards. They took turns calling Sarah's name, their shouts and those of other searchers echoing through the trees. Dalton tried to remember everything he had learned in his training on searches. He had been taught that children would sometimes hide from rescuers, and that kids could walk much farther than most people estimated.

"If somebody grabbed her off the road, she could be miles from here by now," Harper said when they stopped to drink water.

"There was that guy earlier this year who was trying to kidnap kids," Caleb said.

"Yeah, but he went after boys," Harper said. "And he's in jail now."

"There are too many creeps out there," Caleb said.

Dalton remained silent. Was this what had happened to Roxanne? Had William Ledger grabbed her off the street? His attempt to run Roxanne off the road and the break-in of her house pointed to him being in the area. Could he have decided to target another little girl?

They searched until darkness made navigating the thick woods impossible, then regrouped at a clearing a few hundred yards from the campground that had been designated as a staging area. "You look beat," Bethany said when she found Dalton by a watercooler.

"Yeah." He pulled a twig from his hair. "Did your group find anything?"

She shook her head. "Not one footprint or piece of clothing or anything."

Dalton looked past her and spotted the sheriff and Gage walking toward the road. He headed to cut them off. "Dalton, where are you going?" Bethany called, but he ignored her and picked up his pace.

He caught up with Travis and Gage at the road. "Sheriff, wait up!" he called.

They stopped and waited for him. "What is it?" Gage asked. "Did you find something?"

Dalton shook his head. "No. But I was wondering—do you think William Ledger might have grabbed the girl? She's the same age Roxanne was when she was taken, and he had to be the one who broke into Roxanne's cabin and left the doll and the note. I mean, no one else would do that, would they?"

"We're still looking for Ledger," Gage said. "If we find him, we'll certainly question him about this."

"Are you saying he got out of prison and just disappeared?"

"He failed to report even once to his parole officer," Gage said. "He's not leaving an electronic trail under his own name. There are bulletins out to every law enforcement agency in the US and Canada warning that he's wanted for parole violations, but no one has reported seeing him."

"What about the truck he was driving when he ran Roxanne off the road?" Dalton asked. "That was pretty distinctive."

"No one has seen it, either," Gage said.

"He probably ditched it shortly after the accident and is driving something else now," Travis said. "He's using cash, or maybe a stolen credit card, to pay his expenses. He may have changed his appearance and he's certainly using another name."

"Do you know if Roxanne has had any more trouble?" Gage asked.

"I haven't talked to her today," Dalton said.

"An Amber Alert went out this afternoon for Sarah," Travis said. "We'll issue a new bulletin for Ledger as well."

"I hate thinking about that little girl out there, with someone like him," Dalton said.

"We've got deputies combing the county for any sign of her," Travis said.

"Go home and get some rest," Gage said. "We may need you to search tomorrow."

"I'll be here," Dalton said.

The ride back to search and rescue headquarters with his fellow volunteers was silent. Everyone looked worn-out and discouraged. "I imagine the search will continue tomorrow," Danny told them before they dispersed to their own vehicles. "Watch your alerts, if you're available."

Dalton had intended to return to his apartment for a hot shower and whatever he could find in the refrigerator for a quick meal. But instead, he turned the Jeep toward his parents' home. Welcoming light glowed golden in the windows along the front of the house, and he heard laughter as he trudged up the front walk. He let himself in with his key and stood for a moment in the darkened foyer, listening to the sound of conversation from the living room—his father's deeper voice, followed by his mother's familiar tenor, then a softer, feminine murmur that made his heart beat a little faster.

He moved to the doorway of the living room. "Hey," he said.

The three of them were seated side by side on the sofa, Roxanne between his parents, a large photo album open on her knees. She smiled up at him, cheeks flushed and eyes bright. But the smile faded as she took him in. She pushed aside the album and stood, but his mother had reacted even quicker. "What happened to you?" Diane asked. "Have you been in an accident?"

Dalton looked down at himself and realized there was a large rip across the front of his shirt where he had caught it on a thorny vine, and mud streaked the knees of his pants where he had fallen. He probably had scratches on his face from more vines. "I was on a SAR call," he said. "We were looking for a missing girl in some rough country."

"Did you find her?" Roxanne asked.

"Unfortunately, no." He moved to an armchair adjacent to the sofa, dropped into it and closed his eyes. He could have fallen asleep then and there, he thought.

When he opened his eyes again, Roxanne had returned to her seat on the sofa and was watching him. He looked around for his mom and dad. "Your mom went to make you something to eat," she said. "And I think your dad went up to get a room ready for you."

"I can drive home after I rest a minute," he said.

"You don't look like it."

He sat forward and wiped his face with his hands, trying to wake up. "I guess I'm tireder than I thought."

"What happened to the little girl?" she asked.

"We're not sure. She told her mom she was going to walk a hundred yards or so from their campsite and take a picture at the entrance to the campground. A tracking dog followed her scent that far, then she was just…gone."

"Do they think someone picked her up?" Roxanne asked.

He glanced toward the kitchen. He could hear both his parents in there, talking softly, their words reduced to a low murmur. "I was wondering if it was William Ledger," Dalton said.

Roxanne pressed her lips together and gripped her knees

with both hands. "Is that what the sheriff thinks, too?" she asked.

"He says they're looking for Ledger, but they haven't seen any sign of him or that truck he was driving when he went after you. They think he's switched vehicles and is probably traveling under another name and is using cash or a stolen credit card. But no one has seen him."

"He was very good at hiding in plain sight," she said. "I didn't realize how good until years later."

"I brought you some dinner." His mother returned, carrying a tray like the one she'd bring his meals on when he was home sick with a cold. She placed the tray over his knees and the aroma of a hot roast beef sandwich hit him hard enough that his stomach clenched and his mouth watered.

"Thanks, Mom," he said. "I'm starving."

"I called Bethany and Carter while I was waiting for the bread to toast," his mom said, as Dalton ate. "They both made it home safely. Carter said they may need to go out and search again tomorrow, so we'll have to rearrange the tour schedule. I figure Dad and Clayton can fill in for you boys for most of the day."

"They're going to search the woods again tomorrow?" Roxanne asked.

Dalton finished chewing and swallowed. "We have to, unless we get other information to confirm the little girl isn't there," he said.

"Her poor parents," his mom said. "They must be worried sick."

Dalton finished eating, but he watched Roxanne out of the corner of his eyes. She pretended interest in something his mother was saying about her conversation with Bethany, but he thought she wasn't really listening. There was a new stillness to her face, and a pinched look somewhere between worry and fear.

He finished eating and pushed his plate away. "I think I'll go upstairs and take a shower," he said.

"Your old room is ready for you," his mom said. "Go right to bed and rest."

He supposed his mother was never going to stop talking to him as if he was still six years old, instead of twenty-six. Tonight, it was easy to shrug off her words, probably because he had already planned to turn in as soon as possible.

When he emerged from the shower twenty minutes later Roxanne was standing in the doorway of her room, across the hall, as if she had been waiting for him. She glanced down the hallway, as if to make sure they were alone, then motioned for him to come into her room.

Suppressing a grin, he did so. He didn't really think Roxanne was inviting him inside for anything risqué, but he couldn't help but feel like a teenager sneaking around behind his parents' backs. She closed the door behind them, then moved past him into the room. The furniture had been Bethany's before she moved out, though tranquil oil paintings had replaced the posters she had tacked to the wall in her teen years, and the space was more orderly than he remembered his sister keeping it. "I've been thinking about this missing little girl," she said.

"Her name is Sarah," he said.

"Sarah." She nodded. "It sounds like if someone took her, it happened very quickly, is that right?"

"I think so. One camper thought he might have heard one short scream, but no one else heard anything. She wasn't gone that long before her parents went looking for her."

She hugged her arms across her stomach. "When Ledger took me, it wasn't like that," she said.

"It wasn't?"

"No. He didn't go after me directly. He used Alice to get close to me."

He didn't say anything, waiting for her to explain.

She blew out a breath, stirring the tendrils of hair framing her face. "I met Alice at a playground near my home. Ledger must have been nearby, but I have no memory of him. All I remember is this very pretty girl who went out of her way to be nice to me. I told you I was living in a group home at the time, right?"

"Yes."

"I didn't have friends," she said. "None of the other kids in the home were close to my age. They were all much younger. There were six of us and I always felt left out."

He pictured her—a little girl playing by herself at a playground.

"Alice and I played together, then we split an ice cream she bought from a stand there. I never had money for ice cream, so that was a special treat. She promised to come back the next day. I went early and waited and sure enough, she came and we played again. I was so happy. So starved for attention."

She sat on the side of the bed, still hugging herself, not looking at him, but at some point in the past. "After a few days of this, she invited me to come to her house to play. She said her dad had said she could invite me for dinner. I wasn't supposed to do anything like that without permission, but I was afraid the group mom would say no. So I decided I would go anyway and worry about the consequences later. Getting to play with Alice would be worth any punishment." She choked on the last word and Dalton came and sat beside her. But he didn't touch her. She looked so fragile, he feared she might shatter.

"I didn't pay much attention to the man driving the car. Alice and I sat in the back seat and talked the whole way to her house. I don't even know how far we drove. When we got to the house, she took me to her room. It had twin beds with pretty quilts on them, and some toys. We played and talked and I was so happy. But it began to get late. I started to worry I would be in big trouble. I said I needed to go home and Alice told me I couldn't. I had to stay with her now. Something about the way she said it frightened me. I ran to the door, but I couldn't open it. 'You can't get out,' she told me. 'The door is locked.' I started screaming that I had to go home. Alice grabbed me and begged me to be quiet, but I wouldn't be. Then Ledger burst in. He grabbed me and shoved me into a closet. I cried and beat on the door and when I finally wore myself out, I couldn't hear anyone. It was dark and hot in there. Alice told me later I was in there for three days before he let me out."

She leaned against him and he held her tightly. Anger over what had been done to her overwhelmed him. He held on as much to comfort her as to keep himself here in this room, instead of giving into the impulse to go out and search for William Ledger and hurt the man. He tried to focus on Roxanne instead. He thought she was crying, but she was so silent he couldn't tell. He stroked her hair and whispered, "I'm so sorry. I'm so sorry." Over and over.

After a long time she pulled away and wiped at her eyes. She looked at him, more calmly now. "I'm not saying he wouldn't grab a girl off the street," she said. "I don't know that at all. I just… I wanted you to know what happened to me."

The moment felt precious and fragile. He didn't want to spoil it by talking too much. "Thank you for trusting me with that," he said and laced his fingers with hers.

They sat like this for a long minute, then she gently withdrew her hand. "You need to rest now," she said.

"Are you going to be okay?"

She met his gaze. He saw sadness there, but also strength.

"I'm good," she said. "My memories may make me sad, but that's in the past. I'm in a much better place here."

What kind of place was he in? Worried over a little girl he didn't even know. Confused about where he stood with this woman he was growing to care for a great deal. Did she see him as merely a friend, or potentially more?

Because he wanted more. Maybe even more than she could give.

Chapter Eleven

By midmorning the next day, Roxanne gave up trying to focus on work and drove to the campground where Sarah Michaelson had disappeared the day before. A plea for searchers had been broadcast on social media, but Roxanne was still stunned by the number of vehicles crowding both sides of the dirt road leading to the campground.

She followed a stream of people to a field where signs directed volunteers to gather. Dozens of men and women and several dogs milled about while people in orange safety vests tried to direct them to gather in groups. The throb of a helicopter pulsed overhead and a group of ATVs raced by on the road behind the field.

"Roxanne!" The shout carried above the cacophony.

Before Roxanne could even turn around, Debra had hold of her arm and was pulling her out of line. "I need to talk to you," Debra said.

"Debra, I don't want to talk right now." Roxanne pulled free of the other woman's hold.

Debra leaned in so close Roxanne could see where her eyeliner had smeared. "Don't tell me you're not thinking the same thing I am," she said.

"I don't know what you're talking about."

"Doesn't this sound like something Billy Ledger would do?" Debra spoke in a harsh whisper.

"Why do you say that?" Roxanne found herself whispering, too. As if most people overhearing them would even know who Ledger was.

"It's what he did to you, isn't it?" Debra asked. "A ten-year-old girl, taken off the streets near her home."

The words sent a chill through her. "How do you know that?" she asked.

"I read all the newspaper accounts of Ledger's crimes. I've been researching this for years. You don't think I woke up last week and decided to look you up, do you? It took me years to learn how to dig and search in order to find you."

"What did the newspapers say?" Roxanne had never read them. At ten, she had been too young to even think of it. Later, she had no desire to relive her ordeal.

"The foster home reported you missing when you didn't come home from playing in the park. The local police looked for you, but when they couldn't find you they assumed you had run away." She looked around them. "Too bad they didn't do a massive search like this."

Too bad. Roxanne's throat tightened. Alice had told her not to count on anyone looking for her. "People don't miss kids like us," she had said. "Kids without families. It's why Billy picked you. You didn't really have a home, so he could give you one."

It hadn't been a home. It had been a prison, even though Alice refused to believe that.

"What makes you think Ledger did this?" she asked Debra again.

"You know he's out of prison, right?"

"Yes."

"Has he tried to get in touch with you?"

Roxanne recoiled. "Why do you even ask that?"

"He said all that at his trial about how you were 'precious' to him." She made air quotes around the adjective. "He said he would never forget you. I figured that's why you changed your name and made yourself so hard to find—because you were afraid of him."

She hadn't done those things because she was afraid of Ledger. She was only afraid of having her past publicized, so that people only saw her as a victim. "Do you really think he followed me here?" she asked.

"I found you. He could have, too." She grabbed Roxanne's arm again. "You're ghost white. Has something happened? Have you heard from Ledger?"

"Right after I moved here, someone ran me off the road," Roxanne said. "I thought it was Ledger." She wasn't going to mention the break-in and the doll. Debra knew too much about her already.

"Does the sheriff know this?"

"Yes. He knows everything. Law enforcement is looking for Ledger but they don't know that he had anything to do with Sarah disappearing." She pulled away from Debra once more. "If we're going to help look, we need to join the others."

She started to walk away and collided with another woman.

"Oh my gosh, Roxanne." Kara reached out to steady her. "I saw you over here and was coming to talk to you. Are you okay?"

"I'm fine. What are you doing here?"

"I came to help search, but I guess I'm too late." She looked back over her shoulder. "They told us they have too many people. The rest of us are supposed to go home. I guess past a certain point, it's too hard to coordinate all the searchers."

Roxanne felt more relief than disappointment. As much as she wanted to help, she had dreaded coming upon something— or someone—horrible. "Thanks for letting me know," she said. "That poor kid. I hope they find her."

"Me, too," Kara said. "It's just wild that a kid could disappear like that." She patted Roxanne's shoulder. "How are you doing? Any news on your housebreaker?"

Roxanne glanced around, looking for Debra. She didn't want to have to explain the whole housebreaking thing with her listening in. But Debra was nowhere in sight. Roxanne turned back to Kara. "I haven't heard anything. I think the sheriff's department is probably focused on Sarah right now."

"Of course." Kara smiled. "At least you're safe there with the Ameses. They seem like really nice people."

"They are."

"I guess I'd better get going," Kara said. "Take care."

Kara moved off and Roxanne did the same. She wasn't doing anyone good here.

She was almost to the road when a man in uniform flagged her down. Aaron Ames waved her over and she joined him beside a sheriff's department vehicle. "Roxanne, what are you doing here?" he asked.

"I wanted to help," she said. "But I guess they don't need any more volunteers."

He looked out over the field, still crowded with people. "This is chaos," he said. "You're better off back at Mom and Dad's." He looked at her intently. "You should stay there and not wander around by yourself."

"Is that because you think Ledger is nearby? Have you heard something?"

He shook his head. "No. But you've had two close calls already. Better to be safe until we figure out who's behind this harassment."

"Dalton asked me if I thought William Ledger kidnapped Sarah. Is that what the sheriff thinks?"

"Ledger is a known child predator and he might be in the area. It's something we have to consider."

"But you're out here searching the woods."

"Because we don't know she was kidnapped. Maybe she wandered off and got lost. If that's the case, every minute counts."

Roxanne nodded. "I hope you find her."

"You'll go back to the house?"

"Yes." She didn't want another encounter with Ledger. But even more, she wanted to never have to think about him again. That was the only way she would ever feel truly free.

AFTER FIVE DAYS, they called off the physical search for Sarah Michaelson. "We ask the public to continue to keep a look-out for any sign of Sarah," the sheriff said in a statement to the media. "We have conducted an exhaustive search of the area surrounding the campground, utilizing dozens of volunteers, hundreds of man-hours, tracking dogs and both aerial and ground searches. Though we are no longer actively searching, we do ask that anyone who might have seen anything that might pertain to Sarah's disappearance from the Bryson Creek campground around noon on September 17, please contact our office."

Volunteers continued to roam the woods, and the girl's picture was on posters all over town. To Dalton it felt as if searchers had tramped through every inch of the woods and mountainside. The knowledge that no one had found Sarah hung over the search and rescue volunteers. They didn't like to fail in the mission they had trained for.

When Dalton wasn't working, training for SAR or with Roxanne and his parents, he tried to find out more about William Ledger. He didn't tell Roxanne what he was doing because talking about Ledger clearly upset her. But what he found while reading through old newspaper accounts and what trial documents had been released to the public haunted him. Roxanne had been all but abandoned by those who were supposed to protect her. Anger burned in him on her behalf.

So much of a normal childhood had been stolen from her. And the man who did this was walking free.

Despite his previous luck in finding people online who didn't want to be found, he had no luck determining what had happened to Ledger after he was released from prison. One newspaper account mentioned that he was going to live with a "friend" but Dalton could find no further details. He asked Aaron to tell him what the sheriff's department knew, but his brother swore they hadn't discovered anything new, either.

He tried to see Roxanne every day, casually dropping by his parents' house to borrow something or accept an invitation to dinner. Roxanne laughed at his mother's comment that they hadn't seen this much of him since before he moved into his own place, and she always seemed glad to see him, but he didn't think sitting in the living room or on the front porch talking qualified as a real date. He was trying to be Roxanne's friend, waiting for her to see him as more.

"Let's get out of the house and do something fun," he told her a week after she had moved in—the day after the sheriff called off the search for Sarah.

"What do you have in mind?" she asked.

"We could take a hike or something, in the mountains. There are a lot of great trails."

"I'd love that, but Aaron told me I needed to stay close to home until they figure out who's behind my wreck and the break-in. He was so insistent, he kind of scared me."

"Aaron can be that way—a little intense." He thought for a moment. "How about we get you out of the house, but we don't go far. And you won't be alone. I'll be with you." He flexed his muscles in a mock he-man pose and she laughed— the reaction he had been hoping for.

"So what do you have in mind?" she asked.

"What about a picnic at the lake? Or if you'd rather go to a movie or out to eat…"

"A picnic sounds wonderful." She took his hand and squeezed it. "I'll look forward to it."

She was waiting at the curb when he arrived Thursday afternoon. "Is my mom watching out the window?" he asked as she slid into the passenger seat of the Jeep.

"Probably."

"Did you tell her we were going out?"

"No. Though I could tell she was curious when I told her I had a date. But she really is trying hard to respect my privacy. I appreciate that about her."

"I didn't think my mom ever respected privacy," he said. "But I guess that's only with her children."

"When I suggested it was time for me to move back to my own place, she told me she didn't think that was a good idea."

"You were thinking of moving back?" He tried to keep his voice light, but his hands tightened on the steering wheel. "Is that safe?"

"Your mother told me it wasn't. She said she had no idea why, but that Aaron had pulled her aside and impressed on her how important it was to watch out for me." She cleared her throat and when she spoke again, her voice was a little ragged. "I'm touched, really, how much your whole family seems to care."

He reached over and squeezed her hand. "You're an easy person to care about. And I don't think you should move back to that tiny house. It's so remote and you're all alone out there." He also made a mental note to pull Aaron aside soon and find out what made him so insistent on keeping Roxanne from venturing too far alone. Had the sheriff's department heard something about Ledger's location?

"My house isn't that remote," she said. "Kara is just across the drive, and Mr. Lusk lives less than a mile away."

"It's not the same as being in a house with other people."

"Yes, well your mom got so upset I agreed I wouldn't

leave just yet. But I can't stay with your folks forever, and it doesn't seem the sheriff is any closer to finding Ledger—if he was even the one behind those attacks."

"You saw the man who ran you off the road and you recognized him," Dalton said. "And who else would know about the doll Ledger gave you?"

She sighed and sat back in her seat. "I'm glad you believe me. I wonder if the sheriff does, or he's just humoring me."

"Aaron wouldn't insist on you staying safe if he didn't think you were at risk," Dalton said. "I'm not trying to frighten you—I just want you to know we're all taking this seriously."

"I probably should be more frightened, but I'm not," she said. "Mostly, I'm numb. It's so surreal, having to deal with him again after all these years."

"Let's not think about that this evening," he said as he turned onto the road leading to the small reservoir that served as storage of the town's water, as well as a popular fishing and picnic spot. "Let's just enjoy ourselves."

He parked by the restrooms, then they walked the path around the lake. When he took her hand, she moved closer. "I'm glad you suggested this," she said. "It's good to get out."

For a long time, they didn't say anything. They didn't have to. In the week she had been with his parents they had spent more time together, mostly talking. He had learned about the other places she had lived and the jobs she had held. He knew her favorite food, her favorite color, her favorite movie and about her allergy to seafood. She knew the same things about him. These were the boxes people checked off when getting to know one another, but observations counted for more than words. He heard how her voice softened when she spoke about volunteering at an animal shelter at her last home, and her enthusiasm for learning to cook from his mom. She laughed at all his dad's corny jokes and could discuss the intricacies of rehearsal dinner decorations with his sister for a mind-numbing amount of time. She was smart and funny, yet quick to stand up for herself. He was one of the few people here to know how strong she really was.

They picnicked at a table in the shade, sharing fried chicken and deli salads and a bottle of white wine.

When the meal was done, she pushed the leftovers away and turned around to lean against the table and stare out at the lake. "Thanks for suggesting this," she said. "It's so beautiful here."

He slid closer and put his arm around her back. Was he being too daring—asking too much? He didn't think he was the only one feeling this pull of attraction.

She turned her head to smile up at him. He wanted to trace his finger down the curve of her cheek and feel the satiny texture of her skin. He wanted to kiss the corners of her eyes and the tip of her nose and press his lips to hers, to feel her body relax against him and to taste the sweetness of her mouth.

"Dalton?" She whispered his name like a question.

"Roxanne." He leaned closer. "I'd really like to kiss you."

In answer she leaned forward, closing the gap between them, sealing her lips to his. He slipped his arms around her, holding her, but not too tightly, reveling in the feel of her, warm and yielding. Her lips parted beneath his and he accepted the invitation, sweeping his tongue into her mouth. She tasted of the wine they had been drinking and smelled like vanilla and flowers. He wanted to bury his nose in the soft place where her neck joined her shoulder and breathe in the aroma of her.

She pressed her palm to his chest and he slid one hand up her side to cup her breast. They were both breathing hard, wanting more. Or at least, he wanted more.

She broke the kiss, though she kept her hand on his chest.

Her expression was troubled. "Is something wrong?" he asked.

"No. Everything is right. Except…"

"Except what?" He unwrapped his arms from around her and allowed a little more space between them. Her face was flushed, her lips lightly swollen, hair mussed. She was an erotic vision but he forced himself to focus on the pain in her voice.

"Sarah is missing. And Ledger might have taken her. That means he's somewhere close. He could be a danger to you and to your family. I should be telling you to stay as far away from me as you can."

"I'm not going to do that."

"And I'm not strong enough to ask you." She curled her fingers, gripping his shirt, and rested her forehead against his chin.

He stroked her hair, trying to find words for what he needed to say. "After Sarah disappeared, I went online and read more about Ledger," he said.

"So you know more about what happened to me." Her voice was flat. Resigned.

He pulled back enough to look her in the eye. "I know, but it doesn't change how I feel about you."

"It doesn't?" She sounded doubtful. "I guess that saves me the trouble of having to tell you everything that happened."

"You don't have to tell me anything," he said. "Or not anything you don't want to tell me. I guess—I'm just trying to say I understand why you're so afraid of him. I'm afraid for you."

"Then you understand why I don't think we should get involved. Not now. What if he does come for me again? What if he tries to hurt you?"

"What if he tries to hurt *you*? Don't you think I want to protect you?"

"Why would you want to protect me?"

Because I've fallen in love with you. Because you're im-portant to me. The words were so freighted with emotion he shied away from them. "Because you deserve protecting."

She leaned into him again and rested her head in the hollow of his shoulder. "I'm afraid if I start something with you, Ledger will ruin it," she said.

He tried to figure out exactly what she meant. "Because of what he did to you before?" he asked. "Did it change the way you feel about sex?"

She pushed herself away from him and looked him in the eye. "You don't have to worry about that," she said. "I know the difference between what he did and real passion between people who care about each other."

His throat tightened and he was horrified to realize he was close to tears. How was it that every emotion with her seemed more intense? "That's good," he managed to croak.

She smoothed her hand down his chest. "People like Ledger like to break things," she said. "Whether it's people or possessions. I'm worried he'll try to break us."

"No, he won't." He gripped her arms. "He didn't break you all those years ago, and you're stronger now. You make me stronger."

"I love that you're so sure about that. I wish I could be."

He kissed her again, harder, and slid his hand beneath her sweater to trace the edge of her bra. "We could go back to my place."

She pulled back again, a soft expression of longing and regret on her face. "I'd rather wait," she said. "I don't like to rush things."

"And I don't want to rush you." He took his hand from beneath her sweater and kissed her again. A gentler brush of his lips. He was disappointed that he wouldn't be making love to her tonight, but also thrilled that she trusted him enough to be honest with him.

She turned in his arms to look out across the lake once more. "It's a beautiful sunset," she said. "I can't get over how everywhere I look is a picture postcard. I don't want to ever take that for granted."

"Then you're not sorry you came here?"

"No. I've found so much here." She smiled, and he hoped she was thinking of him. Then the smile faded. "I'm not going to lose that," she said. "I'm not going to let Ledger steal that from me."

Chapter Twelve

Roxanne was working on Friday, midmorning, when the doorbell rang. The Ameses were both at work, so she moved downstairs to answer the summons. But instead of a package delivery, which was what she assumed the ringing was about, Debra stood at the door. "Thank goodness, you really are here," she said, bouncing on her toes. "I had to bug people all over town before someone told me they thought you were staying here."

Roxanne was so startled to see her she blurted out the first thing that came to mind. "Why are you stalking me?"

"I'm not stalking you. And this is important. I've found out some stuff about Billy Ledger."

Roxanne knew she was no match for Debra's energy. Better to let her spill whatever she had to say and move on. "Come in." She held the door open wider. "But you can't stay long. I'm working."

"You're going to want to hear this, I promise. The more we know about Billy, the more we can help the authorities capture him."

Roxanne followed Debra into the living room. "There is no 'we.' The sheriff is searching for Ledger. I can't do more than they can."

"Are you sure about that?" Debra sank onto the sofa. "No

one even considered that Bettina might have been one of Ledger's victims until I brought it up. My investigations gave us all the information we know about her disappearance. I'll go anywhere and talk to anyone if I think it will lead to Bettina."

"I already told you—I don't know anything about your sister," Roxanne said. "I'm very sorry, but it's the truth."

"I believe you." Debra hugged a throw pillow across her stomach. "I think my best hope now is for law enforcement to capture Ledger. Then they can question him about Bettina. He's never mentioned her before because no one thought to ask."

Roxanne lowered herself onto the other end of the sofa. "Why are you so sure your sister was one of Ledger's victims?" she asked.

"He was living in the area when she went missing," Debra said. "This was two years before he took Alice. Bettina could have been his first victim. She walked to a store two blocks from our house to buy a loaf of bread and never came back. She just vanished into thin air. Police searched, but Ledger wasn't even on their radar back then."

"What do you think happened to her?" Roxanne asked.

"I think he took her but something went wrong. He killed her. Then he got rid of the body. He lay low for a while until he tried again with Alice and then you. It makes sense."

Roxanne nodded. The neat narrative had appeal. "But you don't have any proof."

"No." She leaned toward Roxanne. "But if the police question him, maybe he'll let something slip. Enough to make them search the house he lived in at the time."

"What will you do if that doesn't happen?" Roxanne asked.

"I'm not going to stop looking for Bettina. I've even thought about trying to buy the house where Ledger held you and Alice from the current owners. Or at least renting it for a while so I could get people in there with ground-penetrating radar or something." She shoved her hands between her knees and looked away. "I know you think I'm extreme, but it's the worst thing in the world not knowing what happened to her."

Roxanne nodded. She could imagine how that would feel. But the chance of Debra getting the answers she was looking for seemed so small. "What did you find out about Ledger that you wanted to tell me?" she asked.

"I started corresponding with a guy who worked at the prison he was at, down in Texas," Debra said. "I got him to tell me all about Ledger's time there."

"How did you do that?"

"Believe it or not, I told him the truth—I think Ledger killed my sister and I'm trying to find proof of that. Anyway, Doug couldn't tell me a whole lot, but he did say that the only visitor Ledger ever had was a woman. She showed up every other week like clockwork. The guards thought at first she might be his daughter. Then they decided she was his girlfriend."

"Wait—Ledger had a girlfriend?"

"I don't think she was a real girlfriend," Debra said. "I think he probably met her after he was locked up. Apparently, there are a lot of lonely women who end up corresponding with prisoners. They send them money and promise to look after them when they get out and visit them. Sometimes they even marry the guys."

"Who was she?" Roxanne asked.

"Doug said her name was Betty Josephs. She was twenty-eight, so too young to be my Betty. When I heard her name, it sent chills up my spine, though."

"Where is Betty Josephs now?" Roxanne asked.

"That's what I need help finding out. I think she met up with Ledger after he got out of prison—gave him a place to live, maybe a car and money. She could even be here with him, helping him."

"Do you know anything more about her—what she looks like?" Roxanne asked.

"Doug said when she visited Ledger she was a bleached blonde. Kind of plain-looking, he said. But she could have changed her appearance—dyed her hair, changed the style. I tried to track her down in Texas, but it's a big state and I didn't have any luck. She might have even changed her name, like you did. But now I'm thinking you could help me find her. Maybe she knows what Ledger is up to."

"Me? How am I going to locate her if you couldn't?"

"You're good at computers, right? Probably a lot better than I am. Can't you—I don't know—hack into the driver's license database or her tax records or something?"

"No! I don't do things like that."

"What about genealogy? Do you know anything about that? Maybe we could find her relatives and talk to them."

"No. I don't know anything about genealogy. You need to tell the sheriff about this woman, not me."

Debra frowned. "The sheriff's department isn't interested in anything I have to say. I talked to them when I first got to town and they were pretty dismissive. Every time I've gone into the office to try to speak to the sheriff, that woman behind the front desk tells me he isn't available. I always leave a message, but I don't hear back. She's probably filing my message slips right into the trash."

Roxanne winced. Unfortunately, Debra could come across as not exactly rational at times. "Dalton's brother is a sheriff's deputy," she said. "I'll try to talk to him about this woman— Betty Josephs. But try not to get your hopes up. This is a small department, and they have a lot to deal with right now, with Sarah still missing."

"All the more reason to find Ledger," Debra said. "I think

Sarah is with him." She stood. "I'll get out of your hair now, but let me know what your boyfriend says."

"Dalton is not—"

Debra laughed. "Gotcha! You may not think he's your boyfriend, but I've seen the way he looks at you. He wants to be more than a friend, trust me."

Roxanne shut and locked the door behind Debra, then returned to the sofa. Yes, Dalton had made his feelings for her pretty clear. And she couldn't deny her growing affection for him. She had dated other men. She had slept with some of them. The first time she had been so relieved to learn that Ledger hadn't ruined sex for her. But just as she never found a home where she fit, she had never found the man with whom she could completely relax and be herself.

Dalton was different. He was the most patient, accepting, strong man she had ever met. When she was with him she only wanted more—more conversation, more touching, more basking in the look in his eyes and reveling in the feel of his body. She had no doubt making love with him would be amazing.

But not yet. Right now, there were too many distractions to spoil the moment.

Her phone pinged and she pulled it out to read the text. I'll be over as soon as my last tour is done, Dalton had written.

Can't wait to see you, she texted back. I have some interesting things to tell you.

She was curious to know what he would think of Debra's latest revelations about Ledger.

Dalton pulled into the driveway just after three o'clock, before his parents got off work, when Roxanne was alone in the big house. "Did you race down the mountain?" she asked as she opened the door for him.

"The tour was three young couples," he said. "They didn't mind going a little fast." He studied her face, with an intensity that sent a shiver through her, as if he was physically touching her. "What's up?"

"Debra came to see me this afternoon."

"Here? At the house?"

"Yes. Apparently, she's determined to keep track of me. I asked her why she was stalking me, but she took it as a joke. She said she had information about Ledger I needed to know and I guess she was right, though I don't know what to do with what she told me."

"Does she know where he is?" Dalton asked. "Is he here in Eagle Mountain?"

"Nothing like that. Come sit down."

He followed her to the sofa and they sat side by side. He took her hand. "Whatever she said, it's upset you. I can tell."

She drew in a deep breath. "Yes, well, this whole situation is upsetting, isn't it? But I'm okay. Apparently, Ledger has a girlfriend. Or at least, a woman who visited him regularly while he was in prison. Debra thinks this woman is probably still helping him now that he's free. She could know where he's hiding and what his plans are."

"I didn't see any mention of a girlfriend when I was digging online for information about Ledger," Dalton said.

She explained about Debra befriending the prison guard. "You've got to admire her single-mindedness," she said.

"The guard could have made up the story to keep her interested," Dalton said. "Or Debra could have made it up to reel you in."

"Maybe." She knew firsthand how manipulative people could be. "But what if it's true? Can you find out? She says the woman's name is Betty Josephs and she thinks she lived in Texas."

"Isn't Betty her sister's name?"

"Bettina. But she says this woman is too young to be her sister. The guard said she was twenty-eight when she was visiting Ledger, at least according to her ID. And she had bleached blond hair."

"I'll see what I can find out." He pulled out his phone and made a note of the name. "I want to look for more information about Alice, too."

"Why Alice?"

"Maybe we can put Debra on to her and she'll stop bothering you."

She laughed. "She doesn't bother me that much. I feel sorry for her, really. I think her whole life is wrapped up in this quest to find out what happened to her sister."

"Maybe you aren't the only person Ledger has come after," Dalton said. "One reason Alice may be so hard to find is that she's hiding from him, too."

"I know she was a victim of Ledger just as much as I was," Roxanne said. "But the way she pretended to be my friend, then betrayed me, hurt as much as anything he did to me. I've never been able to forgive her."

He took her hand and squeezed it. "I'm not judging you," he said.

He never did, which made him so easy to be with. She pulled him close in a kiss. Forget Ledger and Debra and Betty and Bettina. She wanted to focus on the feel of his lips on hers, the way his five-o'clock shadow scraped at her cheek, the spearmint taste of him and the tremor that shook her as he traced his thumb along the curve of her breast.

She was thinking of climbing into his lap and straddling him when the rattle of the key in the front door sent them flying apart. Diane and George Ames stood grinning at them. "Don't let us interrupt," Diane said. She took her husband by the hand and pulled him from the room.

Roxanne put both hands to her heated face. "That was embarrassing," she said. "I feel like a teenager who got caught making out."

"We're not teenagers." He slid over and kissed her again. A thorough kiss that banished embarrassment and had her wanting to pull him up the stairs to her room. Maybe he felt a little of the same, because he groaned when he pulled away from her, a sound that had her arching toward him even as he slipped away. "I'd better go," he said. "I have a search and rescue meeting."

"Let me know if you find out anything about Ledger."

"You'll be the first to know."

Only after he was gone did she remember that she hadn't asked him about talking to the sheriff or Aaron. Maybe she would do that on her own.

But even if Ledger did have someone helping him, what was his purpose in being here, near Eagle Mountain? She didn't buy Debra's reasoning that he wanted to see her again. William Ledger liked little girls. He had no use for a woman like her.

SATURDAY NIGHT, DALTON WAS hunched over the computer, music turned up in the background. He would rather have been with Roxanne, but she was attending a lingerie shower for Bethany. He was trying to distract himself from images of Roxanne in various lacy and diaphanous nightgowns when the door to his apartment opened and Carter walked in. "Ever thought about knocking?" Dalton asked.

"Why knock when I still have my key?" Carter held up the small brass key. "Have you seen my guitar tuner? I can't find it anywhere. Thought maybe I'd left it here when I moved in with Mira."

Dalton turned back to the computer. "I thought you stopped playing guitar." As he recalled, Carter had taken lessons just long enough to discover playing well was much harder than it looked.

"I'm thinking of taking it up again. Are you sure you haven't seen the tuner? It's red plastic."

"I haven't seen it, but feel free to look."

Carter leaned over Dalton's shoulder and peered at the monitor. "What are you working on? Your next million-dollar idea?"

"None of my ideas have made a million dollars," Dalton said.

"I figure it's only a matter of time." He straightened, then moved away. Moments later, the click and thump of doors opening and closing announced Carter's path through the apartment.

Dalton went back to scrolling through the list of names on the screen.

"I found it!" Carter emerged into the living room again, holding aloft a small red plastic box. "It was way back in the closet in my old bedroom." He plopped down onto the sofa, long legs stretched in front of him, picked up the remote and turned down the music. "You really ought to clean this place up. Especially now that you have a girlfriend. She's not going to want to sleep in a dump."

Dalton ignored him, but Carter refused to take the hint. "What is that you're looking at?" he asked. "It looks like you're reading a phone book—if people still used phone books."

"It's the state driver's license database."

"You have access to that?"

"Not officially, no." But he knew a guy who knew a guy who had agreed to let him take a peek in exchange for cheat codes for an online game Dalton knew about.

"Then how—" Carter shook his head. "No, I don't want to know." He got up and came to lean over Dalton's chair again. "Who are you looking for?"

"A woman named Betty Josephs. I found her in Texas,

then I tracked her to Denver, but I can't figure out where she went from there."

"Who is Betty Josephs?"

"Supposedly, she's William Ledger's girlfriend."

"Who is William Ledger?"

How much could he say without betraying Roxanne's confidence? "He's a guy Roxanne used to know. He may be harassing her now."

"The guy who ran her off the road and broke into her house?"

Of course. Everyone in search and rescue knew about those things. Probably a lot of other people in town, too. "Yeah. I figure if I can find the girlfriend, maybe I can find him."

"Does Aaron know you're doing this?"

"No. And don't tell him."

"Like you have to even say that."

"I'll tell him myself when I have more than a name."

Carter pulled a chair close and sat. "So, what have you found out so far?"

"I've tracked her as far as Denver three months ago. She got a speeding ticket and her address is an apartment on the south end of the city. Then she disappears. She's no longer at that address." He closed the file and pushed back from the desk. "I think she's using a different name. I think Betty Josephs was a fake identity, too. At least, I can't find evidence she existed before three years ago. That's when Ledger was moved to the federal prison in Seagoville, outside of Dallas, and she started visiting him."

"Maybe you should quit doing Jeep tours and become a private detective," Carter said.

"Not interested. I just want to help Roxanne."

"Is Roxanne okay?" Carter asked. "She seems pretty chill when I see her at Mom and Dad's, but not being able to go back to her own place because some creep broke in must be kind of a downer."

"She's okay. She's a strong woman."

Carter studied him. Dalton was about to tell him to knock it off when he said, "Mom and Dad like her a lot."

"She really likes them, too."

"And you like her a lot."

"Yeah." No reason to deny it.

Carter nodded. "I figured it would be like this for you."

Dalton shifted in his chair. "Like what?"

"You didn't waste time dating around. You just waited until the one woman came along and wham! You two are together and that's it."

Carter was grinning like he'd won the lottery. Dalton glared at him. "I don't have any idea what you're talking about."

"I'm just saying—some people fall hard right away."

"You fell in love with Mira pretty fast." The two had known each other only a few months when Carter moved in with her and they started planning a wedding.

"Right, but I'd had a lot of experience with women. I knew what I was looking for by the time she came along."

He made it sound like filling out a shopping list or ordering a custom car. Dalton knew that wasn't true—Carter and Mira seemed to really love each other. "Neither of us is rushing into anything serious," Dalton said.

"Nothing wrong with that, but I don't think you're going to change your mind," Carter said. "I've never seen you look at anyone the way you look at her."

"And you're an expert."

"More of an expert than you."

"Thanks for your expert opinion, then." He turned his chair back to face the computer. "Lock the door behind you on the way out."

Carter left and Dalton started a search for Debra Percy. She was easier to find than Betty had been. He scrolled through several pages, then paused and double-checked what he had just read. Huh. Debra had been in Denver at the same time Betty had been there. She had left only a few weeks after all trace of Betty disappeared. Coincidence, or connection? He pondered the question for a long moment, then took out his phone and punched in a number.

"What do you need?" Aaron asked when he answered.

"Can you come over to my place and look at a few things?" Dalton said. "I found some stuff you need to know."

"What kind of stuff?"

"It's about William Ledger."

"I told you not to snoop around on the computer, to let us handle it."

"Since when do I listen to you? Do you want to know what I found out or not?"

"I'll be there in ten."

Almost exactly ten minutes later, Dalton heard Aaron's footsteps on the stairs. He opened the door to his brother, who was in full uniform. "Get in here before the neighbors think I'm in some kind of trouble," he said, ushering his brother inside.

"What have you found out about William Ledger that you think is so important?" Aaron asked.

"Did you know he has a girlfriend? Or had one, at least until recently."

"Betty Josephs," Aaron said. "Yes, we know."

"Oh." He hadn't expected that answer. "Has anyone talked to her? Does she know where Ledger is?"

"As far as I know, several law enforcement agencies are still looking for her. Why? Do you know where she is?"

"I've tracked her to Denver. She was there in July. I have an address. She isn't there now, but maybe someone could talk to her former landlord, see if she left a forwarding address. And ask if anyone who fit Ledger's description was around."

"We know how to do our job," Aaron said.

"Do you want the information or not?"

"I want it." Aaron grabbed a notepad from Dalton's desk. "What's that address again? And the dates she was there?"

When he had finished writing, he tore off the paper, folded it and tucked it into his pocket. "How did you find out about her?" he asked.

"Do you know Debra Percy?"

Aaron nodded. "She thinks Ledger kidnapped and killed her older sister."

"She also thinks—or thought—that Roxanne knows something about her sister. She keeps questioning Roxanne about it. But yesterday she visited Roxanne and told her she had found out about Betty Josephs. Roxanne passed the information along to me to give to you."

"Except you had to do your own research first."

"You're welcome," Dalton said.

"Yeah, thanks. Maybe we need to talk to Debra again."

The *maybe* set Dalton's teeth on edge. "Why haven't you found Ledger yet? He's just one man. He's got to be somewhere close."

Aaron's mouth tightened. "Investigations like this take time. And we don't have a lot to go on. And this isn't the only crime we're investigating."

Dalton heard the frustration in Aaron's voice and noticed the dark circles beneath his eyes. "Sorry. I'm just worried about Roxanne. Do you have any news about Sarah?"

"No. None of us are getting much sleep, worrying about her."

"Do you think Ledger has her?" he asked.

"I don't know what to think. But it's one more reason to

find him. Sooner rather than later." He put a hand on Dalton's shoulder. "Let Roxanne know we'll be following up on this. And you take care."

Aaron left, and Dalton sank into his chair once more. Aaron said investigations took time, but it didn't feel like Sarah—and maybe Roxanne—had much time.

Chapter Thirteen

"Since you've moved in, we're seeing a lot more of Dalton," Diane said as she and Roxanne prepared dinner Saturday night. "As I was leaving work today he asked if I could set a place for him for dinner."

Roxanne focused on the salad greens she was washing, hiding a smile of pleasure at both the prospect of seeing Dalton shortly, and the idea that he was specifically showing up to see her. "He's always raving about your cooking," she said.

"Oh, I don't think my chicken casserole is the big draw." Roxanne didn't have to look to know that Diane was watching her. Though she had been wonderful about respecting Roxanne's privacy, she hadn't hidden the fact that she was curious about Roxanne's relationship with Dalton and about Roxanne's own past.

She finished washing the greens and dried her hands, then turned to face Diane. "I really like Dalton," she said. "He's smart and funny, and kind. He's been a wonderful friend to me during a difficult time."

"But something is holding you back," Diane said. "Don't look surprised. I've raised four young people whose moods I've had to learn to decipher."

"My life is so unstable right now," Roxanne said. "It's not a good time to start a relationship."

"It seems to me having a good man you could count on might be the best thing to have around in the midst of a lot of instability," Diane said.

Roxanne looked away. The next thing she knew, she felt Diane's arm around her. "I'm not trying to tell you what to do," she said. "But now that you're living here with us, I worry about you like you're one of my own. I want you to be happy. And I want Dalton to be happy. He's not like Carter, or even Bethany, who were in and out of love every other week all through high school. He's always slow to give his heart. I've never seen him look at anyone the way he looks at you."

People had told her this so many times she had to believe it, didn't she? She hadn't missed the looks Dalton had given her, but she didn't trust her judgment when it came to most people, especially most men. "You and George have been wonderful," Roxanne said. "I can't thank you enough for opening your home to me."

"Dalton told me you needed a safe place to stay because someone from your past was harassing you," Diane said. "I told Dalton any friend of his is welcome in our home."

Roxanne tried to blink away tears once more but this time they overflowed too fast. Diane patted her back. "In case you felt like you were fighting this alone, you're not," she said. "You've got the whole family on your side. The creep who's after you doesn't know it, but the Ameses altogether are a match for anyone."

Roxanne tried to smile and dabbed at her eyes with the paper towel she snatched from the roll on the counter.

"Hello? Anybody home?"

Dalton ambled into the kitchen. His hair was mussed from a day in the wind, his face flushed by the sun. He wore a red Alpine Jeep Tours T-shirt that stretched over his muscular shoulders and khaki shorts that showed off his strong legs. The shorts were wet around the hem, probably from when he'd washed the Jeep at the end of the tour. "Hey, Roxanne," he said.

She looked away, wondering if he'd noticed her ogling him. "Hi, Dalton. How are you doing?"

"I'm good. I saw your RAV4 out front. Looks like they did a good job restoring it."

"I picked it up this morning." Having her car back had been a big lift to her spirits.

Dalton moved to his mother and hugged her. "Hi, Mom. What are you making?"

"Chicken casserole." Diane swatted his hand as he reached around her and snagged a strip of bell pepper. "Did you remember to set the alarm when you left the office?"

"Yes, I remembered."

"The alarm is new," Diane explained to Roxanne. "We're still getting used to it."

"I took care of everything." Dalton selected an apple from the bowl on the kitchen table and bit into it with a loud crunch.

"You're going to spoil your appetite," Diane said.

"Not a chance." He chewed another bite of apple, then turned to Roxanne. "Do you have any plans for Monday?"

She paused in the act of tearing lettuce. "No. Why?"

"Want to come on a Jeep tour with me?"

"You're doing the Foliage and Falls tour Monday, aren't you?" Diane asked.

"Yeah, and I noticed there's one seat available. I immediately thought of Roxanne." His gaze met hers, and she thought again of May's description of him as having a quiet smolder. Had his mother seen this heat, too?

"That's a wonderful idea." Diane turned to Roxanne. "The waterfalls are still flowing strong and the late season wildflowers are competing with the early-turning aspen. You'll love it."

"I don't know…" she began.

"No charge," Dalton said. "Why not come and keep me company?"

"All right. Thanks."

"Both of you get out of here and let me finish dinner in peace." Diane picked up the chef's knife Roxanne had been using to prepare the salad. "I can handle everything from here."

Roxanne followed Dalton into the living room, where they sat side by side on the sofa. "Thanks for inviting me on the tour," she said. "I've been wanting to see more of the area."

"It would be better if I wasn't working and I could take you up there, just the two of us," he said. "But this will be almost as fun."

"I'm looking forward to seeing you work," she said.

"Now you're making me nervous. Just remember my jokes are geared toward elementary school kids. Seriously, though, the scenery is breathtaking. It's a great stress breaker, to get up there and be in nature." He took her hand and squeezed it gently.

She looked down at their intertwined fingers. "Your mom was asking about us," she said. "If we're, you know, involved."

"I'm sorry about that," he said. "She can be pretty nosy. Do you want me to tell her to back off?"

"No, she's been so respectful. I'm not sure in her position if I could have done as well. I know she's been curious. If she's nosy with you kids, I think it's only that she cares so much." She smoothed her hand down his arm. "Who takes in a stranger, knowing a violent felon might come after them because of it?"

"I guess my mom and dad do. They liked you right off the bat. But you're an easy person to like." He moved closer, bringing them hip to hip and thigh to thigh. "What did you tell her? About us?" he asked.

"I told her my life is so unstable right now that it doesn't seem right to involve anyone else in my troubles."

"I'm already involved." He angled toward her and brushed one finger down her cheek.

She lifted her gaze and looked into his eyes. "I'm here when you're ready," he said. And then he kissed her, his mouth on hers sealing the promise of his words. He tasted of apples and the sweep of his tongue across her lips sent heat pooling between her legs. She pressed one hand to his chest, not to push him away, but to steady herself against the dizzying sensation that spiraled through her. He angled his head to deepen the kiss and a low moan escaped her.

The sound of the front door opening split them apart. They sat back, a little wild-eyed, more than a little breathless. Roxanne touched her still-tingling lips, wondering if they were swollen, then tried to smooth her hair. Dalton cleared his throat and shifted in his seat. "Hey, kids," George Ames called. "Dalton, have you seen my new camouflage ball cap? I can't find the dang thing anywhere and I've only had it a couple of weeks."

"I'm pretty sure it's hanging on the back of the door in the office at the tour company," Dalton said.

"Really? I thought I'd looked there, but I guess I'd better look again." He walked past them into the kitchen, where they heard him greet his wife.

Roxanne looked at Dalton, who patted her thigh, then picked up the half-eaten apple and took another bite.

MONDAY MORNING, ROXANNE CHANGED clothes three times before she settled on jeans and a teal Henley, along with the jacket Dalton had advised her to bring. "It can get cold at the higher elevations," he had said. "Plus, you'll be riding in an open-topped Jeep."

With that in mind, she braided her hair in a single plait and added a black ball cap her employer had given to everyone at the last team-building function. This was the first time she had worn it, but she decided it didn't look half bad.

All this fretting over her wardrobe meant that she was the last to arrive at the tour office. Dalton's relief was plain when she hurried to join the group gathered around him. But there was a tension about him, too—a tightness around his mouth that made her instantly alert. "That's everyone, then," he said. "Why don't you all introduce yourselves while I take this paperwork up to the office." He indicated the clipboard in his hand. "Roxanne, you can come with me and sign your release forms."

She hurried to catch up with him as he crossed the yard to the office. "I'm sorry about this," he said when they were out of earshot of the others. "I swear I didn't know when I invited you that she was on the tour."

"Who?" she asked, confused. She looked back over her shoulder, but could only see the backs of one of the couples around the Jeep.

"Debra Percy is on this tour," he said.

She blinked, surprised. "You're kidding!" Was Debra really so relentless in her pursuit of whatever she thought Roxanne knew that she would book a Jeep tour with her?

"She signed up two weeks ago, according to her reservation form," Dalton said. "We could do this another time, if she makes you too uncomfortable."

She shook her head. "No. It's okay. I'm sure it will be fine." She didn't dislike Debra, really. The woman just made her uncomfortable. Sad. "I want to spend the day with you," she added.

"Yeah. I want that, too. Anyway, you'll be up front with me. I'll put her in the back. That way it will be hard for her to even talk to you."

"I'll be fine. I promise."

Paperwork done, they rejoined the group by the Jeep. Dalton welcomed them, explained some safety rules, then invited them to climb in. "You first, Debra," he said, and motioned for her to climb into the back seat of the open Jeep.

Roxanne settled into the front passenger seat and fastened her safety belt. Dalton got behind the wheel and the tour began. In addition to Roxanne and Debra, there were three couples, all of retirement age, visiting from Florida, Arizona and Manitoba. They exclaimed over the scenery and piled out of the Jeep at the first stop, a pullout on the edge of town that afforded a view of the valley below and the first of what Dalton promised would be six waterfalls on the tour.

"Hi, Roxanne." Debra sidled up as Roxanne was photographing the scenery. "Do you come on Dalton's tours often?"

"This is my first," Roxanne said. "What about you? Have you taken a Jeep tour before?"

"No. I saw the brochure and decided to treat myself."

"Gather 'round, everyone, and I'll tell you a little more about this area," Dalton called.

Roxanne moved in beside him, allowing another couple to fill in the space between her and Debra. As Dalton told them about the history of the area, she took in his words but also enjoyed the opportunity to watch him while his attention was elsewhere. In sunglasses, T-shirt and shorts and a ball cap, he could have been mistaken for a college kid working a summer job. Only she knew he was also a talented software developer and a dedicated search and rescue volunteer. Not to mention a very good kisser.

They moved on, with a stop at the ruins of an old mine, where Dalton delivered an entertaining lecture on the history of mining in the area, including several corny jokes that made them all giggle, if only because his delivery was so humorous. They passed many other vehicles on the four-wheel-drive roads, from other Jeep tours to individuals riding ATVs and motorbikes, and even hikers making their way up the mountain.

The higher they climbed, the more spectacular the views—of golden aspen against achingly blue sky and the mingled gold, orange and red hues of the rocks, like candy tumbled down the mountainside. After two more waterfalls, they broke for lunch. Dalton passed out boxes that contained sandwiches, chips, apples and cookies. "This all looks home-made," one of the men commented.

"My mom makes it all," Dalton said.

Everyone spread out to eat. Roxanne joined him on a large boulder with a view of the waterfall. She half expected Debra to join them, but the other woman was chatting with one of the couples. "You really enjoy this, don't you?" she asked Dalton, keeping her voice low.

"I didn't at first," he said. "I don't have Carter's easy way with people. But when I started learning more about the history and geography of the area and sharing it with people, it got easier. Fun, even."

"Do you ever have trouble with your clients?" she asked.

"Oh, every once in a while you get someone who likes to complain, but most people are really nice, and interesting to talk to."

A shadow fell across them and they looked up to see Debra standing before them. "Sorry to bother you," she said. "But I'm wondering if there's a restroom somewhere nearby."

"Good question." Dalton stood and brushed crumbs from his shorts. He put two fingers to his mouth and whistled loudly. When he had everyone's attention, he said. "If you need to use the facilities, the ladies' room is on that side of the road." He pointed across the road to the left. "The men's room is on this side. You have your choice of any bush you like. Watch where you walk and don't stray too far. If you have to do more than pee, I have some handy little bags for you. We're required to pack out all human waste."

Groans and nervous laughter greeted this announcement. Debra turned to Roxanne. "Want to come with me? We can be lookouts for each other."

"Sure." Roxanne stood. "That's a good idea."

They had to wait for a trio of Jeeps to pass before they could cross the road. Debra headed down a narrow trail between a thick growth of shrubs. After they had walked a hundred yards or so, she looked back over her shoulder. "I guess this is far enough," she said. "Watch to make sure no one else comes over here and I'll do the same for you."

Roxanne turned her back as Debra moved into the bushes. She could see a couple of hikers—a man and a woman, she guessed from their relative sizes—some distance away, but there was no one else near them. She closed her eyes, savoring the warmth of the sun on her skin and breathed in deeply the crisp air that smelled of dust and greenery.

Debra bounced up behind her. "Okay. Your turn."

Roxanne relieved herself quickly, then caught up with Debra, who had moved farther down the trail. "Look at those flowers over there," Debra said, and pointed to a thick stand of fireweed downslope from where they were standing. "I want to get a picture." She started forward.

Roxanne hesitated. "We should probably go back," she said.

"It's not like they're going to leave without us," Debra called over her shoulder. "You go on. I'll catch up."

Roxanne turned and started back toward the road. She hadn't gone far before a yelp, followed by a curse, made her turn around. "Debra?" she called.

Another string of curses, then a single, pitiful "Help!"

Roxanne began retracing her steps. She spotted the cluster of fireweed and headed toward it. But she couldn't see Debra. "Where are you?" she called. "I can't see you."

A pain-filled groan came in answer. Heart pounding, Roxanne increased her steps, but the ground here was rocky and uneven, and she had to focus on where she was going. She heard footsteps behind her. Someone else must have heard Debra cry out and come to help. "Thank goodness—" Roxanne began, and turned to welcome the new arrival.

Something covered her head and tightened around her neck. Strong arms encircled her and pulled her down, into the thick brush and out of sight.

Chapter Fourteen

Dalton checked his watch for the third time. At least fifteen minutes had passed since Debra and Roxanne had left to use the bathroom. They should have been back by now. The other tour participants had already gathered around the Jeep, ready to go. "I'm sorry about the delay, folks," Dalton said. "Looks like I need to go hurry the other two along. I'll be back in a minute."

He crossed the road and headed up the path where he had last seen the two women. "Roxanne!" he called. "Debra! Time to get going." He stopped and listened, but heard nothing but his own breathing.

He turned a complete circle, and tried to remember what they had been wearing. Roxanne's jacket was gray and purple, and she had on a black ball cap. Debra had worn red. That should make her easy to spot, but there was no sign of her. He pulled out his phone and called Roxanne's number. After a dozen rings, the call went to voicemail. "Hey, Roxanne, where are you? It's time to get going again. Let me know you're on your way back to the Jeep."

He pocketed the phone once more, anxiety growing. Even if Roxanne had gotten distracted by something, she should have answered his call. He set out to look for her and Debra, stopping every few steps to call out the women's names.

He reached the top of a long ridge. From here, the ground sloped away to a field of fireweed, the bright pink blooms standing out against the yellowing foliage. Another trail came up from this valley, and he spotted a pair of hikers on it and waved for them to stop. They did so and he ran up to them. "Have you seen two women around here?" he asked. "One has on a red jacket. The other is wearing a purple and silver jacket and a black ball cap."

"I think we saw them a while ago," the man said. "They were up on that ridge." He pointed behind Dalton.

"Did you see which way they went from there?" he asked.

Both shook their heads. "But I thought I heard a scream," the woman said.

Dalton froze. "When was this?" he asked.

She looked at her companion. "Maybe ten minutes ago?"

Dalton checked his watch again. Five minutes had passed since he set out to find Roxanne and Debra. "And you didn't see any sign of them since then?" he asked.

Both shook their heads again. Dalton stared out over the fireweed. Everything around them was absolutely still. The way sound carried up here, with the surrounding peaks acting as amplifiers, he should have been able to hear anyone in distress. The couple were still standing beside him, shifting from foot to foot. "Thanks for your help," Dalton said.

"Yeah, well, hope you find who you're looking for," the man said. He and the woman started down the trail again.

Dalton hurried back to the group waiting around the Jeep. "Did you find them?" one of the women asked.

"No." He pulled out his phone. "I need to make a couple of phone calls. But don't worry. We'll take good care of you."

"Maybe we should spread out and search," the woman's husband said.

"No," Dalton said, even as the others agreed they should search. The last thing he needed was a bunch of people who didn't know the area and weren't accustomed to conditions up here to go stumbling around. "Let's get trained people to do that. We have a terrific search and rescue operation in Eagle Mountain."

Thankfully, he had a good cell signal here. His time with search and rescue had taught him that people often made the mistake of not calling for help soon enough. They thought they could find their own way out of the wilderness or walk down the mountain with a sprained ankle or get back to camp before dark. He moved a short distance away from the group and dialed Roxanne's number again. Still no answer. Then he called his dad. "I need you to come up to Lupine Falls and finish this tour for me," Dalton said. "I'll explain more when you get here."

"I'll be right there, son," his dad said. "Are you okay?"

No. If anything happened to Roxanne, would he ever be okay again? "I'm okay, Dad. Just get here as soon as you can."

He ended the call, then cradled the phone for a moment, fighting panic. He needed to think like a first responder now. What did he do next? He dialed 911. "This is Dalton Ames with Alpine Jeep Tours. Two of the guests on this morning's tour are missing."

Roxanne had the sensation of trying to swim through thick gray muck. She fought to break through to the surface, chest aching, head pounding. With a groan, she opened her eyes, and looked up into a face that was both familiar and strange. "Hello, Mary," the woman said. Her face swam into better focus.

Roxanne gasped. "Kara." She tried to sit up, but a wave of stomach-churning dizziness forced her back down.

"You can call me Alice." Kara smiled. "You didn't recognize me, did you?" She touched her face. "The state paid to have my teeth fixed, then Billy sent me money to get my nose done." She stroked her now petite, straight nose. "He wanted me to look my best."

Roxanne's heart hammered painfully and she struggled to breathe. "Where is Ledger?" she gasped.

"He'll be back soon," Kara said. "He's out making sure no one followed us."

Roxanne's head was clearing. She remembered standing on the mountainside, searching for Debra. "Where is Debra?" she asked.

"You don't need to worry about her." Kara laid a damp cloth over Roxanne's forehead. "That chloroform will probably give you a nasty headache for a while, but it will get better, I promise."

Roxanne batted her hand away. She fought the nausea and forced herself to sit. But when she tried to swing her legs off the bed, she couldn't move them. "Don't strain yourself, hon," Kara said. "Billy didn't want you to hurt yourself thrashing around, so he tied you to the bed."

Roxanne threw back the covers and stared at the chains wrapped around each ankle. She looked over at Kara. "Let me go, now. I promise I won't tell anyone you're involved."

"Oh, I can't do that, hon. Billy wouldn't like it."

Roxanne grabbed the other woman's arm, hard. "What are you doing here?" she asked. "How could you be with William Ledger after what he did to us?"

Kara tried to pull free. "Let go. You're hurting me."

Reluctantly, Roxanne released her hold. Kara rubbed at her arm, where a bruise was already forming, standing out against long red marks that looked like scratches. "Billy loves us," she said. "After we were taken from him, he missed us so much. He wrote me from prison and he sounded so sad."

"He doesn't love us," Roxanne said. "He hurt us."

Kara patted Roxanne's leg. "He doesn't even hold it against you that you ran away and turned him in to the police," she said. "He's forgiven you, and he wants us to all be together again."

Roxanne shrank from the other woman's touch, the nausea returning, but this time not from the chloroform. "You're Betty Josephs," she said.

She smiled. "You're so clever to guess! That was all Billy's idea. He sent me the money to get the nose job and told me to dye my hair and how to get a driver's license in a new name. Then I could visit him in prison. It was so wonderful to see him again." Her eyes shone, and a shiver ran through Roxanne. Kara no longer seemed connected to any reality.

"You moved into the tiny house to spy on me," she said.

"Spying sounds so nasty." Kara pouted. "I was watching over you, making sure you were all right." She smoothed her hand over her hair. "I had to change my hair again. Do you like the red? I'm thinking of keeping it."

"How did you find me?" Roxanne asked.

"Oh, it's not as hard as you might think. I made up a story about looking for my long-lost sister and hired a private investigator who specializes in tracking down people who don't want to be found. Billy was happy to pay the bill."

"How did you find out I was on this tour today?" Roxanne asked.

Kara giggled. "I put a tracking device on your car. Billy gave it to me and told me what to do. Isn't that clever? When you drove to the Jeep tour company this morning, I thought at first you were just saying hi to Dalton. But I cruised by there to check and saw you getting into the Jeep with lots of other people. As soon as you were gone, I called Billy to let him know, then went in to the Jeep office and asked about the tours. All I had to do was ask and the nice lady there told me all about the tour you were taking this morning. From there it was easy enough for Billy and me to catch up with you and just wait for our chance to get you alone."

"Was Debra in on this?" Roxanne asked. Had the big co-incidence of Debra being on the tour not been a coincidence after all?

Kara frowned. "That busybody has been in our way from the first," she said. "I'm glad we got rid of her."

"What did you do to her?" Roxanne asked, alarmed.

"Don't worry. She won't be bothering you anymore."

"Did you put that doll in my house?" Roxanne asked.

Kara grinned. "Wasn't that clever? Billy gave me the doll and the note." The grin faded. "I thought it would remind you of the good times when we were all together. It wasn't meant to make you move out." She raked her fingernails down both arms, leaving white streaks where the nails dug into her skin. "Billy wasn't happy with me about that. He got very angry, until I agreed to help him find a way to get you alone."

She had helped Ledger kidnap her, just as she had all those years ago. "I'm going to be sick," she said.

Kara rushed to shove a trash can under her mouth as Roxanne vomited. When she was done, she collapsed back onto the bed. Kara left the room and returned with another damp cloth and a glass of water. "Drink this," she coaxed and held the glass for Roxanne. "Billy will be back soon and you'll feel so much better then."

GEORGE AMES ARRIVED at the same time as the first search and rescue volunteers. Ryan, Eldon, Sheri and Carrie sped up in Ryan's Jeep, followed by Tony Meisner on a motorbike and Grace, Harper, Caleb and Dr. Rand Martin in the search and rescue vehicle. Rand was the search and rescue group's medical director.

The three couples on Dalton's tour gaped at them all until Mr. Ames herded them back to the Jeep. "These folks know what they're doing," he said. "They'll find the two women.

Meanwhile, let's continue your tour. There's still lots to see up here."

The volunteers gathered around Dalton. He looked for Carter, then remembered he was on another tour. Bethany hadn't shown up yet. Maybe she was busy elsewhere. Danny was working a shift at the hospital, so his partner Carrie was in charge. "Tell us what happened," she said.

Dalton described the two women, then explained that they had gone to use the bathroom across the road and not returned. He detailed his own search for them and his encounter with the hikers who had heard a single scream. He spoke as if the events had happened to someone else, his voice without emotion until he got to the part about not being able to find them. "I knew she could be in danger," he said. "I never should have let her out of my sight." His voice broke, and he had to turn away.

Carrie directed the volunteers to spread out and conduct a hasty search. Dalton pulled himself together and faced her again. "I can help," he said. "Where do you want me to search?"

She put a gentle hand on his shoulder. "You can't be part of the search," she said.

He started to protest, but the arrival of a black-and-white quadrunner with two uniformed deputies distracted him. Gage Walker shut off the vehicle and he and Deputy Ryker Vernon stepped out. "Stay here and tell them what happened," Carrie said to Dalton. "That's the best way you can help."

Dalton repeated his story for Gage and Ryker as the searchers headed out. He described the two hikers he had talked to as a middle-aged man and woman, both with short graying hair and dark green jackets. "Did you see anyone suspicious while you were conducting your tour?" Gage asked.

"There are always a lot of other people around," Dalton said. "But no one was acting strangely."

"Anyone who might have been following you?" Gage asked. "Anyone you saw at more than one stop?"

Dalton tried to think. Had there been anyone? "I don't think so, no," he said after a moment. "But I wasn't really looking for that." He had thought here, in the mountains crawling with tourists, they would be safe.

Gage stared out across the area, which was still busy not only with searchers, but with half a dozen tourists. "They could have fallen, or wandered off the trail and gotten lost," he said.

"I don't think both of them would have fallen," Dalton said. "And we would have heard them calling for help. Or someone would have heard them. And they weren't gone that long."

Gage met his gaze again. "Do you think Ledger took them?" he asked. "Both of them?"

"I don't know what to think." Dalton tried to bring moisture into his dry mouth. "How much do you know about Debra Percy?"

"Aaron shared your concerns about her," Gage said. "So we ran a background check. Her story checks out. Why?"

"She's just always bothered me," Dalton said. "And she kept showing up out of the blue to question Roxanne, even after Roxanne told her she didn't know anything about her missing sister."

"Do you think Roxanne is missing because Debra took her somewhere?" Ryder asked.

"I don't know," he admitted. "Where would she have taken her?"

"Someone posing as a tourist could have stuffed her into a Jeep and driven away," Gage said.

The thought made Dalton sick to his stomach. "Do you think Debra Percy could be Betty Josephs?" he asked. "The woman who was visiting William Ledger when he was in jail?"

"Didn't you tell Aaron that Debra was the one who told you about Josephs?" Gage asked.

"Yes, but maybe she did that deliberately, to deflect suspicion."

"Do you have any other proof of a connection between Ms. Percy and William Ledger?" Gage asked.

"No," Dalton said. "Just a suspicion."

Gage clapped a hand on Dalton's shoulder. "We'll keep that in mind. But first, we have to find both these women." He turned to Ryker. "Get the drone. Let's see if we can spot anything with it."

While an interested crowd of tourists and locals looked on, Ryker launched the drone. Carrie joined them. "If you spot anything worth checking, I'll direct the nearest searchers to take a closer look," she said.

Dalton leaned in closer, watching over Ryker's shoulder as the drone flew over the ridge where the women had disappeared. It hovered over the mass of fireweed before descending the ridge. The ground fell away as it sailed over a drop-off. "Wait!" Dalton shouted. "Back it up. Back it up."

Ryker maneuvered the drone back over the edge of the drop-off. Dalton pointed at the screen. "That red. What is that?"

The drone dipped lower. Something red—Dalton couldn't determine if it was fabric or plastic—lay crumpled among the rocks. The drone flew lower still. "Is that long hair?" Ryker asked. "And that white—is that a hand?"

"I think it is," Carrie said from Ryker's other side.

"Sarge!" Ryker called. "We think we found something."

Gage moved in to take a look. "You said Debra had on a red jacket?" he asked Dalton.

"Yes. And her hair is that kind of maroon color."

"Carrie, get some searchers down there," Gage directed.

"Ryker, get up higher for a wider view. See if you can spot Roxanne."

Dalton stared at the screen as the drone rose once more and panned to take in the surrounding expanse of tumbled rock. No trees grew on this steep slope and very little other vegetation. But there was no sign of a silver-and-purple jacket, a black ball cap or anything else belonging to Roxanne.

Carrie's radio crackled. "We're at the drop-off," Eldon said. "We can see someone below. We think we saw movement, but they're not responding to our shouts. We're going to need to rappel down."

"I'll send more people to help you right away," Carrie said.

Dalton wanted to be there with them—if not climbing down himself, then waiting at the top. But he knew that wouldn't be a good idea. All he could do was stay here, helpless, and wait.

Ryker continued to fly the drone, searching, but Dalton turned away from the screen. Roxanne and Debra had left together. Why weren't they together now? Had Ledger decided to dispense with Debra, now that she was no longer useful to him? Had he taken Roxanne elsewhere, to make her his prisoner again?

Or did he have something else in mind for her?

He shuddered, and hugged his arms across his chest, staring down at the ground and not seeing anything but Roxanne's smiling face as she had waved goodbye to him before crossing the road.

RYAN WAS FASTER on rappel than Eldon, so Eldon set the anchors and took charge of the ropes while Ryan made the descent, a pack of medical supplies on his back. He covered approximately forty feet in minutes. He had scarcely unhooked before he was on the radio. "It's a woman and she's alive," he said. He continued to talk as he moved in to assess her. "She's unconscious but breathing. Bleeding from a head wound. Looks like someone hit her with a rock, or she hit her head on the way down. Her arm's at an odd angle, probably broken."

"I'm going to get Rand on the radio," Carrie said. "Hold on."

Moments later she was back. "We're calling Life Flight, and a rescue copter," she said. "I'm going to send Harper and Caleb down to help stabilize and package her for a short-haul extraction."

Harper and Caleb were stepping into climbing harnesses when Gage and Ryker arrived. "Is she conscious?" Gage asked Eldon. "Has she said anything?"

"Not yet," Eldon said.

The next few moments were a flurry of activity as more volunteers gathered on the ridge. The scene was calm and relatively quiet, but everyone was busy, gathering supplies, setting anchors, laying out ropes or helping the climbers get ready. After only a few minutes, Harper and Caleb moved out of sight over the edge of the ridge.

Dalton walked down the path to join the other volunteers. He didn't say anything, but stood with his arms folded across his chest, waiting. Carrie moved over to him. "How are you doing?" she asked.

"I'm holding it together," he said. "How is Debra?"

"It sounds like she's pretty banged up," Carrie said.

Gage strode over to them. "What are you doing here?" he asked Dalton.

Dalton ignored him, focused on Carrie. "Has she said anything?" he asked. "Does she know what happened to Roxanne?"

"She's still unconscious," Gage said.

The radio crackled. "She's awake," Ryan said. "She says her name is Debra and she was attacked by a man and a woman."

"What about Roxanne?" Dalton asked.

"Does she know where Roxanne is?" Gage asked.

Silence, then the radio crackled again. "When I asked her about Roxanne, she started crying," Ryan said. "I don't want to upset her any more."

The distant throb of a helicopter drew their attention to the sky. Moments later, a yellow-and-white helicopter soared into view. Carrie's radio crackled to life. "We've completed our site assessment." Someone spoke above the rush of air and throb of rotor blades. "Is the patient ready to go?"

"She's ready," Carrie said. "We've got Life Flight on their way to transport her to the hospital."

"We'll be back in about ten minutes," the pilot said, and the helicopter turned away.

"Why ten minutes?" Ryker asked.

"They have to attach the short-haul hook and cable and double-check all their safety gear," Carrie said. She switched to a different radio channel. "Caleb, is everything ready down there? The short-haul crew should be down in a few minutes."

"She's ready to go," Caleb replied.

Moments later, the helicopter was back. It soared over the ridge and hovered just above them, the wash from the rotor bending the fireweed to the ground and kicking up dust. Those watching shielded their eyes and craned their necks as a man clinging to a cable descended from the belly of the chopper. Seconds later, he touched down a few feet from the waiting search and rescue volunteers. Like a well-trained pit crew, they swarmed around the litter containing Debra Percy. In less than a minute, the litter was secured to the cable, with the short-haul rescuer situated to one side. The helicopter rose into the sky, the litter and the rescuer swinging from the cable beneath it. They would be carried this way to a second landing zone, near where the Life Flight had landed, and Debra would be transferred to the Life Flight aircraft for her trip to the hospital in Junction.

When the throb of the helicopter rotors had faded, Gage turned to Dalton. "We're still searching for Roxanne," he said. "We'll talk to Debra as soon as possible and find out everything she knows."

"Hey."

They turned to see Carter picking his way across the rocks toward them. "What are you doing here?" Dalton asked.

"Dad called and told me what was going on," he said. "I've come to take you home."

Dalton looked around. The other volunteers were gathering up equipment scattered along the ridge. "I should stay here, in case they find Roxanne," he said.

Carter took his arm. "You can wait at home," he said. "Come on."

"Go home," Gage told him. "Please."

Dalton let his brother lead him away. The other volunteers watched him go. "Let's get cleaned up here," Carrie said. "Then we've got more searching to do."

Chapter Fifteen

"I was taking a picture of some flowers—some fireweed. I crouched down to try a close-up shot and something hit me in the head. I fell over. I tried to fight, to call for help, but a man came up and hit me again—just punched me right in the face." Debra put a hand to her bruised face. She was sitting up in a hospital bed, an IV trailing from one arm, the other arm in a cast, monitor lines trailing from her chest. She had a black eye, broken ribs, a mild concussion and her legs were scraped raw from where her assailant had dragged her over the rocks.

"What did the man look like?" Gage asked. He stood beside the hospital bed. Ryker sat in the only chair, taking notes on the interview.

Debra frowned. "It all happened so fast. But he was an older guy—maybe in his fifties. Not too tall—kind of stocky. Gray hair. And a mustache. He had a mustache, I'm sure."

Gage nodded. So far, this fit the description they had of William Ledger. Though the same description might apply to many other men. "What happened next?" he asked.

"A woman came running up. She looked…familiar. But I can't remember where I'd seen her before."

"What did she look like?" Gage asked.

"She had short, red hair. And she was little. At first I thought she was a girl."

"By little, do you mean short?" Ryker asked.

"Just…petite. Not very tall, but also not very big all over."

"What did the woman do?" Gage asked.

"She told the man they had to hurry. He ordered her to help him and she grabbed my arm and they started dragging me across the ground. I tried to fight, but the man hit me again and I think I passed out for a little bit. It hurt so bad." She paused. "Could I have some water, please?"

Gage passed her a cup with a straw and she sipped, then returned it to him. "I think they threw me off the ridge," she said. "I just remember pain—in my arm and my head and everywhere. The next thing I really remember was waking up here." She looked around the hospital room, with its blue-green walls and a single window with a view of distant mountains.

"Roxanne Byrne was with you, wasn't she?" asked Gage.

She turned her attention back to him. "She was. But I think by then she had started back toward the Jeep. I told her I wanted to take a few more pictures before I went back."

"Do you remember if Roxanne was nearby when you were attacked?" Gage asked.

"No. I don't think she was there. She had gone back. Why are you asking about Roxanne?" She searched their faces. "Has something happened? What aren't you telling me?"

"Roxanne is missing," Gage said. "She never made it back to the Jeep."

Debra's eyes filled with tears. "That can't be," she said. "I saw her walking toward the road."

Her distress seemed genuine, but Gage had met good actors before. "Do you know a woman named Alice?" he asked.

"Alice?" She stared at him. "Do you mean the other girl William Ledger kidnapped?"

"Do you know her?" Gage asked.

"I've read about her. I've never met her. I asked Roxanne about her and she said she didn't know what happened to Alice. I tried to find her before I started looking for Roxanne. I didn't really know what I was doing back then. There was no trace of her online that I could find, so I moved on to looking for Roxanne and got luckier. I never went back to do more research on Alice, though I always meant to."

"What about Betty Josephs?" Gage asked.

"That's the woman who was visiting Ledger in prison. I told Roxanne about her."

"But you aren't her?" Gage asked.

"What are you talking about?" She clutched at the covers. "My name is Debra Percy."

"Has it always been Debra Percy?"

"Yes. If you don't believe me, ask my mother."

"And you never met William Ledger."

"No."

"You didn't work with him to lure Roxanne away from safety so that he could kidnap her?"

"No!" Her voice rose. "What kind of a person do you think I am? That's horrible."

"I have to ask these things," Gage said.

"Is that what you think happened to Roxanne—that William Ledger kidnapped her?" She leaned toward him. "Is Ledger the person who attacked me? Who was the woman? Do you think it was Betty?"

"We don't know much of anything at this point," Gage said.

"I can't believe I was so close to Ledger and missed the chance to talk to him," she said, her words almost a wail. "I could have asked him about Bettina. Maybe I could have caught him off guard and he would have told the truth."

A nurse pushed open the door and glared at the deputies. "Is everything all right in here?" she asked.

Debra was sobbing, head bent, tears falling onto the sheets. The nurse hurried over to her and put an arm around her.

"We'll go now," Gage said. "Debra, if you think of anything at all that might be helpful, give us a call."

Debra said nothing, continuing to sob.

Gage and Ryker didn't speak until they emerged from the hospital building. "Do you think she was telling the truth?" Ryker asked. "About not knowing Ledger?"

"She was pretty convincing. And we haven't talked to her mother, but we dug pretty deep into her past and it checks out. There is a Debra Percy from San Antonio who had an older sister, Bettina, who disappeared when Debra was ten. If the person in that hospital bed assumed her identity, she covered her tracks really well." He shook his head. "We've asked the state to do a search for Alice but they haven't gotten back to us with anything yet."

Ryker checked his watch. "It's four o'clock."

"You were supposed to be off shift an hour ago," Gage said.

"We're in the middle of an active search for a missing woman," Ryker said. "Not to mention, Sarah Michaelson is still missing, and there's a possible sexual predator on the loose. No one's paying much attention to the schedule right now."

"The sheriff is trying to get some help from the state on these searches," Gage said. "Meanwhile, I need you to stay here with Debra. I'll send someone out to relieve you as soon as I have a deputy available."

"Do you think her attacker will try to finish her off?" Ryker asked.

"I don't know. But I don't want to take that chance."

CARTER HAD TAKEN Dalton straight to their parents' house, where his mother had declared he would stay in his old bedroom for the time being. He spent a miserable night and woke the next morning to find that Carter was still there. "I'm temporarily moving back into my old room, too," Carter said at breakfast. "Mom and Dad thought it would be a good idea."

"I don't need a babysitter," he protested.

He said it again when they were back in his room, after Carter suggested they distract themselves with gaming.

"You'd be a really ugly baby," Carter said.

"Just leave me alone." Dalton sank into the beanbag chair in the corner of the room. How many hours had he spent here as a teen, playing video games or hunched over a laptop, learning to code and create his own programs? "I promise I'm not going to flip out or anything."

"Then what are you going to do?" Carter sat in the ladderbacked wooden chair that went with the student desk where both boys had done homework for years.

"I should be out there looking for her," Dalton said.

"But you can't be, so what are you going to do instead?"

Dalton wanted to shout at his brother to leave him alone. But being alone meant having no one to distract him from the worst-case scenarios that insisted on playing out in his head. Roxanne hurt. Roxanne tied up. Roxanne dead.

He leaned forward and picked up the laptop he had insisted on retrieving from his apartment before they came to his parents' house. "I'm going to try again to find out something about Alice," he said.

"You think Debra is Alice?" Carter asked. Dalton had briefly explained his theories on the drive home yesterday, though he hadn't believed Carter was really listening.

"It makes sense. She came on the same tour as Roxanne and lured her away from the group, so that Ledger could attack her."

"But she made that tour reservation weeks ago," Carter said. "She had no idea Roxanne would be on the same tour."

"Maybe she planned to persuade her to come on the trip,

and I saved her the trouble by inviting Roxanne myself," Dalton said. The knowledge that he was the one who was responsible for Roxanne being on the mountain that day ate at him.

"How are you going to find out the truth?" Carter asked.

Dalton opened the laptop. "I've been starting with Debra and going backwards—and getting nowhere. What if I start with Alice and try to trace her life and see where she ended up."

"How are you going to do that if you don't even know if Alice was her real name?" Carter asked. "And you don't have a last name."

"There are court documents somewhere that will have her real name," Dalton said. "If I can find those, I'll know her name and can start from there."

"Is there anything I can do to help?" Carter asked.

"Leave me alone. Go home to Mira."

"Mira is the one who sent me here. She said I had to help my brother. And she's right." He crossed his arms. "So you're stuck with me."

"Just get out of my hair."

He was dimly aware of Carter leaving the room. All his attention was focused on a search for the court transcripts from William Ledger's original trial. The website for the court was no help, so he went back to the newspaper coverage of the trial. He was able to read dozens of articles, all of which referred to Ledger's captives as "Mary" and "Alice."

Many of the stories were written by a reporter named Andi Wentworth, with the *San Antonio Star*. Dalton pulled up a current issue of the paper and searched. He sat up straighter when he spotted Wentworth's byline, then found the number for the newsroom. Moments later, he was speaking to a woman with a broad Texas drawl who identified herself as Andi Wentworth.

Dalton introduced himself as a friend of Roxanne Byrne's.

"You probably know her better as 'Mary,'" he said. "The girl responsible for William Ledger's arrest."

"I remember her," Andi said. "Such a brave little girl."

"I'm calling you because we're trying to find Alice," he said.

"Why are you looking for Alice?"

"You know that Ledger is out of prison now?"

"Yes. I wrote a piece for the paper when he was released."

"Roxanne has had a couple of unsettling encounters with someone we believe is William Ledger. Threatening encounters." He took a big breath, prepared to spill everything, if it would persuade this reporter to help him. "Roxanne is missing now. I'm afraid William Ledger may have kidnapped her again."

"Wait? What? Say that again. I need to write this down."

"I'll tell you everything," he said. "But I want something from you."

"What do you want?" she asked.

"You covered Ledger's original trial," he said.

"Yes."

"Did you know Alice's real name?"

"That name was never released to the public."

"Yet you recognized Roxanne's name. You knew she was Mary."

"The first name. She had a different last name."

"I need to know Alice's name."

"Why?"

"Because when William Ledger was in prison, he had a woman named Betty Josephs visiting him. That's not her real name. As far as I can tell, she didn't even exist until 2022. I think Betty was really Alice. I believe Ledger got in touch with her somehow and she's helping him."

"Why would she help him?" Andi asked. "He…he tortured those girls."

"She was with him for several years before he kidnapped Roxanne," Dalton said. "I don't know much about psychology, but I can see how that would warp someone. And she lured Roxanne to Ledger's house originally."

"Okay, so you think he got to her again, she changed her name to Betty and started helping him again." He heard the rapid click of a keyboard in the background and pictured her typing furiously. "And she somehow ended up where you are now? Where is that?"

"I'm not saying until you tell me if you can help me."

"Give me a minute, okay? I'm going to put you on hold."

An instrumental version of a song that had been popular when his parents were teenagers played over the phone as Dalton waited. A few minutes later Andi was back on the line. "Your story about Roxanne Byrne missing checks out. In a town called Eagle Mountain, Colorado."

So much for thinking he could keep the information from her. "Do you know Alice's real name?" he asked.

"Brianna Davidson," Andi said. "She had been in the foster system less than a year when Ledger kidnapped her. Her mother was jailed for drug possession. She died of an overdose shortly after being released. Her father had deserted the family the year before and was killed in a shooting the same month Brianna disappeared."

"Rough life," Dalton said.

"It sounds wild, but Ledger gave her a kind of stability she hadn't had before," Andi said. "Still a truly awful life, but I can see how it would twist something in a vulnerable child."

"Do you know what happened to her after Ledger was convicted?" Dalton asked.

"She was thirteen by then. As far as I know, she was still in the foster system, like Roxanne. I didn't keep track of either one of them. I'm sorry I don't have anything else for you."

"Thanks," he said. "This gives me a place to start, at least."

"Now you need to tell me what's going on there in Eagle Mountain."

For the next fifteen minutes, he told her about Roxanne's arrival in the town, the man in a truck who had run her off the road, the break-in of her home and her disappearance the day before. He told the story quickly and dispassionately, betraying nothing until he told about searching for her and finding her gone. "What is your relationship to Roxanne?" Andi asked.

"We're…friends," he said. "Good friends."

"I hope they find her soon," Andi said. "And I hope she's all right."

"I hope so, too."

He hung up the phone and spent a few minutes pulling himself out of the dark place that talking about Roxanne and Ledger had sent him. Andi's words "he tortured those girls" shook him, but he forced them away. He had work to do. He had to find Alice—Brianna Davidson.

Chapter Sixteen

Roxanne lay propped against pillows, still tied to the bed. Her attempts to persuade Kara to release her had been ignored. At one point Kara had stuck her fingers in her ears and sung "La-la-la, I can't hear you" as if they were in elementary school. It seemed as if the grown woman who had been her tiny-house neighbor had reverted to the bullying twelve-year-old who had tormented Roxanne alongside Ledger.

Right now, Kara sat in the room's only chair, knitting a sock out of pink-and-orange striped yarn. The sight of her manipulating needles and yarn struck Roxanne as jarring, given their circumstances.

Roxanne had had time to take stock of her surroundings. They weren't in a house, she had concluded, but some kind of mobile home or even an RV, in a small bedroom with two boarded-up windows. She avoided looking at those plywood-covered windows, which were too reminiscent of the ones in the room where Ledger had kept her and Alice captive all those years ago.

The room had a single bed and a single chair, a single light fixture in the ceiling. The air smelled stale, like old French fries and body odor. Matted gray carpeting covered the floors and the walls were painted flat white over some kind of wall board.

The pop of gravel beneath tires made Kara sit up straight. She gathered up her knitting and stowed it in a bag she shoved beneath the bed. "That should be Billy," she said, and turned expectantly toward the door.

The trailer shook as someone opened the door and entered. Heavy footsteps moving toward them filled Roxanne with dread. The same feeling had sickened her as a child, waiting for Ledger's next "visit."

A key scraped in a lock, then the bedroom door opened.

This was the face that had looked into Roxanne's car the day she was run off the road—graying blond hair cut short, full cheeks, bulbous nose, carefully tended mustache. A Billy Ledger who had been left out in the sun to soften and thicken.

He came to the bed and leaned over her. "Hello, Mary," he said. His breath smelled of cigarettes. "It's good to see you again."

She said nothing. Kara hovered at the other side of the bed. "She was sick, but I think she's feeling much better now," she said.

"Go in the other room," Ledger said and pointed with his thumb at the door.

Kara scurried away, shutting the door softly behind her. Roxanne tried to hide her fear. She remained still, though inwardly she shrank from him. She had two arms free. If he came for her, she would fight with everything she had.

He sat on the end of the bed and put one hand on her leg. "You've grown into a very pretty young woman," he said. He squeezed her calf, and her stomach turned. "Isn't it nice to have our little family all back together?"

She said nothing, but continued to stare, refusing to look away from him.

"You've been very naughty," he said. "You deserve to be punished for making things so difficult for me."

Roxanne clenched her teeth against the whimper that tried

to escape. Ledger had liked to frighten her. She didn't want to give him the satisfaction of thinking he had succeeded now. He stood and removed his belt. She needed to distract him. "What did you do with Sarah Michaelson?" she blurted.

He stilled, the belt half on. "Sarah is being taken care of," he said. "That's none of your concern."

"Sarah isn't part of our family," she said. "Why did you take her?"

"I decide when to add to our family, not you," he said.

"There isn't room for her here," she said. "You're always talking about how the house is too small." He had said those things before—about how he wanted a new house, where each girl could have her own room, instead of Alice and Mary sharing.

Ledger rebuckled the belt. "This place is only temporary," he said. "We'll be moving soon. Someplace where we can all be together."

He left the room, switching off the overhead light as he passed it. The locks thudded into place behind him. Roxanne held her breath, listening, but his footsteps receded. He said something to Alice and she answered, their words indistinguishable. Then all was quiet. Roxanne closed her eyes and gave in to the tears sliding down her face. She would cry a little bit, then she would sit up and start looking for a way out of here. She hadn't given up before and she wouldn't now.

"Alice and Betty Josephs are the same person, I'm sure of it." Dalton had tracked down Aaron at the apartment he shared with Willa.

Aaron, in jeans and tennis shoes and a T-shirt that advertised a local barbecue restaurant, had been in the middle of trying to assemble a bookcase when Dalton interrupted him. Now, sitting in the living room, surrounded by packaging and parts, he looked annoyed but interested. "What kind of proof do you have?" he asked.

Dalton shoved aside a pile of packing paper and set his laptop on the coffee table in front of Aaron's chair. "This is the affidavit showing that on February 16, 2022, Brianna Davidson—that's Alice's real name—changed her name to Betty Josephs."

"How do you know Alice's real name?" Aaron asked.

"A reporter who covered Ledger's trial told me. She obeyed the order not to publish the girls' names, but she knew them."

"And you're sure this is the same person?" Aaron asked.

"Look at this. Same birth date. Same place of birth, same residence. And I found this, too." He scrolled to a second page, this one showing a voter's registry. "Both her names are listed here—cross-referenced to each other—with a note about the name change."

Aaron leaned forward and studied the document. "How did you get this information?"

"It's public record. Skip tracers and genealogists dig into this stuff all the time. You just have to know where to look."

Aaron sat back. "Did you also figure out where Betty Josephs is now? She disappears about the time William Ledger is released from prison. And we don't think she's Debra Percy."

"I don't think it's Debra now, either," Dalton said. "I don't know where Betty is, but I know one thing she did." Dalton scrolled to a screen-capture of a third document. "I had to beg a favor from a friend who works for the DMV for this one," he said. "It's the registration for a travel trailer purchased by Betty Josephs four weeks ago."

"That's three days before William Ledger's release."

"There's also a registration for a truck. I think it might be the same one that ran Roxanne off the road."

Aaron took out his phone. "We need to get a BOLO out on these vehicles."

"If you find those vehicles, maybe you can find Ledger. And Roxanne," Dalton said. He prayed she was still alive. Unharmed would be good, but whatever Ledger had done to her, she would get past that. She was strong, and she had him by her side to help.

ROXANNE LAY ON her back in the bed and inched her way to the edge. She reached down, feeling for the knitting bag Kara had shoved underneath there earlier. The bed was relatively high off the ground, and at first Roxanne couldn't touch the floor. But by shoving her feet against the footboard, arching her back over the side and straining, she could sweep the floor with her fingers.

She brushed something soft, like fabric, and inched her fingers farther beneath the bed. With effort, she was able to coax the item out farther, so that she could grasp it.

Muscles protesting, she levered herself fully onto the mattress again and clutched the knitting bag to her chest. The room was still in full darkness, but as she groped through the bag she was able to identify items by feel.

She had hoped to find scissors but could locate none. No tapestry needle or straight pins. She pulled out something small and round, on an elastic band. As her fingers traced its shape, she pushed down on a button and a light came on. She studied the headlamp. Did Kara have this for knitting in the dark?

She switched off the light and shoved it deep into her pocket, then continued her exploration of the bag. Some papers—a pattern, maybe. A tube of lip balm. Her fingers closed around the knitting itself. She squeezed the partially-constructed sock in frustration, and one of the sock needles poked her. She drew back, even as elation surged through her. Hurriedly, she pulled all four needles from the yarn and shoved them into the pocket of her jeans. There were four of the needles, made of a smooth, hardened wood, short, with sharp points on either end. Then she threw the knitting bag under the bed, just as a key scraped in the lock on the door.

Kara entered first, with Ledger right behind her. He flipped on the light. "Time to go," he said. He took a key ring from his pocket and fitted a key into the lock that secured the chains at her ankles. "Alice, take her other arm," he said as he grasped Roxanne's left arm. "Don't let her try anything."

"I'm not going to try anything." Roxanne tried to sound meek, and prayed Kara wouldn't suddenly decide to retrieve her knitting or notice the knitting needles shoved into the pockets of Roxanne's jeans.

Ledger and Kara heaved Roxanne upright. She wobbled momentarily, but straightened. "I'm okay," she said. "I can walk on my own."

"Then get moving." Ledger dragged her with him toward the door.

"Where are we going?" Roxanne asked. "Is it a bigger place than this? Where did you get this trailer? Do you still have the truck I saw you with before?" She kept up the barrage of questions, determined to distract him.

"When did you become such a chatterbox?" he asked.

"She's just being silly," Kara said. "You know she was always that way." She pinched Roxanne's arm—hard. Another move familiar from their first captivity. Roxanne glared at her, but Kara only smiled.

The three made their way through a tiny living room. "Get the door," Ledger said.

Kara released her hold on Roxanne long enough to unlock and open the door of the trailer. Then she led the way down the steps. Dusk had fallen, the trees around them dark smudges against a gray sky. Roxanne saw no other vehicles and no road, only a narrow dirt track through the trees. The truck sat a few feet away. "Open the truck," Ledger barked, and Kara ran ahead to do his bidding.

Roxanne didn't hesitate. With her free hand, she reached around and grabbed one of the knitting needles. In one forceful movement, she raised the needle and plunged it toward Ledger's face.

He screamed, and she kept driving the needle, into his eye. He clutched at his face, bent double. Roxanne turned and ran. She crashed through underbrush and dodged between tree trunks, Ledger's roars and Kara's screams gradually receding behind her. She ran until her lungs ached and pain pierced her side. When she was finally forced to stop, she could no longer see the trailer or the truck, or hear anything but her own gasping attempts to pull air into her burning lungs. She bent over, hands on knees. She needed to get out of here. To find help. But everywhere she turned, all she saw was trees. She had no idea where she was.

SOMETIMES IN LAW ENFORCEMENT, nothing went your way. The suspect you were sure was guilty had an unbreakable alibi. The proof you needed to make a case turned out to be worthless. And the felon you were chasing had left the state an hour before you got to his house.

But sometimes, you caught a break. Aaron was interviewing his third gas station attendant of the day about whether or not he had seen a truck like the one registered in Betty Josephs's name, or the travel trailer, or anyone who looked like William Ledger.

"Oh yeah, I saw him," the attendant, a tall man with a large, crooked nose and a dime-sized tuft of hair on his chin, said. "He was in here yesterday, filling up with gas. He bought a couple of padlocks."

"Padlocks?" Aaron asked.

"Like those." The attendant pointed over Aaron's shoulder. Aaron turned and saw a row of padlocks on hooks.

"Did he say anything?" Aaron asked. "Where he was going? Where he was from? Why he wanted the locks?"

"Nope. But I noticed the truck. I've been wanting to get one of those big welded bumpers for mine and I asked him about it. He said his girlfriend got it for him."

"Was there anybody with him?"

"No. He was by himself. And he didn't have a trailer. But I'm sure it was him." He tapped the photograph Aaron had laid on the counter. "We've probably still got him on the security video."

Aaron left a minute later with a copy of the security video on a flash drive in an evidence bag in his pocket. He radioed the information to Sheriff Travis Walker. "I think Ledger is holed up somewhere near here," Aaron said. "The gas station attendant said he thought he had been in once or twice before over the last couple of weeks."

"That's a pretty rural area, isn't it?" Travis asked. "Few houses, a lot of public land."

"Yeah, it's pretty dense woods. I'm going to drive down a few roads, see if I can spot anywhere people have been camping."

"Call in anything you see, but don't approach on your own," Travis said.

"Ten-four."

Aaron left the gas station and a quarter mile later turned down a forest service road. Immediately, dense stands of trees closed in on either side, shutting out what little daylight was left. The pavement gave way to dirt after only a few yards. Aaron slowed the vehicle to a crawl and switched on the spotlight mounted to the side mirror of the SUV. He played the beam over the woods on the left side of the road, searching for any space that might serve to hide Ledger's truck or trailer.

Traveling so slowly, it was easy to lose track of how far he had gone. After what seemed like half an hour had passed, he had only driven three miles. Anxiety clawed at the back of his neck, fed by the crowding trees and narrow road. Full darkness had descended, distorting shadows and making every tree appear menacing. He could easily end up trapped in a place like this. If Ledger had seen the spotlight, he might move ahead or behind and ambush Aaron, picking him off with a long gun as he drove past.

His search for Ledger's hiding place became a search for a place to turn his SUV around. He spotted a section of trees ahead that seemed less dense and aimed for it. As he neared it, he could see tire tracks turning off the road. He stopped, and aimed the spotlight past the tracks.

The trailer crouched in a clearing hacked out of the forest, the raw stumps and severed branches glowing white in the harsh glare. Beside it sat a black truck, a large welded bumper on the front. Aaron couldn't see the plate numbers from here, but he didn't have to. He switched off the spot, slammed the vehicle into Reverse and backed down the road until he could turn around in a series of awkward back-and-forth shifts.

Then he picked up the phone, afraid to use the radio in case Ledger was listening in on a scanner. "Sheriff, I've found him," he said. "The truck and trailer are right here, on Forest Road 4624. About three miles down. I'm going to pull over and watch the place until backup arrives."

"I'll get a team out there ASAP," Travis said. "Let us know if he moves."

Aaron ended the call and settled in to wait. If the truck drove past him, Aaron would follow it, lights off, keeping track of Ledger, but not approaching him.

But Ledger didn't drive past. The road was silent and still. Aaron rolled down his window and listened. Somewhere an owl hooted, and a second owl replied. The chatter of the radio was a barely audible hum. He checked his service weapon, then freed the rifle from its holder between the seats. He hoped he wouldn't need any of these weapons, but he wanted to be prepared.

He thought about texting Willa, to tell her where he was and what he was doing, but decided that would only worry her. Better to wait to tell the story after this was all over.

It seemed a long time before he heard a car approaching, though in reality it was less than twenty minutes. The sheriff's truck pulled up alongside him and Travis lowered the window. "Anything we should know?" Travis asked.

"No one has come this way," Aaron said.

"Ride with me," Travis said.

Aaron exited his SUV and came around to the passenger side of Travis's truck. He brought the rifle with him. Travis said nothing, merely waited until Aaron had shut the door and secured the rifle, then the truck rolled forward. Lights came up behind them. "Gage is back there with Ryker, with Shane and Jake behind them," Travis said. "I've got a SWAT unit out of Junction on call if things get hairy, but I'm hoping we can go in and arrest him without much trouble."

They approached the truck and trailer and Travis switched off his headlights. The others did the same. They parked side by side across the entrance to the clearing, blocking the exit. Then they got out of their vehicles, moving as silently as possible in the darkness.

Travis took out a microphone. "William Ledger!" he said, his amplified voice filling the clearing. "This is the Rayford County Sheriff's Department. We have you surrounded. Come out with your hands up."

No answer. The silence stretched until Aaron thought his

nerves would snap. He wiped his damp palms on his thighs and stared at the door of the trailer, willing it to open, yet fearful of what would happen when it did.

"William Ledger," Travis said again. "Come out now, with your hands up."

They had three spotlights trained on the trailer, so everyone saw when the door began to ease open. "Don't shoot me!" a plaintive voice called.

"We won't shoot," Travis said. "Put your hands on top of your head and walk out slowly."

The door opened wider and a small woman—not even five feet tall, with short hair that looked black in this light, descended the steps. Her face was streaked with tears. "You have to help him," she wailed. "I'm afraid he's dying."

Travis and Aaron moved in to take the woman by the arms. Aaron cuffed her hands behind her back. She didn't resist, merely stood between them, sobbing. "Who's dying?" Travis asked.

"Billy! He's hurt. He's in the trailer and there's so much blood."

They passed the woman over to Shane and Jake and, with Ryker and Gage, approached the trailer. At a signal from the sheriff, Ryker and Jake moved around to the back of the trailer. Travis and Aaron positioned themselves on either side of the front door. Travis reached over to pound on the door. "This is the sheriff! Open up!"

No answer. Travis tried again, but still no response. His shoulder-mounted radio crackled and Jake said. "I can see in the back window," he said. "Someone's lying on the floor. He looks to be in bad shape."

"Ten-four." Travis looked to Aaron. "On three."

Travis counted down, then together, they burst through the door into chaos.

The first thing Aaron noticed was the blood. The air

reeked of it, the metallic aroma overcoming even the funk of cigarette smoke. The carpet around the door was wet with it. A man lay on his back in the middle of the floor. He was clutching his face and moaning. The three deputies and Travis descended on him. Aaron helped roll the man on his side and cuff his hands. His fingers and wrists were slippery with blood, and it took several tries to secure him.

Ledger—Aaron was sure it was Ledger—thrashed and wailed. "My eye!" he cried. "My eye!"

Travis keyed his mic. "We need an ambulance," he said, and relayed their location. Meanwhile, Ryker shone a flashlight at Ledger's bloody face. His left eyelid was closed and swollen shut, though blood continued to seep from beneath it. "What happened?" Travis asked.

Ledger's only answer was a sound like a wounded animal.

Travis crouched in front of Ledger. "We have an ambulance on the way," he said. "I need you to tell me where Roxanne Byrne is."

"I don't know a Roxanne," Ledger said.

"Mary," Aaron said. "Where is Mary?"

"She's dead!" Ledger roared. The two words echoed in the silence that followed.

"How did she die?" Travis asked, his voice tight.

"I killed her."

"What did you do with her body?" Travis asked.

"I burned it. And I buried the ashes. You'll never find her."

Aaron's mouth was dry. His throat burned. "Who did that to your eye?" he asked.

Ledger turned to him, face mottled red and white, the grotesque, weeping eye giving him the appearance of a gargoyle. "She got what she deserved," he said.

The ambulance arrived and Ledger, accompanied by Ryker and Gage, was transported to the hospital in Junction. Shane and Jake took the woman, who had refused to give her name, into the sheriff's department for booking.

Aaron and Travis surveyed the bloody living room of the trailer. "Do you think he was telling the truth?" Aaron asked. "About killing Roxanne?"

"I don't know," Travis said. "But someone stabbed him in the eye and I don't think it was the woman we just arrested."

"Roxanne would have fought back," Aaron said. "At least, I think she would."

"We need to look for her," Travis said. "We won't know for sure she's dead until we find her body."

Chapter Seventeen

The day after Roxanne's disappearance a mandatory training session for search and rescue volunteers was scheduled. Dalton had no plans to go, but Carter and Bethany appeared in the doorway of his room shortly before 6:00 p.m. "I've got your pack right here," Carter said, and hefted the backpack Dalton had assembled with first aid supplies, extra food and clothing, and other supplies he might need on a search and rescue mission.

"And I've got your jacket," Bethany said. She tossed him the blue-and-yellow jacket with SAR across the chest and back.

Dalton looked down at the jacket bunched in his hands. "I'm not going tonight," he said.

"The meeting is mandatory," Carter said.

"You're not helping anyone, holed up in this room moping," Bethany said. "Come with us and get out of your own head for a while."

He wanted to protest. To shout at her, even. It would feel good to be angry with someone besides himself. But he couldn't summon the strength. Instead, he followed his brother and sister out to Bethany's Subaru. "I'll wait in the car when we get there," he said.

But when they arrived at search and rescue headquarters, he followed his siblings inside. His fellow volunteers greeted him when he entered. They didn't stare or murmur expressions of sympathy or ask him what had happened the day before in the mountains. They treated him the same way they treated him every time he saw them—as another member of the team. As if they trusted him with their lives and the lives of others.

"Tonight's topic is assessing and treating compound fractures." Danny spoke from the front of the room.

But before he could elaborate, alerts started going off all over the room. Dalton pulled out his phone and stared at the message from the search and rescue app. "This says someone reported a distress signal from the cliffs over by Cub Creek," Caleb said.

Danny was on the phone. When he ended the call, he said. "Someone saw SOS flashing from the cliffs above Cub Creek about 6:00 p.m.," he said. "They tried to spot whoever it was through binoculars, but the terrain in there is so heavily wooded, they couldn't make out anything."

"Where is Cub Creek?" Dalton asked. He thought he knew the area around Eagle Mountain pretty well by now, but this was a new one to him.

"East of here," Grace said. "There's a trailhead at the end of Forest Road 4624 for a couple of trails in that area, but I don't think they're very popular. It's pretty dense forest in there."

"I have the details about the location of the person who called this in," Danny said. "We'll have to go around the long way. The sheriff's department says they've closed off the forest service road because of an incident."

"What kind of incident?" Carter asked.

"Don't know. But we can get to where we need to go if we cut over on County Road 7, then across the Everson Ranch. We'll start there and see if we can see anything."

Chairs scraped and papers rustled and everyone present prepared to respond to the call. Dalton put on his jacket, slipped on his pack and joined the line of volunteers transferring rescue gear to their vehicles. He rode with Carter, Bethany and Caleb to a ranch gate, where a man in a buff-colored Stetson unlocked the gate and let them in. From there they followed a narrow dirt track up a slope and into the woods, and stopped beside a shallow creek.

Danny pulled out a portable spotlight, equipped with a movable cover. "From the description the caller gave, they saw the signaling up there somewhere," he said. He switched on the light, then aimed it at what to Dalton looked like a steep, tree-covered slope. Three short bursts of light. Three longer bursts. Three short bursts.

They waited. A cry rose up when a light flashed in answer. Three short, three long, three short.

Someone pulled out a map and spread it on the hood of the rescue vehicle. Tony sketched out a route to take them to the ledge. "We'll need to cross the creek and bushwhack up the slope," he said.

"We need a couple of people in front with chain saws, with people behind them to move the brush out of the way," Danny said. "Tony and Harper, you get the medical gear and be ready to hustle up to that ledge. The rest of us will follow. And be careful."

Something in his voice made them all freeze and look at him. "Something wrong?" Sheri asked.

"I'm just thinking there's still a fugitive loose out there," Danny said. "We don't want to risk walking into a trap."

Dalton walked over and pulled a chain saw from the back of the rescue vehicle. "I'll go first," he said. If William Ledger was up there, he'd welcome the chance to be the first to confront him.

It took an hour of cutting and clearing brush to reach the

ledge where the light continued to flash periodically. Dalton remained at the front of the group, still carrying the heavy chain saw, when they emerged at one side of the ledge. At first, he didn't see anyone. Then someone stepped from the shadows. "Dalton," Roxanne said.

He dropped the saw and reached for her. She wrapped her arms around him tightly, and began to sob. "It's okay," he murmured and rested his face against her hair. "You're safe now. You're safe."

ROXANNE MANAGED TO pull herself together and reassure the search and rescue volunteers who gathered around her that she was all right. "I'd like some water," she said, and someone handed her a bottle.

"Is anyone else up here with you?" Danny asked.

"No one," she said. "I've been signaling for hours." She held up the little headlamp she had taken from Kara's knitting bag. "I was afraid the battery was going to run out soon."

"Where is William Ledger?" Dalton asked.

"I don't know." She turned to him. Though her knees threatened to give way, she kept her voice defiant. "I stabbed him in the eye with a knitting needle and ran away. I didn't care if I was lost in the middle of the forest. At least I got away from him."

Danny radioed that they had located Roxanne. "She's okay," he said. "She says she stabbed William Ledger with a knitting needle." He cleared his throat. "In the eye."

The person on the other end of the line chuckled. "So that's what happened to him. Ledger is in custody, along with his accomplice."

"His accomplice?" Dalton asked.

"Kara Lee," Roxanne said.

It took Dalton a second to place the name. "Your neighbor?"

She nodded. "She was Alice."

"Her real name is Brianna Davidson," Dalton said. "Then she changed it to Betty Josephs. And now I guess she's going by Kara Lee. She was helping Ledger?"

"She put a tracking device on my car so she could follow me around town," Roxanne said. "She led Ledger to me. She…she's not right. I think the things he did to her, when she was so young—they destroyed her."

Dalton pulled her close once more. "Come on," he said. "Let's go home."

She pushed away from him, agitated. "I almost forgot." She turned to Danny. "You need to tell the sheriff to go to Kara's rental—the tiny home on County Road 3. They need to look for Sarah Michaelson there."

"I'll tell him," Danny said.

"Ledger really did take Sarah?" Dalton asked.

"Yes. He wouldn't tell me where he was keeping her, but things he said made me think she was still alive. I thought Kara's tiny home might be a good place to stash the girl until Ledger was ready to bring us all together."

Dalton turned to look her in the face. "How are you really?" he asked. "Did he hurt you?"

She shook her head. "He tied me to a bed, but I got away before he could do anything more," she said.

"Where did you get a knitting needle?" he asked.

"Kara knits. I took them from her knitting bag."

"Huh."

"I've been afraid to ask," she said. "What happened to Debra?"

"Ledger hit her and threw her off a cliff, but she's going to be okay," he said. "She's recovering in the hospital."

"That's good."

"I thought for a while she might have been Alice," Dalton said. "She was so fixated on you."

"I wondered about that, too," she said. "But I think she really was just wanting very badly to find out what happened to her sister."

"I don't guess Ledger said anything about Bettina?"

"No. But it is odd that he had Alice—Brianna—change her name to Betty. I'm sure the name was his idea. I got the impression Kara didn't do anything he didn't tell her. She told me he even paid for her to have a nose job." She leaned against him. "I don't want to talk about her anymore. I just want to go home."

Dalton started toward the Ameses' house, but when he signaled for the turn, Roxanne put a hand on his arm. "Can we go to your place instead?" she asked. "I'm not really ready to see a bunch of people yet."

"Sure." He drove on, to his apartment, and led the way up the steps to the front door.

The air smelled musty, like a place that hadn't been open for several days. "I've been staying with my folks," Dalton said. He moved ahead of her, picking up dropped socks and an empty soda can along the way. "Do you want something to eat or drink?" he asked.

"I want a shower and a nap." She yawned. "I'm exhausted."

Fatigue dragged at Dalton, too. "The bathroom is here," he said, and led her down the short hall. "The bedroom is across from there."

"Maybe you have some clothes I could borrow," she said.

"Sure."

He came up with a T-shirt and a pair of athletic shorts. He handed her these, along with a pair of socks. "They'll be too big for you," he said.

"It doesn't matter." She took the clothing and shut the door gently. He hurried away to change the sheets on the bed, glad for once of his mother's insistence that he needed two sets of sheets at all times, a belief he had considered overkill until now.

When Roxanne emerged from the shower she was pink-cheeked and smelling of his shower gel. Her wet hair curled around her face and her nipples tented the front of the T-shirt. His response was immediate and he turned away, hoping she didn't notice his erection. "You can sleep in here," he said, pointing out the freshly made bed. "I'll sleep in Carter's old room."

Roxanne took his hand. "I'd rather if you slept with me. I'd feel safer."

He waited until she had crawled under the covers and switched out the light before he joined her. He wore a T-shirt and boxers, and the sheets were cool against his bare legs. Roxanne curled on her side, her back to him. He lay on his back, a few inches separating them. "Good night," she said, her voice already blurred with the beginnings of sleep.

"Good night." He closed his eyes, sure he would never go to sleep with Roxanne so close, but the events of the past few days had drained him, and slumber soon pulled him under.

ROXANNE WOKE TO soft warmth. She sighed and settled more firmly under the covers, pressed against something warm and firm. She opened her eyes, shocked awake by the realization that she wasn't alone in this bed. Someone—a man—was with her. Someone who had one arm firmly around her waist, pulling her tight up against his erection.

"Dalton?" she whispered. She had a vague memory of them crawling into bed together before sleep engulfed her.

"Hmm." He nuzzled against her. It wasn't an unpleasant sensation. In fact, she liked it a lot. She put her hand over his at her waist and adjusted it to rest on her breast. Automatically, his fingers shaped themselves to her, and squeezed her gently. She let out a breathy sigh and squirmed against him.

His hand stilled. "Roxanne?" he asked.

"Good morning."

He took his arm away and tried to scramble back. "Sorry," he said. "I didn't mean. I mean…"

She rolled over to face him and grabbed his hand before he could exit the bed altogether. "It's okay," she said. "Don't leave. I was enjoying myself."

To his credit, he didn't hesitate, but slid over to pull her close once more. "You feel amazing," he said.

"All I wanted while I was trapped in that trailer was to get back to you. To show you how much I love you." She kissed the side of his neck, and slid her hands over his abs and up his chest, pushing his T-shirt out of the way.

He sat up and pulled off the T-shirt, then reached for hers. "Not that you don't look sexy in it, but right now it's in my way."

She laughed, and stripped off the shirt, then pulled him to her. They knelt facing each other, and she cradled his head in her hands as he lavished attention on each breast in turn. She threaded her fingers through his hair and arched her back, sensation vibrating through her with every stroke of his tongue. She moaned and he looked up at her. "Tell me if I'm doing something you don't like," he said.

"You're doing great." She pushed his head back down. "Keep going."

He slid down, trailing kisses to her belly button, then lower still. He helped her out of the shorts and made a pleased sound when he saw she wasn't wearing any underwear. Soon his mouth covered her center, the area becoming the focus of all his attention. She eased down onto her back and he shifted with her. She had a glimpse of his erection tenting the front of his boxers, a teaser of things to come.

And then she stopped thinking about anything as his mouth went to work on her in earnest. He was nothing if not attentive. And thorough. While his mouth worked, his fingers weren't idle, stroking in and out of her, until the building tension had her vibrating beneath him. She brought her hands to her breasts, touching herself, swamped by sensation.

Her climax surprised her with its intensity, wave upon wave of sensation rocketing through her. Tears stung her eyes and she blinked them away, but a sound like a sob still escaped her.

Dalton was at her side almost instantly, looking at her with alarm. "What's wrong?" he asked. "What did I do?"

"You didn't do anything wrong." She cradled his face in her hands and smiled at his blurry image, still blinking back tears. "You did everything so right. I'm just…overwhelmed with how wonderful it is."

He pulled her close and held her so tightly she could scarcely breathe. But she didn't pull away. She wanted to be this close to him.

After a few moments, he began to move against her, his hands tracing patterns across her hip and lower back, his erection nudging at her entrance. She lifted one leg and invited him in.

But instead of accepting the invitation, he leaned back and groped at something on his bedside table. A second later, he held up a condom packet. "Bet you thought I forgot."

She laughed and held out her hand. "Allow me to do the honors."

She loved the feel of him, hard and hot in her hand. But she loved even more the glazed look in his eyes as she fit the condom to him, the little gasp that escaped him when she squeezed him.

Their eyes met and that overwhelming feeling of being so cherished and cared for—and of wanting to cherish and care for him—returned. She pulled him to her once more and this time they fit together easily and began to move in a rhythm that seemed to light up every nerve ending in her body.

They kept their eyes open, reading the passion in each

other's eyes, moving faster, then slower, then deeper, until they were both panting and trembling. He bent his head, focused now, thrusting harder. She closed her eyes and gave herself up to the sensation. His body tensed and his climax shuddered through them both. She wrapped arms and legs around him and rocked with him until he was spent.

He got up and went into the bathroom, and emerged smelling of mint toothpaste. He slid into bed and lay beside her, cradling her head on his shoulder.

She couldn't remember the last time she had been this happy. She thought he was asleep and started to slip from beneath his arm, but he clutched at her. "It's all right," she said. "I'll be right back."

She went to the bathroom, cleaned herself and brushed her teeth and her hair and returned to find him awake, hands behind his head, watching her as she walked, naked, to the bed. "I could get used to this," he said.

"Hmm." She pulled back the covers and nestled in beside him. He put his arm around her.

"I love you," he said. "I've loved you for weeks now."

"I've known it for weeks, too," she said. "I was just afraid to say it. Love seems so fragile."

"It isn't fragile," he said. "It might be the strongest thing there is. At least that's what it feels like to me."

"Can you deal with someone with so much baggage?" she asked. "I've had a lot of therapy over the years but there are still things that live in my head that come out sometimes."

He raised himself up to look her in the eye. "I love you. That means all of you." He shaped one hand to her breast. "Not just the sexy parts or the smart parts or the funny parts or the talented parts. All the parts make you *you*—that includes your baggage. And I've got plenty of faults of my own. Can you put up with those?"

"I want to try."

"Then let's try." They kissed to seal the promise, a simple kiss full of tenderness tempered with passion. A promise she hoped to keep.

Her phone jangled from the table beside the bed. She picked it up. "It's the sheriff," she said, reading the screen.

Dalton sat up again and watched as she answered the call. "Hello?"

"Roxanne, this is Sheriff Walker. I wanted to let you know we found Sarah Michaelson at Kara's tiny house. She was locked in a closet, but she's alive and with her parents right now. She's going to be okay."

The tears flooded back. Dalton had to take the phone from her and tell the sheriff they were thrilled to hear about Sarah and would be in touch so Roxanne could give her statement about everything that had happened with Ledger and Kara. Then he held her while she sobbed. "I don't know what's wrong with me," she said. "I'm just…so overwhelmed."

He stroked her hair. "Maybe you're remembering another little girl," he said. "Another girl who escaped Ledger and went on to survive and grow into a wonderful woman."

She sobbed harder at his words, and held on tighter. She was never going to let him go. Never.

Epilogue

An organ fanfare played the opening strains of the "Bridal Chorus" and the crowd in the open-air chapel shuffled to its feet. Dalton turned to watch his sister progress up the aisle on the arm of their father while, in the row ahead of them, his mother began to softly weep.

"She's so beautiful." Roxanne squeezed Dalton's arm and dabbed at her own eyes. Next to her, Mira stood with Carter and Aaron had his arm around Willa. Much of the rest of the chapel was filled with various cousins, aunts, uncles and other friends and family members.

At the front of the chapel the groom, Ian Seabrook, wearing a suit that probably cost more than Dalton made in a month, beamed at his bride, the huge grin a little goofy on a man who was usually so serious. He shook Mr. Ames's hand, then took both of Bethany's in his own. The two stared at each other, entranced. The officiant had to clear her throat to get their attention, and the crowd chuckled, then settled once more into their seats.

The vows elicited more tears from the Ames women—or those who would soon be part of the family. And then the organ trumpeted again and they rose to watch the bride and groom recess to the Wedding March.

Half an hour later, the Ames siblings, minus Bethany,

stood on a patio outside the hall where the reception dinner was to be held. They held glasses of champagne and watched as, in the distance, the bride and groom and parents posed for photographs.

Aaron and Willa moved over to stand beside Dalton and Roxanne. "Some news today, about Debra Percy," he said.

"Oh?" Dalton still wasn't sure what to think about Debra. He knew she had recovered from her injuries and moved back to San Antonio. He expected they would see her again at William Ledger's trial, though that had not yet been scheduled.

"What news?" Roxanne asked.

"She was right about her sister, Bettina," Aaron said. "She was Ledger's first victim—or at least, the first we know about. The owners of the house he lived in at the time decided to remodel and found her body buried in the crawl space."

"That's so sad," Roxanne said. "Though at least now Debra and her family know. I hope that brings her the closure she was looking for."

"Can we talk about something more cheerful?" Willa asked. "After all, we're at a wedding."

Carter and Mira joined them. "I saw Sarah Michaelson today," Mira said. "She looks happy and her mother says she's doing well."

"I'm so glad to hear it," Roxanne said. She nudged Dalton. "Dalton has some good news."

"What is it?" Carter asked. "Are you coming back to work at the tour company?"

"No." Dalton had stopped giving tours after Roxanne was found. He couldn't face giving another cheerful spiel at the site where he had almost lost her. He looked into his empty champagne glass, then set it on a side table. "I'm starting my own software company."

"He had big offers for both his first responder and resort

reservation programs," Roxanne said. "But he'll do better marketing them on his own."

"We'll do better." Dalton put his arm around her. "We're starting the business together."

"What are you going to call the business?" Carter asked.

"We're thinking Ames Solutions," Dalton said.

"I thought you said you were starting the business together," Willa said. She turned to Roxanne, who was grinning. "Or does this mean you're going to be changing your name?"

Dalton took her hand in his. "We don't have a ring yet. We didn't want to steal Bethany's thunder at her wedding, so don't go spreading this around. But yeah, we're engaged."

"I'm so happy for you." Willa moved in for a hug, followed by Mira, and then Aaron and Carter.

"Mom's going to be over the moon," Carter said.

"So don't tell her yet," Dalton said. "We want to keep things low-key for a while longer." He kissed Roxanne's knuckles.

She lifted her glass in a toast. "To a wonderful future," she said.

"To a wonderful future." Dalton no longer had a glass of champagne, but he drank from hers. This was what he wanted for the future—them sharing in everything, good and bad. No matter what happened, they were both stronger together.

* * * * *

COMING SOON!

We really hope you enjoyed reading this book.
If you're looking for more romance
be sure to head to the shops when
new books are available on

Thursday 15th January

To see which titles are coming soon, please visit
millsandboon.co.uk/nextmonth

MILLS & BOON

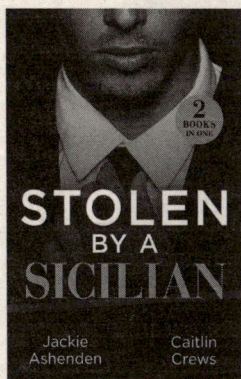

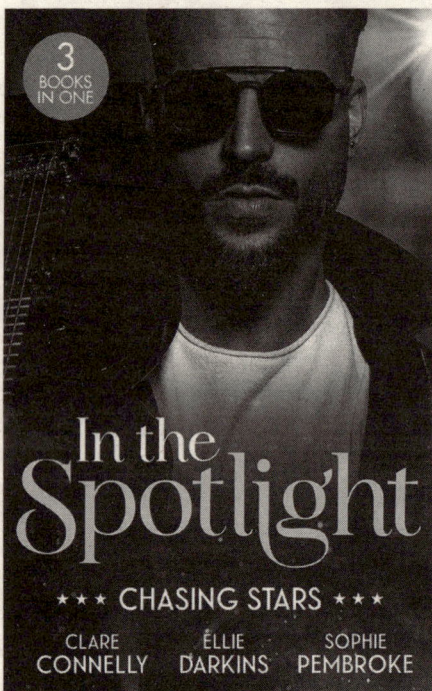